When jet-s
to p

Mother's Day

Pamper yourself this Mother's Day with
three breathtaking stories from Abby Green,
Chantelle Shaw and Fiona McArthur

Escape for Mother's Day

ABBY GREEN
CHANTELLE SHAW
FIONA McARTHUR

Mills & Boon, an imprint of Harlequin (UK) Limited, Eton House, 18-24 Paradise Road, Richmond, Surrey TW9 1SR

ESCAPE FOR MOTHER'S DAY
© Harlequin Enterprises II B.V./S.à.r.l. 2012

The French Tycoon's Pregnant Mistress © Abby Green 2009
Di Cesare's Pregnant Mistress © Chantelle Shaw 2008
The Pregnant Midwife © Fiona McArthur 2004

ISBN: 978 0 263 89751 7

012-0312

Printed and bound in Spain
by Blackprint CPI, Barcelona

THE FRENCH TYCOON'S PREGNANT MISTRESS

ABBY GREEN

Abby Green worked for twelve years in the film industry. The glamour of four a.m. starts, dealing with precious egos, the mucky fields, driving rain…all became too much. After stumbling across a guide to writing romance, she took it as a sign and saw her way out, capitalising on her long-time love for romance books. Now she is very happy to sit in her nice warm house while others are out in the rain and muck! She lives and works in Dublin.

CHAPTER ONE

'WITH a nail-biting finish like that, I think we can safely say that this tournament is wide-open and set to be one of the most exciting yet. This is Alana Cusack, reporting live from Croke Park. Back to you in the studio, Brian.'

Alana kept the smile pasted on her face until she could hear the chatter die away in her earpiece and then handed her microphone to her assistant, Aisling, with relief once she knew she was off air. She avoided looking to where she knew the man was still standing, his shoulder propped nonchalantly against the wall, hands in the pockets of his dark trousers, underneath a black overcoat with the collar turned up. He'd been talking to one of the French players, but now he was alone again.

He was watching her. And he'd been watching her all through the Six Nations match between Ireland and France. He'd unsettled her and he'd distracted her. And she didn't know why.

That was a lie; she knew exactly why. He was dark and brooding, and so gorgeous that when she'd first locked eyes with him, quite by accident, it had felt as though someone had just punched her in the stomach. There had been an instant tug of recognition and something very alien and disconcerting. Certainly something that no other man had ever made her feel.

Not even her husband.

The tug had been so strong that she'd felt herself smiling and raising a quizzical brow, but then she'd seen an unmistakably mocking glint in his dark eyes. Of course, she didn't know him; she'd never seen his long, hard-boned face before, had never seen that mouth, which even to look at from where she sat, had the most amazingly sensuous lips. Immediately she'd felt herself flushing with embarrassment at her reaction to him.

He had to be French, as he shared the quintessential good looks of so many of the crowd today, quite exotically different from the more pale-skinned home crowd of Irish supporters. And he'd been sitting in the seats reserved for VIP's, situated just below the press area. He looked like a VIP. She'd only had to look once to know that he effortlessly stood out from the rest of the crowd. But her gaze had been inexorably drawn to him again and again, and to her utter ongoing mortification their eyes had met more than once. When he'd stood intermittently with the crowd during a try or a conversion, he'd stood taller and broader than any of the men around him—and in a crowd full of rugby supporters, that was something.

Yet was he waiting now because he thought that she'd been giving him some sort of come-on? Everything in Alana clammed up and rejected that thought. She would never be so blatant.

'Do you need a lift, Alana?' Aisling and the others had finished packing up, and Derek the cameraman was looking at her. Suddenly she felt very flustered. She didn't *get* flustered. She was often teased for appearing cool, calm and collected at all times.

'No,' she answered quickly, aware that the stranger had moved out of her peripheral vision. A sense of panic threatened her—that he might be right behind her, waiting for her. 'I have to go to a family dinner later, so I have my car here.'

'So no glitzy after-party to see the French celebrating for you, then?'

She mock-grimaced, secretly relieved that she had an excuse. 'I'll only have time to stop in to show my face on my way, just to keep Rory happy.'

He shrugged and was about to walk away after Aisling and the other assistant, with their small amount of gear, when he stopped and turned again, distracting Alana.

'Good reporting today, kid.'

Pleasure rushed through her. This was so important to her; Derek was practically a veteran of TV. She'd been slogging for a long time to get a modicum of respect. She smiled. 'Thanks, Derek. I really appreciate that.'

He winked at her and turned to walk away again. With the fizz of pleasure staying in her chest, she checked around for anything left behind and made to follow the others, before stopping and cursing as she remembered that her laptop and notebook were back in the press seats.

Derek's words were forgotten when that prickling awareness came back. She turned around with her heart beating hard, fully expecting to see the man again. She had a curiously insincere feeling of relief when he wasn't there. He'd obviously gone, bored with waiting around. Taking the lift back up to the upper level, she told herself to stop being ridiculous, that she'd merely imagined that they'd had some kind of silent communication...

He thought he'd missed her when he'd gone to look at the pitch for a moment, and he didn't like the momentary sense of panic that thought had generated.

But she was still here.

Now Pascal Lévêque stood back with arms folded and surveyed the enticing sight in front of him. A very shapely bottom was raised in the air, encased in the tight confines of a pencil skirt. Its owner was currently bending over, hauling a bag out from under a seat. His eyes drifted down. Long, slim legs were momentarily bent and now straightened to their full length—which was *long*, all the way from slim, neat ankles right up to gently flaring hips which tapered into a neat waist. He wondered if she was wearing stockings, and that thought had a forceful effect on the blood in his veins.

He wondered, too, then, what it was about her that had kept him looking, that had kept him here, when he should have long gone. What was it that had kept drawing his eye back again and again, uncharacteristically taking his attention away from the riveting match?

Neat.

That was it. She was neat. Right from her starchy, buttoned-up stripey shirt complete with tie, down to her sensible court-shoes and shiny, straight hair neatly tucked behind her ears, a side parting to the left. It was tied back in a small ponytail, but he could well imagine that if let loose, it would fall ever so neatly into a straight shoulder-length bob, framing her face. And since when had he been into *neat*? He was famously into seductive, sensual women, women who poured their beautiful, curvaceous bodies into clothes and dresses designed to fire the imagination and ignite the senses. Women who weren't afraid to entice and beguile, using all their powerful charms for his pleasure.

She was shrugging into a long, black overcoat now, hiding herself, and bizarrely, he felt all at once irritated, inflamed and perplexed. What the hell was he doing, practically slavering over some vacuous TV dolly bird? He knew that any second now she'd turn round, and he'd see that up close her face wasn't half as alluring as he'd imagined it to be from a distance: with a healthy glow, full, glossy lips and doe-shaped eyes under dark brows which contrasted with her strawberry-blonde hair.

No; she'd turn round and he'd see that she was caked in orange make-up. Her eyes would flare with recognition—hadn't she already recognised him earlier, and given him those enticingly shy looks? And then he'd be caught. He was already trying to think up something to excuse his very out-of-character behaviour when she did turn round. He opened his mouth and suddenly his mind went blank.

Alana had no warning for what or who faced her. That gorgeous, brooding stranger was right in front of her. Just feet away. Looking at her. They were standing alone in an eighty-thousand-seat stadium, but to Alana in that moment it shrank to the four square feet surrounding them. And it was then that she had to acknowledge that the prickling awareness she'd been dismissing had just exploded into full-on shock. The blood seemed to thicken in her veins; her heart pounded again in recognition of some base appreciation of his very masculinity.

He stood with his head tilted back, hands in the pockets of his trousers. His coat emphasised his broad shoulders, the olive tone of his skin. But it was his eyes that she couldn't take her own shocked gaze from. They were wide, dark, intelligent and full of something so hot and brazenly sensual that she felt breathless.

Her hands gripped her notebooks close to her chest, and she was absurdly relieved that she was wearing a long coat, feeling very strangely that this man could somehow see underneath, as if with just a look he could make her clothes melt away. She shook her head, unaware of what she was doing, and to her intense relief, she found her voice.

'Excuse me, can I help you? Are you looking for someone?' Since when had her voice taken on the huskily seductive tones of a jazz singer? Even though they were alone, Alana felt no sense of fear. Her sense of fear came from an entirely different direction.

'You were looking at me.'

Pascal winced inwardly at the accusing tone of his voice and the baldness of his statement, but he was still reeling from coming face to face with her. His recent assumption that she would prove to be entirely unalluring was blasted to smithereens. She was all at once pale and glowing. Dewy. Cheeks flushed red from the cold breeze…or something else? That thought had blood rushing southward with an unwelcome lack of control. Her eyes were a unique shade of light green. Her lips were full and soft, not covered in glossy gloop. He'd never seen anyone so naturally beguiling.

'Excuse me?' Alana welcomed the righteous indignation that flowed through her, and told herself it wasn't adrenaline. But since when had righteous indignation made her shake? She'd been right; he was obviously just a tourist looking for a little fun. He'd misconstrued her meaning when she'd smiled at him. Well, she wasn't on the market for that sort of thing.

'From what I recall you were doing a fair amount of looking yourself.' She hitched up her chin. 'I thought I recognised you, but I was wrong, so forgive me if I led you to believe that something more was on offer. Now, if you'll excuse me, I have work to get back to.'

The man smiled, revealing gleaming, strong white teeth, and Alana felt momentarily dizzy. 'I am well aware that you are working, after all, didn't I just see you interviewing Ireland's manager? I was making an observation, that's all. And you were looking at me.'

'No more than you were looking at me.' She desperately tried to claw back some semblance of control.

He rocked back on his heels and a different light came into his eyes. An altogether more dangerous light. And Alana could see that she was effectively trapped. The space between the seats was far too narrow for her to even attempt to push past him, and the only alternative would be to jump into the next aisle—far too unladylike and desperate. And, in the skirt she was wearing, impossible.

Alana felt unbelievably threatened. She called up her best brisk manner and hitched her laptop-bag strap higher on her shoulder, hoping he'd take the hint. 'This conversation is getting us nowhere. Now, really, I have to get back to my office, and I'm sure you have somewhere far more exciting to be.'

After a long, intense moment, to her utter relief, he stepped back and indicated with his arm that she should precede him out of the row of seats that led into the press area. Alana gritted her teeth and walked past, but, even though she tried to arch her whole body away as she moved past him, she was aware of his height which had to be at least six foot four, the sheer breadth of him and an enticingly musky smell.

The smell of *sex*.

Oh God, what was wrong with her? Since when had she ever thought she could smell *sex*? And since when had she even been aware of what it smelt like? She felt weak in the pit of her stomach, but thankfully she was now past him and hurrying back up the main steps to the lift, which would bring her down to ground level and back to reality.

Her silent prayers weren't answered when she felt his presence beside her, yet he said nothing as the lift doors opened. When he stepped in with her, Alana punched the button, silently pleading for the journey down to be quick. It was excruciatingly intense, sharing the small confined space, and she practically bolted as soon as the lift juddered to a halt and the doors opened. As she walked towards the main gates at the back of the stand, Alana could see her car parked on the road outside. And then she heard his steps stop behind her.

Of course, he'd kept up with her effortlessly; she had the unsettling feeling that she was on a tight leash. He was like a predator indulging his prey, not moving in for the kill just yet. And knowing that, against all rational thought in her head, Alana stopped, too, and turned round. Her heart was still pounding from the close proximity in the lift, and she just realised then that she must have held her breath the whole way down.

He was looking at her with those intense eyes. And then he said, 'Actually, I do have somewhere more exciting to be. Maybe you'd care to join me?'

The full effect of his accent washed through her now; it was as if she'd blocked it out when she'd first heard him speak, having been too much to cope with along with everything else. He was absolutely devastating, and he *was* coming on to her. Alana couldn't believe it. She knew perfectly well she was nothing special; she looked like a million other girls. What on earth could this man want with her? Anyone could see he was in another league. Alarm bells rang, loud and insistently.

She shook her head and started backing away towards the gate and her car, but the physical pull to stay in this man's orbit was something she had to actively fight against. Simultaneously a sleek, dark Lexus pulled up beside them. Clearly his car—his chauffeur-driven car—which had of course been parked here in the VIP parking area.

She was shaking her head. 'I'm sorry, Mr…?'

'Lévêque.'

'Mr Lévêque.' Even his name sounded sexy—purposeful. Important. 'I have to get back to work.' She repeated it then, as if to drive a point home. 'This is work for me. Enjoy your weekend in Dublin. There are plenty of other women out there.' *Who won't be stupid enough to walk away*, the voice mocked her. But as she finally turned and walked towards her car she told herself she was glad. He hadn't looked put out; he hadn't even tried to get her to change her mind. He was just a rich tourist over for the match. And she knew all about sports supporters. She used to be part of that crowd, used to *be* a professional supporter. Not any more.

Pascal refused to give in to the desire to look to where she was getting into her car as his own swept past and away from the stadium. He couldn't really believe that she'd refused him. A woman hadn't walked away from him since…he couldn't remember when. His mouth thinned. She was right: there were plenty of other women out there. She really wasn't anything special.

So why was it that all he could see were those invitingly soft lips? And those huge, green eyes, full of changing depths? And that alluring body in its veritable uniform that made his hands itch to rip it off and see what it hid?

He was bored. That was it. And he'd been without a lover for some weeks. He was going to a party tonight. If all he was looking for was a quick lay, then he'd get it in spades.

Feeling his equilibrium start to settle again was a welcome relief, because it hadn't been normal since he'd laid eyes on her. He settled back and relaxed. And then promptly tensed again, all recent justifications out the window. He hadn't got her name. And he didn't even know if she was married. He couldn't remember seeing a ring, but now it glared at him. That *had* to be it. Equanimity rushed through him again. This time he firmly cast her out of his head as a weird, momentary diversion and looked forward to the fast-approaching evening and the promise of fulfilment that was now a dull, throbbing ache in his body.

'Alana, you can't leave yet.'

'But, Rory, I've got to get home, it's my brother's fortieth.'

Her boss ignored her and pulled her firmly by the hand, back into the throng of people she'd just battled her way through to get out. She rolled her eyes in exasperation.

'Alana, you have to meet him, you're interviewing him tomorrow. He rang in person after the match, specifically asking for you—must have seen you reporting or something, but who cares? Do you have any idea what a coup this is? He's an important sponsor of the Six Nations…famously reclusive… billionaire.'

Alana was getting bumped and bashed by people along the way as she struggled to keep up with her hyper TV-boss. She couldn't hear half of what he was saying. Something about an interview? That was nothing unusual; she did interviews most days. Why was he making such a big deal about this one? She cast a quick, worried look at her watch on the wrist not held captive by Rory. The surprise party would be starting in half an hour, and it would take her that to get out to her parents' house in Foxrock. If she missed the start of it, her life wouldn't be worth living.

Then Rory stopped abruptly and she careened into him. He turned and gave her a worried once-over. 'You'll do; it's a pity you're not more dressed up, you know, Alana, you could have made more of an effort. Really.' His mouth pursed in disapproval.

Irritation rankled; all too frequently people seemed to expect her to be what she had been—before. 'Rory, I'm dressed for a family party, remember? Not the French team's celebrations.'

Which she had to privately admit now were something else. Clearly someone had a lot of money to spend. They were taking place in the lavish ballroom of the Four Seasons hotel just on the outskirts of Dublin city-centre. She wasn't dressed in the glittering half-sheath dresses that most of the women seemed to be sporting, but she was perfectly respectable. And she preferred it that way. She had too many uncomfortable memories of being paraded in fashions that had been too tight, too small, too *everything*. And not her. She knew she went out of her way in situations like this to draw the line between the woman she had been and the woman she was now.

Rory looked over her head, tensed visibly and then looked back, taking her shoulders as if she were a child. 'He's just arrived. Now, I can't impress upon you how important this man is. Apart from his role in the Six Nations, he's the CEO of one of the biggest banks in the world. I'll introduce you and then you can go, OK? No doubt he's got bigger fish to fry tonight than meeting you, anyway.'

Rory grabbed her hand again, and before Alana could say anything, he was leading her over to where a man stood with his black-suited back to them, surrounded by obviously fawning people and a couple of scantily dressed women. And suddenly Alana's legs turned to jelly. Even before they reached him she felt her heart start to pound in recognition. It got about a million times worse when Rory hissed in her ear, 'His name is Lévêque. Pascal Lévêque.'

'I believe I saw you covering the match earlier, no?' He said this innocently with that deeply sexy voice, as if they'd never met.

For the second time that day Alana looked up into those eyes. Those eyes that she hadn't been able to get out of her head. Her mouth turned dry, her hands clammy. Her reaction was alarming; she'd sworn off all men, and had no time for frivolous flirtations, and she couldn't understand why this man was having such an extreme effect on her. Other men flirted with her and asked her out, and she dismissed them with barely a ripple of acknowledgement or reaction. But this was different. And she'd known it from the moment she had met him, which was why she'd all but run.

Silence lengthened, and Rory nudged her discreetly but painfully. Automatically Alana held out a hand. She spoke on autopilot. 'Yes. Yes, you did.'

Pascal Lévêque then took her hand in his much larger one, but instead of shaking it he bent his head, his eyes never leaving hers. Alana saw what he was going to do as if in slow motion, but still the feel of his mouth on the back of her cool hand sent shockwaves through her entire body. Immediately she tried to pull her hand away, but he wouldn't let her go. He straightened slowly. She felt his index finger uncurl to caress the point under the wrist where her pulse beat fast, and then he let her hand go. The gesture was fleeting but utterly earth-shattering.

He broke their eye contact, leaving Alana feeling curiously deflated, and with a brief, succinct question Rory left, muttering something about getting drinks. The rest of the crowd the man had been talking to melted away too. He turned back, fixing on her with that intense gaze again.

'You've had time to change, I see. Tell me, is this still classed as work?'

Alana bristled. Hot, burning irritation was rising. 'Of course I changed—it's a party. And, yes, this is still work.'

His eyes swept down, taking in what she knew to be a perfectly suitable albeit very unexciting dress. It was a black shift, high-necked and under a matching jacket. Unrevealing.

'You've changed, too,' she pointed out, feeling ridiculously self-conscious. But, whereas she felt sure she merged into the background, he was managing to stand out in a crowd of identically dressed men in a traditional black tuxedo, white shirt and black bow tie.

His eyes met hers again. 'Don't you want to take off your coat? It's warm in here.'

Warm!

She could feel a trickle of sweat roll down between her breasts as if his words had just turned the room into a sauna. 'No, I'm fine.' But all at once the jacket which had felt positively lightweight now felt like a bear skin. To be confronted with him up close and personal was overwhelming. Her eyes wanted to look their fill of his broad, lean body, wanted to rest and dwell and see if he filled out his suit as well as she suspected he did. Who was she kidding? As well as she *knew* he did. She didn't have to look to feel the latent power of his taut body envelop her in waves.

Before she knew what she was doing, she felt her hand come up in a telling gesture to smooth her hair behind her ear. It was a nervous habit. His eyes narrowed and followed her movement, and Alana flushed. Damn. She did not want to look like she was in any way aware of him.

A smile quirked his mouth. 'Your hair is perfectly…tidy.'

Was he laughing at her? And then she remembered what Rory had said. She glared up at him. Her hand dropped. 'Is it true that you requested me for this interview?'

He shrugged nonchalantly. 'It's tiresome, but every now and then I have to give in to press demands. So, yes, I requested you…in the hope that, perhaps with you asking the questions, it would prove a more diverting experience than I'm used to.'

His eyes were hot and sensual. Everything professional in her reacted to his dismissive and high-handed manner. She smiled sweetly, and something treacherous ignited in her belly when she saw a flare of something in his eyes. She ignored her body's response. 'Mr Lévêque. If you think that just because I'm a woman I'm going to confine my questions to what your favourite colour might be, then you're sadly mistaken.' At that moment she made a mental note to stay up all night if she had to, to research this man.

His eyes narrowed and cooled, and she shivered slightly.

'And if you think that because you're a woman I would dismiss your ability on that basis alone, then you are much mistaken. Any interest I have in you as far as the interview goes *is* purely professional. I've had your work investigated, and you impressed me.'

Alana was completely taken aback, and immediately felt like apologising. But, looking up at him now, she felt that cool wind still washing over her. She could almost believe that she had imagined his hot look of just moments ago. That she had imagined everything leading up to this point. She had an uncanny prescience of what it would be like to be this man's enemy.

'Well, I'm… That is, I hadn't thought that—'

He cut off her inarticulate attempt to apologise. 'Like I said, my interest in you is purely professional…as far as the interview goes. However…' He stopped and moved closer. The air around them changed in a heartbeat. Became charged.

Alana sucked in a breath. His eyes were hot again, making her feel very disorientated.

'I can't promise that my interest doesn't extend beyond the professional.'

As with earlier in the stadium, Alana felt as though the huge, packed ballroom had just shrunk around them. Adrenaline pumped through her along with the desire to flee.

'Mr Lévêque. I'm very sorry, but you see—'

'Are you married?' he asked so quickly and abruptly that Alana was stunned.

'Yes,' she answered automatically, and saw something dark flash across his face. And then she stepped back and shook her head. What was this man doing to her brain? 'No. I mean I am, I *was*, married.' She bit her lip and looked out to the room briefly, desperately willing Rory to come back and interrupt them. She looked back up at Pascal with the utmost reluctance. His eyes glittered, and a muscle twitched in his jaw. She wondered how they'd got onto such personal territory so quickly, and then his words came back: *I can't promise that my interest doesn't extend beyond the professional.*

A whole host of emotions and memories was threatening to

consume her. And the fact that she was here, in an environment so evocative of her past, was quickly becoming claustrophobic. She took a breath, deeply resenting that he was making her talk about this. 'I *was* married. My husband died eighteen months ago.'

Pascal opened his mouth as if to say something, and Alana was already tensing in anticipation. But her prayers had been heard, and Rory bounded up at that moment with drinks. He thrust a glass of champagne at Alana before handing what looked like a whiskey to Pascal. And then panic struck. She put the glass on a nearby table, some of the champagne sloshing out over the rim.

She opened her bag to pull her phone out. Ten missed calls. She groaned, 'I am in *so* much trouble.'

She turned to Rory. 'I have to go.' She looked at Pascal briefly, welcoming the feeling of panic which was distracting her from his overpowering presence.

'I'm sorry, but I'm already late for another engagement.'

She started backing away, valiantly ignoring Rory's none-too-subtle facial expressions. She bumped into someone and apologised. She felt her hair come loose from its sleek chignon and pushed it behind her ear. She was literally coming apart.

'It was nice to…meet you, Mr Lévêque. I look forward to the interview.' *Liar*. He just watched her, a small, enigmatic smile playing around that hard mouth, and stuck one hand deep into a pocket. Alana could already see women hovering, ready to move back in again, and something curdled in her stomach.

'Me, too,' he said softly, and lifted his glass like a salute—or a threat. 'Á demain, Alana.' *Till tomorrow.*

It was disconcerting to say the least to try and conduct a coherent conversation while the remnants of the hottest lust he'd ever experienced still washed through his body in waves. Even the welcome knowledge that she wasn't married failed now to impinge on his racing mind. He was still trying to clamp down the intensely urgent desire to know exactly whom she had gone to meet and where. Was it a date?

'So, what made you decide to ask for Alana Cusack to interview you?' Her boss, Rory Hogan, the head of the sports division of the national TV channel, laughed nervously. He was beginning to intensely irritate Pascal with his obsequious behaviour—and also by drawing his attention to the uncomfortable fact that, in the space of the short car journey earlier, Pascal had gone from dismissing Alana Cusack from his head to making a series of calls to find out exactly who she was, and then requesting her for his interview the next day.

Following an instinct, he decided not to dismiss this man straight away. 'I decided to use her because she's the best reporter you've got, of course.'

Rory's flushed face got even more flushed. 'Well, thank you. Yes, she is good. In fact, she's rather surprised us all.' The other man looked round for a second and then moved closer. Pascal fought against taking a step back; Rory was becoming progressively more drunk.

'The thing is, you see, she was only given a chance because of who she is.'

Pascal's interest sharpened. He injected a tone of bored uninterest into his voice. 'What do you mean?'

Rory laughed and waved an arm around. 'See all these women hanging on?'

Pascal didn't have to look; they were practically nipping at his heels. His lip curled with distaste. Situations like this always attracted a certain kind of woman—eager for marriage to a millionaire sportsman, and the platinum-credit-card lifestyle his wages could afford. The women who had achieved that status lorded it over the ones who hadn't, but it didn't make them any less predatory.

'Well, she was one of them. The queen of them, in fact. Y'see, she was married to Ryan O'Connor.'

Pascal sucked in a breath, shocked despite himself. Even he had heard of the legendary Irish soccer-player. That knowledge fought with the mental image of Alana in front of him just now, in that unrevealing black dress that had covered her from neck to knee, her hair as tidy and smooth as it had been earlier.

Rory was on a roll now. 'When they got married, it was the biggest wedding in Ireland for years. The first big celebrity-wedding. The Irish football team were having back-to-back wins. Alana was seen as their lucky mascot; she went to all the matches. It was an idyllic marriage, a great time…and then she wrecked it all.' Rory flushed. 'Well, I mean, I know she's not personally responsible, but—'

'What do you mean?' Pascal was rapidly trying to remember what he knew about Ryan O'Connor, still slightly stunned at what Alana's boss was revealing.

'Well, she threw him out, didn't she? For no good reason. And Ryan went off the rails. Ireland's luck ran out, and then he died in that helicopter crash just days before the divorce was through. We ended up giving her a job because she was unbelievably persistent, and she knows sports inside out. It's in her blood; her father played rugby for Ireland.'

Pascal was still trying to reconcile the image he had of Alana with the women around him in their tiny dresses that left little to the imagination. And yet, he could see her now as she'd been backing away just moments ago; she'd been flushed in the face, and a lock of hair had been coming loose. It had been that which had sent his lust levels off the scale. He'd had a tantalising glimpse of her coming undone, of something *hot* beneath that über-cool surface.

But the thought that she had been one of those women made everything in him contract with disgust. Yet she certainly hadn't been flirting with him, despite knowing who he was. Unless it was just a tactic. In which case, he vowed to himself now, he'd play with her to see how far she was willing to go and walk away when he'd had enough. One thing was for certain—he wanted to seduce her with an urgency that was fast precluding anything else.

The next day Alana looked at herself in the mirror of the ladies toilet at work. Nervously, and hating herself for feeling nervous, she smoothed her already smooth hair. She'd tied it back in its usual style for work, and now tucked it firmly behind her ears. She leant close to check her make-up. She'd had to put slightly more on than usual today to cover the circles under her eyes. She'd arrived home late last night, and had then stayed up researching as much information about Pascal Lévêque as she could.

The fact that she hadn't had to stay up long said it all. He rarely gave interviews; the last one had been at least two years previously. He was the CEO of Banque Lévêque, and had reached that exalted position at a ridiculously young age. Now in his mid-to-late thirties, he had brought a conglomerate of smaller archaic banks kicking and screaming into the twenty-first century, turning them into Banque Lévêque and making it one of the most influential financial institutions in the world.

Alana saw the flush on her cheeks and scrambled for some powder to try and disguise it. There had been little on his childhood or family, just one line to say that he'd been born in the suburbs of Paris to an unwed mother. Nothing about his father.

Her mouth twisted cynically. She wouldn't have been surprised in the slightest to learn that he was married. From her experience, the holy sanctity of marriage was a positive incitement for men to play away. She stopped trying to calm her hectic colour down; it was useless, and if she put any more make-up on, she'd look like a clown. She met her own eyes and didn't like the glitter she saw.

The wealth of information she'd found on his personal life—quite at odds with the paucity of information on his family or professional life—had put paid to the suspicion that he could be married. Picture after picture of stunning beauties on his arm abounded on the Internet. It would appear that he'd courted and fêted an indecent amount of the world's most renowned actresses, models and it-girls. However, no woman ever seemed to appear more than twice.

The man was obviously a serial seducer, a connoisseur of women. A playboy with a capital *P*. And Alana Cusack, from a nice, comfortable, unremarkable middle-class background, with a relatively attractive face and body, was not in his league. Not even close.

He was rich. He was powerful. He was successful. He played to win. He was the very epitome of everything she'd vowed never to let into her life again. She packed up her make-up things and gave herself a quick once-over. Her dark-navy trouser suit, and cream silk-shirt buttoned up as high as it would go, screamed *professional*. She adjusted the string of *faux* pearls around her neck. With any luck he'd have met and seduced one of the many women at the party last night, and not even remember the fact that he'd shown any interest in her.

'Let's get started, shall we?'

Alana spoke briskly, and barely glanced up from her notes when Pascal was shown into the studio. But she felt the air contract, the energy shift. The excitement was tangible. She hadn't even experienced this level of palpable charisma from some of the world's most famous sportsmen. She'd been given a thorough briefing from an attendant PR-person not to stray into personal territory, and above all, not to ask him about relationships with women. As if she even wanted to go there.

She felt rather than saw him sit down opposite her. She could hear the clatter of people getting ready around them with lights and the camera. Derek was with her again today, and he said now, 'Just a couple of minutes; I need to check the lights again.' Alana muttered something, feeling absurdly irritated. She just wanted to get this over with.

'Late night last night?'

She looked up quickly and glanced round to see if anyone had heard. No one appeared to have. She hated the intimate tone he'd used, as if drawing her into some kind of dialogue that existed just between them. It was less than twenty-four hours since she'd met him in the first place. She *had* to nip this in the bud. She looked at him steadily, ignoring the shock-waves running through her body at seeing him again.

'No.' She was frosty. 'Not particularly. You?' Why had she asked him that? She could have kicked herself.

He smiled a slow, languorous smile that did all sorts of things to her insides. She gritted her teeth. He was immaculate again today in a dark suit and pale shirt, a silk tie making him look every inch the stupendously successful financier that he was. 'I went to bed early with a cup of hot cocoa and dreamt of you in your buttoned-up suit.'

Before she could react to his comment, his eyes flicked over her in a brazen appraisal. 'A variation on a theme today, I see. Do you have a different suit for every day of the week?'

A molten, heated flush was spreading through Alana like quickfire. She was so incensed that he was already toying with her that she couldn't get words out. They were stuck in her throat.

'OK, Alana, we're ready to go here.'

Derek's voice cut through the fire in her blood. She glared at Pascal for a long moment and struggled to control herself. He hadn't taken his eyes off hers, and now he smiled easily, innocently. With a monumental effort, Alana found her cool poise. And after the first few questions had been asked, and Pascal had answered with easy, incisive intelligence, Alana began to relax. She'd found a system that was working. She just avoided looking at him if at all possible.

And that was working a treat until he said, 'I don't feel like you're really connecting with me.'

She had to look at him then. 'Excuse me?'

His eyes bored into hers, an edge of humour playing around his lips that only she could see. 'I don't feel the connection.'

Alana was very aware of everyone standing around them and looking on with interest. She wanted to get up and walk out, or hit him to get that smug look off his face. 'I'm sorry. How can I help you feel more…connected?'

He gave her an explicit look that spoke volumes, but said innocuously, 'Eye contact would be a help.'

She heard a snigger from one of the crew in the room. A familiar pain lanced her. There was always the reminder that people wanted to see her fail. She smiled benignly. 'Of course.'

Then the interview took on a whole new energy because, now that he was demanding that she make eye contact with him, she couldn't remain immune to the effect he had on her. And he knew it. She struggled through a few more questions, but with each one it felt as though he was sucking her into some kind of vortex. The sensation of an intimate web enmeshing them was becoming too much.

In a desperate bid to drive him back somehow, she deviated from her script, and could sense Rory's tension spike from across the room as she asked the question. 'How did a boy from the suburbs in Paris develop an interest in rugby? Isn't it considered a relatively middle-class game?'

Now she could sense the PR-person tense, but they didn't intervene. Clearly Pascal Lévêque was not someone to be *minded*, unlike other celebrities. He would stay in absolute control of any situation. For the first time, he didn't answer straight away. He just looked at her, and she felt a quiver of fear. He smiled tightly, but it didn't reach his eyes. 'You've done your research.'

Alana just nodded faintly, sorry she'd brought it up now.

But then he answered, 'It was my grandfather.'

'Your grandfather?' She avoided looking down at her notes, but she knew there had been no mention of a grandfather.

He nodded. 'I was sent to the south of France to live with him when I was in my teens.' He shrugged minutely, his eyes still unreadable. 'A teenage boy and the suburbs of Paris isn't a good mix.'

Something in his eyes, his face, made her want to say, 'it's OK; you don't have to answer', and that shocked her, as she never normally shied away from asking tough questions. And she didn't know why this question was generating so many undercurrents. But he continued talking as if the tension between them didn't exist.

'He was hugely involved in league rugby, which is a more parochial version of the game. Very linked to history in France. He instilled in me a love for the game and all its variations.'

Alana had no doubt that she'd touched on something very personal there, and the look in his eyes told her she'd be playing with fire if she continued. All of a sudden, she wanted to play with fire.

'You never considered playing yourself?'

His eyes were positively coal-black and flinty now. He shook his head slightly. 'I discovered that I had a knack for using my head and making money. I prefer to leave rolling around in the dirt to the professionals.'

Alana coloured. Was he making some reference to the fact that *she* was playing dirty, straying into the no-go area of questions into his past? She looked down for a moment to gather herself, and realised that she'd asked all the scripted questions. And then some. She opened her mouth to start thanking him and signing off, when he surprised her by leaning forward.

'Now I have a question for you.'

'You do?' she squeaked. His eyes had changed from black and flinty to brown and...decidedly unflinty.

'Will you have dinner with me tonight?'

Shock and cold, clammy fear slammed into Alana. And then anger that he was asking her in front of an entire crew. The camera was still rolling. She could feel tension snake through the small studio. She tried to laugh it off, but knew she sounded constricted. 'I'm afraid, Mr Lévêque, that my boss doesn't approve of us mixing business with pleasure.'

Rory darted forward, while motioning for the crew to start wrapping up. 'Don't be silly, Alana, this is an entirely unique situation, and I'm sure you'd be only too delighted to show Mr Lévêque gratitude for taking time out of his busy schedule to do this interview.'

Pascal sat back, fully at ease. 'This is my last evening in Dublin. I thought it would be nice to see something of the city. I'd like your company, Alana, but if you insist on saying no, then of course I will understand.'

He stood up and looked down at Rory, straightening his cuffs. 'Can you have the tape of the interview sent over to my hotel? I'm sure it's fine, but I might take the opportunity to approve it fully if I've got some time on my hands.'

In other words, surmised Alana from the tortured look on Rory's pale face at the possibility of losing their biggest scoop to date, Pascal could turn right round and deny them the right to broadcast it. She stood up then, too, and spoke quickly before she could change her mind.

'That won't be necessary, Mr Lévêque. I'd love to have dinner with you. It would be a pleasure.'

CHAPTER TWO

'I DON'T appreciate being manipulated into situations, Mr Lévêque.'

Pascal looked at Alana's tight-lipped profile from across the other side of the car, and had to subdue the urge to show her exactly how much she might appreciate being manipulated. He knew she felt the simmering tension between them too. At one point during the interview earlier, when she'd had the temerity to dig so deep—too deep—their eyes had stayed locked together for long seconds and he'd read the latent desire in those green depths even if she tried to deny it.

'I prefer to think of it as a gentle nudging.'

She cast a quick look at him and made some kind of inarticulate sound. 'There was nothing gentle about it. Your unspoken threat was very clear, Mr Lévêque—the possibility that you could deny us the right to the interview.'

'Which is something I could still very well do,' he pointed out. As if on cue, Alana turned more fully in her seat. Her eyes spat sparks at him, and he felt a rush of adrenaline through his system. He was so tired of everyone kowtowing to him. But not so this green-eyed witch.

'Is this how you normally conduct your business?' she hissed, mindful of the driver in the front.

He moved closer in an instant, and Alana backed away with a jerk. She could smell his unique scent; already it was becoming familiar to her. One arm ran along the back of the seat, his hand resting far too close to her head, his whole body angled towards her, blocking out any sense of light or the dusky sky outside, creating an intimate cocoon.

'There's nothing businesslike about how you make me feel. And let's just say that I don't normally have to use threats to get a woman to come for dinner with me.'

Alana was reacting to a million things at once, not least of which was her own sense of fatal inevitability. 'No, I saw your track record; it doesn't appear as if you do.'

'Tell me, Alana, why are you so reluctant to go out with me?'

And why are you so determined? she wanted to shout. Her hands twisted in her lap, and Pascal caught the movement. Before she could stop him, he had reached down and taken her hands in his, uncurling them, lacing his fingers through with hers. Alana could feel a bizarre mix of soporific delight and a zing of desire so strong that she shook.

'I...don't even like you.'

'You don't know me enough to know if you like me or not. And what's flowing between us right now is nothing to do with *like.*'

It's lust. He didn't have to say it.

'I...'

His hands tightened. She could feel his fingers, long and capable, strong, wrapped around hers. She looked down, feeling dazed. She could see her own much paler, smaller hands in a tangle of dark bronze. The image made her think of other parts of her body—limbs enmeshed with his in a tangle of bedlinen. With super-human effort, she pulled her hands free and tucked them well out of his way. She looked at him, and she knew she must look haunted. She felt hunted. Ryan had never reduced her to this carnal level of feeling, and the wound he'd left in her life was still raw. Too raw.

Pascal was close, still crowding her, his eyes roving over her face, but something had changed in the air. He wasn't as intense. He reached out a hand and tucked some hair behind her ear.

'I like your hair down.'

'Look, Pascal…'

He felt something exultant move through him at her unconscious use of his name, and not the awful, prim 'Mr Lévêque'. He dropped his hand. 'Alana, it's just dinner. We'll eat, talk and I'll drop you home.'

At that moment she could feel the car slowing down. They were pulling up outside a world-class restaurant on St Stephen's Green. She seized on his words, his placating tone. She told herself she'd get a taxi home, and then she'd never have to see him again.

She looked at him and nodded jerkily. 'OK.'

Alana was burningly aware of the interest she and Pascal had generated as they followed the maître d' to the table. While the establishment was much too exclusive for the clientele to seriously rubberneck, nevertheless their interest was undeniably piqued.

It was another strike against the man who sat opposite her now, broad and so handsome, that despite her antipathy she couldn't help that hot flutter of response.

He sat back in his chair. Alana could feel the whisper of his long legs stretching out under the table, and she tucked hers so tightly under her chair that it was uncomfortable.

'You don't have to worry, Alana, I'm under no illusions; you're compartmentalising this very much in the "work" box.'

She just looked at him, and he quirked a brow at her.

'The fact that you insisted on meeting me at my hotel

rather than let me pick you up from your home, the fact that you haven't changed out of your work clothes.'

Alana felt stiff and unbelievably vulnerable at the way he was so incisively summing her up. 'I didn't have time to change. And, yes, for me this is work.' She leaned forward slightly then. His perceptiveness made her feel cornered. 'I've had the experience of living with a level of public interest that I never want to invite into my life again. Being here with you, being seen with you, could put me in an awkward position. I don't want people to think we're here on some sort of date.' She sat back with her heart thumping at the way his face had darkened ominously.

'So who do you date, then, Alana?'

'I don't.'

'But you *were* married to Ryan O'Connor.'

The fact that he'd already found that out made her feel inordinately exposed. Her mouth twisted cynically. 'No doubt you didn't have to dig too deep to find that out.'

'No deeper than you dug to find out about my life.'

'That was for a professional interview.'

'Do I need to remind you that your questions didn't exactly follow the script?'

She flushed hotly. His eyes flashed with that same icy fire she'd witnessed earlier. She said defensively, 'You must know that if you open yourself up to any kind of press attention, then there's a risk that you'll be asked about things that are off-limits.'

He inclined his head, the ice still in his eyes. 'Of course; I'm not so naïve. But somehow I hadn't expected that of you.'

Ridiculously, Alana felt hurt and guilty. He was right; with another person who wasn't pushing her buttons so much, she would never have taken the initiative to ask unscripted questions. It had been her reaction to him that had prompted her to try and provoke a response that would take his intense interest off her, that playful teasing he'd seemed set to disarm her with. Again she wondered what she'd scratched the surface of earlier.

She opened her mouth, but at that moment a waitress arrived and distracted them by taking their orders. Conversation didn't resume until she had returned with a bottle of white wine. They'd both ordered fish. Once they were alone again, Pascal sat up straight. 'You can tell yourself that you're here for work, Alana, but I did not ask you here to talk about work. It's a subject I have to admit I find intensely boring when we could be discussing much more interesting things....'

'Such as?' she asked faintly, mesmerised by the way his eyes had changed again into warm pools of dark promise.

He took a sip of wine and she followed his lead unconsciously, her mouth feeling dry.

'Such as where you went last night, if you don't date.'

Initially Alana had felt herself automatically tensing up at his question, but then something happened. She found herself melting somewhere inside, and there was nothing she could do to stop it. Some part of her was responding to his heat, and it was just too hard not to give in just a little. So she told him about her brother's fortieth birthday. And that led to telling him about her six brothers and sisters. And her parents.

'They're *all* happily married with kids?'

Alana had to smile at the vague look of horror on his face. She knew people sometimes couldn't get over the entirely normal fact of large Irish families. She nodded, but felt that awfully familiar guilt strike her. She was the anomaly in her family. She tried to ignore the pain and spoke lightly. 'My family are a glowing testament to the institution. I have a grand total of fifteen nieces and nephews and my parents have been happily married for fifty years.'

He shook his head in disbelief. 'And where do you come?'

'I'm the baby. Ten years younger than my youngest

brother. Apparently I was a happy mistake. The age gap meant that despite coming from such a big family I've always felt in some ways like an only child. For most of the time that I can remember, it was just me and my parents.'

Alana fell silent as she thought of her parents. She was acutely aware of their increasing frailty, and especially her father, who had had a triple bypass the previous year. With her older siblings busy with families and their own problems, the care and concern of their parents largely fell to her. Not that she minded, of course. But she was aware nevertheless that they worried about her, that they wanted to see her settled like the others. Especially after Ryan.

Alana took a quick gulp of coffee and avoided Pascal's laser-like gaze. They'd finished their meal, and the plates had been cleared. It was as if he could see right through her head to her thoughts. She hoped the coffee would dilute the effect of the wine, which had been like liquid nectar. She'd shrugged off her jacket some time ago, and the silk of her shirt felt ridiculously sensual against her skin. And she found that it was all too easy to talk to Pascal Lévêque. He was attentive, charming, interested. *Interesting.*

But then he cut through her glow of growing warmth by asking softly, 'So what happened with you?'

At first she didn't understand. 'What do you mean?'

'Your marriage. You were about to divorce your husband when he died, weren't you?'

Immediately the glow left, Alana tensed. She could see his eyes flare, watching her retreat.

Unconsciously she felt for her jacket to pull it back on, instinctively seeking for some kind of armour. Her voice felt harsh. 'I see that whoever your source was didn't stop at the bare facts.'

Pascal's jaw clenched. 'I'm not judging you, Alana, or anything like it. I'm just asking a question. I can't imagine it was easy to take a decision to divorce, coming from the family that you've described.'

Her arms stilled in the struggle to get her jacket on; his perceptiveness sneaked into some very vulnerable part of her. He didn't know the half of it. Her own family still didn't know the half of it. They'd been as mystified and dismayed as the rest of the country at her behaviour. Something her husband had ruthlessly exploited in a bid to win as much sympathy as possible.

She broke eye contact with effort and finished the job of putting on her jacket. Finally she looked at him again. 'I'd really prefer not to talk about my marriage.'

Pascal was tempted to push her, but could see her clam up visibly. She'd become more and more relaxed over the course of the meal. He'd had to restrain his eyes from dropping numerous times to the soft swell of her breasts under the fine silk of her shirt. He still had no idea why she seemed so determined to cover up as much as possible. But, instead of his interest waning, the opposite was true. He had to admit that was part of the reason he'd asked her out—some kind of bid to have her reveal herself to be boring or diminish her attraction—yet she was intriguing him on levels that no other woman had ever touched.

He was not done with this, with her. But he knew that if he pushed her now, he could very well lose her. This was going to test all his patience and skill, but the chase was well and truly on. So now he flashed his most urbane smile and just said, 'No problem.' And he called for the bill. The abject relief on her face struck him somewhere powerful.

Pascal wouldn't listen to Alana's protests. He insisted on dropping her to her house, which was only ten minutes from the restaurant. Tucked in a small square in one of the oldest parts of Dublin, her house was a tiny cottage. Pascal's car was too big to navigate past all the parked cars at the opening of the square, and she jumped out. But he was quick, too, met her at the other side of the car and insisted on walking her up to her door.

She turned at the door, feeling absurdly threatened, but by something in herself more than him. Standing close together, her eye level was on his chest, and she looked up into his dark face. The moon gleamed brightly in a clear sky, and the February air was chill. But she didn't feel cold. She had the strongest feeling that if he attempted to kiss her, she wouldn't be able to stop him. And something within her melted at that thought. She blamed the wine. And his innate French seductiveness.

But then suddenly he moved back. Alana found herself making a telling movement towards him, as if attached by an invisible cord and she saw a flash of something in his eyes as if he, too, had noted and understood her movement.

Before she could clam up, he had taken her hand in his and was bending his head to kiss the back of it, exactly as he had the previous night in the hotel. His old-fashioned gesture touched and confused her. Her hormones were see-sawing with desires and conflicting tensions. And then, with a lingering, unfathomable look, he started to walk away down the small square and back to his car. Against every rational notion in her head, Alana found herself calling his name. He half-turned.

'I just...I just wanted to say thank you for dinner.'

He walked back up towards her with an intensity of movement that belied his easy departure just now. For a second she thought he was going to come right up to her and kiss her. She took a step back, feeling a mixture of panic and anticipation, with her heart thumping, but he stopped just short of her. He reached out a hand and tucked some hair behind her ear. It was a gesture he'd made earlier in the car, and she found herself wanting to turn her cheek into his palm. But then his hand was gone. And his eyes were glittering in the dark.

'You're welcome, Alana. But don't get too complacent. We will be meeting again, I can promise you that.'

He turned again and strode back to his car. He got in, shut the door and the car pulled away. And Alana just stood there, her mouth open. Heat flooded her body and something much worse—*relief*. She knew now that she had called his name and said thanks, because something about watching him walk away had affected her profoundly. She had an uncontrollable urge to stop him.

She had to face it—even though she'd been telling herself she wasn't interested in him from the moment their eyes had locked at the match, she *was*. He was smashing through the veritable wall she'd built around herself since she'd married Ryan O'Connor and her life had turned into a sort of living hell. It was frightening how, in the space of twenty-four hours, she found herself in a situation where she was actually feeling disappointed that a man she barely knew hadn't kissed her. Her famously cool poise, which hid all her bitter disappointments and broken dreams from everyone, even her own family, was suddenly very shaky.

By the time Alana was standing in her tiny galley-kitchen the next morning drinking her wake-up cup of tea, she felt much more in control. She only had to look around her house, in which she quite literally could not swing a cat, to feel on firmer ground. This was reality. This was all she'd been able to afford after Ryan had died. Her mouth tightened. Contrary to what everyone believed, she hadn't been left a millionairess after her football-star husband had died in the accident.

She was still picking up the pieces emotionally and financially from her five years of marriage. And, while her emotional scars might heal one day, the financial ones would be keeping her in this tiny cottage and working hard for a very long time. The truth was that Ryan had left astronomical debts behind him and, because their divorce hadn't come through by the time he'd died, they'd become Alana's responsibility. The sale of their huge house in the upmarket area of Dalkey had barely made a dent in what had been owed to various lenders.

Alana swallowed the last of her tea and grimaced as she washed out the cup. Pride was a terrible thing, she knew. But it had also given her a modicum of dignity. She'd never confided in anyone about the dire state of her marriage, had never told anyone about the day she'd walked into her bedroom to find Ryan in bed with three women who'd turned out to be call girls. They'd all been high on cocaine. He'd been too out of it to realise that it wasn't even his bedroom. By then, it had been at least three years since *they'd* shared a bed.

That had been the day that her humiliation had reached saturation point. The pressure of having to maintain a façade of a happy marriage had tipped over into unbearability. She'd left and filed for divorce.

But her wily husband had quickly made sure that it looked as though Alana had coldly kicked him out. She hadn't suspected his motives when he'd sheepishly offered to move out instead of her. But she should have known. The man she'd married had changed beyond all recognition as soon as he'd started earning enormous fees and tasted the heady heights of what it was to be a national superstar.

Admitting that she'd failed at her marriage had been soul destroying. She hadn't wanted to confide the awful reality of it to anyone. Even if she had wanted to, her father's health had been frail, and her mother had been focused solely on him. And, around the same time, one of her elder sisters had been diagnosed with breast cancer. With her sister having three children, and Alana being the only childless sibling and suddenly single again, she had moved into her sister's home to help her brother-in-law for the few months that Màire had spent getting treatment. Alana's marital problems had taken a backseat, and she'd been glad of the distraction while the divorce was worked out. She'd kept herself to herself and shunned her family's well-meaning probing, too heart-sore and humiliated even to talk about it.

It was exactly as Pascal had intuited last night, and she hated to admit that. It *had* been so hard, coming from a family of successfully married siblings, to be the only one to fail and to cause her parents such concern. Her monumental lack of judgement haunted her to this day. She obviously couldn't trust herself when it came to character assessment, never mind another man. And Pascal Lévêque was ringing so many bells that it should make it easy to reject his advances.

Alana brusquely pulled on her coat and got her keys. She refused to let her mind wander where it wanted: namely down a route that investigated the possibility of giving in to Pascal Lévêque's advances. Alana reassured herself that by now he'd have forgotten the wholly unremarkable Irish woman who had piqued his interest for thirty-six hours.

Thirty-six hours. That's all it had been. And yet it wasn't enough. Pascal stood at the window of his Paris office and looked out over the busy area of La Défense with its distinctive Grande Arche in the distance.

Alana Cusack was taking up a prominence in his head that was usually reserved for facts and figures. Ordinarily he could compartmentalise women very well; they didn't intrude on his every waking hour. They were for pleasure only, and fleeting pleasure at that. The minute he saw that look come into their eye, or heard that tone come into their voice, it was time to say goodbye. He enjoyed his freedom, the thrill of the chase, the conquest. No strings, no commitment.

But now a green-eyed, buttoned-up, starchy-collared, impertinent-questioning witch was making a hum of sexual frustration throb through his blood. He had to get her out of his system. Prove to himself that his desire had only been whetted because she was playing hard to get, and only because she *seemed* to be a little more intriguing than any other woman he'd met. The fact that she'd been married intrigued him too. Her marriage had obviously left her scarred. That had been clear from a mile away. Was that why she was so prickly, so uptight and defensive, so wary? Was she still grieving for her husband?

Pascal ran a hand through his hair impatiently. Enough! He turned his back on the view and called his PA into the room. She listened to his instructions and took down all the details, and she was professional enough not to give Pascal any indication that what he'd just asked her to do was in any way out of the ordinary.

But it was.

'There's something for you on your desk, Alana.'

'Thanks, Soph,' Alana answered distractedly as she flipped through her notes on her return from a lunchtime interview and walked into her tiny cubbyhole office just off the main newsroom. She looked up for a quick second to smile at Sophie, the general runaround girl, and her smile faltered when she saw the other girl's clearly mischievous look. With foreboding in her heart, Alana opened her door, and there on her desk was the biggest bunch of flowers she'd ever seen in her life. Her notebook and pen slid from her fingers onto the table. With a trembling hand, she plucked the card free from amongst the ridiculously extravagant blooms.

She cast a quick look back out the door, and seeing no one, quickly shut it. She ripped the envelope open and took out the card, which was of such luxurious quality that it felt about an inch thick between her fingers. All that was written on the card in beautiful calligraphy was one mystifying letter: 'I…'

She was completely and utterly bemused. Her dread was that they would be from him. But the card was enigmatic. They could actually be from anyone.

Not one person looked at her oddly afterwards, though, not even the junior reporter who covered current affairs who had drunkenly admitted at the office party last Christmas to having a crush on her. It wasn't her birthday, and she hadn't done an especially amazing babysitting-stint lately for any nieces or nephews, which sometimes resulted in flowers as a thank-you.

For the rest of the day Alana was like a cat on a hot tin roof. Distracted. She only left and brought the flowers home once she was sure nearly everyone had left the office.

The following day, as Alana walked in, flicking through her post, Sophie again said, 'Morning! There's something for you on your desk.'

Alana's heart stopped. It was like groundhog day. She went into her office with a palpitating heart and shut the door firmly behind her. Another bunch of flowers. Slightly different, but as extravagant as yesterday's. Her hands were sweating as she repeated the process of opening the envelope and taking out the card. This one read: 'will…'

By the end of the week Alana sat at the wooden table in her sitting room and felt a little numb. The smell of flowers was overpowering in the tiny artisan-cottage. A vase sat in the centre of the table abundant with blooms. And also on the table in front of her, neatly lined up in a row, were the five cards that had accompanied a different bunch of flowers every single day of the week.

All together, they now made sense: 'I will see you tonight'.

But of course she'd known what the full meaning of the

cards was when she'd received the fifth one that morning. All day she'd experienced a fizzing in her veins and a sick churning in her belly. She'd vaguely thought of going to the cinema, or seeing if friends wanted to go out, anything to avoid being at home where she was sure he was going to call. An awful sense of inevitability washed over her. She wasn't ready for this. She would just have to make him see that and send him on his way. But still…the gesture, the flowers, and his obvious intention to fly all the way back to Dublin just to see her, was nothing short of overwhelming.

Her phone rang shrilly in the silence and she jumped violently, her heart immediately hammering. Her mouth was dry. 'Hello?'

'What's this about you and Pascal Lévêque?'

Alana sagged onto the arm of her sofa. 'Ailish.' Her oldest and bossiest sister was always guaranteed to raise her hackles. Twenty years separated them, and sometimes Ailish came across as a little overbearing to say the least. She meant well, though, which took the sting out of her harsh manner.

'So? What's going on? Apparently one of the world's most eligible bachelors took you out for dinner last weekend.'

Tension held Alana's body straight. 'How did you hear about it?'

'It was in the tabloids today.'

Alana groaned inwardly, wondering how she'd missed that. Someone at work must have leaked the story. God knew, enough people had heard him ask her. And it wouldn't have taken a rocket scientist to work out who the flowers had been from, either.

'Look, I interviewed him and he took me for dinner, that's all. Nothing is going on.' The betraying vision of her house full to the roof with flowers made her wince.

Her sister harumphed down the phone. 'Well, I just hope you're not going to be gracing the tabloids every day with tales of sexual exploits with a Casanova like that. I mean, can you imagine if Mam and Dad saw that? It was bad enough having to defend you to practically the whole nation after you threw Ryan out—'

Alana stood up, her whole body quivering. The memory of her parents' lined and worried faces was vivid. And her guilt. 'Ailish, what I do and who I see is none of your business. Do I comment on your marriage to Tom?'

'You wouldn't need to,' replied her sister waspishly. 'We're not the ones being discussed over morning coffee by the nation.'

Alana heard her doorbell ring and she automatically went to answer it. 'Like I said, what I do is none of your business.' Her sister's 'judge and jury' act made anger throb through her veins, and she knew her voice was rising. She struggled for a minute with the habitually stiff lock, and tucked the phone between her neck and shoulder to use both hands.

'I am a fully grown woman and I can see who I want, go where I want, and have sex with who I want whenever I please.'

The door finally opened. Her words hung on the cool evening air as she took in the devastatingly gorgeous sight of Pascal Lévêque just standing there, turning her inner-city enclave into something much more exotic. Her heart-rate soared. She'd forgotten all about him in the space of the last few seconds, and the high emotion her sister had been evoking. In her shock she lifted her head and her phone dropped to the ground with a tinny clatter.

Pascal swiftly bent and picked it up.

An irate voice could be heard: 'Alana? *Alana!*'

Alana couldn't take her eyes off Pascal. She took her phone back, lifted it to her ear and said vaguely, 'Ailish, someone's just arrived. I'll call you back, OK?'

Words resounded in her head: *too late to escape now.*

CHAPTER THREE

BY THE time Alana had stepped back into her house, followed by a tall, dark and imposing Pascal Lévêque, the shock was rapidly wearing off. She crossed her arms and rounded on him with a scowl on her face. Once again he was demonstrating that ability to suck in the space around him and make everything seem more intense—dwarfed. She tried to block out the fact that he was quite simply the most handsome man who'd ever stood feet away from her and looked at her with an intensity that bordered on being indecent.

'That phone call was a conversation that shouldn't have had to happen. And it was all your fault.'

He inclined his head slightly. He looked *huge* in her tiny sitting room. 'I apologise, but, as all I heard was the intriguing last sentence, you'll have to forgive me as I don't know what I've done. And *we* certainly haven't had sex yet.'

Alana flushed when she recalled what she'd been saying to her sister as she'd opened the door. 'Did you know that apparently our dinner date was in the papers today?' Defensive, angry energy radiated off her in waves. She could almost see them, like a heat haze.

He shook his head, his eyes never leaving hers, hypnotising her. 'No. I wasn't aware of that. But of course, there were people at the restaurant, and I would imagine that one or two people heard me ask you at the studio; perhaps it was leaked.'

Alana laughed out loud. 'One or two? Try the whole crew standing in the room. It's recorded on tape, for God's sake.'

He started to shrug off his big, black overcoat and proceeded to whip out a bottle of wine from somewhere, like a magician. Panic flowed through Alana. She put out her hands as if that might halt him. 'What do you think you're doing? Stop taking off your coat right now.'

She shook her head emphatically. 'No way; you are not coming in here with a bottle of wine, and we are not going to be having a cosy chat.'

For a big man he moved swiftly and gracefully. His coat was already draped over one arm, the bottle of red wine in one hand, long fingers visible. She remembered him holding her hands, entwining those fingers with hers. A pulse throbbed between her legs.

She looked up at him and knew she must look slightly desperate—she felt desperate.

'I don't mind where we go, Alana, but I've come all this way to see you, so you're not getting away.'

His voice was like deep velvet over steel. He meant what he said.

She gulped. 'What do you want?' she asked weakly. He was threatening and invading every aspect of what had been up till now her impregnable defence.

Pascal restrained himself from telling her exactly what he wanted. He didn't want to frighten her off. But what he wanted very much involved a lot less clothes and a flat, preferably soft surface. She was dressed all in black, her hair tied back. Not a stiff shirt this time, but a roll-neck top that effectively concealed everything. And yet the material had to be cashmere or something, because it clung to her torso and chest, and for the first time he could see the proper shape of her. The thrust of her breasts against the fabric was sensual torture. They were perfectly formed, high and firm. He could imagine that they would fill his hands like ripe, succulent fruits, their tips hardening against the palm of his hand... He slammed the door on his rampant imaginings. His arousal was springing to life. He forced himself to sound reasonable, calm.

'What I would like is to share this bottle of wine with you and to talk. We can go somewhere else if you'd prefer.'

Alana looked at him suspiciously, hating this invasion of her space. He was as immoveable as a rock. If they went somewhere else that would involve more time. If they stayed here, he'd be gone sooner. She made her reluctant decision and reached out a hand.

'We might as well stay here. It's a Friday night; most places in town would be like cattle markets by now.'

Despite her obvious lack of delight at the prospect, Pascal carefully masked the intense surge of triumph he felt and handed over the wine, even being careful to make sure their hands didn't touch, knowing that could set him back. *Dieu!* This woman was like an assault on his every sense. He hadn't imagined her allure, she was more vivid, more sexy, more *everything*, in the flesh.

As Alana went into the galley-kitchen, she was aware of him moving into the sitting room, hands in the pockets of his trousers and looking around. She sent him a surreptitious glance. He was dressed smartly—dark trousers and a light shirt, top button open as if he'd discarded a tie somewhere. He must have come straight from work—on a private plane? Somehow she couldn't imagine him queueing up with lesser mortals for a scheduled flight. He was the kind of man who would stride across the tarmac and climb into a sleek, snazzy jet.

'You got my flowers, I see.'

Alana's hand stilled on the bottle opener for a moment. She looked at him. 'Yes, thank you.' She cringed inwardly. Had he seen the cards all laid out in a row on the table as he'd come in? 'You shouldn't have, though. It caused no amount of speculation at work, and I'd really prefer if you didn't.' God, she sounded so uptight. And what was to say he'd ever send her flowers again anyway?

'As you can see, this house isn't exactly big enough to take them.'

Pascal looked around and thought privately that this was hardly what she must have been used to, as Ryan O'Connor's wife. It made her even more enigmatic. She was fast proving that, whatever scene she'd been a part of in the past, that was not who she was now. 'No, I guess not. I'm sorry if I embarrassed you, Alana, I merely wanted to show you that I meant what I said, about seeing you again, and I didn't have your number, so…'

Alana stabbed the cork with the bottle opener. 'It's fine; forget it. The old-folks' home around the corner were delighted, as they got the other half of the flower shop you sent.'

She sent him a small, rueful smile then, unable to help herself. She didn't like being ungrateful for gifts.

Pascal was looking at her with an arrested expression on his face, his eyes intent on the area of her mouth. Her lips tingled. Alana's hands stopped on the cork. 'What is it?'

But then his eyes lifted to hers as if she'd imagined it, and he went back to looking at her books and prints. 'Nothing.'

Eventually she pulled the cork free with a loud pop and got down two glasses from her open shelves. She poured the wine and handed him a glass, keeping one for herself.

He stood looking at her for a long moment and then held his glass out. Her heart thumped at what he might say, but all he said was, *'Santé.'*

She clinked her glass to his and replied with the Irish, *'Sláinte.'*

They both took a sip. She couldn't quite believe that he was standing here in front of her. The wine was like liquid velvet, fragrant, round and smooth. Clearly very expensive. Alana indicated for him to sit on her couch. He did, and dwarfed the three-seater. She sat in the armchair opposite. The lighting was soft and low. The space far too intimate. This was her sanctuary, her place of refuge. And yet, having him here wasn't generating the effect that she would have expected. She was still angry, yes—but more than that was something else, something like excitement.

She thought of something then as her stomach growled quietly. 'Have you eaten?'

He took another drink from his glass and shook his head. 'No.' He just realised then that he'd hardly eaten all day; he'd been so consumed with getting out of Paris and over here. It made him feel uncomfortable now.

Alana put down her glass and stood up. 'I was going to make myself something to eat…that is, if you want something, too?'

'That would be great, I'm starving.' He smiled, and the room seemed to tilt for a second.

Alana picked up her glass and backed into the kitchen, which was just feet away from where he now sat with an arm stretched out over the back of the sofa. At home, as if he dropped in all the time from Paris. She couldn't think of that now.

'It's just fish, lemon sole, nothing too exciting. But I have two…'

He nodded. 'That sounds perfect. Thank you.'

Alana busied herself turning on the oven and putting potatoes on to boil. When she looked back over to the sitting room, she could see that Pascal was looking through her CDs.

She had a moment of clarity. What was she doing? She was meant to be rushing him out of the house, not cooking him dinner! But, she had to concede, it had been easy to ask him. And he *had* sent her all those amazing flowers. If she was never going to see him after tonight, then what was the harm in a little dinner?

Happy that she'd justified her actions to herself, and not willing to pay attention to the hum of *something* in her blood, when she heard the strains of her favourite jazz CD coming from the sound system, she found it soothing rather than scary.

'I hope you don't mind?'

She looked over to where Pascal was hunched down at the system, the material of his trousers and shirt straining over taut, hard muscles in his thighs and back. She shook her head, her mouth feeling very dry.

'No…no.' She took another hasty gulp of wine. *Oh God.*

By the time Alana was taking his cleared plate from him, and apologising again that their dinner had been on their knees, she was smiling at something he'd just said. As she'd been preparing the dinner, they'd started up an innocuous conversation, and in the course of eating had managed to touch on films, books, French politics, the Six Nations and rugby. She'd found herself telling him about her father's career playing for Ireland, unable to keep the pride from her voice. And she hadn't mistaken the gleam of something unfathomable in his eyes. Even though he'd told her he hadn't wanted to play, had he harboured ambitions?

She came back and sat down, tucking her legs under her. She'd slipped off her shoes. She felt energised, zingy, as if she could stay up all night.

To her surprise, she saw Pascal look at his watch and then he drained his glass of wine. He stood up and Alana felt unaccountably disorientated. She stood too. The space between them was electric.

'I'm afraid I have to go.'

Alana immediately felt crushed, silly, exposed. She should have been grinning from ear to ear, racing to hand him his coat, saying good riddance—so why did she feel her stomach hollowing out at the thought? The old pain of past misjudgements rose up like a spectre.

'Oh, well. I can imagine you must have some business here. Somewhere else to be?'

He shook his head and came close. Alana couldn't back away as the chair was just behind her legs. Her heart was thumping so hard she felt it must be visible under her top.

'I've got important meetings at home all weekend. It's too boring to go into. But I need to make my flight slot tonight, otherwise I'll miss my first meeting in the morning.'

Alana's jaw dropped. 'You're going back to *Paris*? Now?'

He nodded.

The knowledge was having trouble sinking into her brain: he had come all the way to Dublin just to see her for a few hours; it was too much for her to take in.

'I…I…'

Her shock was obviously transparent.

He pulled a quirky, sexy smile. 'It was worth it, Alana. Just to see you again. I've been thinking about you all week. I can't seem to get you out of my head.'

'I…' Her powers of speech had been rendered null and void. He was coming closer, making speech even more elusive and unlikely.

He was now so close that her head was tipped back to look into those dark, dark eyes. She felt a warm finger come under her chin, stroking the smooth skin, his thumb on her chin. She couldn't move.

His scent enveloped her in a haze of desire, desire that

she'd never felt before. She fancied that she could hear his heartbeat too. Then he spoke and his voice was harsh. 'I told myself I wouldn't do this now. But…I can't *not*. You're more intoxicating to me than anything or anyone I've ever known. And all week I've been imagining what it would be like.'

She swallowed, 'What *what* would be like?' But she knew. And heaven help her but she'd been imagining it too. She knew she had; she'd just been denying it.

He said the words and something awful like relief flowed through her.

'To kiss you.'

With his finger still under her chin, no other parts of their bodies touching, he bent his head to hers. Past, present and future collided in the moment that her eyelids fluttered closed, and she felt his mouth touch hers. It was a brief press of his lips to hers, a testing, tasting. But it ignited a flame of raw desire along every one of Alana's veins.

When he drew back slightly, she made a treacherous sound in her throat. She wanted more than that brief all-too-chaste kiss. And so did he evidently.

This time it wasn't chaste and benedictory, this time it was forceful, both their mouths pressing together, tasting, experiencing. The finger at her chin was gone. His hand slid round to the back of her head, flicked away the band tying her hair in a ponytail and threaded through the soft, silky strands to cradle her skull in his hand. His other arm slid around her slim waist and pulled her into him. Her arms automatically went to his shoulders and clung for support.

The feel of his body pressed up close to hers was short-circuiting her system. He was hard all over, and so strong. She could feel his chest muscles flex against her soft curves when his arm tightened around her, pulling her even closer.

While their bodies melded together, their mouths remained fused. Pascal pulled back briefly and Alana looked up into those amazing eyes that were burning, reflecting a fire she felt deep in her belly, where a very hard part of him was making her want to move restlessly. She was stunned by everything. She felt confused; she could feel herself tremble with reaction. She frowned slightly, her mouth opened.

Pascal pressed a finger to her mouth. The softness of her lips and her warm breath made him harder, and he almost groaned out loud with the need to take her now, to sink into her yielding, silky warmth. But he knew that she wasn't far from letting her head take over, from possibly pushing him away. 'Don't think. Don't speak. Just *feel*.'

This time when his mouth touched hers it was slightly open. Breaths mingled and wove together, and for one split second neither of them breathed. And then Pascal slid his tongue between her lips and Alana's hands clutched at his shoulders. She'd been kissed like this before; of course she had. But whenever Ryan had kissed her, it had always been rough and with no finesse.

But this was in another league. Pascal's tongue danced erotically with hers, advanced and retreated, inviting her to follow him. And she did. Winding her arms tight around his neck, pressing even closer, she slid her tongue into his mouth and was rewarded with a low guttural moan. It was the sexiest feeling, and she was controlling the pace, the movements. She savoured his full lower lip, felt it with her tongue, let it glide across the surface before allowing their tongues to duel again.

When she felt him snake a hand under her top, to feel the skin above her trousers, the curve of her waist, her legs trembled in earnest. Their kisses stilled for a second, as if he was waiting to see what signal she would give. She nipped his lower lip gently and she could feel him half-smile against her mouth.

His hand slid higher over her smooth back, to just below the clasp of her bra. His hand was so big she imagined it could span her entire back. With a practised flick of his wrist and fingers, he opened the clasp. Alana felt her bra loosen, but she was lost in a maelstrom of lust so strong that she wanted nothing more than for him take the weight and fullness of her breast into his palm—which he promptly did, sliding his whole hand around her ribs as if loath not to caress every part of her. The sensation was so shockingly electric that she gasped and wrenched her mouth from his, breathing jerkily.

His other hand still cradled her head; their bodies were still fused at every conceivable point. She was on her tiptoes to try and keep his hardness there, at the apex of her thighs where a loud, heavy beat of blood called to her. She couldn't do anything but look up into his glittering, aroused gaze as his hand cupped her heavy flesh and his thumb moved back and forth over the tingling, tight peak of her nipple.

She bit her lip, and he bent his head to whisper hotly in her ear, 'I want to take it into my mouth until you come apart in my arms…until you're so wet that sliding into you will be the easiest thing in the world.'

A million things were hurtling into Alana's head. Past experiences, warnings, wants and confusion reigned. What was happening to her? She should be shocked, but she wasn't. She'd never thought in a million years she could respond like this, and yet they had done little more here and now than she'd already experienced at teen discos years ago. Or during her marriage.

Pascal could see the way her eyes were clearing, the way those green depths were starting to swirl. He had to pull back, even if it was going to kill him. Gently he closed her bra again and stepped back slightly to pull down her top. He'd been right; her body with its gentle curves was infinitely more alluring than he'd ever expected it to be, her breasts fuller. It was a crime that she hid under those structured tops and dark colours.

He put his hands on her shoulders and stepped back completely, and tried to ignore the inferno raging in his pants.

'I have to go. I wish I didn't, but I do. You could come with me?' he asked then, but already he could see her start to tense, stiffen.

'No,' he answered for her. 'It's too soon.' He castigated himself for his lack of control.

He walked over to get his coat which was draped on the back of a chair, and pulled it on. He saw the cards that had accompanied the flowers neatly lined up to show the sentence they'd spelt out. Something forceful struck him then. He'd never gone to such trouble before. Women always said yes; it was always easy. But recently his experiences with women had always proved somewhat unsatisfactory. And now merely kissing Alana was making him feel like a randy teenager again.

Alana welcomed the distance as she watched him put his coat on, accentuating his shoulders, his broad back. His shoulders that she'd just been clutching with complete abandon, because if she hadn't, she'd have dissolved at his feet. What had he done to her? What the hell did he think he was doing, waltzing in here for just a few hours only to mess up her carefully controlled world? She crossed her arms over still tight and sensitive breasts.

He turned around and saw her look immediately. 'Don't look at me like that.'

Alana's jaw tensed so hard she felt it might break. 'I don't want this. I don't want you.'

He covered the paltry distance between them in a couple of steps, floorboards creaking under his weight.

'I think I've just proven that you *do* want me. And I want you. Badly.'

In a shocking move he took her hand and brought it down to where she could feel his agony for herself. Hectic colour flooded her cheeks.

'There's something rare and powerful between us, Alana, and I won't let you shut me out just because you're scared.'

She snatched her hand back from where the hard evidence of his arousal was threatening to overheat her brain again. 'I am *not* scared.' *Liar.* 'I just don't want this. I really don't want this.'

His stance was strong, legs planted wide, face implacable. 'It's already happening. We can't go back now. You could have sent back the flowers, or thrown them out.' He flung out a hand. 'But you didn't. You could have refused to let me come into your house tonight, but you didn't.'

Humiliation coursed through her. He was right. She'd put up absolutely no fight whatsoever. What was she doing? Had she learnt nothing?

'You're covering the match in Italy next weekend in Stadio Flaminio?'

His abrupt change of subject caught her unawares. 'Yes. Yes, I am.'

'I have an apartment in Rome. Come over on Friday night and stay with me for the weekend. I have to go to the match, too, and my bank is sponsoring a charity ball on Saturday night—you could come with me.'

Alana automatically shook her head and quailed slightly under the harsh light in his eyes.

'My flight on Saturday morning is booked already. I'm going with colleagues. And I'm due back on Sunday morning. It's all organised.'

'And do you always do what you're told?' he asked softly, softly enough to disarm her for a second. It made a poignant memory rise up. She hadn't always been so conventional, so careful to stick to the rules. There had been a time when she'd been very much a free spirit. That was how she'd met Ryan; she'd fallen for the passionate free spirit she'd seen in him. But she'd had it all wrong. His passion had never been for her or even life. It had been for money, fame and adulation. And then he'd slowly killed any such impulse in her, reducing her to a shadow of her former self.

Alana looked up. Caught between two worlds and painful memories, she found herself instinctively clinging on to something in Pascal's eyes.

'I will have my plane at your disposal.'

'But that's crazy.'

He shushed her. 'At your disposal. It will be at Dublin airport on Friday evening, ready to take you to Rome to meet me. I would like you to use it, Alana. I would like you to stay with me. I won't force you into anything you're not comfortable with. Or ready for.'

She would have laughed, but the intensity in his face stopped her. He was holding out a card. She took it warily.

'Those are all my numbers, and my assistant's numbers. If you're going to come on Friday, just call her and give her your passport details and she'll give you all the information and arrange for a pick-up to deliver you to the plane.'

To deliver her to him like a gift-wrapped parcel.

Everything in Alana rebelled at the thought of being so easy, so compliant. But another part of her was beating hard at the thought of how easy it would be to just…do this. Had she really envisaged living her entire life celibate? While she knew well that Pascal took women for just a finite amount of time, perhaps that was what she needed—a no-strings affair. He was already smashing the awful, soul-destroying belief that somehow she'd been frigid. But then, if Pascal discovered the extent of her lack of experience, would he be turned off? Doubts crowded her mind again. How could she even be seriously contemplating this?

And now he really was leaving, opening the small hall door, ducking his head to go out through the front door.

She forced her stricken limbs to move, and followed him.

When he turned round, she was on her step. Before she could move, he'd pulled her into him and pressed his mouth to hers, sliding his tongue between her lips, making her heart beat fast and her blood turn to treacle in seconds. She could already feel herself melting. And then he pulled away and set her back.

'See?' was all he said, was all he had to say. He backed away and then turned to walk down the square. As if by magic a sleek, dark car pulled up at the bottom of the square and then he was getting into the back and was gone. Alana's hands curled into fists at her sides, her emotions and hormones in chaotic turmoil. Every carefully erected piece of defence was crashing and burning. There was no way she would take him up on his offer. No way.

Those very words came back to mock Alana as she sat in the back of a very familiar, luxurious Lexus which was speeding through the usual tangled Dublin Friday-night rush hour like a hot knife through butter, almost as if Pascal had decreed it. Not even the traffic was giving her a chance to stop and think, to change her mind. Her small weekend-bag was in the boot. And she couldn't even reassure herself that it had been a last-minute decision; she'd packed her bag last night as if on autopilot, as if somehow it hadn't really been her doing it.

And then she'd brought it to work that morning, and had coolly informed her boss that she'd made alternative arrangements for getting to Rome. And then she'd rung Pascal's assistant, and told her that she'd be on the plane that evening. His assistant had been brisk and efficient, ringing back within ten minutes with the details of who would be picking her up, leaving her no time to think about backing out.

And now here she was.

On the way to becoming Pascal Lévêque's newest lover.

And her only reaction was one of intense anticipation. She'd finally had to give into it. She'd vacillated each torturous day that week, from vowing absolutely that she would do no such thing, to staring into space, remembering what it had been like to have him kiss her, and wanting him with a hunger that shocked her.

He'd called to speak to her every evening, too, having made sure to take her number, but had never mentioned Rome. He'd ask her about her day, and tell her a little about his. He was a master tactician, slowly but surely wearing down her defences. She'd found herself looking forward to speaking to him. It was when she'd woken in the middle of the previous night, to find herself in tangled sheets damp with sweat after an intensely erotic dream, that she'd got up and packed. It was only after she'd done that, she'd been able to go back to sleep.

Another dark, sleek car with tinted windows was waiting on the tarmac at the airport in Rome. She'd seen it out of the window as they'd landed. Now she took a deep breath, her case in a white-knuckle grip as the air steward waited for the door to open. Alana straightened her short jacket over her dress. She hadn't changed from her work clothes, her *armour*. A black pinafore dress, complete with shirt and tie, stockings and high-heeled shoes.

The clunking noise of the steps being wheeled to the aircraft made her jump, and she smiled nervously at the steward, wondering in a fleeting, scary moment how many women he'd escorted to meet Pascal like this. All of a sudden she wanted to go, leave. She'd made a huge mistake.

But then the door opened and there was nowhere to go but forward.

And there he was. It was too late to turn back now.

It was dark and slightly chilly as she walked down the steps. Pascal was waiting at the bottom, dressed casually in jeans, looking relaxed, vibrant and beautiful. He didn't move to touch her, and he didn't look triumphant. And she was grateful, because if he had she might have scuttled back up the steps and ordered the pilot to take her back home.

'Here, let me.' He took her case and the driver transferred it to the boot of the car. Pascal indicated for her to get in. And then he shut the door and walked round to the other side. The door closed and they were moving.

Enclosed in the intimate space, Alana felt as if she were on fire. Suddenly her shirt and tie were ridiculously restrictive. She couldn't look at Pascal. Silence thickened, but it wasn't awkward. As they approached the city, Pascal started pointing out landmarks in a neutral, deep voice. Just that alone had an effect on her body, the fine hairs standing up all over her skin. Yet it was also calming, as if he were trying to soothe her. She still hadn't looked directly at him, but then she felt his hand, warm and very real on her chin and jaw, turning her head towards him.

Did she have any idea how beautiful she looked? Did she have any idea what her effect on him was in those clothes? That damn shirt and tie had featured in every fantasy that had kept him awake, tossing and turning, all week. Her eyes were huge, staring at him with a mixture of fear and trepidation.

'Thank you,' he said huskily.

She swallowed, and he could feel the small movement. He couldn't take his hand from her chin. He wanted to smooth and caress the silky skin all over her body.

'I'm still…not sure that I'm doing the right thing.' She looked for a second as if she were gearing herself up for something, and then she said in a rush, 'How many women have you had delivered to you by plane like that?'

Her honesty hit him between the eyes. He knew this was important. This could determine the weekend—*them*. He didn't have to lie. 'No one. I have travelled on that plane with women, but I've never sent it especially for someone before.

Alana, you wouldn't be here if you didn't think this was right. Don't you trust your own judgement?'

The minute he'd said the words he could feel her tense, could see her withdraw mentally and physically. What had he said?

She reached up and took his hand down. 'That's just the problem,' she said with a sterile voice. 'My track record when it comes to judgement leaves a lot to be desired.'

Her husband—she had to be referring to her marriage. It made him want to quiz her, ask her what she meant. But he wasn't in the habit of wanting to know extraneous personal details of his lovers' past experiences, and he rejected the desire now. Pascal wanted her attention back with him with an urgency that bordered on the painful. He found her hand and wound his fingers through hers, not letting her pull away.

'Alana, this thing between us is too important to ignore. Trust *that*, if nothing else.'

She knew that it would have been the height of naïvety to assume that Pascal had never taken another lover on his plane. She gave up trying to pull her hand away and let it rest in his. She also gave up trying to avoid his eyes. They glowed with dark embers of sensual promise.

A hum of electricity flowed between them. He wasn't exaggerating; she'd never ever thought anyone would make her feel this way. She'd once foolishly and romantically thought that this was the way she'd feel with her husband.

But she hadn't.

And she'd blamed herself for that—but for the first time she could see more clearly that it had been just as much Ryan's fault as her own.

Perhaps this was her chance to start living again, to stop closing herself off to the world in some kind of misplaced penance she felt she owed. Her husband had taken enough of her life and soul. It was time to take some back for herself.

'We're here.'

Alana's hand tightened reflexively in Pascal's. He didn't rush her. He let her take a look outside the car. They were on a quiet street. Old stone steps led up to a foliage-covered walkway through which Alana could see a massive, ornate door.

When the driver had taken out her case and walked round to open her door, Pascal finally released her hand and she got out. The Rome night air was cool and fragrant. Pascal picked up her case and took her hand, leading her up the garden path; she wasn't unaware of the metaphor. He let go of her to open the door. All was darkness when they walked in at first, but then Pascal flicked a switch nearby and lights came on, low and intimate. Alana gasped. It was stunning.

A huge, lofty high-ceilinged room with massive windows led in one direction into a large kitchen, and the other direction into a huge open-plan living area. It was all decorated in white, prints on the walls and dramatic cushions on the couches adding splashes of colour. Inexplicably, this heartened Alana. She wasn't sure what she had been expecting, but she knew that if Pascal had shown her into some kind of sterile bachelor-pad all her misgivings would have returned with a vengeance.

'Come; I'll show you upstairs.'

Wordlessly, she followed him up a wide staircase to the side of the living area. Upstairs were huge windows. He showed her into a big bedroom. The feel of deep, luxurious carpet underfoot made her instinctively bend to take off her shoes. She saw him look and grimaced slightly, holding her shoes in her hands. 'I hope you don't mind. My feet are killing me.'

He shook his head. 'Not at all.' He put her case down at the bottom of the king-sized bed that was dressed in Egyptian cotton. 'This is your room, Alana.'

He walked to the door and gestured across the hall to where she could see in through an open door to another dimly lit large room, dressed in more masculine tones. 'That's my room.' He turned then and stuck his hands in his pockets. 'Obviously I would prefer you to share my room with me, but it'll be your move to make.'

Alana bit her lip. He couldn't know how important it was to her that he wasn't pushing her. 'Thank you. I appreciate that.'

He held out a hand. 'Leave your things there. You must be hungry; I'll prepare us something to eat downstairs.'

Alana shrugged off her jacket to lay it over the back of a chair, and felt the energy zip up her arm when she took his hand.

'You can cook?' she asked a little breathlessly as he led her out in her stockinged feet.

He glanced back with a smile. 'I can just about manage to burn some pasta and tomato sauce. Are you hungry?'

Just then her stomach rumbled. She smiled too. 'Starving.'

With a full stomach and a languorous feeling snaking through her bones, Alana walked around the downstairs living-area with a glass of wine in her hand, looking at Pascal's prints and sculptures. She was transfixed by one photograph; something about it was very familiar. It was black and white, an old man's face, gnarled and lined, very dark, even a hint of some other exotic lineage. His eyes were remarkable, deep set and black, holding such a wealth of emotion that Alana could feel it reach out and envelop her. There was everything in that expression: regret, pain, love, passion, disappointment, hope.

'That's my grandfather.'

She turned round. Pascal was a few feet behind her, looking at the photograph. She could see the resemblance now, except Pascal's eyes were unreadable.

'Did you take it?'

He shook his head. In an instant Pascal knew instinctively that Alana had seen the same things he saw whenever he looked at the picture. No one else had ever stood transfixed by it before. It made something feel weak in his chest. He avoided her eye, his voice gruff. 'No; my talents lie solely in facts and figures. This was taken by an American photographer who was travelling around the south of France. After my grandfather died, I tracked him down and got a print.'

'You must have been very close; you mentioned that you spent time with him.'

Pascal just nodded. She didn't probe any more. She understood the need to keep things back. She knew he was watching her as she continued to walk around, taking sips of wine, feeling the surface of a smooth Roman bust beneath her fingers.

Every one of Pascal's senses was pulled as taut as a bow string as he watched her hand smooth over the head of the bust, wanting her hand to be smoothing over him. He had to wonder if perhaps her air of vulnerability, her apparent lack of experience, was all an act, designed to entice, tease, seduce. She'd let her hair down, and it was slightly tousled from where she'd run her hands through it, but it wasn't tousled enough for him yet.

She turned then, and he could see that her glass of wine was empty. He made as if to get the bottle and top her up, but she shook her head jerkily. She was going to make him wait; he knew it. She wasn't ready. His desire, already at boiling point, would have to settle to a simmer for now.

Alana had turned with every intention of asking for some more wine, but she could already feel the effects. Desire hung between them, heavy and potent. *Too much too soon.* Pascal stood just feet away, but when he moved as if to give her some more she shook her head. She couldn't do this now. She wasn't ready, and she could see that he'd already read that in her expression before she'd known it herself. That disconcerted her. She wasn't used to people intuiting her intentions.

'You must be tired.'

She forced a smile. She was anything but. 'I was up early. Would you mind if I went to bed?' *'Alone'* hung between them along with the desire, but it seemed to make it even heavier, denser. Was she doing the right thing? Her body told her no, her head said yes.

He shook his head, jaw rigid, eyes black. 'Of course not. What time do you have to be in work tomorrow?'

Such banalities.

Alana glanced at her watch, but didn't even register the time. 'I have to meet the crew in Stadio Flaminio at midday; the kick-off is at 3:00 p.m.'

He nodded. 'My car will take you in and come back for me.'

'If you're sure? I could get a taxi.'

He shook his head almost violently, and Alana knew the sudden urge to leave, get away now. It was as if his control was barely leashed.

He took the glass from her hand. *'Dors bien*, Alana.'

CHAPTER FOUR

WHEN Alana reached her room, she was breathing hard. She went straight into her *en suite* bathroom and looked in the mirror. Her cheeks were flushed, eyes over-bright. Her body was too sensitive, and an ache throbbed down low in her belly and between her legs. She dropped her head, hands gripping the edge of the sink.

She went back out into the bedroom and fooled herself into believing that she was doing what she wanted by unpacking her clothes and taking out her toiletries. A silk dress slithered out of her trembling hands to the ground. She picked it up. She'd pulled it out of her wardrobe on a whim. It was one of the very few dresses she'd kept from her days with Ryan, and she hadn't worn it since her marriage had ended. Ryan had derided her when she'd worn it first, as it hadn't been revealing enough for him…or, more accurately, for the press, who he'd constantly wanted to impress. But in actual fact it was plenty revealing, and way more than Alana had been comfortable with. *Up to now.*

She hung it up abruptly, refusing to think about why she'd brought it.

As she was about to start undressing, she stopped and sat on the edge of the bed. Her heart was thumping slow, heavy beats. She was shaking. Adrenaline washed through her system. Her body already knew what was inevitable. She couldn't deny it to herself. It was as if the centre of her being had become magnetised and could only go in one direction.

She walked back over to the door and opened it. The only light came from downstairs. She paused at the top of the stairs. He was still down there, sitting on the couch, long legs splayed in front of him, in bare feet, the dregs of a glass of wine in his hands into which he was staring broodily. Fear assailed Alana again, and she almost fled, but then he looked up.

Tension snaked up from him to her and an unspoken plea: *don't go*. She realised that she couldn't, even if she'd wanted to. She came down the stairs, clinging onto the rail as she went. She was melting inside as she came closer and closer. Her clothes felt restrictive.

She got to the bottom. Without taking his eyes off hers, he carefully placed his glass on the small table at his feet and stood up. She concentrated on his eyes—dark, molten.

'I couldn't sleep.'

He didn't smile, but she heard the smile in his voice. 'You were only gone ten minutes.'

'I know I won't be able to sleep.'

'What do you want, Alana?'

She shook her head. 'I want…I want…' Her face flamed. 'You know what I want. Don't make me say it, please.'

'Show me what you want.' His voice was soft, silky, heavy with erotic promise.

He was making her come to him all the way. Making sure.

Alana stepped forward jerkily until she was standing right in front of him. She could barely breathe. They hardly touched, and now she lifted her hands to his shoulders. They were so much wider and higher than she remembered. She took another couple of awkward steps. He was making no move to help her.

She looked up at him, a hint of desperation on her face; she could feel sweat on her brow. 'Can't you just…?'

'You want me to take you? To take the decision out of your hands—so on some level you don't have to actually make it clear what you want?' He shook his head. 'No. I need to know that you really want this. I won't indulge regrets and recriminations in the morning.'

Damn him. Since when had he become a psychoanalyst? But Alana's need was too great.

She moved even closer and wound her arms around his neck, bringing her whole body flush against his, leaning into him. Her breasts were crushed into his chest, and she felt him suck in a deep breath. It made her exultant. He might be displaying control, but she guessed it was shaky.

She pulled his head down to hers, her fingers threading through dark, silky hair. She lifted her face to his and angled it to try and kiss him. She felt so awkward. She aimed for his mouth, but ended up bumping his nose, his chin. She pulled back, letting him go. This was ridiculous. No doubt he'd expected her to sashay up to him, throw him down on the sofa and seduce him into mindless ecstasy. Well, he'd be waiting.

Her voice was stiff with humiliation. This was exactly what she'd feared. 'I'm sorry. I haven't…done this in a while. I think you expect me to be something…more than I am.'

She turned to go but he caught her wrist and pulled her back. She fell against him, caught off-balance. With the practised ease which she lacked and so envied, he immediately cradled the back of her head with a big hand, the other holding her close against him.

'Not at all. I just wanted to be sure you were ready for this.'

'Maybe I'm not, after all,' she breathed up, mesmerised by his eyes.

'I think you are.' And then he bent his head and kissed her, exactly how she'd been aching to be kissed since the last time. Both hands now threaded through her hair, messing it up, cradling her head. Her hands rested on his chest and wound higher until they were tight around his neck. They barely paused for breath; there was no awkwardness now. First their kiss was slow, sensual, a tentative touching of tongues, tasting. Then it developed into full-on passion, igniting an inferno between them.

Somehow, Alana didn't know how, Pascal had manoeuvered them and now her back was against a wall. He lifted his head. One hand was high on the wall behind her, the other resting on her hip. She felt as boneless as a rag doll. She looked up, her eyes glazed, her lips plump and tingling.

His index-finger traced around her jaw and down to the top button of her shirt. Her heart stopped and kick-started again. Faster.

'Do you have any idea what this outfit has been doing to me since I saw you arrive in it?'

She shook her head. All she knew was that she wanted to be out of it. As soon as possible.

He started to undo her tie. 'As much as this turns me on,' he said gruffly, 'I think I'm going to have to burn it.'

'I have ten more at home,' Alana said matter of factly, distractedly.

He threw it aside and it landed in a sliver of dark colour on the wooden floor. 'Then it'll be a bonfire.'

His fingers were at her buttons now. She tipped her head back to give him access, and she felt him drop his head and press a kiss to the exposed, delicate skin of her throat. Alana moaned softly. She was in a sensual land that she'd never thought she'd experience. She'd heard other women talk of lust and chemical attraction, and had always secretly disbelieved them or thought it was overrated. Now…she *knew*.

She could sense Pascal's growing impatience when he

couldn't undo any more buttons as the dress got in the way.
He growled, 'How do you get this thing off?'

Alana stood and turned around to face the wall. 'The zip.
At the back.'

She could feel it whisper down, and then he turned her
round again. Bending to take her mouth with his, she could
feel his hands go to the shoulders of her dress and push it
down; it snagged on her hips, and then his hands were there
and pushing it off completely until it fell at her feet, a pool
of pleated black.

She brought her hands to the bottom of his sweater to pull
it up. He lifted his arms and pulled it off the whole way, and
then he stood in front of her, bare chested. She could feel her
eyes widening as she took in the bronzed magnificence.
Whorls of dark hair dusted his pectorals and then met in a
silky line that descended down and into the waist of his low-
slung jeans which barely clung to lean hips.

Heat. All Alana could think of was *heat*.

He pulled her into him and she gloried in the sensation of
his bare chest, running her hands round his back, feeling the
satin-smooth olive skin, warm beneath her fingers. He gathered her close and his mouth closed over the beating, throbbing pulse at her neck; his hands travelled down to her bottom
and caressed it before searching further and finding the bare
skin at the top of her thighs over her stockings. He jerked back
and looked down, eyes glittering, breath coming harshly.

'*Mon Dieu.*'

'What?' she asked uncertainly, feeling exposed.

He just shook his head and a huge grin split his face.
'Stockings. Proper stockings. And suspenders.' What was
turning him on even more was the suspicion that she dressed
like this all the time, that it hadn't been just for him.

He looked at her then. 'I knew that underneath all that
starch was someone earthy, sensual…'

He kissed her, and she felt his hands undoing the rest of the buttons on her shirt, the slightly cooler air hitting her torso as he pulled it apart. He looked at her for a long moment before pushing it off, down her arms, until it too joined her dress on the floor.

The carnal appreciation in his gaze made her throb in response. She was glad now that bizarrely she'd always had an instinctive desire for nice underwear, although she hadn't indulged it while married, as Ryan had mocked her for trying to be sexy whenever she did. Her breasts were straining against the satin cups of her bra, peaks tingling painfully. Pascal pushed one strap down over her shoulder and dragged down the cup, baring one pale breast to his gaze...and mouth.

He whispered in her ear, 'Remember what I said before?'

She nodded jerkily, anticipation lasering through her veins.

Then he bent his head and blew softly and enticed, before flicking out his tongue to taste and then drawing that tight, extended peak into his mouth. Alana's head fell back. She couldn't stop the moan, and wondered at this woman she didn't recognise.

As Pascal suckled, a tight spiral of intense sensation connected directly with Alana's groin. She found herself pressing closer, seeking, wanting more, arching her back. He had taken down the other cup, so now both her breasts were bared, upthrust and framed by the satin black material.

He was torturing her with his mouth. She couldn't breathe. He reached down, lifted one leg and hooked it around his thigh. His other hand was on the leg that was barely able to keep her standing. His fingers danced over the suspenders; she felt him snap open the ties, then smooth around to cup the cheek of her bottom before slipping his hand between her legs.

She stopped breathing entirely for a long moment as he pushed her panties aside and slid his finger into her, into a caress so intimate that she would have closed her legs if she'd been able to. He was relentless, his mouth on her breasts, his finger sliding in and out, until finally, as if he'd been teasing her, he found the centre of where she throbbed unmercifully and, with one flick of his thumb, she came violently. She could only cling to him as the sensation ripped through her body in case she'd be swept away too.

Her leg that was lifted fell. She couldn't quite believe what had just happened. A bit like chemical attraction; she'd read about it, heard about it. But amazingly...

'Alana, was that your first orgasm?' He sounded slightly stunned, and Alana cringed inwardly at how gauche she must seem.

He stood upright and let her settle against him, cradling her with a disconcerting level of tenderness. As if he could sense her turmoil, he tipped her head back. 'No, don't do that. You're amazingly responsive, but it's nothing to be embarrassed about. It's a compliment.'

She looked at him shyly, mortified. 'I'm—'

'Don't say it.' He shook his head. His expression was enigmatic. 'You were married; did you never...?'

She shook her head quickly, her body still pulsing in the aftermath, making her feel a little out of this world. Spaced out. 'My husband never...made me feel like that. We didn't sleep together for the last three years of our marriage.'

'And you were married for...'

'Five years.' Unwelcome reality was trickling back in. Alana resented the questions now; she didn't want to think of Ryan. This was her new start for herself. Ryan was in the past.

'Alana—'

She pressed a finger to Pascal's mouth and could feel his breath feather there, could feel a delicious tightening in her belly. 'Please. I don't want to talk about it, OK?' He didn't say anything for a long moment, and then finally he nodded.

Alana gave a huge sigh of relief, and then yelped as Pascal lifted her into his arms against his chest.

'Time to go somewhere more comfortable, I think. Much as I could take you standing against that wall right now, I'll resist the temptation.'

She buried her head in his shoulder as he climbed the stairs and shouldered his way into his room.

A part of her wanted nothing more than that carnality, but another part of her was grateful that he was being so considerate.

He looked down at her briefly, his face tight with need. 'Is this OK?'

She nodded. She knew one thing for sure for the first time in ages. 'Yes.'

Alana woke to a delicious sensation of someone running a finger up and down her bare spine in a tingling caress. Pascal. Warmth flooded her even as she registered aches and pleasurable pains all over her body. She opened one eye to see him smiling at her, looking clean, vital and very awake. He smelt fresh, delicious. And sexy. Heat flooded her belly.

The previous night came back in Technicolor: the pathetic fight she'd put up before giving in, the amount of times they'd made love, the amount of times she'd reached ecstasy because of him.

He bent his head and his mouth hovered near her ear. 'No regrets and no recriminations. We agreed, remember?'

Alana turned her face into the pillow so he wouldn't see her blushing. She just nodded into the pillow. She heard a soft, sexy chuckle and then felt a playful swat on her bottom. The bed dipped and she could feel him standing up.

'Come on; my car will be here for you in half an hour, and if you're anything like the rest of your species, you'll be struggling to get ready in time.'

Alana lifted her head with a squeak. 'Half an hour?' She cursed under her breath and went to get up, and realised that she had no cover, as her clothes had practically melted off her last night in the heat of passion that had consumed them. She was stuck. Pascal stood between her and the door from where she could get to her own bedroom. She was not ready to parade around naked in broad daylight.

He watched, amused, as she pulled the sheet from the bed and wrapped it around her before getting up and trailing it after her.

Before she was clear of him, he caught her and pulled her against him. He pressed a hot kiss to her mouth. 'Take the sheet for now, but I'll have you walking around naked in no time.'

'Never…'

He kissed her again, and suddenly the vortex was opening up around them, and in a shamingly small amount of time Alana knew she would be saying yes to anything, even going to work naked. But then he drew back, showing her that ultimately he was in control, whereas she was not. He pushed her gently towards her room.

Under the powerful spray of her shower, Alana hugged her arms around herself and gave into the stream of images. She groaned out loud as she remembered one moment, half in mortification, half in a state of arousal, even now. Pascal had been poised above her, skin gleaming, slick with sweat, his erection nudging her moist entrance. As if he'd been testing her again, he'd waited until her nerves had been screaming for release. She'd arched up to him, willing him to impale her, but he'd waited until she'd brokenly begged him. And then he'd slid into her slowly, deeply.

With a curt flick of her wrist Alana turned the shower to cold and endured it for a minute. Anything to dampen her flaming hormones.

* * *

At the match later Pascal came and found her at half time, and took her by the hand. She was distracted; she'd been trying to set up an interview for after the match with the England manager.

'Pascal, I'm working, you can't just walk up and drag me away,' she said with a mixture of reproach and breathless anticipation.

He ignored her and took her down into long corridors before ducking into a room full of equipment. He closed the door behind them.

Still holding her hand, he pulled her to him. She was helpless not to respond, her body welcoming his heady proximity. How quickly she'd become consumed by him. Alarm bells weren't just ringing, they were now joined by sirens and flashing lights.

With quick hands, he undid her ponytail and pocketed the band.

'Hey!'

Then he put two hands in her hair and mussed it up. He looked at her critically. 'Much better. And now…'

'Now what?'

'Now this.' He hauled her into him and kissed her deeply, with barely checked passion. She wound her arms around his waist and found her hands lifting his shirt from his trousers, searching for and finding that smooth, taut flesh where the small of his back curved out to firm buttocks. Warmth flooded her. He was opening the buttons of her shirt; she'd tried to put on her tie that morning but he'd kept taking it off her. She could feel the air on her heated skin as he opened her shirt and palmed her breast, her nipple aching against the confines of her bra. She pressed a feverish mouth against his throat.

And then suddenly the spell was broken as someone tried to come in the door behind them. Pascal said something quickly in Italian and started to do up her buttons again. Alana didn't know how she was going to be able to go back out there and string two words together.

Her brain was mush for the rest of the match and the ensuing interviews, but somehow she managed to keep it together. Pascal was waiting for her, exactly like he'd been waiting and watching that first day in Dublin. Only now... A wave of heat engulfed her...only now it was totally different. She was different.

Her crew feigned extreme lack of interest in the fact that Pascal Lévêque was hovering like a bodyguard. But once the last interview was done, and she'd been given the all clear from the Dublin studio, effectively the rest of the weekend was hers.

In the back of Pascal's car a short time later, he pulled her over so she was practically on his lap. She'd given up trying to pull away and retain a more dignified position for the sake of the driver. He pressed a kiss to the underside of her wrist and looked up at her.

'Are you glad to be here now?'

Alana looked down at him and felt the earth move bizarrely beneath her feet even though they were in a moving vehicle. Something very suspicious tightened her chest. She nodded, because she had to admit it. 'Yes. I am glad.' She bent her head and pressed a kiss to his mouth, revelling in the freedom she had to do this. They'd achieved an immediate level of intimacy that would be frightening if she thought about it too closely.

She was embarking on an affair with a world-renowned playboy and that was going to be her protection: at no point would she be deluded. At no point would there be talk of love, marriage. It would end when it would end. And she'd take the gift of herself that he'd given back to her, like a guilty, delicious secret. That was all she wanted. This was all she wanted.

Later that evening Alana took one last look at her reflection and turned to leave the room, but just then her door opened. Pascal stopped dead for a moment, his gaze raking her up and down, and then he clapped his hand over his eyes. 'I can't believe it.'

Alana felt like a fool. She knew she shouldn't have worn the dress—it was ridiculous, too tight, too revealing. 'Look, I can change, I'm not even that comfortable.'

Pascal wasn't moving.

She took a hesitant step forward. 'What, what is it? Is it really that bad?'

Alana tried to look back at the mirror self-consciously when she heard something suspiciously like a grunt coming from Pascal.

He'd taken his hand down and was laughing. Then he stopped and walked towards her. 'I'm sorry. I couldn't help it. It was the shock of seeing so much exposed flesh at once.'

Alana all at once felt like laughing and angry. She picked up a small cushion from the chair beside her and threw it at him, but he caught it deftly and kept coming. Dressed in a tuxedo, with his hair still damp from the shower, he was magnificent.

She had to speak to try and negate the effect he had on her, the way his teasing wound through her and impacted a place that was so deep, so vulnerable.

'I'm going to change right now; I knew this dress was a mistake.'

She went to undo the zip that was under her arm, and Pascal reached her and captured her hand. 'Don't you dare. That dress is beautiful.'

Alana's face flamed. 'It's not. It's too—'

'So why did you bring it, then?'

She couldn't answer. He walked her over to the full-length mirror and stood her in front of him. His hands rested on her hips. She could feel him, tall and hard and lean behind her, and it was so seductive.

'Look at yourself.'

Alana closed her eyes, her cheeks still scarlet. She shook her head. 'I hate looking at myself.'

'Alana, *look* at yourself.'

Something in his voice made her open her eyes, and she immediately looked at him through the mirror. She could feel him sigh behind her.

'Not at me, at yourself.'

With extreme reluctance, she did. She saw the black silk dress that was cut on the bias and fell to just below her knees in an asymmetric line. She saw one shoulder, pale and bared, and just a hint of a curve of her breast. She saw the strap that held the dress up over her other shoulder with its flamboyant red-silk flower, a splash of vibrant colour.

'Now, what's wrong with this picture?'

Alana groaned inwardly. This was so embarrassing. She would bet a million dollars that not one of his previous lovers had had to be reassured about a dress before.

She tried to turn. 'Look, it's nothing, I'm sorry. Let's just go, shall we?'

He wouldn't let her. He held her fast, and something in the air changed. It became electric.

'You're beautiful, Alana. This dress is beautiful on you. It's not too revealing. In fact,' he growled with mock lasciviousness, 'it's not revealing enough.'

He turned her then to face him, his hands warm on her shoulders. She could feel her breasts peak against the silk of the dress.

He tipped up her chin so she couldn't avoid his eyes. 'What did he do to you, Alana? I bet you weren't always like this.'

Alana struggled not to let the tears brighten her eyes, but there was a lump in her throat. She shook her head. 'No, I wasn't. He just…he just made me feel cheap. That's all.'

She pulled free of his arms and looked at her watch. 'We should really go.'

He heard the emotion in her voice and watched her precede him out of the room, the dress emphasising her gently curved shape, the jut of her rounded bottom. He could recall only too clearly the thrust of her breasts against his chest.

He stalled a moment before following her out. She was so totally different from any woman he'd known before that he couldn't quite begin to rationalise how she made him feel. Physically, he burned for her. Earlier at the match he'd quite literally *had* to see her, touch her at half time or he'd felt he would have gone insane. She'd been preoccupied. First of all, he wasn't used to any woman being preoccupied around him, and secondly, he wasn't used not to being in complete control with his lovers. They turned him on, yes, that was what he chose them for, but never to the extent that he felt with this woman. This was something different.

He straightened his cuffs before walking out, uncomfortably aware of his near-constant state of arousal. She was just different because she wasn't one of the polished socialites that littered his social scene, who threw themselves at him, that was all. It was still just an affair, and he'd no doubt that he'd soon look at her and wonder what he'd been hot and bothered about.

A little later, in the exclusive hotel which was hosting his bank's lavish charity-ball, Pascal felt extremely hot and bothered. Alana was generating a veritable tsunami of attention in her sexy dress. After having spent the last two weeks trying to get her out of her buttoned-up uniform, now he wanted to march her right out of there and make her change back into it.

Clamping her to his side was a need born out of a violent emotion that he'd never felt before as acquaintance after acquaintance came up under the pretext of talking business, whereupon they did nothing but stare at Alana. She seemed oblivious, but Pascal was too inured to women and their wily ways. And he was all too aware of how beguiling her natural beauty was to these men, who were jaded and cynical. As jaded and cynical as he was. Was he no better than these men? He'd just seen her first. All sorts of conflicting, unsavoury thoughts were being unleashed within him. Not least of which was the sensation that perhaps he'd been fooled, fooled by her act, her apparent vulnerability. *How* could she really be so different?

He dragged her attention back from where she was looking in awe at the room around them, and muttered something about getting drinks. He saw a flash of uncertainty in her eyes and ignored it, and the feeling it generated through him. He needed space.

Alana looked to where Pascal was cutting a swathe through the glittering crowd. She couldn't help but notice the intense interest he generated among every cluster of women in the room, who also followed his progress with avid attention. Some of them turned then to look at her, and she felt extremely self-conscious. Trying to shrug off the immediate insecurity that their looks generated, she walked to where ornate doors led out to a small, idyllic garden. Even though it was cool, one or two people mingled outside. The hotel was pure opulence, one of the oldest and grandest in Rome, situated with a view of the Spanish Steps.

She couldn't help but think of similar situations with Ryan. He'd always dumped her as soon as they got in the door and made straight for the bar. Invariably she'd be left on her own all evening and would return home alone, only to wake up in the morning and find that he hadn't even returned. She'd stopped worrying about his whereabouts soon into the marriage when it had become clear he'd never seemed to miss her.

She rubbed her arms distractedly, as she had that sensation of someone walking over her grave.

'*Bella.*'

Alana jumped and turned to see a tall man standing beside her, looking her up and down. She looked nervously over his shoulder back into the room, but couldn't see Pascal. She smiled tightly. 'I'm sorry, I don't speak Italian; I'm just waiting for someone, actually.'

'Then it's lucky that I speak English. You are a very beautiful woman.'

Alana blushed. 'That's very…nice of you to say.' The man was attractive in a heavy-set kind of way, but there was something faintly menacing about him. He'd moved subtly and now he effectively blocked her from the room. In order to move, Alana would have to push past him or go into the garden. She didn't want to retreat to a dark area where he might follow her.

'Please.' He held out a hand. 'Can I know your name?'

Alana sent up a silent prayer for Pascal to find her. Where *was* he? She couldn't ignore the man, as that would be unaccountably rude. So she shook his hand very perfunctorily and whipped hers back before he could clasp it. 'Alana Cusack; I'm very pleased to meet you. Now, please, my friend will be looking for me.' *Except patently he wasn't.* A very familiar feeling of pain clutched her deep down inside.

She went to move past the man, but he stopped her with an arm. Alana flinched back from the contact.

His voice now held a distinctly threatening tone. 'But I haven't told you my name yet, and your accent—where are you from? It is so pretty.'

Alana was beginning to feel desperate. Even though Ryan had never physically harmed her, the latent threat had always been there, and now the memory was making her feel panicky. 'Look, I don't mean to be rude, but I don't really want to know your name, OK? Now, I'm sorry, but would you *please* get out of my way?'

After a long, tense moment, he stepped back with hands held high and spread. 'Go then, if you want, it's your loss.'

Alana seized the opportunity and fled. Her heart was hammering, and she had an awful, sick feeling in her chest, an overwhelming sensation of foreboding. She pushed through the crowd and then she saw Pascal, and the whole room tilted crazily, the chatter dulling to a faint roaring in her ears.

He was at the bar, talking to a woman. He didn't look as if he was in a hurry to go anywhere, much less to look for Alana. The woman was stunningly beautiful—blonde, tall, slim, in a sparkling gown with a thigh-high slit that was being provocatively displayed. She had a hand on Pascal's waist and was leaning in, her whole body arching seductively into his. His head was bent towards hers as if she were telling him something intimate.

It all hit Alana at once, and again she felt acutely self-conscious in her revealing dress. She hated the compulsion that had led her to wear it now. But, worse than that, she'd let herself be taken in *again* by a man who lived his life searching for the next thrill, the next pleasure-point. The next adoring female. She could see all too well, in a room like this, how she must have been such a novelty. The innocent Irish cailín. And then, like watching a car crash in slow motion, she saw Pascal's hand go to where the woman's rested on his waist. He was about to thread his fingers through hers, lift her hand to his mouth. Alana knew it. But just before she could turn away her humiliation became complete. They both turned, as if they could sense her watching them.

The glittering, too-bright icy-blue gaze of the woman was mocking, triumphant. Pascal's was… She didn't wait to find out. Turning, Alana stumbled and pushed through the crowd until she was finally free of the room and burst out into the spacious and hushed lobby. She walked quickly to the door on jelly legs, where a doorman rushed to open it for her.

CHAPTER FIVE

ALANA stood on the steps, shivering.

'You would like me to get you a taxi, madam?'

'Yes, please,' Alana said gratefully to the nice doorman. She had no idea where she would go—all her stuff was at Pascal's—but she just wanted away from here.

'She doesn't need a taxi, she's with me. Can you send for my driver, please?' a familiar deep voice, throbbing with anger, came from behind her and she stiffened in rejection.

A harsh hand on her arm pulled her round. She met furious dark eyes, and everything in her rebelled against *his* anger. The fact that the doorman had already scurried off to do his bidding made things even worse.

'I believe that I just ordered a taxi; thanks all the same for the offer of the lift.'

'What the hell just happened back there?'

'Why, I believe what just happened is that you saw a better option and decided to pursue it, leaving me at the mercy of a…a creepy, slimy lounge-lizard.'

His hand tightened on her arm. 'What are you talking about? Did someone come on to you? Did someone do something to you?'

'No,' she dismissed him furiously, while trying to shake him off unsuccessfully. 'Not that you would have noticed anyway. But, thanks, you've saved me going back in to look for you. If you could give me the keys to your apartment, I'd appreciate it; I'll get my things and be gone by the time you get back. No doubt you'll be wanting the place to yourself tonight?'

'And why would that be?' His voice was arctic, but Alana was on fire.

'Do you really need me to spell it out, Pascal? I thought you were more sophisticated than that.' She berated herself bitterly now for having allowed herself to be seduced by him.

'Apparently not so sophisticated that I can go to the bar to get a drink for my date and turn around to find she has disappeared, only to find her again and have her run from the room as if I'd chased her out myself.'

He'd been looking for her? A reflex to stop, to apologise, was quashed as she remembered the woman. They'd looked far too cosy. She'd only known Pascal two weeks. Did she really think she could trust him? Her astounding naïvety mocked her mercilessly.

'Your companion might have another impression. She seemed to think that you were quite interested in what she had to offer.'

Pascal could recall only too noxiously what the British model Cecilia Hampton had been offering. She'd all but wrapped herself around him like a clinging vine, and had spoken in an absurdly quiet, jarring little-girl voice—a well-worn ploy to get a man to come closer, whereupon she'd all but thrust her enormous fake bosom in his face. He'd been feeling foolish ever since he'd stalked away from Alana to get drinks, and had turned back to get her, imagining all the predatory males in the room moving in on her, but she'd disappeared.

His car drew up at that moment and, heaving a sigh of relief, he hurried Alana down the steps and into the back, making her slide along the seat and getting in beside her, not giving her a chance to get out. Or say a thing.

In the back of the car Alana ripped her arm from Pascal's grasp, her skin hot and tingling. 'How dare you? I want you to let me out this minute. I'll get a cab.'

She sat forward and opened her mouth to speak to the driver, but Pascal hauled her over and she lay sprawled inelegantly against him. With his other hand he flicked a switch and the privacy window slid up with a hiss.

The air was electric around them. Alana was very aware of how she lay practically across his lap, in a pose of supplication that galled her. His body was tense and taut, and unmistakably hard. It made her feel sick, that he could so easily transfer his desire from one to another.

'Isn't there something wrong with this picture?' she gritted out, holding herself as tense and as far away as possible.

'Yes,' Pascal ground out. 'You're wearing far too many clothes for my liking and I want you *now*.'

Alana tried to pull free, but he was remorseless and held her still. 'You don't want me, you want *her*.'

In an instant Pascal had shifted and lifted Alana with an ease that shocked her. She found herself straddling his lap, knees pressed either side of his powerful thighs. His hands were on her waist, holding her captive. A wave of anger and humiliation at her own helpless response, her lack of strength, drove her to try and move but she couldn't.

Her arms were rigid, either side of Pascal's shoulders on the seat behind them. With his hands firmly on her waist he shifted her slightly so that she could feel where his erection strained between them against the confines of his trousers. A rush of desire made her suck in a betraying breath. And then his hands came up to her dress, to undo the clasp hidden underneath the flower. If he undid that, her dress would fall to her waist.

'Don't you dare.' She caught his hands, but he swatted hers away with ease. He undid her dress and it fell. Alana caught it. The motion of the car made her fall against him, and made the apex between her legs grind into Pascal's hardness. She could hear his breath coming harshly, see the colour slash across his cheekbones. She felt sick inside, knowing that he could just as easily be doing this with any other woman.

She heard him sigh, and he looked up at her with a curiously unguarded expression. She was caught by it.

'Alana, please believe me: if I were in the unfortunate position of having Cecilia Hampton straddle my lap right now, I can assure you that she would not be feeling what you're feeling.'

He snaked a hand around the back of her neck. Alana tried to hold herself stiff, but it was too difficult. His voice was low, reasonable, and oh, so sexy. 'You'd disappeared when I went looking for you, so I went back to wait at the bar, thinking you'd come find me there. Cecilia approached me. If you'd watched for another few seconds before running out, you would have seen me extricate myself from her extremely unwelcome embrace.'

Alana looked down at him. He looked sincere. Had she read it wrong? She found herself wanting to believe him so much. And that was beyond scary in its implications. But right now she could avoid thinking about it without a huge amount of effort. The need consuming her, consuming the air around them, was too great. Desire flowed, hot and urgent, between them. This was all-encompassing, and she had to give into it and deal with the fallout later.

Pascal slowly moved his hand from the back of her neck, over her shoulder and down to her hands. He exerted a little bit of pressure and Alana let him pull her hands away, giving in to a need too great. Her dress fell to her waist, baring her breasts. She put her hands back onto the seat behind Pascal. He took her face in his hands and kissed her softly, reverently. It made something hard melt inside her. She sank into him, found her hips moving sinuously against his. Urgency rose. His kiss became more forceful. He dragged his mouth away and held the weight of one breast in his hand before flicking out a tongue and laving the distended peak. Alana's back arched.

She pressed kisses feverishly to his face, mouth, neck, her hands seeking to rip open his shirt. Buttons popped and his bow tie disappeared down into the cracks between the seats. She blindly sought his belt buckle and opened it impatiently.

'You're like a fever in my blood, Alana. There's no one else I want.'

His words set her aflame even more, and she bent to kiss him again. He lifted her slightly and she braced her hands against his shoulders. She bit her lip as she heard his zip come down, and as he pulled his trousers down with a rough urgency. Then he settled her back and she almost cried out at the sensation of his hard, virile, unsheathed heat, *right there*.

He lifted her dress at her waist, and she heard fabric rip as he brought two hands to the side of her knickers and pulled. He pressed a kiss to her throat as she felt the material being pulled away. 'I'm not sorry and I'll buy you new ones.'

She didn't care. She wanted him inside her, right now. The ache was killing her.

As if he heard her silent plea, he lifted her again, and she could feel his hand on himself as he guided his rigid length to the apex of her thighs. He slid in easily, and as Alana sank down onto him, he surged upwards. She was so turned on, and the sensation was so shockingly thrilling, that she came right there and then, her inner muscles clamping around him in a series of minor convulsions.

She dropped her head into his shoulder. He was still rigid within her, filling her. 'Oh God, I'm sorry…' She was breathing heavily.

He pulled her back, tipped her head up, pressed a kiss to her mouth, slid his tongue between her soft lips. She could feel him stir within her, and inexplicably she could feel herself start to respond again, not being allowed to fall back to earth; she was kept on a high plateau of sensation that threatened to go even higher.

'We've only just started.'

With a slow, burning intensity, Pascal moved within her like a devil magician. He brought her to the edge only to stop, then start again. In a fever of prolonged ecstasy, skin slick with sweat, it was only when he knew he couldn't hold back that he allowed free rein to his movements, which became urgent. His big hands moulded her back, held her hips steady. Alana was beyond words. Everything in her was reverent, the orgasm that broke through her just before his was so powerful that she had to keep her eyes locked on Pascal's or she would have disintegrated into pieces.

Pascal had never felt anything like it. He'd almost have believed that she hadn't climaxed, if he hadn't felt her body contracting powerfully around his. But she'd done it with such quiet intensity that it had made his own completion burst up in a never-ending stream of exquisite pleasure. Only her biting her lip at the zenith of sensation had shown any of her internal experience.

Alana shook all over. Pascal pulled her into his chest and cradled her against him. They were still joined intimately, and at that moment she couldn't ever imagine being separated from this man. She'd never felt like this with her husband, not even in the early days of their marriage when she'd had so many hopes and dreams of a happy future.

Something extraordinary had just happened, and she hated to admit it.

* * *

When they reached his apartment, Pascal carried her straight up to his bathroom and ran them a bath. Then they made love. Again. And now she lay here, blissed out. Replete. Complete.

She heard a movement and looked up. Pascal was holding out a big robe.

'Come on, or you'll turn into a prune.'

Something in his eyes made her hold back a quick, joky comment. She stood up and reached for the robe, only to have him pull it back from her reach.

'Pascal, come on.' She groaned and immediately went to cover her breasts. She was totally exposed in the low lighting of the intimate bathroom. And it was silly to feel this way when they'd just made love, first in the back of his car and then in the bath. She flushed.

'Let your hands down. Please.' His voice sounded rough. 'I want to look at you, Alana—will you let me look at you? As you are?'

Fear and embarrassment gave way to something else. The desire in his eyes emboldened her. She carefully and slowly climbed out of the bath and stood beside it. She dropped her arms and watched as his eyes travelled down, resting and dwelling on parts of her body that she'd certainly never inspected so intensely herself.

After a long, long minute his eyes met hers again. They were dark. He stepped forward and put the robe around her, drying her, before slipping her arms into the sleeves and tying it securely around her waist. He smoothed back her damp hair and ran a finger down her cheek.

'I could quite easily have you again right now, on the floor… And all sorts of other images came into my mind as I looked at you.' Pascal wrestled for a moment inwardly with the very real and disturbing reality that he could take her again right now. The knowledge made him cautious. 'But there's time…'

'Time,' Alana said stupidly, suddenly wanting very much

instead that they could make love on the floor right now. She had an erotic flash of an image: kneeling at his feet and taking him into her mouth. The shocking heat that inflamed her made her feel weak. Where had that desire come from? She'd never even done that with Ryan. She'd never even thought that she found it sexy. But the thought of driving Pascal to the edge of all endurance was intoxicating in the extreme.

'Yes, time. Let's eat and have some wine.' He cut through the fevered images in her wanton imagination and pushed her towards the bathroom door, and then out and down the stairs to the sitting room. A bottle of wine sat open with two glasses. Alana felt stone-cold sober all of a sudden, which wasn't surprising as she hadn't drunk all evening, but bizarrely she also felt drunk, heady…something very nebulous and disturbing.

He poured wine into their glasses and busied himself with something at the oven. Although Alana was in a robe, Pascal wore faded jeans and a plain shirt that was haphazardly buttoned, showing the light smattering of hair on his chest and a sliver of hard-muscled, olive-skinned belly. Alana took a quick sip of wine. He really did have the honed body of an athlete—again something niggled at her about that, but it was wispy and eluded her.

'Look,' she started nervously. 'I'm sorry about…running out like that. I'm not normally so dramatic.'

Pascal closed the oven door and slanted her a look before taking a sip of wine from his own glass.

Alana flushed. 'We should still be there. Didn't you have to make some kind of speech?'

Pascal shrugged noncommittally. 'My assistant did it. It's no big deal, really; I wouldn't have even been here necessarily if it hadn't been for the match happening on the same day. It was an opportunity to drum up publicity and kill two birds with one stone. But, no.' He smiled disarmingly. 'I would much prefer to be here with you.'

She flushed again, unused to being flattered. 'Well. Thank you. Next time—'

She stopped abruptly, her eyes flying to his with a sickening feeling as she realised what she'd been about to say— she'd been about to imply that there would *be* a next time.

'That is, I don't mean—'

Pascal hushed her and came round the counter, pulling her into him. 'Next time I'm not going to let you out of my sight, so there will be no room for any confusion or misinterpretation, OK?'

Her mouth was dry and she just nodded.

He let her go and moved back, smiling easily, charmingly, and her world tilted all over again. 'Now, how about you tell me about this lounge-lizard of yours?'

Alana shuddered delicately at the memory, realising that it had shaken her more than she cared to admit, but talking about it would lessen it. She told Pascal and acted out his slimy manoeuvres, and by the time she'd finished they were both laughing, and Pascal admitted that he knew exactly who she was talking about. Apparently the man was famous for pouncing on vulnerable-looking women. Their easy intimacy and Pascal's ability to make her feel protected, to make her feel like she could *trust* him, was sucking Alana into a veritable whirlpool that she feared it would be nigh impossible to climb back out of.

The following evening, as Alana looked at the Italian capital grow smaller and smaller beneath her, she got hot in the face again thinking of the previous night. The erotic fantasy she'd had in the bathroom had become a reality. Pascal had let her push him to the edge of his endurance. She groaned inwardly; she seemed to be in a permanent state of heat since she met him.

She was alone on his private jet on her way back to Dublin. He was taking a commercial flight back to Paris, and he hadn't taken no for an answer when she'd objected. He'd flown her to him, and now he was flying her home. Just like that. As if flying someone on a private jet was banal, ordinary. Easy. And she had to concede, for someone like him who strode through life and got what they wanted with a click of their fingers, of course it was easy. Accolades, money, women, beautiful houses—easy come, easy go. And she'd put herself firmly in that category, made no bones about the fact that she was fine with that.

She finally turned away from the view and recalled the stern set of his features as he'd sent her off, having insisted on accompanying her to the airport. They'd had their first row, of sorts. Except it had been more like a non-row. Alana still couldn't quite figure what had happened but all she knew was that he hadn't been happy.

They'd woken late, well into the early afternoon. Pascal had insisted that she see something of Rome, and had taken her to the nearby Trevi Fountain and then to a tiny restaurant tucked away from the hordes of tourists. The food had been sublime, authentic Italian cuisine at its best. The experience had been intimate, the table so small that their legs had been all but entwined underneath, and it had been easier for their hands to stay linked, too, separating only when the food arrived.

It was when they'd got back to his apartment so that Alana could pack; they'd been standing in the kitchen and she'd been watching Pascal percolate some coffee. He'd turned round and said easily, 'There's so much more you should see. But we can do it again.'

Alana had immediately reacted to his words at a very deep, visceral level, an instant negation of something very fleeting and wishful rising up inside her. 'Oh, well, yes. I'm sure I'll be back at some stage.'

It was the way she'd said *'I'* that got his attention, and she knew it. Even though he said nothing—at first. And then he did say, 'I meant when you come back here with me.'

Alana took the coffee he handed her and walked away into the living room, holding the cup between suddenly chilled hands. She schooled her features and turned back round to face him, forcing her voice to sound as casual as she could. 'You really don't have to say that, you know.'

He took a sip of coffee, his eyes narrowed disconcertingly on her face. She was glad that he was still behind the island in the kitchen.

'And what's that supposed to mean?'

Alana gave a little laugh, which sounded fake to her ears. 'I mean, you don't have to do this…reassurance thing. I really don't expect you to make me feel like you want me to come back…' Her words trailed off, diminishing some of the vehemence with which she'd started the statement.

He walked round the island, ridiculously small coffee cup in one hand, his other in the pocket of his jeans. He looked astoundingly gorgeous in a dark sweater. Unconsciously, Alana backed away.

'Believe me,' he said throatily, 'the only thing I want to make you feel right now involves a soft surface and no clothing in our way.'

Alana gulped and took a quick swig of coffee.

'Look,' she said weakly, 'all I'm saying is that I know what this is and I'm fine with that. Really.'

'And what would *that* be?'

She shrugged one shoulder; they were still doing a bit of a backward dance around the room, she backing, and he advancing.

'It's an affair. A fling.'

His eyebrows raised high. 'Oh, so that's what this is?'

Alana winced. No doubt his other lovers were far too experienced and suave to put a name on their experience with him. Suddenly she felt anger rise up. Why was he being so obtuse? Surely she was doing him a favour? She stopped backing away and put her coffee cup down carefully on the low table by the sofa.

She straightened and folded her arms. 'Look, that's exactly what it is. We both know that. I'd prefer if we could just be honest about it. What I'm saying to you is that I don't need to be given any kind of platitudes. I'm not going to be clingy or want anything more. If you said to me right now that this is over, and thanks but goodbye, I'd have no problem walking out of here.'

Pascal had gone very still, his eyes very black. No doubt he wasn't used to lovers calling the shots, Alana thought cynically. And why did her flip words cause an ache somewhere in the region of her chest? She pushed it aside. The truth was this: Pascal was not a man she could trust in a million years. And she'd vowed to herself never to trust again. Never to be so silly, naïve.

Pascal put down his coffee cup, too, and walked towards her slowly. Alana stood her ground, but had the impression that she'd woken a sleeping dragon.

'I'll admit that your honesty is both tantalising and refreshing.'

'It is?' she asked.

Pascal nodded. He was close enough to touch now.

'Yes. We both know that when the time comes, we'll walk away without a backward glance, happy with what we've had.'

'Exactly.' Alana nodded vehemently. 'I don't mean to sound…crass, it's just that I've been married. I've had that experience and I never, ever want to go near it again. Not even in the form of a tenuous commitment—and I know you're not even offering that.' She stopped and cursed herself; she sounded like a bumbling idiot. 'What I'm trying to say is that I'm not looking for anything. I know you're a playboy.'

His eyes flashed, and Alana's insides clenched painfully

but she ploughed on. 'I'm not expecting anything more. I can't begin to tell you how comfortable I am with that.'

'A no-strings, no-consequences affair—we both walk away when we get bored.'

She nodded. She knew that time wouldn't be far off. A man of Pascal's voracious tastes wouldn't be content with someone like her for long. Not when there were other, more beautiful women waiting in the wings.

He came very close and snaked a hand round the back of her head. His eyes were still dark, unreadable, and his jaw had a rigidity to it that made Alana instinctively want to smooth it, relax it.

'Well, then, seeing as how it's doubtful you will ever be back here with me, now that the sands of time are slipping away from us, we should make the most of here and now, *n'est-ce pas?*'

'What do you mean?'

'What I mean, Alana—' his voice had a hard edge '—is that we're wasting too much time talking when we could be saying goodbye to Rome and this weekend in a very satisfactory way.'

He kissed her for a long, drugging moment, hauling her whole body against his. When he pulled back, and Alana fought to regain her breath, she said, 'But your plane...we have to leave.'

He shook his head, eyes flashing dangerously. 'That's the beauty of being a playboy—my crew are very used to last-minute changes.'

Alana felt a knife skewer her inside, so hurt for a moment that she felt winded. And yet this was exactly what she'd asked for. Demanded. And when he bent his head to kiss her again, and started to open her shirt, she couldn't stop him because if she did he'd know that all of her proclamations were built on a very flimsy foundation.

With the lingering heat of their recent impassioned love-making still in her blood and heavy limbs, Alana's focus came back to the present. The earth below was an indistinct mass of brown mountains seen through breaks in the cloud. She sighed and let her head fall back against the seat, closing her eyes. She was playing with fire; she knew it. And all the trust issues in the world weren't going to keep her safe from harm.

As his private jet winged Alana home in style and comfort, the novelty and charmlessness of commercial travel was quickly reminding Pascal how far he'd come. Although, he could never forget his upbringing; it was branded onto his skin like a tattoo. He could remember how close he'd come to being one of the lost youths of the Parisian suburbs: lost to a life of crime and drugs, hopelessness. Until his mother had died and had thus saved him, by ensuring that he would go to live with his grand-father. She had redeemed herself and her woeful mothering by making sure he'd take another path, despite the fact that he'd been a representation of everything that had failed in her own life.

Pascal strode free of the gnarled mass of human traffic in Charles de Gaulle airport and sank into the back of his car which was waiting just outside the doors. Why was he thinking of such things now, when he hadn't thought of them in years?

Alana.

A woman was making him think of these things, when no other lover had ever done so. He had to concede that no other lover had taken him by the scruff of the neck and rattled him so completely. No other lover had evoked within him a com-pelling need to obey instinct over intellect. He hadn't lived like that for a long time. She connected to something within him, primitive and long-suppressed, deep and visceral. He searched desperately to justify this feeling, to rationalise it, but his brain wouldn't cooperate.

When she'd stood there earlier and had coolly informed him that she was fine with their temporary affair, that above all she didn't expect commitment, he should have been rejoicing. Wasn't it a man's ultimate fantasy? For a man like him, happy to take lovers for a short time until they bored him, or until they started looking for more.

Here he was, being offered this fantasy on a plate, and he well knew that she meant every word she'd said. It wasn't some kind of devious reverse-psychology. So why had he felt anything but relieved? Why had he wanted to challenge her? Why had that instinct not to let her go felt so strong? He'd certainly never aspired to the empty heights of marriage, either; he'd learnt at an early age that searching for that elusive happiness only bred disillusionment and pain. His parents had both proved in their own ways to be prime examples of that. His father had seen him as nothing but a threat to his own marriage, and had rejected him outright because of it.

Yet Alana was making him question the very bedrock on which he'd built his life. His sluggish brain finally kicked into gear: attraction. That had to be it. A rare form of lust. He just hadn't met a woman who'd taken possession of his body and mind before, that was all. That had to be all. OK, so she wasn't into anything permanent—well, neither was he. He just wasn't used to being on the receiving end of the ultimatum, that was all. He relaxed. Their affair certainly wasn't over yet. Not by a long shot.

'You know we're just concerned, love.'

'I know, Mam, I know.' Alana sank into her couch, still wearing her coat.

'He seems like a very nice man. He's awfully important, isn't he?'

Alana bit back a rueful smile. *'Nice'* hardly did him justice. 'Em, yes, he's quite important. But, Mother, don't go getting any ideas, now. It's nothing special.' *Liar*.

Her mother trilled a laugh down the phone. 'I might not quite understand these new relationships, but, love, I know how hard it was for you when Ryan died. It's OK to move on now, it's been long enough. No one would expect you to mourn for ever.'

Alana felt a wave of isolation come over her. Her parents had never really acknowledged the fact that she'd been divorcing Ryan; it had simply been too painful for them to admit that one of their children had failed in their marriage that way. So, when Ryan had died so tragically just before the divorce had come through, Alana had known that in some awful way, it had allowed her parents to believe in the myth of her fairy tale. Was it any wonder she hadn't been able to confide in them?

After a few more words they finished the conversation, and Alana was relieved that her mother hadn't mentioned Pascal again. She shook her head and then resolutely turned off her phone before she could get another acerbic call from her sister, Ailish, who would no doubt have seen the same gossip rags as her mother. She and Pascal were all over the press; the reporters had been waiting at Dublin airport. She knew she'd been naïve to think for a second that perhaps people wouldn't be interested.

Why did she have to go and meet someone who made her feel alive again, someone she couldn't resist? Someone in the public eye on a level that made Ryan O'Connor seem as if he'd been in the Z-list celebrity pile? It was as if she'd had a list of things to avoid and had blithely ignored each and every one of them. Alana just hoped that she could look at Pascal one day soon and not feel that burning desire rip through her entire body like a life-sustaining necessity.

CHAPTER SIX

THREE heady, passion-filled weeks later, that day was eluding Alana spectacularly as she looked down from her position in the press box to the VIP area in Croke Park. Déjà vu washed over her as she caught Pascal's eye and made a face before turning her attention back to the game between Ireland v England. Her heart was singing, her breath was coming fast, and her blood was zinging through her veins. She put her intermittent feelings of nausea down to that see-sawing feeling and tried to forget that she'd been compelled to buy an over-the-counter pregnancy test that morning on her way to work after Pascal had said goodbye to her from her own modestly sized double bed.

She wouldn't think about her late period or the pregnancy test now. It couldn't be possible. And yet, a small voice niggled, *it could.* But in the years of her marriage to Ryan, while they'd still been sleeping together, she hadn't had one scare despite not having used contraception. It had been the source of some of their main problems, and, while Alana had got checked out and been told everything was fine, Ryan had refused, clearly unable to deal with the fear that it could be something on his side.

The match picked up in pace just then and Alana let it distract her. At the end, Pascal found her as the usual scramble started.

'I've agreed to go on the post-match analysis panel to give my opinion on how I think the tournament is going to go. They're doing it in the press centre here.'

'OK,' Alana said, feeling slightly breathless and hating herself for it. 'I've some interviews lined up, and then I've got to head back to the studio, so I'll see you later.'

He nodded and bent close to her ear for a moment. 'I want to kiss you so thoroughly that you're boneless in my arms, but I don't think you'd thank me for that in front of the entire pressbox.'

Alana felt boneless already, and fought the rogue urge to let him do exactly that. She just shook her head swiftly, alternately disappointed and relieved when he stepped away with a cool look on his face.

His tall, powerful frame disappeared down through the seats, taking a little piece of her with him. She sighed. She was in so much trouble, and she was potentially in a whole lot more trouble too. The kind of trouble that Pascal Lévêque wouldn't thank her for. And yet… She placed a hand on her belly. Right at that moment she thought that, if she was pregnant, it was something she'd always have for herself. A baby, a child.

Just then the cameraman signalled that they were ready to go with the first interview, and Alana gathered up her stuff and hurried down to the pitch.

By the time they were onto the last interview with one of the Ireland players, Alana was feeling exhausted. She glanced up and her stomach contracted painfully when she saw who it was—Eoin Donohoe, one of her late husband's partners in crime. He was a huge, intimidating presence, one of the biggest players on the team. Like Ryan, he, too, was married, but that hadn't stopped his own hedonism. Waves of old mutual antipathy flowed between them as Alana prepared to ask the questions. Eoin smiled at her, but it held a nasty edge which she ignored.

They were almost done with the live interview when Eoin said quietly, 'So, we see that you're moving on with your life. Poor Ryan's barely cold in the grave.'

The air went very still around them. Alana fancied she could hear a pin drop. 'Excuse me?'

'Everyone knew you couldn't wait to get rid of him and suck him dry so you could move on, but you've got the best of both worlds now, don't you? You've got all of Ryan's money, and now you've got one of the richest men in the world eating out of your—'

'I beg your pardon, Eoin,' she cut in quickly, having no doubt he'd not stop at saying something unbelievably crude. 'My husband has been dead for a year and a half, and it's no business of yours and never has been what I do with my personal life.' The vitriol in Eoin's eyes made Alana quail inside, but something else was starting to rise up, too, something she'd held down for a long, long time—the truth.

Eoin continued with ugly menace in his voice and face. 'Except that it's your fault he died, your fault the Irish team never recovered from Ryan's death. If you hadn't thrown him out when he was so vulnerable—'

It came up from somewhere deep and reflexive. Alana laughed. She actually laughed. And it felt so good that she kept laughing. She knew it was verging on hysteria, but the truth had risen so far now that she couldn't help it coming out. She'd had enough of being the scapegoat for Ryan O'Connor.

She stepped forward and pushed a finger into Eoin's massive chest, emboldened by the fact that he looked distinctly nervous now at her reaction.

'Let's get a few things straight here and now, shall we?' She didn't wait for an answer; everything was forgotten as she was borne aloft on a wave of something like mad euphoria.

'My husband was a lying, cheating, womanising, gambling, pathetic excuse of a man. And I'm not the only one who knew it. My only sin was that I helped to perpetuate the myth, that I helped the world to see and believe in Saint Ryan. He made my life a misery. And *you* were part of that. I know all about you, too, Eoin Donohoe; don't you think people or even your wife would like to hear about your drunken, whoring binges in—'

'Shut up, you little bitch.'

His stark language, the threat in his tone and the way his face had twisted, made Alana step back in fright. Someone jumped in and physically restrained Eoin, he looked so angry.

The world came back into focus and Alana was stunned. Had she really just said all that? She looked around at the cameraman wildly. It wasn't Derek, it was a new guy, young and scared-looking. Derek would have had the sense to stop filming. Her stomach went into free fall.

She said through stiff, cold lips, 'Please tell me you stopped filming?'

He gulped and went puce, lowering the camera. 'I—'

Alana raised a shaky hand to her face; her other one was still wrapped around the microphone. 'Oh God.'

A low, threatening voice sounded near her ear, turning her blood cold. 'Well done, Cusack. You've done it now; you'd better be prepared for the fallout.'

She took down her hand and watched as Eoin sauntered away. He hadn't even tried to stitch her up. She'd done it all by herself. The minute he'd come out with his first provocative comment she should have wrapped up the interview and that would have been that. It was no worse than some of the barbed comments people had thrown at her since Ryan had died. Yet she'd never felt the need to defend herself till now.

In the temporary studio set up at the other end of the pitch for the after-match analysis, there was a deathly lull as the panel absorbed what had just happened. Luckily they had just cut to a commercial break, but the damage was done. Pascal's face was like granite.

When she finally let herself into her house later, Alana felt shell shocked, as if she'd been put through a wringer and left flat and limp on the other side. When she'd walked back into the newsroom, she'd been summoned immediately to Rory's office and had been fired on the spot. The entire slanging match had been aired on national television, in front of the country and in front of the panel of experts discussing the match. And Pascal. Apparently he'd held his tongue on air, but afterwards had voiced his concerns for the image of the tournament, and the image of his bank's involvement in the face of the rapidly escalating scandal. That was what Rory had told her as he'd all but flung her contract at her.

'I knew you were liable to be a problem when I hired you!'

'And yet,' Alana had pointed out in a desperate bid to try and save herself, 'I proved myself to be reliable, well informed, and you even told me last week that I was the one you trusted most to do the hard-hitting interviews.'

'Yes, Alana,' he'd replied wearily, sitting down behind his desk. 'But you brought your baggage with you, didn't you?'

She'd kept it together and had just said quietly, 'I guess I did.' Even from the grave her husband was having the last laugh.

As Alana sat on her couch now and thought of everything that had just happened she couldn't stop the nausea rising. She just made it to the bathroom in time and emptied the contents of her stomach. As she washed her face, she thought of something, and with a fatal air went back out to her bag and extracted the chemist's bag. She went back into her tiny bathroom.

The day couldn't get any worse.

And then it just did.

* * *

She tried to ignore the doorbell which was ringing persistently, the door-knocker banging violently. But the thought of her neighbours hearing the commotion finally made her move off her couch and out of the state of shock that had held her immobile for the past few minutes. She opened the door and didn't wait to see who it was. She knew.

Pascal came in and towered over her, the door shut behind him.

'What the hell was all that about?'

Alana moved around to her armchair and sat down, because she was afraid she might fall. 'That was me, finally airing my dirty laundry. In front of the nation, no less.'

Pascal had moved to the centre of the small sitting-room, and glared down at her. 'And in front of the entire Six Nations public too. I believe the news is hitting the airwaves as we speak. The hotel where the after-match party is being held has had to call for police assistance in dealing with the hordes of paparazzi already camped outside.'

Alana winced.

Pascal grunted something unintelligible and sat down on her couch. She was still a little too numb to react.

'So? Are you going to tell me what happened?'

Alana shrugged. She looked at him, but didn't really see him. 'He pushed me too far. For months people have been making snide comments about how I was so cruel to Ryan—how could I have thrown him out?—and the truth was exactly what I said.'

Pascal drove a hand through his hair. 'But it's crazy. The things you said—'

'Were all true.' Alana felt life-force coming back into her bones, the shock wearing off. This man and his concern for appearances was the reason she'd just lost her job, and the reality of what that meant was beginning to sink in.

She stood up and crossed her arms. 'I'm not really in the

mood to discuss this actually, would you mind leaving? I think you've done enough for one day.'

He stood, too, bristling. He pointed at his chest. '*Me?* I'm not the one that has just ripped the rose-tinted glasses from a nation of mourners. Whatever your husband might have been, Alana, surely there was a more decorous time and place to tell the truth?'

She stepped up to him, shaking. 'Do you really think I thought it through logically for one second Pascal—and then went ahead thinking it would all be OK?' She stepped back again, breathing heavily. 'Of course I didn't. It just came out. And in all honesty, I probably couldn't stop myself if it happened again. He provoked me.'

Pascal recalled what Eoin Donohoe had said, and recalled, too, his urge to go and lift Alana bodily out of his way so that he could shield her. He'd been genuinely concerned for her safety as he'd watched her confront the huge man. She'd looked so tiny and fragile, standing up to him. The protective instinct had caught him unawares as the events had unfolded in front of him, but then he'd also had to assess the potential damage as a barrage of calls had immediately jammed the phone lines in the studio.

Pascal couldn't keep the censure from his voice. 'He may have provoked you, but you've unleashed a storm now.'

He saw how Alana paled dramatically. But his own head was still ringing from the board of his bank wanting to know what on earth was going on, why a storm in a teacup was threatening to reduce the famous rugby-tournament to the level of a sideshow. And what it was already doing to their reputation on Europe's stock markets.

Alana felt a wave of weariness. 'It'll die down soon enough. It's not as if people are going to be faced with me, anyway; I've been sacked.'

Pascal's head reared back. '*Sacked?*'

She nodded and looked at him, hardening her heart and insides to the way he made her feel, even now. The weariness fled and anger rose, hot and swift. How could he be so cavalier about her life? Her independence was gone, everything she'd built up destroyed. 'Rory sacked me as soon as I got back. And as it was in part to do with your reaction, you needn't act so surprised.'

Pascal's face darkened ominously, features tight. 'I didn't know he'd done that.'

'Well, he did.' Her hands were clenched into fists at her sides.

'I would have never have advocated that you lose your job over this. To suggest that is ridiculous.'

His words rang with conviction, and he seemed affronted that she thought he would be so petty. She knew she couldn't blame him for the fact that Ireland was so small that the merest whiff of scandal could run for weeks and weeks and wreck a career overnight. The immediate future lay starkly ahead of her, especially with the brand-new knowledge that she held secret in her belly. The anger drained away and she felt weary again; it was too overwhelming to try and get her head around it. And at the centre of everything stood this man who was turning her upside down and inside out.

She sat down again when a wave of dizziness went through her. Immediately Pascal was at her side, bending down, a hand on her knee. She tried to flinch away, but he wouldn't release her.

'What's wrong?' he asked harshly.

'Nothing,' she answered quickly, restraining the urge to place a hand on her belly. Then hysteria rose again. 'Unless you count the fact that I'm now jobless and about to be homeless, too.'

'What are you talking about, Alana? You're not making sense.'

'Sense! If I had *sense* I wouldn't have opened my mouth

earlier.' She was already hoping he'd forget what she'd just said. But of course he didn't; his logical brain was sifting through everything.

'What do you mean, homeless?'

She wished he'd move back. He was crowding her, exactly as he'd done that first time they'd met and had been in the car on the way to the restaurant. She cursed her runaway mouth inwardly.

'What I mean is that, without a job, I'm going to be homeless. I have this month's mortgage paid, and after that... nothing.'

He stood up again and she looked up.

He was remote, more remote than she'd ever seen him. 'How is that possible? You must have been left a fortune.'

Alana felt his coolness touch her deep inside. She stood up, too, moving back towards her galley-kitchen as if seeking refuge. This was the first time she'd ever contemplated telling anyone the whole truth. She grimaced inwardly, apart from her recent exposé.

She shook her head. 'That's just it. It's a myth. Ryan gambled everything away with people like Eoin, on stupidly lavish expensive weekends to places like Las Vegas. They'd hire private jets, stay in the best hotels—drink, drugs, girls, gambling. They did it all. When Ryan died, he had debts to the tune of millions, and no one knew. He kept up the pretence all along. If we hadn't had the house to sell in Dalkey, I'd have had to declare myself bankrupt. Thanks to my own savings, which didn't amount to much, I was able to buy this house and set up a loan agreement with Ryan's debtors to pay the rest of the money back. Without my job, the repayments will fall behind immediately. This house is the least of my worries; the minute the repayments stop, they'll come after me.'

Alana didn't glean any comfort from Pascal's shocked

look. She knew well that on some level he'd still had her cast in the role of an ex-WAG—the derogatory term for the wives and girlfriends of sports stars. She couldn't blame him; she'd seen the way he'd look at her sometimes, as if waiting for her to trip herself up, reveal herself to be the silly bimbo that most of those girls were.

'I'll talk to Rory.'

Alana shook her head vehemently. 'No, that'll make things even worse. The last thing I need now is to be pushed to the forefront of everything again.'

'But maybe he can keep you behind the scenes for a while.'

'It wouldn't work.' She could just imagine the snide comments, the looks.

'What about your family? Don't they know about this?'

A spasm of pain clenched Alana's insides. She hated admitting this, knowing it would be hard to understand. 'No; they don't know. I was as guilty as Ryan for keeping up the pretence.' She avoided Pascal's eye. 'They just…they don't have the kind of resources I needed. They had their own things going on, and my parents are old, frail. They didn't need to hear about my problems.'

Pascal's tone was frigid. 'It sounds to me like it was a problem worth sharing.'

She looked at him, feeling defensive. 'It was my decision, OK? My family aren't that wealthy, my parents certainly aren't any more. They live comfortably, but they've earned that. I couldn't burden them with the mistake I made.'

'Is that how you saw your marriage?'

The way Pascal asked the question so softly made Alana feel even more vulnerable. She had to push him back; she knew well it was only a matter of time now before he ran as fast as he could from her car wreck of a life.

'For a long time, yes I did, which is why I'm determined not to make the same mistake twice.'

He started advancing towards her, and Alana backed away further.

'Is that what you see happening here—a mistake in the making?'

Alana shook her head, confused. Did he mean *them*? 'I don't... What are you talking about? This isn't anything like that.' *It's worlds apart.*

He was still advancing into her kitchen, making the space become tiny. Alana was starting to feel desperate. She felt so raw and vulnerable right now that if he so much as touched her... She stopped abruptly as her hand that had been sliding along the counter hit something. Instinctively, she covered it. She knew immediately what it was; she'd left it there in her shock and confusion just minutes before. Pascal's eyes darted to where her hand had made the betraying, concealing movement. Alana gulped as he looked back to her. She felt guilty. She looked guilty.

'What's that, Alana?'

'Nothing,' she said, almost hopefully.

'So why are you trying to hide it?'

'I'm not.'

'Show me what it is.'

'It's nothing, just rubbish.' Desperation tinged her voice, and in a rising surge of panic and rejection at the thought of confronting this, too, when so much had just happened, she whipped it off the counter top and whirled around to put it in the bin. But before she could a strong arm wrapped itself around her midriff and pulled her back into a hard body. With effortless strength, Pascal reached round and pulled the object from her hand. She closed her eyes. Their breathing sounded harsh in the small space, and she could imagine him trying to make sense of what he was looking at.

Alana could feel the tension come into Pascal's body. His arm grew even more rigid around her. She knew it wouldn't take long for him to make sense of it. These days pregnancy tests were idiot proof and the results immediate—the word *'pregnant'* wouldn't have taken a six-year-old long to figure out.

And then abruptly, so abruptly that she stumbled a little, Pascal released her. She turned round to look up but he wasn't looking at her, he was looking at the pregnancy test. After a long, tense moment he finally looked at her and she fought not to wince under his almost-black look.

'It's pretty self-explanatory.'

He nodded. 'Yes, crystal-clear.'

He turned and walked back into the sitting room, holding the test in his hand. Alana followed warily. He turned then, and she stopped in her tracks at the harsh lines on his face.

'And were you planning on keeping this little secret to yourself, too, shouldering this as another burden? Another mistake?'

Pain lanced her. 'I did the test just before you arrived. My period is late… I've been feeling a bit sick, so I bought it this morning on my way into work. Of course I would have told you.' *Eventually.*

'Oh, really?' His voice could have turned milk sour. 'I find that hard to believe, when you were about to throw it in the bin as nothing more than a piece of rubbish. Perhaps you've already decided what you want to do with our baby.'

Our baby.

The simple words of acknowledgement and acceptance rocked through Alana like an atom bomb. She put her hands instinctively on her still-flat belly. 'Of course I haven't decided anything, and certainly not what you seem to be implying. And I *was* going to tell you. It's just…I've barely had time to take it in myself. I think you can agree that today has packed more than its fair punch.'

Hating herself for feeling so weak as another wave of dizziness washed over her, she couldn't help swaying slightly. Words resounded in her head: *jobless, homeless, pregnant.* She'd really made a mess of things this time.

With a muttered curse Pascal was by her side and made her sit down on the couch.

'When was the last time you ate?'

Alana had to struggle to recall. Pascal cursed again colourfully. 'Don't tell me you haven't even eaten all day?'

He threw off his coat and went into her kitchen and started opening the fridge and looking on her open shelves. Feeling totally bemused and numb, Alana watched as he took out bread, butter, cheese, tomatoes and made a sandwich. He brought it back over on a plate and handed it to her, watching her until she'd eaten the whole thing, even though it was the size of a doorstep.

When she was done, he took the plate and set it aside, then he stood up and started to pace. He ran a hand through his dishevelled hair. He looked dishevelled all over, and Alana could feel her pulse stirring to life. His shirt was coming out of his trousers, the top button of his shirt undone. He rounded on her then, taking her by surprise. Her eyes had been on his bottom, and she coloured guiltily. How could she be thinking of that at a time like this?

But it seemed as if she was not the only one. Pascal dropped down onto the couch beside her, coming close, and before she could stop him he was undoing the top button of her shirt.

'That's better. I can't concentrate when you're all buttoned up.'

Alana backed away into the corner of the couch. Pascal's brows rose. 'It's a bit late for that, don't you think?'

She was beginning to feel stifled, threatened—sensory overload. She shimmied out from under him and stood up. Pascal sat back and looked up from under hooded lids. Alana's insides clenched.

'So when do you think it happened? I thought we were careful.'

'We were,' she said crisply, and then remembered the back of the car that night in Rome. Colour washed through her cheeks again. She looked down and caught his eye. She couldn't read his expression. But it seemed as if he could read her mind.

'Yes, there was that time. Or the bath afterwards.' Pascal had known well he was being careless, but for the first time in his life that concern had assumed secondary place to fulfilling his physical needs. And in the intervening days he hadn't even thought about it. More fool him. Yet, even more astounding to him right now was the equanimity he felt in the face of this news. In fact, what he was feeling was an inordinate sense of *rightness*. A sense of something his grandfather had passed onto him, something he'd never realised he possessed before: a sense of family.

Along with it came the memory of what it had been like to be shunned, rejected, and surging up within Pascal now was a zealous desire to give this child, *his* child, the kind of acknowledgement he'd never had. The revelation stunned him.

Alana started to pace, anything to avoid looking at him, wanting him. She had to sort her head out. She couldn't let him distract her.

'Look. This has happened. It was reckless and silly, but we both know where you stand on this kind of thing.'

He stood up and was immediately dangerous, towering over her. 'Oh, we do?'

Alana felt like stamping her foot childishly. 'Yes! I can't imagine you're happy to be faced with a pregnant—'

'Mistress?' he asked equably.

'I hate that word. I'm not your mistress.'

'Then what are you? Go on—say it, Alana.'

He was goading her, teasing her, even now. She glared up

at him, arms crossed. 'I'm your latest lover. The one in between your last one and your next one.'

His expression hardened, his eyes flashed. 'Yes. But now
you're my pregnant lover, so that changes things somewhat.'

'Are you trying to tell me that you're seriously happy
with this?'

'Not happy, exactly, no,' he bit out, feeling defensive. 'But
how do you know that I haven't always wanted a child someday?'

'Have you?' she shot back.

Now Pascal was the one backing away, feeling a little
poleaxed again. His recent revelation was too new, too raw
to articulate. This whole afternoon was taking on an unreal
hue, as if he'd stepped into some mad time-warp. He was in
a tiny house in the middle of Dublin with a woman who'd
stepped into his life and turned it upside down. She'd just told
him she was pregnant, and he was still there. He wasn't running as fast as his legs could carry him away from her, which
was how he'd always envisaged reacting to such a scenario.

He looked at her steadily and tried to ignore the way her
hair was escaping the confines of its neat bun, the way he
could see the hollow at the bottom of her throat where he'd
opened the button. Even now, more than ever, he wanted her.
He answered almost distractedly, 'Yes…of course I did. On
some level.' *Someday.*

His mind cleared and fixed on Alana. 'What about you?'

He saw her hand go to her belly again; she'd done that a
few times, almost as if to protect the unborn child from
something—*their* unborn child. Something in his chest felt
tight.

Alana turned away from Pascal's gaze for a moment. He
was looking too deeply, seeing too much. When she turned
around, his expression had lost that intensity; it was more innocuous.

'Yes. I always wanted children. We…myself and Ryan… tried, but nothing happened. And I was always grateful then that we hadn't. No child deserved to be born into our sham of a marriage.'

'And what will this be, Alana?'

She looked up into his eyes, panic trickling through her. He was so powerful, a million times more powerful than Ryan ever had been. He was cold, remote, and she had that prescience again of what it would be like to cross him—she wouldn't win.

'This will be just us, having a baby. I'm not going to marry you, Pascal.' She was shaking her head, moving away. He advanced.

'I wasn't aware that I'd asked you,' he said silkily.

She flushed. 'Well, isn't that…how you people operate?'

He threw back his head and laughed, but Alana knew he wasn't amused. 'What do you think I am, a masochist? Why would I want to marry a woman who doesn't want to marry me?'

And who I don't want to marry, he should have added. Alana shrugged, feeling silly now. 'So that you can have control over our baby. Child.'

He was very close now.

'Oh, I'll have control, Alana, as much as you do. We don't need to be married for that. It'll be my name on the birth certificate, and I expect to be involved every step of the way.'

'But…' Alana's throat was dry. 'But how is that going to work?'

Pascal's hand reached out and she felt his finger trail from her jaw down to her neck, to the hollow where her pulse beat fast and unevenly.

'It's simple—for now you'll come back and live in Paris with me. We can sort things out from there.'

CHAPTER SEVEN

THREE days later Alana finally had to acknowledge that she really hadn't had a choice. Not that it made her feel any better. What could she have done? Her family was reeling from the revelations. The country was reeling. Reporters had camped out on her parents' front lawn until Pascal had hired security guards to protect them and drive the reporters away. She'd created an unholy row. She'd never confided in her brothers and sisters, so to seek help now—and in doing so bring the media circus behind her—would be unforgivable. The best thing she could do was to disappear. But unfortunately that could only happen with the one person she really didn't want to have to face: Pascal. By coming to Paris, she knew she'd tacitly agreed to stay for an indeterminate amount of time— till things calmed down at home, or until she could get another job. Either way, she was in no position to call the shots for now.

Yet she'd prevaricated, resisted, and watched with mounting horror as the story had taken hold in the press, had watched as her tiny house and square had come under siege. Pascal had finally battled through reporters the previous day, his face rigid with censure as he'd rounded on her once inside the tiny space.

'This is ridiculous. If you don't leave and come with me

right now, *today*, you're going to turn this into something even bigger. They know where you live, where your family lives. You'll have to leave the house at some stage, or were you planning on surviving on air and water?' His scathing glance had taken in the already bare-looking shelves in her kitchen.

Alana had never felt so undone, so threatened, in all her life. Even when Ryan had been at his worst, she'd had a level of freedom, space. He hadn't touched the part of her deep down that this man was trampling all over. She'd shaken her head as much in negation of that as anything else. 'Please. Don't make me; I can't leave. I'll manage somehow.'

'How?' he'd asked curtly. 'As of next month, you're facing repossession. You're hardly in a position to go out and seek employment within a two-hundred-mile radius of this country. I've stayed here out of concern for you and your family, but I have to return to France.' He'd gestured to the curtains drawn over her window. She could hear the jostle of people outside. 'Are you really ready to take them on by yourself?'

Alana had looked at him and let easy anger rise. She'd lashed out as much at herself as him, but made him the target. 'This is all your fault. If you hadn't pursued me, if you hadn't wanted me—'

Her words were cut off as he bridged the gap between them and gripped her upper arms, hauling her close. Words died in her throat as she felt her body come flush against his. She'd never seen him look so angry.

His mouth was a thin slash of displeasure. 'I wanted you, yes, but you acquiesced, Alana. I'm not the reason your marriage failed, and I'm not the reason you never spoke the truth before now, and I'm certainly not the reason you felt compelled to spill your guts the other day.'

Alana gulped as she looked up, held captive in his hands, her body already responding to his. The problem was, he *was* the reason, but she knew she couldn't blame him. He'd changed her; since the first moment their eyes had met, something in her had started to melt and breathe again. 'I'm sorry,' she said quietly, soberly. 'You're right. It's not your fault.'

'Damn right it's not my fault. If anyone is to blame, then it's you because *this*, the way you make me feel, is all your fault.'

He looked at her for a long, searing moment before hauling her even closer into his chest, and claimed her mouth with his. It was passionate, bruising, all-encompassing. Pascal's hands held her easily, pressing her close into his fast-burgeoning arousal. And she did nothing to stop him because she couldn't. Didn't want to. He hadn't touched her since it had all come out. And she needed this, wanted him so badly that nothing else mattered but him here, right now, with his mouth on hers, giving her life. Restoring sanity, while taking it away spectacularly.

He pulled back after a long, incendiary moment. They were both breathing fast, hearts thumping in unison. She looked up at him helplessly, aghast at how even now he had the power to render her speechless with just a kiss.

When he spoke, it made something cold descend into Alana's belly; his voice was so cool, so devoid of the passion she felt in his body. 'Have you also forgotten that you're carrying my child? And for that reason alone, if nothing else, you will be afforded my protection whether you like it or not. This isn't just about us any more, Alana.'

Now Alana stood at the window of Pascal's top-floor apartment near the Champs-Elysées in Paris, arms folded. The view over the Parisian rooftops was stunning, taking in the Arc de Triomphe in the distance. Where the apartment in Rome had had something homely about it, something Alana had instinctively preferred, this was sumptuous on another level. The antiques and priceless art, the luxurious curtains and ankle-deep carpets screamed decadence.

She sighed and turned to survey the room again. Despite

its objects, its gilded antique furniture, it felt empty somehow. They'd arrived yesterday evening. Pascal had overseen her pack her things in her house and had then escorted her through the crush in the square. In his car on the way to the airport she'd made her calls, explaining to her parents that she was going away for a while to let things die down. They had been understandably concerned, and to her surprise Pascal had taken the phone out of her hand and had reassured her father that she would be fine, giving him his phone numbers and also assuring them that their protection wouldn't be lifted until Pascal was sure they would be left in peace. His easy reassurance had made her hackles rise, but had also conversely alleviated her awful, burning guilt.

Pascal had shown her to a separate bedroom when they'd arrived, clearly having had no expectation that she would share with him, and Alana had to wonder now what her role would be. And why she felt so confused about that—about what she wanted. This was exacerbated by the fact that she'd barely seen him since then. After having showed her where everything was, pointing out some food ready-prepared for eating, he'd informed her that he had work to do and had disappeared into a study.

Then this morning, he'd been up and gone to work when she'd emerged from her room, feeling like a train wreck, even after an amazingly deep sleep. He'd left a note on the kitchen counter with a long list of numbers and assistants' names. His writing was as distinctive and boldly authoritative as him:

If you need anything, just call. I've set up an account in your name at my bank with funds, should you need anything. My assistant will be around shortly with bank cards. Please make yourself at home. I will be back late, so don't wait up. I'll be eating out.

Pascal.

And just like that, here she was—pregnant with Pascal Lévêque's child, at the centre of a storm of controversy at home and conveniently sidelined to…where, exactly?

'I've made an appointment with a gynaecologist near here for tomorrow morning. You need to start thinking about yourself and the baby.'

Alana bristled; as if she'd had time to think about anything else. She'd hardly seen Pascal, had walked what felt like the length and breadth of Paris on her own, and now he was ordering her around only minutes after coming in the apartment door at the end of a long, lonely week for her. She lashed out at his easy assumption that she was here for good. 'I'd prefer if I could choose my own doctor, thanks, and there are plenty of gynaecologists in Dublin.'

A muscle clenched in his jaw. Alana was trying to ignore the way he looked so sexy in his suit. Suddenly to be faced with him after days of not touching him was making her equilibrium very shaky. She had to wonder if she'd imagined that kiss in her house the day he'd taken her away. Was their affair, in fact, over for him? Had the pregnancy killed his desire?

'She's the best in Paris. And who said anything about having the baby in Dublin? You're here now, Alana.'

Her eyes clashed with his, and her hands clenched at her sides as she regarded him across the kitchen where she'd followed him when he'd arrived home. Now she regretted the puppy-dog-like impulse. And her insecurity. 'I don't believe we've actually discussed this, Pascal. I have every intention of having my baby at home. As far as I'm concerned, I'm just here until things die down.'

'You mean, *our* baby.'

'I mean, *my* baby. This is not a traditional relationship. I've no problem with you being involved, but I'm making the decisions to do with my body and how I want this to proceed.'

'The medical system here is one of the best in the world,' he declared arrogantly, and Alana opened her mouth but faltered. He was right.

'That may be so. But when this baby is born, I'm going to want the support of my family. Here I've no one.' Alana felt a rising sense of panic that Pascal would just keep her here, like some kind of animal in a zoo.

She had her hand on her belly again, in an unconscious gesture of protection. She was dressed down in jeans and a loose shirt, and Pascal could see the outline of her bra underneath, white and plain, and yet more seductive than the flimsiest lingerie he'd seen on her yet—the memory of which was all too vivid. His jaw ached from holding it so tight. His belly burned with a fire that only the woman in front of him could quench, and he knew that would only be momentary. One taste of her and he'd want more. Much more. His body thrummed with sexual hunger, but it was a hunger he feared would hurt her, it was so strong.

That was why he found himself in the novel position of holding himself back. His head was scrambled. Alana wasn't just his lover any more, she was the mother of his unborn child. That elevated her to a place he wasn't quite sure he knew how to navigate. He knew nothing about pregnant women. So he'd done what he thought was best, given her some space—himself, too, if he was honest. The knowledge of impending fatherhood was bringing up all sorts of long-unexplored emotions and memories, not least of which was this desire to nurture and protect. He'd buried himself deep in work to try and avoid being alone with her as much as possible. But his good intentions were feeling very elusive now as she stood in front of him with bare feet, hair down, looking as sexily undone as his most rampant fantasy. Not a scrap of artifice or make-up.

'You're telling me that you will expect the support of your family, when up until now you've had no problem shunning it?'

Alana blanched. How was it that he could see her coming from three-thousand miles away? And why had she felt compelled to tell him all about her family?

'You haven't even told your parents yet.'

He was remorseless, and Alana felt exposed. 'I'm not going to tell anyone until the three-month mark, when it's safer. Anything could happen between now and then. It's such early days, we might not... It might not even...'

Pascal negated her fears with a slashing movement of his hand, a quick, violent surge of something protective rising up within him. 'Don't even say that. You will be fine. This baby will be fine.' The strength of the emotion that gripped him made him feel a little shaky, even Alana had stepped back, her eyes growing huge.

'Look.' He forced a reasonable, steady tone into his voice, belying what was under the surface. 'You need to have an initial check-up appointment, admit to that at least?'

Alana forced herself to take a deep breath. She was feeling overwhelmed, all at sea, itchy under the surface of her skin, unbelievably vulnerable and...homesick. The sting of tears burnt the back of her eyes, and a lump lodged in her throat. To her utter horror and chagrin, she saw Pascal's eyes narrow on her face. He came closer, and she feared even moving in case she shattered and fell apart.

'What is it, Alana? What's wrong? You seem...edgy.'

She could have laughed out loud if she'd had the wherewithal—*edgy?* She'd been on a knife-edge ever since she'd laid eyes on this man. He was standing so close she could smell him. She shook her head faintly and tried to control her emotions.

He came closer and the air seemed to swirl headily around them. It was the bizarrest sensation; the closer he came to her, the better she felt, the less isolated, the less lonely. But also the more confused.

'Alana, I can see *something* in those expressive eyes of yours.'

She tried to step back, but her legs wouldn't move. She threw out a hand as if to gesture around them. 'What on earth could be wrong, Pascal? Within a week I lost my job, found out I was pregnant, have moved homes and now I just… I've been alone all week, and it's just…' This time she couldn't stop them. The dam she'd been holding back burst and tears fell, hot and thick, down her face; her throat worked convulsively.

Through her blurred vision Pascal loomed large, and then Alana felt herself being enfolded in his arms, and held so tenderly and carefully against his chest that it made her cry even harder. And this wasn't pretty, silent crying, this was loud, snotty, shuddering, gasping crying. For what seemed like an age. And as she cried Alana realised that she'd never cried once in all the years of her marriage, even at the end. Even at Ryan's funeral. She'd locked her pain deep inside and it felt like it was all pouring out now, along with all her fears for the future and for her baby. *Their* baby.

Without her knowing how he did it, Pascal had taken Alana into the sitting room and she found herself sitting on a couch, still cradled against his chest. When her crying finally began to stop and became deep, shuddering breaths, she pulled away a little. His shirt was soaked.

'I'm sorry.' She couldn't look at him, and tried ineffectually to wipe at her damp face, which she could well imagine was not a pretty sight. Her eyes felt sore. He pulled a handkerchief from his pocket and handed it to her. She took it and blew her nose loudly, moving away from him. She was mortified. She'd never cried like that, even in front of her own mother.

He moved away for a second and came back. She saw a glass with dark liquid appear in front of her face. She looked at him swiftly. 'I don't think I should…' He made a very Gallic facial expression. 'I'm sure a small sip won't do any harm.' So she took a tiny sip. She could feel reaction start to set in, her legs and hands start to shake, and was glad of the burning sensation of the liquid as it entered her stomach and its comforting warmth spread outwards. She put down the glass carefully.

'I'm sorry. I don't know where that came from.' Alana felt her hands taken in Pascal's and he pulled her gently round to face him. His face was cast slightly in the shadows of the softly lit room.

'No, I'm the one who is sorry. I shouldn't have left you alone all week.'

She felt something flutter in her chest, and Alana immediately wanted to scotch his obvious suspicion that she might have missed him. Or that she needed reassurance, like some wilting heroine or, God forbid, a lover who was falling in love with him. 'Don't be silly, you were busy. I understand that.'

His mouth tightened momentarily. 'I created more work for myself to avoid being alone with you.'

A severe pain lanced Alana. She shouldn't be feeling pain, yet she also couldn't quite believe he was being so harsh. So this is what it would feel like when the time came. Well, the time had come. She tried to pull her hands from his. He wouldn't let her go. A spark of anger restored her equilibrium. 'Pascal—'

'Let me explain. I don't think you know what I mean.'

Oh God, he was going to explain, and she'd just blubbered all over him. She spoke quickly, 'No, really, I do; it's fine.'

'Alana, *tais-toi!*'

Pascal's exasperation was palpable. She shut up.

'I've avoided being alone with you, because if we're in any kind of close proximity for more than two minutes, I want to take you to bed with an urgency that is not necessarily good for someone in your condition.'

Her *condition*. For a second Alana didn't even know what he meant. Her heart was thumping, and a treacherous surge of joy in her chest was threatening to strangle her. He did still desire her. But then at the intent, serious look on his face her mind and vision cleared. He was worried that he'd hurt her?

That all-too-familiar melting sensation was spreading through her chest, warming her like the brandy. 'Oh.'

'Yes. Oh.'

Alana tried valiantly not to let the desperation she felt sound in her voice. She knew it was there, though, when she stumbled over the words. 'Well…I don't think— That is, as far as I know, it's OK. I mean, lots of people don't even know they're pregnant at this stage.'

Her face was getting warm. Could he see how badly she wanted him? She prayed not.

'How are you feeling now?'

Like I want you to rip my clothes off and make love to me right here: the words resounded in Alana's head. She gulped and could feel a trickle of sweat roll down between her breasts. 'Fine. Absolutely fine. I haven't been sick once this week. So, unless it comes back…'

Pascal stood up and paced. Immediately Alana wanted him back by her side. 'You see, that's what I mean, you need to go and speak to the doctor so we know what to expect.'

He looked down at her with a stern expression, all hunger and desire erased from his gaze and eyes. Alana felt as if she was a dog in heat, and struggled to control her libido. Was this a side-effect of the pregnancy—like the way her breasts felt so heavy and tender? If so, how was she going to cope with the next eight months?

'So, we're agreed, we'll go to see the doctor tomorrow?'

Alana just nodded, only half-taking in what he was saying. Her whole being was focused on the fact that he still desired her and had been holding back.

He came back and sat down beside her. Alana tried not to let the hunger she felt show on her face.

'Look, Alana, you need me now. Let me take care of you…and the baby. Ireland is not somewhere you can go back to anytime soon. Let things calm down. In the meantime, let's just concentrate on the baby and preparing for that…'

He made it sound so easy. And, while Alana felt it was important to assert her independence, she knew he was right. For now. It wasn't just about the two of them any more. She'd worry about the shifting parameters of their affair later. The knowledge that he still desired her was intoxicating, she went to bed that night and slept properly for the first time all week.

'The doctor said it's OK.'

Alana immediately winced and froze inwardly at how baldly she'd let the words come out. She'd had no intention of even saying anything, but standing here, back in the apartment, holding all the bumph from the doctor's office and the baby books Pascal had insisted on buying, something primal was rising up within her—a need that had to be acknowledged. Pascal turned to face her. He was dressed in faded denims and a dark coat, cheeks slightly reddened from the brisk breeze outside. Alana's heart clenched. She'd never grow tired of looking at him.

He walked towards her, a glint in his eye. 'What's OK?'

Alana flushed but looked at him steadily, not backing down. 'If we…you know…wanted to—'

'Make love?' he asked innocently, that glint looking decidedly suspicious.

'Yes,' Alana bit out through a clenched jaw, and wished that she didn't feel the way she did—that she wasn't enslaved by this man and his body and how he could make her feel. The doctor had pointed out that it was entirely natural to be feeling more desirous at the moment, the result of hormones. But Alana knew well that the pregnancy was only heightening what was already there in raw form.

Pascal came very close and took Alana's jaw in his hand, its delicacy testing all of his powers of restraint. His thumb smoothed the satin-soft skin of her cheek. He saw her pupils dilate and it had a direct effect on his body.

'We'll go for dinner later.' He had to put some kind of control on this wanton craving he had. She was *pregnant*, for God's sake.

Her jaw moved against his hand and he hardened, his erection straining painfully against the constricting material of his jeans.

'OK. Where?'

'You choose. I have to go to the office to pick up some papers; I'll be back in an hour.'

'You've booked us a table where?'

Alana looked at the guide book again, slightly mystified by Pascal's incredulous reaction. 'A restaurant called Lapérouse.'

His face looked slightly pained. 'Are you doing this on purpose?'

Alana was nonplussed. 'On purpose—why? It just sounds nice. It's one of the oldest restaurants in Paris.' She held out the book for him to see.

Pascal took the book and put it down. 'I know the restaurant—or, should I say, I know what it's famous for.' Then he took her hand to lead her out of the apartment and Alana followed.

'What do you mean "famous for"? Because Émile Zola and Victor Hugo used to go there?'

'Something like that,' he muttered. 'You'll see.'

It was now late evening. Pascal had been held up at the office, and the sky in Paris was darkening to an inky blue, stars popping out. She'd changed into a simple black dress. Pascal had showered and changed into dark trousers and a dark sweater under his black overcoat.

Alana shivered slightly despite her big padded coat when they got outside. Pascal went to flag down a cab, but she wasn't shivering from the cold; it was a shiver of anticipation. Because ever since this morning, and her brief, excruciatingly naked declaration that it was OK to have sex, something heavy and tangible had been humming between them. Alana was confused as to how things were going to go in general with this relationship, but one thing she knew for sure was this: Pascal's desire for her was finite, and soon—as soon as the pregnancy started to progress in earnest, she guessed— he'd be moving on. She just didn't know where that would leave her. Oh, she wasn't so silly to have fallen for him. Even now she could say with pride that she'd protected her heart. But...

'Here we go.'

Pascal was helping Alana into the back of a warm cab, stopping her train of thought. And then, with him so close to her on the backseat, his fingers tangled in hers, she was finding it hard to think any more.

They got out of the cab in front of an ornately decorated restaurant situated on the corner of a street, right on the banks of the Seine. It had old murals of lavishly dressed women on the panels outside, windows full of ancient books, bottles and delicate filigree balcony-railings around the first-floor windows.

'This is gorgeous,' breathed Alana as she looked up.

Pascal just grunted something unintelligible in reply. When they went inside and Pascal gave Alana's name, as she had made the booking, she saw him exchange a few words with the head waiter. The man looked at her curiously and smiled, leading them up through the main part of the dining room and then off to the side and to a door. There were rooms off to all sides, creating a warren-like ambience of hidden nooks and crannies.

Pascal looked at her with an indecipherable expression on his face as the waiter opened the door and indicated for her to step in. When she did, her heart stopped, and then started again with slow, heavy beats. It was a tiny, private dining-room, more like a salon, with a table set for two, a mirror along one wall and a banquette seat at the back on which sat plump, inviting velvet cushions. The colours were dark and earthy, unbelievably sensual. It was like a *boudoir*.

Alana heard the door click shut and turned to face Pascal, her face flaming.

'I had no idea this was here.'

His mouth quirked, his eyes glittering in the soft light. 'I believe you.'

Alana was very aware of the look in his eye, the lines of tension on his face. No wonder he'd reacted the way he had. She'd led them to a veritable seduction scene straight out of a fantasy. She walked further into the intimate space. 'What *is* this place?'

She could sense him close behind her and her body trembled.

'It's where the wealthy could dine privately in peace and seclusion, and also, it's said, where clandestine affairs took place. Look here.'

He directed her attention to crude scrapings on the mirror. 'This is where the women would test the diamonds they'd been given by their lovers to see if they were real or fake. Where they would write love messages.'

Alana leant close but couldn't make out what the faint, scrawled writing said. She was very aware of the space, their breathing, *them*. A discreet cough sounded outside the door, and Pascal opened it to let the waiter back in with menus and water. He took their coats and left again. Pascal indicated for Alana to sit down. They were practically side by side at the table. The banquette seat loomed large in Alana's imagination just behind them.

Pascal sat back easily, his huge body taking up most of the space, and drawled softly, 'Good choice.'

Alana felt prim. 'You know very well I had no idea about this.'

He sat up then and captured her hands, coming close. 'I know, I'm only teasing. The table you'd booked was in the main part of the restaurant, quite innocuous. *I* asked for one of these rooms.'

'You did?' she all but squeaked.

He nodded. 'I've heard about this place, but never been. It's been something of a fantasy of mine to see what it was like.'

'It is?' Alana was barely breathing now; her whole body was igniting and melting. She'd all but forgotten that they were even in a restaurant. The thought of inadvertently fulfilling one of Pascal's fantasies was so heady, so...

A discreet cough came from outside again, and Pascal let her hands go and called, *'Entrez.'* But his eyes barely left hers or her face as the waiter took their food order.

Alana wasn't entirely sure how or what she ate during that meal. The whole experience in that small space became about the senses. It felt as though she and Pascal had been removed from the world and set adrift in this little cocoon of sensuality and decadence. She knew courses came: Dublin Bay prawns to start, amazingly enough, and a ham dish as a main course, and then a wickedly dark chocolate-praline sorbet. Or she could have been completely wrong, because she knew she wouldn't be able to recall what they'd had if asked. The things she would be able to describe in detail had more to do with Pascal's gestures, the way his eyes crinkled appealingly when he smiled or laughed, the way he made her feel so hot inside.

A waiter had cleared the plates and was leaving small cups of coffee with an after-dinner liqueur for Pascal. He was almost at the door when Pascal issued a few rapid words in French. The waiter inclined his head, and when he'd left, Alana asked, 'What did you say to him?'

Pascal looked at her with a heavy-lidded gaze. 'I said that we would call if we needed anything else.'

He came close and his arm brushed across her breasts, making her breath stop as he drew her attention to a cord descending from the wall beside her. She hadn't even noticed it. 'We won't be disturbed again unless we pull that.'

Alana looked from the cord to Pascal; he didn't move back. His scent wrapped around her like a cloak of heavy desire. The sheer sexiness of him, and the room, overwhelmed her, and she lifted a hand to run her fingers through his hair, feeling the beautiful shape of his strong skull. And then, unable to wait any longer, the promise of fulfilment so close, she pulled his head to hers and their mouths touched.

A week of not touching blew up around them instantly. It could have been a lifetime, the way things escalated so rapidly. Without breaking contact, Pascal lifted Alana from her seat and moved them over to the lush banquette behind them. He took his mouth from hers and she followed him momentarily, as if loath to break even that point of touch. He laid her back against the huge cushions, gently, reverently.

He shrugged off his sweater, revealing a dark shirt underneath, and Alana watched with heavy-lidded eyes as he smoothed a hand down one of her thighs. She arched her back even at that chaste touch; every part of her seemed to be so sensitive, tingling. She wore thigh-high black socks and zip-up leather ankle-boots; she felt Pascal bend down and slip them off her feet before his hand travelled back up one leg, right up to where the sock ended and her flesh screamed for his touch. He smoothed that hand further up her thigh, causing her dress to ride up, and when his hand reached where her panties covered the moistening apex of her thighs, she stopped him.

Desperate need tinged her voice even as she said, 'We can't, not here. They could walk in.'

Pascal just shook his head. *'Non;* they know better.'

Alana's head sank back. Pascal's hand was covering her now, moving back and forth; she was helpless not to push herself into him, wanting more. He bent over her and kissed her deeply, before she felt air whisper over her skin and she realised that he was undoing the buttons at the front of her dress. With one hand, he pushed the sides apart to reveal her breasts, covered in blood-red lace.

'So beautiful…' he breathed, before gently pulling the lace of one cup down and rubbing a thumb back and forward over one tight tip. Alana bit her lip. Her breast was almost painfully sensitive; her body felt as though it was on fire. Pascal lifted one of her legs and brought it up and over so that it was bent on the seat beside him, opening her up to him even more. His hand still moved between her legs, and she could feel herself plumping, ripening, getting ready.

With her legs spread, Pascal moved even closer, and Alana finally found some autonomy of movement and stretched out her hands to open his shirt. Her fingers shook, and she could feel sweat break out on her brow. She needed that contact so badly, his naked chest against hers.

When his shirt was finally open, he bent again to take her

mouth. His hand had pulled down the sliver of lace covering her other breast, and to feel him like this was heaven. Alana moaned deep in her throat when his mouth moved away, and at the same time as his hand stopped teasing her and his fingers slipped in behind her panties to seek the passage to the wet hot heart of her, his mouth and tongue closed over one nipple, pulling it into his mouth and suckling fiercely.

Alana cried out; she couldn't help it. Although she bit back the next cry, her hands were speared in his hair, wanting to make him stop the torturous pleasure he was inflicting on her breasts, and also never wanting him to stop. Her hips bucked towards his hand. He was wringing every ounce of her being out in a never-ending stream of pleasure, but the pinnacle was elusive. It wasn't enough.

She managed to pull his head from her breast and looked up into dark, glittering eyes. She felt wild and wanton. 'I need more, I need *you*.'

'Alana,' he groaned softly, his own body throbbing so painfully that it genuinely hurt. 'I've no intention of taking you here; I just wanted to kiss you.'

'And see where that gets us? You said they wouldn't disturb us.' A part of her couldn't believe she was being like this. Talking like this. Demanding this.

Pascal looked into her green eyes that were darkened with desire, pupils so large and dilated that it was simply too much not to give into temptation. But, even so, he was not comfortable with this base part of him, a part of him that reminded him of other times he'd left behind. He'd done so much to be civilised, sophisticated. And yet patently there was still something untamed within him, something he'd already realised this woman tapped into effortlessly.

With a sense of futile inevitability, Pascal pulled down Alana's pants, slipping them off one leg. Pressing kisses to the fragrant inner skin of her thigh, he opened his own trousers, pushing down constricting underclothes. He manoeuvred them so that, while she was still reclined on the seat, her legs were around his waist, and he leant over her. 'You're sure about this?' As if he could turn back!

Alana could feel the heat of his erection as it pulsed near her body. The heady, musky scent of arousal permeated the air. She felt exactly like one of the courtesans from long ago.

She nodded. This was where her universe began and ended.

That was all he needed. He couldn't turn away from this. Shifting his hips forward slightly, he entered her with one smooth thrust, all the way, burying himself so deep that he saw her head fling back, muscles corded in her neck. Her arms gripped his biceps. Her breasts were like lush fruits framed by red lace.

He bent his head and paid homage to each hard peak, rolling and suckling them against his tongue. He could feel her hips twitch and buck towards him, drawing him down and in, holding him tightly before releasing him again. When he looked up, she was looking right at him. It hit him straight between the eyes, and he almost lost control there and then.

She was on the edge. He felt the delicious tension coil through her body. A darker flush stained her dewed cheeks, and then he felt the growing ripples of her release start around his shaft as he drove in and out. And then he came, too, his body thrusting rapidly until he had nothing left to give. It had been fast and furious. In the aftermath, he rested on one elbow, shielding her from his weight. He still lay within her, and could feel the after-tremors of her body.

When he could, he moved back and then scooped her up against his chest where she curled up into him. He sat like that with Alana curled into his body for a long moment. Sweat glistened on their skin. He could feel her soft breasts move against him with her breath, and unbelievably he could feel himself stir again. She felt it, too, and wriggled a little. Pascal gritted his teeth and jaw. As much as he wanted this to be an oasis, to take her again and again, he had to remove her from here. Again he felt that untamed part of himself emerge, and he really wasn't comfortable with that. It made him forget about being in control. And what was compounding this feeling now was the fact that Alana wasn't just a lover any more, she was the mother of his child. And, he had to acknowledge uncomfortably, even that knowledge didn't seem to diminish his impulses around her.

As Pascal held her cradled against him for those moments, heart rates returning to normal, a vision of the future opened up before him, the clarity of which stunned him. In an instant he realised that the image, the desire forming in his head, was something he hadn't been able to articulate before now, it had simply been too alien to him. He never would have imagined that he would feel this way about it. That he wanted it so badly he could taste it. The chaotic tumult of emotions and desires whirling through him became secondary as he finally saw the way to reconcile the way she made him feel, to put order on things. He tried to make sense of what had just happened. He had to pull back. He had to exert some control. Everything had just changed irrevocably.

In the taxi on the way home Alana was wrapped in a delicious haze of satiety. She still couldn't quite believe what had happened in a *restaurant*, albeit a private room, and she couldn't stop looking at Pascal. She lifted a hand to smooth the unruly tendrils of hair on the neck of his shirt. He caught her hand, lifted it to his mouth and kissed her palm. She felt like a different person, and a deep fear-inducing moment of panic gripped her. Was it already too late? Had she already allowed him in so far that she wouldn't be sane again? Would walking away from him, which would inevitably happen, destroy her?

All she knew was that even when she'd believed she loved her husband it had never felt like this, and she had a sick feeling that she couldn't keep pinning these feelings on sex.

Pascal was kissing her hand and looking into her eyes, but she felt a distance there. She'd felt it in the room after they'd made love. He'd been considerate and even tender, helping her to dress again. But there'd been a coolness there. As if he'd been embarrassed. By her wanton behaviour? She cringed inwardly even as he still captured her hand. And she wondered how she'd come to read him so well that she knew something had changed.

CHAPTER EIGHT

SOMETHING was definitely wrong. Since that night in the restaurant a week ago, Pascal hadn't made another move to touch her.

Yet he hadn't left her alone like he had the first week. He'd come home early every day, they'd cooked or eaten out, but with an impregnable wall growing between them. Alana was too nonplussed and unsure to ask what was wrong. But all the time she was burning up inside, aching with desire, aching for Pascal to just reach out and touch her, kiss her. She wanted to make the move, but she was too scared of what his reaction might be, and she couldn't help but be afraid that this was the start of the end of his attraction for her. There had been something finite about the way he'd made love to her the other night.

All he seemed to want to do now was talk. About everything.

'Have you thought any more about what you want to do?'

Alana's attention came back to the present and the discreetly exclusive restaurant that Pascal had taken her to, which was round the corner from his apartment. She looked across the table at him and tried to bury the spike of lust that clenched her insides whenever their eyes met.

'I'm going to enrol in French classes to improve my

French. And I wouldn't mind looking for a job at some stage. I know there are English-language TV and radio stations here; they might be looking for temporary sports presenters.'

He inclined his head. 'I'll check it out, too, and I'm sure there's information on the Internet about job opportunities. I've told you, you're more than welcome to use my study whenever you want.'

Alana nodded. 'Yes, thank you.' She was a little bemused at how easily he was giving her autonomy; she wasn't sure what she had expected. She must have looked a little shocked, because Pascal sat back with a wry look on his face. 'What did you expect—for me to refuse you the chance to take up employment again? To become independent?'

She thought of the irony behind his words—she'd never been less independent. Alana flushed and said tightly, 'I appreciate you paying off Ryan's debts and looking after my mortgage while I'm here, but it just means that now I have to pay you back.'

The ease with which he'd sorted out her tangled finances had rankled with her. But she hadn't been in any position to fight him.

He sat forward now and she sensed the waves of tension coming off him. His voice was clipped, accent more pronounced. 'You know very well those debts were a drop in the ocean for me, and you're the mother of my child. I was careless in protecting you from getting pregnant. I was instrumental in you losing your job. It's the least I could have done. So please, don't mention it again, and I do *not* expect you to pay me back.' He was genuinely angry.

She cradled her coffee cup in her hand and forced herself to meet his gaze. 'I was careless in protecting myself, too, Pascal, it wasn't just your responsibility. I don't want to seem ungrateful, but we both know we're not exactly talking about a loan of a few-hundred euros here.' She shrugged and looked away for a second. 'It's just…Ryan didn't want me to work, even though I'd done a degree in media studies. I can't help but think that if I'd worked during my marriage, our finances wouldn't have been in such dire straits. When he died, I was allowed to become independent for the first time, and I vowed never to have to depend on anyone again.'

Pascal sat back slightly, grimly. 'Which is why you never confided in anyone and why you fought so hard to get a job, no doubt.'

Alana looked at him quickly. 'How did you know that?'

'Rory Hogan told me.'

Alana's mouth tightened. 'When he also told you about my marriage?'

Pascal nodded.

'Why did you marry him, Alana? Surely you could see what he was like?'

Alana shrank back. She really didn't want to talk about this—it was too deep, too personal, still too raw—and especially with this man so close. So she glossed over it as best she could, avoiding Pascal's eye. She knew she sounded clipped, tense. 'I married him because I loved him, of course.' If she could fool herself, maybe she could fool Pascal. 'We met at a function that was celebrating my Dad's career playing rugby, and he just came up to me and started talking.' She smiled then; this bit she didn't have to fake. 'He had what we call at home "the gift of the gab".' She sobered again. He'd made her believe in the dream, that marriage was for her. His gift of the gab hadn't lasted long. But by then it had been too late.

'Somehow I don't think you're telling me everything, Alana, but don't worry; one day you will.'

Alana looked at him swiftly. His gaze was penetrating, incisive, too knowing, and too much—alluding to a future that stretched ahead which she knew couldn't exist. She lashed out to take that intensity off her and her choices.

'What about you, Pascal? Why haven't you been snapped up by now? I'm sure some of the women you know aren't beyond asking you to marry them.'

Her use of the present tense, and dispassionate tone—as if she didn't care that he hadn't married before now—irritated Pascal intensely, and he fought against it, saying coldly, 'I never let any get that far.'

Or that close? Alana had to wonder. She shivered a little at the way he'd suddenly closed up, and could see what countless other women must have been faced with once the desire was on the wane. The only difference with her was that she was pregnant with his child.

He shrugged then, and surprised her by elaborating, 'We're not so dissimilar, you and I. My upbringing, with a single mother bent on finding an elusive state of happiness through marriage, has taught me never to view it with rose-tinted glasses.'

Alana was stunned into silence. 'What do you mean? Why did she want to get married so badly?'

His eyes seemed to bore into hers. 'My father was a married man from her home town that she had an affair with when she was eighteen. He told her he was going to leave his wife and children and marry her, but he never did. She moved to Paris in disgrace to have me, and made it her life's mission to find another man to marry. But no one wanted to take on a single mother and demanding child.

'When I went to live with my grandfather, my father was still in the village; he'd never moved away. He knew exactly who I was. I'd pass him in the street perhaps twice a day and he'd look through me as if I didn't exist. Then he'd go home and play happy families with his wife and my three half-brothers and sisters. *That's* why I never wanted to get married. If it can induce a man to turn his back on his own child, if it can induce a man to make a mockery of his vows...'

Alana's heart ached. She wanted to reach out and touch him but held back. She just said gently, 'You would never do that, Pascal. And there are plenty of people out there who have kids and manage to meet someone new; it's just unfortunate that your mother didn't. She must have been very lonely.'

Pascal felt a jolt in his abdomen at Alana's immediate assertion that he wouldn't do what his father had done; again that hitherto-unacknowledged sense of family that his grandfather had instilled in him rose up, shocking him anew. For a second Pascal forgot everything. Alana was getting close, seeing too deeply; it made him want to draw back, protect himself.

He knew he sounded curt. 'My mother blamed me for her pain and loneliness. But it got her in the end; she died of cancer when I was fourteen.'

Alana shook her head. 'I'm sorry. No matter how difficult your relationship was, she was your mother. That was when you moved down to your grandfather?'

He nodded abruptly, still feeling raw, exposed.

She thought of something then, something that had been niggling at her on and off. She leant forward. 'What's the connection between you and your grandfather and rugby? There's something there that you're not talking about.'

His eyes went flinty, exactly as they had that day in the interview. Alana had an impression of him feeling cornered. 'Are you asking now as the reporter? Hoping to get a scoop for your first piece from France?'

Alana straightened up, unbelievably hurt that he would think that after everything he'd just told her. 'Of course not.'

Their eyes were locked, brown and green. But Alana refused to back down and then she saw Pascal's eyes change, become less hard, his face softened. He reached out a hand and captured hers, and held it when she would have pulled away. The contact was making her blood race through her veins.

'I'm sorry. That wasn't fair. I know you're not like that.'
He'd looked down at their hands, and now he looked back up,
stopping her breath. 'The truth is, you speak of a subject that
is…very personal, something I've never discussed with anyone.'

Alana was utterly consumed by him at that moment; nothing else existed around them. Unbeknownst to them a waiter
was trying to get their attention, but gave up and walked
away.

'I'm sorry, I don't mean to pry. If it's that hard to talk…'

'No,' he said quickly, his hand tightening on hers. His eyes
locked onto hers. The sympathy he saw in their depths reminded him of what he wanted, what he'd vowed to set out
to achieve after that cataclysmic night in the restaurant. If he
wanted that, then he had to tell her everything. 'It's not that.
I can take you somewhere tomorrow, if you like. Perhaps it'll
be easier to explain then.'

She just nodded, every part of her warming under his gaze,
but then conversely she also felt like running as fast as she
could in the other direction. There was something about this
moment, this conversation. It was inviting a deeper intimacy
into their already ambiguous relationship, and yet that cool
distance was still there, confusing her. Alana's well-worn
alarm bells were coming back to clanging life.

The next day Alana's nerves were jangling. She could remember coming back to the apartment the previous evening,
how badly she'd longed for Pascal to make love to her so she
didn't have to contemplate all the mounting confusion,
worries and fears in her mind. Fears that were incoherent and
tantalisingly out of reach. Pascal had been preoccupied and
distant again. He'd merely said goodnight and shut himself
in his study.

Then he'd reminded her that morning that he wanted to

show her something. 'Don't you have work?' she'd asked over the rim of her tea cup, trying not to let her eyes wander down over his jeans-clad legs and his dark sweater. He'd just shaken his head.

So now Alana was waiting outside the apartment for him to bring his car round. When he appeared and pulled into the kerb in front of her, her jaw dropped.

He got out and looked at her over the hood of the car. 'What is it?'

'This isn't your car.'

Amusement laced his voice, but something very panicky was taking off in Alana's belly.

'I have a lot of cars. But you're right; this is a new one.'

'But…you had a sports car.'

'You said you hated those cars. You said they represented inadequacy, and the inability of men to function sexually and in the world.'

'I know I did.' Alana felt like wailing, remembering that it had been a laughable argument to throw at him. But right now she would have given anything to see his Porsche. She actually felt slightly as if she were going to hyperventilate. Or get sick.

'But this…this is…' She looked at him helplessly.

He quirked a brow in her direction and she was transfixed by his eyes. 'A family car?'

That was exactly what it was. She tore her eyes away from his. It was a sleek, brand-new, beautiful top-of-the-range Mercedes family car.

When he came round and held the passenger door open for her, she was too scared to look in the back and see if he'd actually bought a baby seat too. Panic gripped her like a suffocating vice around her heart. He got in beside her and pulled out from the kerb, and she could feel him send her a quick glance.

'Are you OK? Are you feeling sick?'

Alana alternately shook her head and nodded; she didn't know *what* was going on with her. When he went to slow the car for a second, as if to stop, she put a hand on his arm, and even that brief touch sent a whole host of other feelings and sensations through her body. She jerked her hand away.

'No, I'm fine. Really.' She was a mess.

He flicked her another sideways glance as if to make sure and then said, 'I got the car for you. You'll need something. But I know the traffic in Paris can be daunting, so you can get used to it with me driving first.'

Alana's stomach stopped churning as if a switch had been flicked. It was the most bizarre and curiously deflating sensation. Of course; silly her. He didn't mean that the car was for *them*. He wasn't buying it as a symbol of commitment. If anything, it was a sign of his belief that she should be independent. Automatically her breath came easier and her stomach settled and, even though a feeling of emptiness hollowed out her belly, she told herself it was just relief.

She turned to face him finally. 'Where are we going?'

'You'll see,' was all Pascal said. He was intent, quiet.

He'd told Alana to dress down and warmly. He'd brought a bag that looked like a gym bag, and must have thrown it in the boot as she couldn't see it anywhere now. She looked out the window and could see the picture-perfect Paris start to retreat, and as they veered onto a motorway with high graffiti-covered walls on either side, they left it behind completely.

After driving for about twenty minutes, Pascal took a slip road off the motorway, and the Paris he drove into now was a million miles from the Paris they'd just left. This was the suburbs. Unconsciously, Alana straightened in her seat and looked out at the bare streets, dilapidated buildings and bleak-looking, towering apartment-blocks in the distance.

'Is this where you grew up?'

He didn't look at her. He was grim. 'Near enough to here, yes.'

Groups of youths stood on the streets, along with women and children, going about their daily business. They passed a school and Alana could see children playing behind a high barbed-wire fence.

Pascal finally pulled into the car park of what looked like a well-kept community hall, but Alana guessed that it looked well kept thanks to the beefy security-guard posted on the gate who'd waved them through. Pascal parked and they got out. He still hadn't said anything, but Alana knew that he was watching her reaction closely, and suddenly it was very important to her that she pass whatever unspoken test was going on.

He grabbed his bag from the boot of the car, and just then a group of gangly, well-built youths burst from the hall. They surrounded them and the car in seconds, greeting Pascal with slang catcalls and jeers that must have been good-natured, as Pascal was smiling at them and answering back. He had her hand in a tight grip. A couple of the more menacing guys stood back and looked Alana up and down, and then walked round her, making comments. But she wasn't scared. If anything, she'd never felt safer with Pascal beside her, and even when one of the youths brushed close to her as if to test her reaction, and Pascal made a protective move, she gripped his hand to tell him it was OK. She knew this was a deeply ritualistic place, any kind of ghetto area was.

So she stood tall, even though they all towered over her, and after a long moment the tension was dissipated when the guys started laughing and one even clapped a hand on her shoulder. Pascal led her into the centre and sent her an enigmatic look before saying, *sotto voce*, 'You've just been accepted by one of the most notorious gang leaders in the area.'

She shivered then despite herself, because she knew well that being in one of these gangs meant life and death. Literally. Suddenly she could see how Pascal's move to live with his grandfather had undoubtedly changed the course of his life.

He left her alone for a few minutes under the watchful gaze of a kindly woman, who appeared to be the cook, and returned in faded sweats and a well-worn T-shirt. He was joined now by another huge well-built man who she recognised as a recently retired French international rugby-player. He'd featured in the last Six Nations tournament. He recognised Alana, too, and they spent a few minutes chatting amiably.

It was only when she followed them outside that she understood the full import of where they were and what was going on. It was a rugby pitch, and all of the youths she'd just met and many more were warming up and throwing rugby balls back and forth. Some were doing scrum-practice. Apart from Pascal and Mathieu, the retired player, there were also at least three coaches on hand. Pascal was in the thick of it, too, and all of Alana's suspicions were suspicions no longer. He had the easy athleticism of a top player.

The cook brought Alana a steaming cup of hot chocolate, and she settled down on a bench outside to watch, fascinated by how much raw talent was on the pitch in front of her.

A while later Pascal finally tore himself away from the action and sat down beside her, breathing heavily. His sweat-soaked and mucky clothes should have repelled her, but she found that all she could think about were his muscles—which she could imagine were hot and taut and gleaming after exertion—and the way his top clung to his stomach, clearly delineating his defined abdomen. She swallowed painfully and had to block a wanton desire to pull him into the hall behind them and beg him to make love to her. In all her years of avid sport watching, she'd never found a sweaty, mucky man arousing. Pregnancy hormones; that had to be it. She spoke as much to try and defuse her hectic pulse as anything else.

'I'm guessing this isn't just a few guys who come out here once a week to knock a ball around?'

He shook his head. 'They're part of a rugby academy I set up. I know at first glance they don't look it. I've set up a scholarship for kids who want to get to school or college through sport.' He shrugged. 'Rugby was always my love, so I've done it through that. I wanted to introduce the sport into the area.'

He looked at her then and she felt hot again.

'You were right—it is largely a middle-class game—but through something like this we're not letting it become exclusive. After all, I came from here, too.'

Her suspicions were confirmed. 'So you did want to play it too. Anyone watching you out there could see what a natural talent you have. Why didn't you go for it?'

He looked out to the men on the pitch and then spoke with a kind of resigned modesty. 'My grandfather could see how good I was. He had played all his life, and he was a great player. But it never got him anywhere. Originally he played it for acceptance into the community. He was half-Algerian, and he always felt like an outsider. That's why he took it so badly when my mother disgraced the good name he'd built up by having an affair with a married man.'

Alana looked at his profile. It was proud and harsh. A warrior's profile.

'He'd always regretted his actions towards her, so when she told him she was dying, he saw his chance to make it up to her and took me in. A few years after I'd started living with him and playing rugby, I was approached by a rugby scout, but my grandfather wouldn't let me go back to Paris to pursue the opportunity.'

'Why not?'

Pascal sighed. 'Because for one thing he didn't want me to end up in the suburbs again. He knew that if I got caught up in that world I might make it, I might be a star for a short time. But he also knew that ultimately I'd burn out and have nothing. It was only when I went to school in his village that I discovered I had a good brain. He saw it, too, and asked me to follow that route…college and a proper career. And not rugby.'

'You sacrificed your chance of a successful sports career to abide by your grandfather's wishes?'

He heard the incredulity in her voice and looked at her again, smiling ruefully, making something in her chest flip over. He jerked his head towards the pitch. 'These boys have brains too. I'm hoping that they get the best of both worlds. All my grandfather could see was one or the other. He was the only family member who showed a real interest in me. I couldn't turn my back on him.'

Alana shook her head, shocked at the level of sacrifice he'd made. It was so far removed from the kind of person her husband had been that her mind boggled.

His face sobered then, and he said quietly, 'The truth is that if I hadn't been taken in by my grandfather, there's a good chance I would have ended up in jail.' Alana held in a gasp and frowned slightly. His eyes were dark pools. She could sense that he was holding his emotions tightly in check.

'The gang I was with were getting more and more heavily involved with drugs, crime…we were the worst of the worst, Alana.' He gestured abruptly towards the field. 'The stuff we got up to makes these guys look like a girls' tea-party. I was on the periphery for a long time, but was about to be sucked right into the middle of it all. Part of the initiation rituals involved making a clear statement of intent, a show of bravery.'

'What do you mean?' Although Alana suspected she had a very good idea.

He looked away from her. 'The week after I left, a member of a rival gang was shot dead. If I'd still been there, I would've been picked to do the job; it was my turn.'

Alana grabbed his hand, making him face her. 'But you didn't do it, Pascal. You got out of here.' She had no idea how close he'd come to being lost for ever. She felt icy inside. She tried to show him that the horror she felt wasn't for what he'd been.

His face was bleak. He held up a hand, thumb and forefinger inches apart. 'Yes—but I was *this* close to doing it. That's scarier to acknowledge than you can imagine.'

Alana was fervent; she took his hand again. 'You can't say that for sure. You don't know what you would have done in that moment, what choice you would have made. Don't condemn yourself so easily.'

Pascal looked at her. Somewhere deep inside, he'd always felt as though another part of him still existed in this wasteland, lost for ever. Wild. Capable of awful things. But was she right? Would he have made another choice if he'd been faced with that scenario? Had he been carrying around the guilt all his life for something he wouldn't have even done?

He pulled his hand from hers, just as a rugby ball shot through the air towards them. Pascal stood easily and caught it deftly. He looked down at her for a long moment before turning and jogging back onto the pitch with easy grace. Alana felt a little shell shocked. She could only imagine how hard it must have been over the years to come to terms with how close to the edge he'd sailed. Or how painful it must have been to turn his back on something so dear to his heart for the sake of a family connection that had come so late in his life. She could see now that he'd channelled all of his ruthless, competitive energy into his professional life. It was no wonder he'd achieved what he had. And yet he hadn't become so embittered that he didn't want to help others achieve what he never had.

Later that afternoon they were in the car on the way home, dusk falling over the suburbs as they left them behind. 'So what did you think?' he asked innocuously.

Alana thought for a long moment before turning towards him. He'd showered with the guys in the community centre and changed, so thankfully her hormones had settled to their normal level of craziness around him. There was something deep inside her that begged to come out, some emotion, but it was too big for her to deal with. What he'd told her earlier was huge in its implications of a deepening intimacy between them, but she knew she was too cowardly to look at how it made her feel. She kept her voice light and deliberately stuck to neutral waters. 'I think what you're doing is amazing. Especially considering your own history. How many of those kids know how close you got to being a player?'

He shook his head. 'None. But Mathieu knows; we've been friends for years. He's from the same town as my grandfather. He was picked by the scout too. So, in a way, I got to follow his progress and see where he went.'

He looked at Alana before turning them back onto the motorway and seamlessly entering the manic Paris-bound traffic. 'My grandfather was right you know. Mathieu has this now—coaching, and perhaps some commentating—but apart from that he doesn't have much else. He's told me himself that sometimes he wishes he'd taken my path.'

Alana smiled. 'And you wish you could have taken his.'

Pascal shrugged. 'Who knows if I really missed out on all that much?'

After a companionable silence Alana could feel tiredness wash over her, and she stifled a yawn. She couldn't help sinking down a little into the comfort of the seat. She felt safe and

protected and warm. And before she knew it, she was slipping
into a welcoming dark abyss. So she didn't see when Pascal
looked over, and she didn't see the intense look on his face
as his eyes swept down over her body. And she only had the
barest of sensations when he reached over and tucked some
wayward hair behind her ear.

Pascal tore his eyes away from Alana as she fell easily into
sleep. He couldn't believe he'd revealed so much earlier, even
though he'd intended to tell her about his life, his past. But it
had been easy. And she hadn't looked at him with horror,
she'd understood. He couldn't even begin to fathom how that
could be possible when she'd lived such a different life—a
secure life, loved and surrounded by a big family. Telling her
had been like letting go of a huge weight around his shoulders.

He glanced at her again, his chest tight with emotion. She
was his now. He knew that he never wanted to let her go, that
he would do whatever it took to show her that they had something beyond the physical. That they had something that could
work, that could last. And to do that all he had to do was avoid
the physical. He grimaced. When every part of him burned
up just looking at her, he knew it would be the hardest thing
he'd ever done—yet at that moment it was the only way he
knew how to show her, to demonstrate to her his intention.

Alana woke the following morning to find herself naked but
for her underwear in her bed, and she couldn't believe it when
the clock said 10:00 a.m. She'd slept for the entire previous
evening and night. Had Pascal undressed her? Who else could
it have been? And she'd slept through it?

She showered and dressed quickly, feeling completely disorientated. When she emerged into the main drawing room
after finding no note in the kitchen, she jumped with fright
when Pascal's study-door opened and he strode out, dressed

head to toe in his successful-billionaire gear. A world away from the mucky rugby coach of yesterday. Her heart clenched.

She folded her arms defensively, not sure why she was feeling like that. Prickly. 'I'm sorry, I was obviously more exhausted than I thought. It must be the pregnancy.'

Pascal stopped a few feet away from her; he looked so stern and grim that Alana felt a little scared.

'It's me who should be sorry,' he surprised her by saying. 'I shouldn't have had you sitting out on a cold bench all day. You could have caught cold or anything. How are you feeling? I think we should go to see the doctor just in case. I was going to call her if you didn't wake up soon.'

Alana couldn't help laughing, and it completely defused the tension she was feeling. 'Pascal! Don't be ridiculous; I'm fine. I'm a hardy Irish girl. Sitting on a cold bench for a few hours will not bring on early labour or pneumonia.'

'All the same…' He looked genuinely worried, and Alana's heart clenched again. She rolled her eyes, ignoring her worrying reaction; maybe something *was* wrong with her? 'Pascal, really, I haven't slept that well the last few nights, I'm sure that's all it was. Here—' she reached out, took his hand and brought it to her forehead '—see? No fever. I'm fine.'

His hand felt warm and strong on her head, and she could feel his pulse at his wrist. It had an immediate effect on her body, and she felt herself respond, her own pulse tripping. She hurriedly took his hand down again. If she kept it there, she *would* feel feverish in a minute. She stepped back to put some space between them and he looked utterly unmoved by the physical contact. She was still confused by this wall, this distance, that existed between them. It had to be because he just didn't find her attractive any more, and that was becoming harder for her to bear than she'd imagined it would be.

He finally seemed to be satisfied that she was OK, and

started to walk back to his study, throwing over his shoulder, 'I've lined up some places for us to look at today.'

Alana followed him, glad of the distraction from her roiling emotions and hormones. 'Places? What do you mean?'

She followed him into his light, airy study and looked around with interest. Shelves from floor to ceiling were packed with all sorts of books. A huge table stood in one corner, where he told her he sometimes held impromptu meetings. It was a hub of energy, but Alana knew that once Pascal walked out, the energy would dissipate.

He was round the other side of his desk, and he gestured for her to come and have a look at something on the computer screen. She walked over feeling a little apprehensive and tried to stay as far away from his body heat as possible.

'What am I meant to be looking at?'

He pressed a key, and what looked like a property page came up with pictures of houses and gardens.

'These are all houses and apartments for sale around Paris, mostly around Montmartre. You mentioned that you liked that area.'

'I…well…I know, but what do you mean? Why are we looking at these?' He looked at her as if she were slightly dim, and she could feel herself getting hot.

'I don't think that this place is going to be ideal for when the baby comes, do you? Even though we have the lift, we're on the top floor, and it's hardly kitted out to accommodate a baby.'

Alana started to back away, her belly churning again. No, she could imagine very well that this wouldn't suit him. This apartment screamed 'billionaire bachelor'. There was no room for a baby. Alana still felt a little too stunned to say anything else but, 'I guess you're right.'

'Good. Now, I've arranged some viewings for today, if that's OK?' He didn't wait for an answer, he strode over, took her arm and herded her out of his study. 'You should have some breakfast and then we'll head out to see them.'

By that evening Alana's head was spinning. She'd seen stunning art-deco ground-floor apartments in the Latin Quarter. She'd seen beautiful town houses in Montmartre, with idyllic gardens tucked away from prying eyes. She'd seen opulent, airy, studio-style apartments near the Eiffel Tower. Then she'd seen some more in the upmarket eighteenth-*arrondissement*. All of them had the same thing in common: they were all exclusive and awe-inspiringly, jaw-droppingly expensive. The *crème de la crème* of Paris real-estate. When she'd hissed to Pascal about the cost, he'd waved her concerns away and talked over her head to the agents about what it would take to make the properties baby-safe.

Clearly setting up his ex-lover and his baby in a suitable pad was something he was prepared to pay for. And it was also quite clear to Alana that Pascal meant to live in his own apartment and have her living independently, complete with family car, just across town or around the corner; if she liked the first apartment they'd looked at that morning. But she didn't think he'd be too thrilled at the prospect of running into her and the baby with his new lover. There had been no talk of 'we'; it had been all down to her to say if she liked a place or not.

Her life had transformed so completely in such a short space of time that Alana felt light headed as they walked back into Pascal's apartment. Compounding everything had been his careful restraint from touching her all day. Even if she'd brushed off him, he'd moved away as if he couldn't bear to be near her. She stopped dead inside the door and Pascal glanced back at her briefly. 'I have a business dinner to attend tonight. I'd ask you along, if you want, but I'm sure you're tired after today.'

Alana could have laughed. She had so much adrenaline

running through her body at that moment that she felt she could run a marathon.

'I'm fine.' She pushed herself off the door. 'Tell me, have you done this before? You seem to have everything pretty well arranged for setting us up.'

He turned fully then and looked at her suspiciously. 'Us?'

Alana's hand went to her belly. A fear of the isolation that lay in store for her made her feel panicky. 'Me and the baby. How do you know I even want to live here permanently, Pascal? I never said I wanted to live here. I told you, I fully expect to go home at some stage.'

He turned away in an abrupt negation of her words. 'Don't be ridiculous. You're having my baby; I told you, I'm going to be involved every step of the way.'

The fear rose up even stronger. 'Just as long as we're on opposite sides of the city, you mean.'

He turned again, his mouth a thin line of displeasure. 'What are you talking about, Alana? I don't have time for this.'

'Well, neither do I.' Alana could feel tears sting her eyes. All she did want right then, despite the evidence of his lack of desire, was for Pascal to stop this autocratic confusing behaviour, walk over and pull her into his arms, to tip her face up to his and kiss her deeply and soundly until she didn't have to think any more—and certainly until she didn't have to think about becoming a rich man's brood mare, relegated to the sidelines. However lonely things had got with Ryan, at least there had been the pretence of some kind of union, togetherness. And yet she knew she didn't want that, either. Her head was so fried that it hurt. And it was all this man's fault. She glared at him.

Pascal stepped towards her as if to say something, and his mobile rang abruptly. With a muttered curse, he pulled it out of his pocket and turned away to speak rapidly. Alana walked past him and into the kitchen. After a few minutes he came to the door. He looked and sounded weary, and Alana's heart lurched before she clamped down on the rogue impulse to worry about him or tell him he looked tired. She'd been a wife before; she would not do that again. And especially not with a man like Pascal.

'Look, I have to go out now, they've moved dinner forward. We'll talk tomorrow, OK?'

Alana sent him an airy, 'Fine,' and she resolutely turned away and started opening doors and drawers at random. When she stopped and looked around again, he had gone.

CHAPTER NINE

As soon as she knew she was alone, the tears came, and through them Alana ranted at herself—what was wrong with her? She wanted Pascal and yet she didn't want him. She wanted to be independent, and then when he brought her out to show her places where she could live independently, she didn't want that, either.

All she knew for sure, as she wiped away the tears and prepared some dinner, was that she *wanted* him with a bone-deep ache that ran through her body like a dull pain. It got worse every time he came near. She'd been having erotic dreams nearly every night about what had happened in the restaurant, waking with sheets damp and twisted around her body. She needed the physical. It was as if that would make all her confusion go away, if she could just bury herself in that release that only he could give her…

As Alana sat and ate, not tasting any of it, an intense desire rose up within her to seduce Pascal, making it hard to think of anything else. Her blood felt heavy and her pulse throbbed. She told herself she had to know for sure if he was simply not attracted to her any more. If that was the case it would make things so much easier. She would go home and face the music. She wouldn't let him set her up in Paris like some ex-mistress. But she had to know. Feeling much better all of a sudden, Alana hopped down from the stool, washed up her plates and headed for her shower.

She hummed and hawed over what to wear, and then she found herself going into Pascal's room. She opened up his wardrobe and his scent reached out and enveloped her. Her pulse sped up to triple time and her breathing quickened; he didn't even have to be here in person and he could turn her on. She shook her head and reached in to pull out one of his silk ties. She'd seen a scene in a movie once that involved a woman waiting for her man dressed in nothing but a tie, but Alana didn't think she had the balls for that, especially with the slight thickening of her waistline. So she pulled out a shirt too.

Dressed in the shirt and tie, she left her hair down and put on the slightest amount of make-up, just enough to enhance her eyes. Feeling slightly silly but quashing it, she pulled on pants at the last minute, and then she got a bottle of wine with a glass and went into the sitting room to wait.

The minutes ticked by, and Alana alternately felt confident, bolshy, insecure and then gravitated back to feeling silly again. But she was determined to stick it out. She needed him too badly. She needed to know too badly. Even if he rejected her, it would be better than this awful ambiguity, this wall of distance. She had to put a stop to the way things seemed to be escalating out of her control, as if Pascal knew something she didn't, as if he was reading from a different script.

She made herself some hot chocolate. She opened the wine to let it breathe. She watched the news. She watched a French film and couldn't understand a word. The shirt started feeling constrictive, so she opened the top button and loosened the tie. And in the end she could feel tiredness washing over her. She fought it for a long time, but the cushions were so luxurious it was hard not to sink into them a little, to just close her eyes for a few minutes. Confident that she would hear him coming in, she let herself doze.

When Pascal let himself quietly into the apartment he became alert immediately. The light was on in the sitting room, so he went in there. He stopped in his tracks and the breath locked in his chest at the sight in front of him. Alana was asleep on the couch. Dressed in one of his shirts and ties. Long, bare legs flung out, hair in disarray around her head, one hand on her belly, the other by her head, palm up. All at once innocent and so wickedly sensuous that he felt dizzy with lust.

He barely took in the full bottle of wine and the glass, the empty mug of something. He came close, but didn't want to break the spell. Had she dressed like this on purpose for him? He shrugged off his jacket and undid his tie, barely aware of what he was doing. He felt constricted, and his body was so hard and so hot that time seemed to stand still. She was temptation incarnate. Her lips were soft, inviting him to just bend down and press a kiss. It would be so easy to do that—to kneel here beside her, to slip his tongue between those lips, have her wake and take his tongue deeper into her mouth, mimicking the way she would take another part of him deep inside her.

Pascal fought the most intense battle as he stood there. The memory of undressing her as clinically as he could the other night was still fresh and painful in his memory. But his resolve was strong. He could exert it again even if he felt like it would kill him. With his face set in rigid lines of ultimate control, a control he hadn't had to call on before, he bent down and slipped his arms underneath her pliant, sleep-relaxed body. She made a small sound, a mere breath, and her body automatically curved into him as he lifted her up effortlessly. Her breasts pressed against his chest. Pascal had to stop for a moment and grit his jaw so hard that it hurt. He was so aroused that he didn't think he'd make it to her bedroom. But he had to. He was doing this for *them*.

Alana knew she was fighting her way through layers of sleep for a reason. She felt so safe and so secure that she wanted to stay there for ever. And yet, another feeling was making her wake up, something within her, an urgency that was starting down low in her abdomen and spreading outwards, making everything tingle deliciously. She finally started to wake as she became aware of being carried in strong arms against a hard, muscled chest. *Pascal.* And at that moment he was putting her down, letting her go. Every part of her screamed rejection at that.

'Wait, what are you doing?' she asked, still feeling drowsy.

His voice rumbled low and near her ear, setting off another chain reaction of sensations, waking her more. 'You're half-asleep. You should go back to sleep, Alana.'

'But…' Alana struggled through the waves that wanted to suck her back down. 'I stayed up to seduce you.' She knew somewhere rational that it was only because it was dark and she was still half-asleep that she was being so honest.

Pascal's body tensed, she could feel it as he rested momentarily over her on his hands after depositing her on her bed. Finally, after a long moment, he just said enigmatically, 'You only have to look at me and I'm seduced. Go to sleep, Alana.'

He stood and swiftly left the room, and suddenly Alana was wide-awake and alert. She sat up in the bed, in the dark. *You only have to look at me and I'm seduced.* Had she dreamt that? She didn't think so, she'd felt the tension in his body; it was the same tension running through her right now.

She threw back the covers and got out of the bed. With her heart thumping, she went back out to the sitting room, where she instinctively knew he'd be. She stopped at the door. He was standing at the window, one hand deep in the pocket of his trousers, pulling the material taut over one buttock, and she could see the wineglass was gone. Just then his head tipped back and she saw him drink deeply from the claret liquid.

She saw the lines of tension come into his body before he turned round, and a part of her hated that tension. Alana crossed her arms. His eyes were narrowed, his face had that stern expression, but she couldn't let that stop her.

'What's that supposed to mean—you only have to look at me to be seduced? So if that's the case, then why…?' She couldn't say it, even now, even after waiting up to seduce him.

'Why don't I make love to you?' he asked harshly.

Alana nodded jerkily. He put down his glass and now both hands were deep in his pockets, his frame huge and powerful, awe-inducing. Alana felt that ever-present quiver in her belly.

'Because I was attempting to show you that what we can have is more than just…lust, desire, *sex*.'

Alana shook her head and walked a little closer. 'I don't understand.'

Pascal took out a hand and raked it through his hair, mussing it up, making him look even more rakishly attractive.

'From the moment we've met it's been about physical attraction, unprecedented physical attraction, for the both of us.'

She flushed.

'But now that you're pregnant, we're having a baby and I just wanted to try and elevate things to another level. The way you make me feel… That evening in the restaurant, I had no intention of allowing things to get that far, but within seconds we couldn't turn back.' That lack of control still stung him.

Alana's flush deepened. She saw Pascal's eyes narrow even more on her face, and a stain of colour washed his cheeks too. The air around them was saturated with their desire. Alana didn't know how she was still standing. She felt weak and trembly. And a little angry.

'What are you talking about, Pascal—elevating things to another level? We're just… We were lovers. I'm here while things settle down at home. Nothing's changed.'

He crossed his arms at that, and his face got even sterner. 'Why do you keep saying that? I've told you, we're together now. I'm not going to be apart from you or this baby.'

Bitterness and something else indefinable washed up through Alana. 'And yet you've spent the day showing me places where you'll happily shelve me and our child.' She shook her head. 'I won't have that, Pascal. I'd prefer to go home than become just your responsibility.'

He came towards her, stopping her words, a look of exasperation crossing his face. 'What are you talking about? The places we looked at today are for the three of us, not just you and the baby. What made you think that?'

At that moment he could have knocked Alana down with a feather. She just looked at him. He read her in an instant.

'Did you really think I was going to go on living here and have you living a separate life in another part of the city?' His eyes glittered and he was so close now that Alana could touch him if she wanted. But right now, for the first time, she didn't want to. She backed away.

'Yes, I did think that. We've never discussed this, Pascal. I told you I was happy with no commitment. But just…not like this…' That panicky feeling was surging back, a painful vicelike feeling around her heart. He made her feel so confused, so mixed up.

'That was before you got pregnant. Things are different now.'

'But I don't want that. My God,' she breathed as she finally saw what he had been doing. The suspicion she'd had when she'd seen the car, the way it had made her feel, surged back to haunt her now. 'The car, the apartments… You've been planning this all along, haven't you?'

'Well, one of us has to face the reality, Alana. Tell me, how *do* you see the future for you, me and our baby?'

'I see me going home as soon as I can, and you can visit whenever you want.' Her voice sounded high and constricted to her ears. At that moment she also knew that any feelings about her precious independence being threatened were so flimsy it was laughable. To acknowledge that fact now made her feel even more exposed. If her independence, which she'd guarded so zealously after Ryan's death, could so easily be forgotten, then what did that mean?

He advanced and she backed away. This was exactly what she didn't want to look at; she didn't want to have to clarify her feelings. She knew now that was why she'd craved the physical contact so badly. She'd sensed he had an agenda. He'd been intent on weaving her into the fabric of his life with an ease that scared her. He was threatening the very foundation of her life, the life she'd built so carefully after Ryan died. She shook her head, begging him silently to understand.

'Can you honestly tell me that when I'm like a beached whale, you'll still be happy with me in your life? That when we have a screaming baby waking every hour on the hour for feeds, that you'll not regret failing to maintain your independence?' His relentless advancing goaded her further, making her lash out. 'Or perhaps you're planning on keeping this apartment and having it for your mistresses? Well, I won't stand for that, either.'

He finally caught up with her and grabbed her arms in his hands; they burned through the thin material, and it was only then that Alana became aware of how she was still dressed in his shirt and tie. It mocked her now, the thought that she could have used the physical to avoid talking about this.

'Dammit, Alana, I won't live up to the box you want to put me in. I have no intention of taking a mistress. I was going to sell this place.' He laughed harshly, and the sound grated on Alana's nerves. 'I never thought I'd say this, but for the first time in my life, I've even been contemplating marriage—you've made me believe that perhaps it can be different for me, *us*, despite our pasts. Although I know the mere mention of it would send you running. So I've been bending over backwards to try and show you that we can have a life here, that we can have something that's not just about sex. I'm prepared to commit to you, but you won't even give the thought of family life a chance, not even for our child.'

Alana was starting to shake. His words... What was he saying? It was too much for her to deal with. 'But you...you're a playboy. You like being single. You don't do this. How can you want this?' A treacherous flutter of hope mocked her loudly amidst the panic.

'When you're the *woman* and you don't?' he asked caustically. He laughed then, harshly, his hands still around her arms. Every small hair seemed to stand on edge along Alana's skin. She saw his eyes drop to take in her attire, and her breasts felt heavy and sensitive. She'd thought he'd killed her desire with all his words and scary rationale, but now it was flaming back, yet she wanted to fight it. But Pascal, it seemed, had other ideas.

His mouth was a cruel line. 'It seems an awful pity to waste this, after all.' He ran a long finger around her jaw and down to the pulse beating hectically in her throat.

'No, Pascal, not like this; you don't want this.'

'Don't I?' He arched a cynical brow. 'You seem to know me so well, Alana. You think that I'd be turned off by your pregnant, blooming body, or that I'd hate to hear my own baby call for food, that I'd hate to take it in turns to do night feeds to give you a break. That I'd grow tired of domestic life, that I'd keep this place to house my mistresses. As you seem to know me so well, perhaps you'll also know that I'm done with talking. I'm done with trying to show you another side to this relationship when clearly all you're interested in is physical gratification. It never went beyond that for you, did it?'

Before Alana could take in his words, before she could formulate anything, even a thought, as the hurt rippled through her, he brought his hands to the tie and pulled it open and off in a fluid move. Then he brought his hands to her shirt, *his* shirt, and calmly, without violence, ripped it open. Alana gasped as the air whistled over her naked breasts and buttons popped and fell to the floor, scattering loudly.

'Right now, I'm also done with denying myself what you're so generously offering.'

With that Pascal hauled Alana's semi-naked body into his, one hand around her back, the other spearing through her hair as his mouth drove down onto hers, taking and plundering. Her world became a ball of fire that she couldn't step away from, even though she knew it was going to burn her badly. After so much build up Alana was helpless not to respond, even though she knew in some small, still-rational part of her brain that it would be much better for her to step back and say no. But her body had other ideas. Her hands were already scrabbling for his shirt, pulling it out of his trousers. She was aching to feel his skin. She reached for buttons, found them and opened them impatiently, and somehow managed to push the shirt off his broad shoulders where it fell to the floor unseen and already forgotten beside hers.

Pascal pulled back, breathing harshly. 'You turn me into something… You make me feel like I've still got my past in my blood. Like I'm untamed.'

Alana reached up a hand and curved it around his jaw. Everything that had just happened previously was forgotten. 'It's not a bad thing, it's a part of you.' She reached up and pressed a kiss to his jaw, and she felt it clench. 'I can handle it. Show me what it's like.'

Pascal bent and lifted Alana into his arms, striding into her bedroom and depositing her on the bed. He ripped off the rest of his clothes and then he was standing in front of her, naked and massively aroused. Alana sat up on the side of the bed and reached for him, pulling him to her. She looked up at him as her hand closed around his hard length and as she took him into her mouth.

She could feel that he was trying to control himself. He brought a hand to her head; she felt it shaking. But he wouldn't let her bring him to the edge or beyond. He stopped her and pulled back, and then his big hands reached underneath and lifted her bodily back onto the bed. With a flick of his wrist, he smoothed her pants down and off her legs. He ran a hand over the slight swell of her belly, the only indication of their child growing within. He pressed a kiss to it, and inexplicably Alana felt tears threaten. As if to drive the emotion away, she reached down and pulled Pascal up her body. She could see a harsh glitter in his eyes, as if he knew what she was doing.

'Please,' she begged, opening her legs around him, feeling his weight and strength between them. 'I want you now.'

He rested over her on his hands for a long moment and Alana bit her lip. She couldn't take her eyes away from his; she knew there was a silent battle of wills going on. But finally, just when she thought he was going to make her beg, he slipped a hand under her buttocks, tilting her up towards him, and then with one deep, cataclysmic thrust, he entered her and she felt as if he'd touched her soul.

She wrapped her legs around him as far as she could, drawing him in deeper and deeper, going with him when he pulled out, and drawing him in tight again when he thrust back. She reached up and wrapped her arms around his neck, her mouth blindly finding and pressing kisses to any bit of exposed flesh, and he took them higher and higher. When the pinnacle came after an excruciatingly exquisite climb, Alana reached a hand down to his buttock and with her other held on tight as the waves of pleasure and release washed through her. She felt his own release burst free inside her, as his back tautened and tensed. His whole body was rigid as helpless after-shocks rushed through him too.

He came down over her and rolled them so that he lay on his side. Their breath mingled, and came harsh and swift. Alana was tucked into his chest, his weight off her belly. Still entwined with Pascal from arms down to legs, intimately joined, Alana fell immediately into a deep sleep, not even waking when Pascal extricated himself, or moved her under the covers or left her alone in the bed to go back to his own room. He sent one brief glance back to her in the bed, the set of his features grim.

The next morning when Alana woke, she had a delicious feeling of satisfaction. She was aware of pleasureable aches and pains throughout her body before the entire previous night came back in vivid recall. Instantly, the warm feeling seeped away and she tensed. Even though she was lying down, the world spun on its axis for a moment.

She didn't have to look to know that Pascal hadn't spent the night in the bed with her. She didn't hear any sounds from the apartment. Getting up, she grimaced when she felt tender. After washing and dressing, she went outside, but she knew Pascal had gone to work. She found a note in the kitchen:

We need to talk.
Pascal.

Fear and trepidation rushed through Alana's body as she recalled everything that had preceded their explosive love-making the previous night. Had he really told her that he wanted to make a go of this, create a proper family life? He'd even said that he'd respect her wish not to marry, knowing that she wouldn't want that. But that truth rocked her: he'd contemplated *marriage*?

Pascal was offering her security, more than just an extension of their affair. She knew she couldn't keep ignoring the fact that strings were very much a part of it now. Her hand went to her belly; they weren't strings, they were ropes, binding her and Pascal together for ever whether she liked it or not.

That panicky feeling was back, and even stronger this time. It threatened to consume Alana utterly. Feeling claustrophobic, she picked up the apartment keys and went out to walk. Anything to try and clear her head.

She came back later, feeling just as muddled as ever. When her mobile phone rang, she picked it up gratefully, wanting any distraction, even if it was her sister Ailish, to take her away from her tortured conscience. But it wasn't her sister. After talking to the person on the other end for a few minutes, she terminated the call. It was a sign—a welcome sign. Pascal didn't know what he was talking about, offering her this life. She'd seen it before. He'd change to adapt, but ultimately he would revert back to what he was.

And Alana didn't want to look at why that cut her so deeply. She told herself it was because she couldn't put herself through trusting someone again, but in her heart of hearts she knew she wasn't being honest with herself. That was only the half of it.

'I'm flying home tonight, Pascal, on the late flight from Charles de Gaulle. It's all booked. I've got a taxi coming any minute.'

Pascal stood just inside the door of the living room where Alana had been waiting to confront him all afternoon. And now she'd blurted the words out with little or no finesse. They hung baldly in the air between them.

Pascal looked utterly cold and remote. This was what Alana had had a glimpse of when she'd first met him, the side of him she'd always thought would be formidable. And it was. He put down his attaché case and walked over to the drinks cabinet on the opposite side of the room. He poured himself a neat drink of something powerful before turning back to Alana.

'What do you want me to say, Alana?'

She crossed her arms even tighter across her chest as if she could stop her heart beating and feeling so much pain. Pain that she still denied to herself. 'I don't want you to say anything. You don't have to say anything.'

He gave a short, curt laugh and downed the liquid in one, before turning back to pour himself another. 'No, I forgot. You're not into conversation, are you? I tried that. I think all you want is a gigolo.'

'Stop that. That's unfair.'

'Oh, really? And how is it that our best communication was in bed last night?'

Alana blanched.

'Look, I appreciate what you wanted to do.'

His voice was icy. 'Don't patronise me, Alana. Do what you want, but don't do that. I'm not asking you to marry me.' He ran a hand through his hair, the first signs of anger coming out. 'God forbid I might do that! I'm offering you everything on a plate. And a chance to build a life together for the sake of a family. Not even your husband offered you that.'

'Don't bring him into this.'

'Why not?' Pascal taunted. 'Isn't he the reason you've got that Fort Knox of defences around you? The reason you won't let anyone close, not even the father of your unborn child?'

'There's more to it than that,' Alana gritted out, shamingly aware that Pascal spoke the truth. She felt cornered again, panicky. 'What you've been doing is tantamount to…a…a deception. You could have told me what you had in mind, but you let me believe that you wanted to set me up as some sort of mistress. And then you bring me out to the suburbs and make me see what you're doing, tell me about your past…' Alana couldn't stop the incoherent jumble of thoughts spilling out. 'It's almost as if you're trying to get me to—' *Fall in love with you*… The words flashed into her head and she stopped, stunned. She knew they were wrong, but that word *'love'* made her feel weak. Even more claustrophobic.

Pascal stayed where he was, rocking back on his heels, surveying her coolly. 'To what, Alana? *Trust* me? Is that it?' He downed the rest of the liquid and slammed the glass down, making her flinch. 'Is that such a crime?'

Alana shook her head; her arms felt numb now, she held them across her body so tight. 'No…it's not. I'm sorry, I just can't…can't do this. With you.'

'You can't trust me, you mean. You can't even try. And what do you think is waiting for you back in Dublin? No job, a family you don't confide in and a mortgage you're hardly equipped to start paying off again.'

Alana winced at his condemnation. She hitched up her chin. 'I had a call from Rory earlier. He's offered me my job back. Eoin Donohoe's wife came out and revealed the truth behind their marriage. She's seeking a divorce now too. And some of the women who were with Ryan have come out and sold their stories. So, you see, I can go back now.' It sounded weak and pathetic to her ears, but she'd never been so grateful for an escape route.

Pascal's mouth twisted. 'How fortunate. And what do you think you're going to do about our child?'

Alana felt bleak and hollow inside. 'I told you from the

start, you can have as much access as you want. I'd never deny you that, Pascal.'

Just then the doorbell rang. It was obviously the concierge ringing up to tell her that the taxi was outside. Alana moved forward on wooden legs. She avoided Pascal's eye, but just when she drew alongside him, he gripped her arm and pulled her round.

'I *am* the father of your child, and I won't have you sideline me. I can't lock you in here. If you want to go, then go, but I'm not going to come running after you. I don't chase women.' His eyes burnt right through her with a fierce black intensity.

'I know,' she said through stiff lips. *This was it.* Already she could feel herself anticipating the pain of one day seeing him with someone new, but she had to bury it deep, because if she even thought of that for a second now, she wouldn't make it out the door.

CHAPTER TEN

'HEY, Alana, nice to have you back, we missed you.'

Alana smiled at Sophie, but it felt forced as she walked into her old office. 'Thanks.'

She closed the door behind her. Everything had felt wan since she'd come home just a few days ago. She felt listless, as if a vital source of energy had been taken from her body. She smiled bleakly to herself. She knew what that was: *Pascal*. She sat down behind her desk heavily.

Just then a knock came on her door, and before she could answer, it opened and Rory barrelled in. 'Alana! Great to have you back. Sorry about all that business before, but you know my hands were tied.'

Alana couldn't help a wry smile as Rory's words flowed into one another and washed over her aching head.

'…Pascal Lévêque for the charity bash in the K Club this weekend.'

Alana's body straightened up as if she'd been given a shot of adrenaline. 'What did you say?' Her heart was already beating fast. Out of control.

Rory rolled his eyes. 'I was talking about the Rugby fund-raising party at the weekend. It's at the K Club in Kildare. Your friend Lévêque is hosting it.' The K Club was an exclusive golf club and hotel about an hour out of Dublin. The rich and famous regularly helicoptered in for a few days there. Alana felt her blood run cold. 'Rory, you don't want me to cover it, do you?'

She could have wept with relief when he said, 'No, I think it's still a bit soon to put you at the forefront of such a high-profile event.' He laughed nervously. 'Never know who you might run into!'

He rambled on for a bit about what he wanted her to concentrate on, and Alana was relieved when he got up to go. He stopped at the door though, and looked back for a minute, his eyes shrewd on hers. 'I suppose things didn't work out with Lévêque?'

Alana felt protectively for her belly, which seemed to be swelling each day now. She shook her head quickly and forced a smile.

Rory smiled too. 'I'm sure it's for the best. He's not exactly in our league, is he?'

Alana shook her head again and held her breath till Rory left. When he did she sagged like a rag doll.

Hearing Rory mention his name now had somehow finally made Alana face up to the reaction that still held her body in its grip. She'd known it all along, if she was honest with herself, she'd just been in a pathetic state of denial.

She loved him. She loved him so much that even to think about it or acknowledge it made her feel dizzy. It was all so clear now, and what came with the clarity wasn't panic, or claustrophobia; they had all been symptoms of the futile denial of her feelings. She actually felt relief, relief for being honest with herself for the first time in weeks.

She'd craved the physical contact with Pascal in order to feel connected to him without having to look at her feelings. When he'd maintained that ridiculous distance, it had nearly killed her. The extent to which he'd been prepared to commit to her still made her shake, and she knew that walking away hadn't been a fear of commitment or a lack of trust—it had been the fear that he didn't love her, that he'd been doing it solely out of a sense of responsibility. He'd turned his back on his dream of becoming a rugby sporting-hero to fulfil his grandfather's wishes. So Alana knew he was capable of making big sacrifices. But she didn't want to be a sacrifice.

That was what it came down to. Ultimately she had to concede now that Ryan had never truly killed her spirit. He'd only dampened it. Meeting Pascal had brought it back to life. But she wanted him to love her too. She could do anything if she had that, even contemplate getting married again; she knew that now. Her real fear had been of committing to a life with Pascal only to witness his inevitable decline in interest and his taking of a mistress or leaving her.

Yet, was she being unfair? He'd already accused her of trying to read his mind and she'd got it spectacularly wrong. Could she risk it? Could she put her heart on her sleeve and walk away in one piece if he said 'no thanks'?

Somehow, Alana knew that, whether or not she could survive his rejection, she owed it to herself and their baby at least to be honest. Properly honest. The only thing was, it could already be too late.

'Look, Alana, I'm sorry but I don't know where he is. He's probably gone to a club in town or something. He was here earlier and now he's not, OK?' Rory shrugged apologetically, too wound up and hyper even to ask her why she was looking for Pascal. He hurried off again.

Alana stood inside the main reception door of the K Club. She could see the glittering dresses of the women through the doors of the main ballroom in the distance, the men in their tuxedos. And somehow she knew Rory was right; he wasn't there. She left and got back into her car outside the main door. It had taken all of her guts just to drive down to the K Club, and now this. She'd asked at Reception, and after much cajoling Alana had found out that he was booked in there for the night.

A part of her knew she should wait for him to return, but another part of her urged herself to follow a hunch. She knew if she was wrong, then she was going miles in the opposite direction, but she turned her car round and headed back for Dublin anyway.

The security-guard at the gates of Croke Park recognised her and let her in, saying, 'What is it about this place tonight? It's not as if there's a match on.'

Alana felt hope bloom in her chest, and it solidified when she drove in and saw the familiar lines of a sleek black Lexus. With a palpitating heart and clammy hands, she got out of her car and walked in through the dark tunnel to get to the pitch.

He was here.

Alana's heart clenched painfully. He was sitting on a seat up near the press and VIP boxes, looking out broodily into the moonlit pitch. He looked darkly mysterious, his tuxedo visible underneath a black overcoat. At that point her heart swelled in her chest. She'd never felt that happen when she'd looked at Ryan. So much was different, and that was what she had to trust. She was stronger now, clear for the first time in her life. If he didn't love her the way she loved him, then she'd let him go. But she at least owed it to him to let him know why she wouldn't commit to him: she couldn't without his love.

She walked up the steps and then into his row of seats. He seemed lost in another world. Her foot scuffed a discarded plastic cup, and at that he looked up. Alana stopped in her tracks, just feet away. She was very aware of her old jeans, woollen jumper and jacket, hair down and blowing in the breeze. She couldn't read the expression on his face, but she could see the deep grooves beside his mouth. His eyes flicked dispassionately over her before he turned away again.

'What are you doing here?'

The harshness of his tone made her quail inside, but she wouldn't let it daunt her.

'I was looking for you.'

He gave a sort of curt laugh and stared fixedly back out to the pitch. 'Correct me if I'm wrong, but I think the last time we saw each other you couldn't wait to see the back of me.'

Alana forced herself to move forward and sat into the seat beside him. She could feel him move his body away imperceptibly. Her hands were clenched deep inside the pockets of her coat. One hand was curled around what she'd brought with her, and it burned like a mocking brand into the palm of her hand.

She fixed on a point out in the pitch and took a deep breath. 'I'd like to tell you something.'

She felt him shrug one powerful shoulder near her but then he stood up. Alana acted on instinct and whipped out a hand, catching his. She looked up at him.

'Please. Hear me out.'

With a hard expression, no emotion, he took his hand from hers. She held her breath and let it out again unsteadily when he finally sat again, clearly tense.

She forced herself to speak. 'I never really loved Ryan. I grew up believing in the sanctity of marriage. I grew up believing that that was what I wanted, to be like the rest of my family. When we met, Ryan swept me off my feet, made me believe in the dream. He told me he wouldn't stop me working, but then he did. He told me we'd be happy, but we weren't. And the thing was, by the time doubts were crowding my head just days before the wedding, I couldn't stop it. So much money had been spent, so much emotion invested. My parents were old. I knew they wanted to see me settled before it was too late. And I just…I couldn't stop it. I knew I was making a mistake. I'd isolated myself spectacularly in a bubble of make believe. And yet still I hoped for the best, put my trust in what I'd witnessed growing up, thought everything would work out OK.'

Alana felt Pascal turn towards her, but couldn't look at him. Her eyes stung with tears but her voice didn't waver. 'I was a baby, Pascal, just twenty-two. I hardly knew myself, never mind Ryan. I subjugated myself, put myself through hell with him to try and make things work, and I just…I just couldn't believe how easily I'd let someone like him take over my life. I should have seen it. I should have had more self-respect to know—'

Pascal reached out and took her hand that was twisting on her knee, stopping her words. Stopping her heart. She still couldn't look at him.

'Alana, look at me.'

Very reluctantly, she turned her head. His eyes were dark and molten, like she hadn't seen them for a long time, and she wanted to dive right in and drown in their depths, but she held herself rigid. She had so much more to say. He spoke before she could.

'You said it yourself, you were so young and you obviously felt you had to live up to the expectations of your own family.'

She nodded jerkily, relieved that he was stalling her for a moment. 'I know, I know that now. And I can't regret it, because it taught me so much. I know now, too, that my family would have been there for me if I'd confided in them. But I just always felt so distant, removed from them, like I couldn't go and bother them with my petty problems.'

Pascal shook his head. 'They weren't petty.'

'I know that now, too,' Alana said quietly.

She turned away again and Pascal released her hand. She was about to make another choice, take another fork in the road of her life, and, while this one had the potential for so much more pain than Ryan had ever inflicted, it was different this time because she knew this was the right thing. The right choice. It all came down to Pascal and what he would choose, and she couldn't control that.

She took another deep breath and turned to face Pascal again, her eyes roving over his face. Everything about him was so dear to her. So necessary for her well-being. He was looking at her, too, but warily. His expression was guarded again.

With her heart thumping, Alana moved off the seat to kneel before him on the cold stone ground. Pascal reared back, surprised. 'What are you doing?'

Alana rocked back on her heels. 'I'm following my heart, Pascal, but this time I know why I'm doing it and I know it's right—because from the first moment I saw you it's felt right, in here.' Alana put a hand to her belly and then touched her heart. 'And most of all in here. It just took me a while to trust that. To trust myself again.'

Pascal said nothing, but his eyes gleamed with some indefinable emotion and Alana put her trust in that. She took her other hand out of her pocket; it was still clenched over her precious cargo. She looked at Pascal. 'You asked me to consider committing to a life together, to consider that we could try and make things work.'

He cut in harshly. 'I never asked you to marry me, Alana; you've made it abundantly clear how you feel about it. All I wanted was for us to give family life a chance. To give our child a stable foundation.'

'I know,' she said gently. 'And I do want that too.'

He raised an incredulous brow.

She forged on. 'I do, Pascal. But the truth is, I want so much more. I said no to you in Paris, I came back here to try and get some space, because I was afraid of what you were asking, and what might happen if I said yes—that you'd grow tired of me, or take a mistress. I always said I'd never marry again, yet I want to believe in the dream again. And it scares the life out of me, when it had become such a dangerous myth to me. I'd thought I'd given up on that dream for ever.'

She looked back into his eyes, willing him to see what she was feeling, what was in her heart. 'I walked away because deep down I couldn't bear the thought that you didn't love me. I've fallen in love with you, Pascal, and I've realised that I still do want the dream. I can't settle for anything less, no matter how much pain might be in store, even if you say no.' She opened her palm then, and she saw his stricken gaze look down to take in the heavy platinum band nestling there.

'Pascal, I...' God, she couldn't falter now. She kneeled up straighter and held out the ring in her hand, but she could feel it starting to shake. 'Pascal, will you please marry me?'

His eyes met hers, and Alana stopped breathing. Time stopped for an infinitesimal moment and started again in slow, heavy beats and then she realised that it was her heart.

Pascal felt as though a two-tonne lorry had just crashed into his solar plexus. And all he could do was look at her, this woman he loved more than life itself, on her knees in front of him, *proposing* to him. Because she loved him. Finally the momentary shock wore off. He felt a ripple of pure incandescent joy surge upwards through his body. He could see her hand shake, her lips tighten momentarily as if to ward off the inevitable rejection, and ridiculously tears stung the back of his eyes. He was in awe, transfixed by her strength and bravery, and he felt humbled.

He summoned control and held out his left hand. 'I thought you'd never ask.' Alana just stayed there, dumbstruck. Speechless. Pascal fought against tumbling her straight to the ground and kissing her senseless. 'Do you want me to marry you or not?' he said throatily, a smile starting to break through.

She still held back. There was a waver in her husky voice. 'I only want you to marry me if you love me, Pascal.'

His heart ached for her uncertainty, but he had to make her trust just another little bit. To show her trust in him. 'Put the ring on my finger and you'll find out.'

Dammit, couldn't she see? His heart was singing.

With endearing concentration and unbelievable trepidation on her face, Alana took his hand in hers and carefully slid the ring onto his finger. But before she'd even reached the second knuckle he'd pulled her up off her knees and onto his lap. She trusted him, that was all he needed to know.

Alana felt Pascal's arms secure around her waist, and looked down into his eyes. Her world had just been upended. He was shaking his head. 'You put me through hell the last week. You've turned my life inside out and upside down. Letting you walk out of that apartment was the hardest thing I've ever done, but I had to let you go…and I just prayed that you'd come back to me. And you have.'

He reached up a hand and pulled her head down to his, kissing her deeply. Alana was still struggling to get her breath back, still in shock at what she'd just done, at what he'd just said. As if reading her mind, he pulled back before they went up in flames. He smoothed some hair behind one ear and looked into her eyes.

'I love you, Alana. How can you not know that?'

She shook her head faintly; awe made her voice shake. 'I couldn't allow myself to hope it for a second. I knew I had to do this, to tell you how I felt, but I couldn't contemplate your rejection or else I would never have had the guts to tell you.'

He shook his head and pulled her closer. 'I fell in love with you right here, in this stadium. See how I had to come back? It's as if I had to be near the place I saw you first.'

Alana was melting into his warm, strong embrace. She shook her head faintly. 'But how is it possible? It was just an affair.'

His eyes gleamed. 'It was never just an affair. From the moment we first kissed it was more than that. When our eyes met we *knew* each other. We were made for each other.' He smiled then, and it made her chest ache. 'Although, of course, all I saw at the time was you in that shirt and tie, all buttoned up, and all I wanted to do was unbutton you, undo you.'

Alana pushed back to look down at him again, a blush staining her cheeks. 'You undo me every time you look at me.' She caressed his cheek with the back of her hand. Tears stung her eyes; she could feel her lip wobble. She'd come home, finally.

Pascal caught it and wouldn't let her go. 'You do realise that, just because you've put a ring on my finger, you're still going to have to marry me in a church and make an honest man of me?'

She nodded and smiled tremulously, not a hint of her past or any fears in her eyes any more. 'I'm counting on it. I want the world to know you're mine.' Her voice rang with possessiveness, making Pascal's heart sing even more, making his body hum with urgent desire.

He knew now that he could embrace the way she made him feel, knowing that she could contain every part of him, even the part that felt untamed. He knew now that it had just been her instinctive ability to connect with every part of him from the moment they'd met that had unsettled him. He pulled her head back down to his. When they were finally able to stop kissing, Alana sat back and smiled at him shyly. She brought his hand down to cover her belly where their baby was growing strong and bigger every day. 'I have all I need right here, right now. Anything else is a bonus.'

Pascal pulled her head down to his, and just before he kissed her he whispered against her mouth, 'I love you, very much.'

EPILOGUE

ALANA relaxed back into the luxurious cushions of the huge, comfortable couch. The tiny baby suckling at her breast was inducing a deliciously soporific effect in her blood. A familiar flood of happiness and contentment made her smile as she looked up from her daughter and took in the warmly decorated open-plan sitting room, and the big windows that looked out into a large garden littered with toys. Situated right in the centre of Montmartre, you could be forgiven for thinking you were in the countryside, the hum of Parisian traffic barely discernible through the high trees guarding the property.

This had been one of the first elegantly palatial town houses she and Pascal had looked at that day so long ago, when she'd believed that all he wanted was to set her up in isolated seclusion. When she'd been so confused about how that made her feel. She shook her head mentally at how far removed that image was from the reality of their life now.

Her heart rate zinged up a notch when a familiar scent teased her nostrils and the couch dipped beside her. As if sensing her father's presence, Orla's head jerked away from Alana's breast, big, brown eyes opening to seek him out. Pascal came close and kissed the baby's head before nuzzling a kiss to Alana's neck, making exquisite shards of desire race through her blood. She marvelled that even while she was breastfeeding, with her baby belly still evident, Pascal's attraction for her didn't seem to diminish. It was the most heady feeling. It got even more heady when he growled into her ear, 'How is it that I can be jealous of my own daughter?'

Alana turned her head to meet his mouth in a brief, searing kiss and then said dryly, 'Well, it's not as if you haven't been through this before; I'm sure you'll survive.' Pascal smiled wolfishly, but then took Orla from Alana to place her on his shoulder and pat her back with all the dexterity of someone well practised in the art. Just then the fruits of his earlier practising efforts exploded into the room.

They were two black-haired, dark-eyed miniature versions of Pascal, one slightly smaller than the other. They were both pulling at a green rugby jersey emblazoned with the Ireland logo. The taller one wailed, 'Papa, it's my turn to wear the Ireland jersey, I don't want to be French today, tell Sam it's his turn to be French. Anyway, it's too big for him!'

The smaller of the two boys clinging desperately to the jersey—three-year-old Samir, named after his paternal grandfather—stood with a bottom lip quivering and tears glistening on ridiculously long lashes.

Pascal shot a wryly accusing look to Alana, whose mouth was twitching as she unsuccessfully held in a grin. She looked at him reproachfully, 'What? You knew I came from a large family.'

'Yes, but that's not it,' he said with mock severity. 'Do we have to encourage our sons to support either one country or the other?'

Alana started to do up her bra and shirt and stood up from the couch, looking down at her husband sprawled before her with Orla successfully burped and falling asleep contentedly on his shoulder.

With her hands on the buttons of her shirt, and seeing the way Pascal's eyes were lingering there explicitly, she valiantly ignored his look and said, 'On the day of the Six Nations match between Ireland and France? It's only natural that our eldest, most discerning son will want to support the team about to win a Grand Slam. And don't blame me for their competitive streak; I think we can safely say they got that from you.'

She flashed him a cheeky grin and turned to go and deal with her sons' spat, but Pascal grabbed her wrist and she laughingly fell back as he pulled her onto his lap and claimed her mouth for a kiss.

On cue, the two boys forgot all about the rugby jersey and started making loud vomiting noises. 'Ugh! Gross!' declared Patrick as he dragged his younger brother away. 'You two better not get all kissy at the match. *So* not cool.'

Alana finally pulled away breathlessly and smiled into Pascal's face. She imitated Patrick. '*So* not cool, but *so* much fun.'

'Hmm,' murmured Pascal appreciatively, settling Alana into one arm while holding Orla with the other. 'Have I told you yet today how much I love you, Mme Lévêque?'

She lifted her head to look at him and smiled coquettishly, running a finger down his chest. 'I don't believe you have, M Lévêque, but you could make it up to me.'

'How?'

Alana pretended to think for a second, her head on one side. 'Let me see. As our lovely nanny has offered to babysit tonight, you could take me out for dinner….'

His eyes darkened and she felt his body grow taut underneath her. 'Anywhere in mind?' he asked with a gruff tone, vivid images already filling his head.

'Oh, I'm sure I can think of somewhere…' Alana came close and pressed a kiss to his mouth '…nice and cosy.' She moved down and pressed another kiss to his neck where his pulse beat fast. 'Somewhere intimate…private…'

'Where we won't be disturbed?' His voice became gruffer.

She pulled back and looked at him, and smiled, her eyes shining with love for him.

'My thoughts exactly.'

Pascal felt his daughter squirm slightly against his shoulder, and felt his wife wriggle on his lap, making lust arrow straight to his groin. He heard the scuffle of his two sons playing nearby, and his heart swelled in his chest. The moment was huge, buoyant, and though his life was filled with such moments now, this didn't diminish it in any way. Alana just looked at him with innate understanding in her eyes. She smiled and said simply, 'I know—and I love you, too.'

And that was all that needed to be said.

DI CESARE'S PREGNANT MISTRESS

CHANTELLE SHAW

Chantelle Shaw lives on the Kent coast, five minutes from the sea, and does much of her thinking about the characters in her books while walking on the beach. She's been an avid reader from an early age. Her schoolfriends used to hide their books when she visited—but Chantelle would retreat into her own world and still writes stories in her head all the time. Chantelle has been blissfully married to her own tall, dark and very patient hero for over twenty years and has six children. She began to read Mills & Boon® novels as a teenager and, throughout the years of being a stay-at-home mum to her brood, found romantic fiction helped her to stay sane! She enjoys reading and writing about strong-willed, feisty women and even stronger-willed sexy heroes. Chantelle is at her happiest when writing. She is particularly inspired while cooking dinner, which unfortunately results in a lot of culinary disasters! She also loves gardening, walking and eating chocolate (followed by more walking!). Catch up with Chantelle's latest news on her website: www.chantelleshaw.com.

CHAPTER ONE

'THAT'S Tamsin Stewart—walking into the ballroom now. And there's my father rushing over to her. I can't believe Daddy is making such a fool of himself. She's young enough to be his daughter, for heaven's sake!'

The waspish comment caused Bruno Di Cesare to turn his head and follow Annabel Grainger's gaze across the ballroom to the blonde who had just walked into the room. His first thought was that the woman looked nothing like he had expected, and his eyes narrowed as he lifted his glass to his lips and savoured a mouthful of vintage champagne while he studied her.

When Annabel—younger daughter of his friend and business associate James Grainger—had phoned him and sobbed that her father was involved with a 'bimbo', he'd pictured a brittle bleached blonde wearing some skimpy outfit that revealed acres of overly-tanned flesh. Tamsin Stewart was certainly blonde, but she bore no further similarity to the image in his head.

Her slender figure was emphasised by her silk dress: an elegant, floor-length navy sheath that moulded her breasts and skimmed her flat stomach and the gentle curve of her hips. Her delicate oval face was dominated by huge eyes, although he could not make out their colour from this distance, and her mouth was wide and full and deliciously tempting, coated in a pale pink gloss. Her hair was swept up into a chignon, leaving her long, slender neck exposed, and the ornate diamond necklace she was wearing was almost as eye-catching as the woman herself.

She was beautiful, Bruno conceded, irritated by his reaction to her. The last thing he had expected was to feel physically attracted to a woman he had good evidence to suggest was a callous gold-digger with her sights set on James Grainger's fortune.

Annabel snatched a champagne flute from the bar. 'Look at her—she's all over him,' she muttered disgustedly, downing half the contents of her glass in one gulp.

Bruno reminded himself that Annabel was eighteen now, and entitled to drink alcohol. Over the years that he had been friends with the Graingers he had come to regard her as a little sister, and he frowned at the stark misery on her face.

Across the room Tamsin Stewart was smiling warmly at James as she reached up and brushed a speck of confetti from his jacket. The gesture spoke of an unusual level of intimacy between employer and employee, and Bruno's jaw hardened. Initially he had dismissed Annabel's claim that her father was besotted with a woman half his age. James Grainger was one of the shrewdest businessmen Bruno had ever met, and for the last eighteen months had been grieving the death of his adored wife. It was impossible to imagine him starting a relationship with any woman—especially one who was the same age as one of his daughters.

Nevertheless, Bruno had requested a report on Miss Stewart from one of his many contacts, and he had been sufficiently concerned by what he'd learned to cancel a trip to the US and fly to England to attend James daughter's wedding.

The marriage of Earl Grainger's eldest daughter, Lady Davina, to the Right Honourable Hugo Havistock had taken place in the private chapel on the Grainger estate, followed by a sit-down meal for family members and close friends at a nearby hotel. Now another two hundred guests had arrived at the Royal Cheshunt for the evening reception, and Tamsin Stewart was one of them.

Annabel watched her father lead the beautiful blonde onto the dance floor, and then rounded on Bruno. 'You see! I'm not imagining things,' she said angrily. 'Tamsin seems to have *bewitched* my father.'

'If that's the case, then we will just have to find a way to release him from her spell, *piccola*,' Bruno murmured softly.

Annabel stared at him. 'But how can we?' Her face clouded. 'I thought Daddy had bought that necklace for me,' she choked, lifting her glass to her lips to take another long sip of champagne.

Frowning, Bruno glanced at the diamonds around Tamsin Stewart's swan-like neck.

'Daddy bought all the bridesmaids one of these,' Annabel muttered, fingering the string of pearls at her throat, 'but when I was tidying his study—' she flushed faintly '—I found the diamond necklace and thought he was going to give it to me. I am the chief bridesmaid, after all,' she added sulkily. 'I couldn't believe it when he said it was for Tamsin, in thanks for her work on Davina's flat.'

'If only he hadn't decided to employ an interior designer as part of Davina and Hugo's wedding present, he would never have met her,' Annabel continued dolefully. 'Davina thinks Daddy is lonely, and just wants someone to talk to, but she's been so wrapped up in the wedding that she doesn't understand what a hold Tamsin has over him.'

Annabel drained her glass and held it out to the barman to

refill it. 'Oh, Bruno, I don't know what to do. I wouldn't be surprised if Tamsin has set her sights on becoming the next Lady Grainger. Daddy has been so unhappy since Mummy died,' she said thickly. 'I couldn't bear it if she hurt him.'

'She won't, *piccola*, because I won't allow her to.'

Bruno caught the shimmer of tears in Annabel's eyes and a hard knot of anger settled in his chest. He had known Annabel and Davina since they were children, when Lorna and James Grainger had welcomed him into their home on his frequent business trips to England. He had been saddened by Lorna's untimely death from cancer, and understood the raw grief of the family she had left behind. He felt protective of Lorna's daughters—and in a strange way of James too, as the older man struggled to come to terms with the loss of his beloved wife.

He took another sip of champagne, following James and Tamsin's progress around the dance floor while he considered what he knew of her. She was twenty-five, and single since her divorce two years ago. After university she had worked for a top London design company, where she had gained a reputation as a talented designer, and she had recently joined her brother's property development and design company, Spectrum.

Almost certainly Tamsin's move to Spectrum would have meant a drop in her salary, but the lady had expensive tastes, and Bruno was curious to know how she had afforded her recently purchased new car and spent two weeks at an exclusive holiday complex in Mauritius—not to mention her penchant for designer clothes. The dress she was wearing tonight was from a well-known fashion house—although not his own, Bruno noted—and he was sure it would have been out of her price range. Someone had bought it for her—and Bruno had a good idea who that someone was.

He knew that James Grainger travelled to London every

week to meet Tamsin. Did she persuade him to take her shopping for clothes and jewellery? Or had she seen the diamond necklace and hinted that she wanted it?

But shopping trips were one thing—investing a huge sum of money in Tamsin's brother's company was quite another, Bruno mused grimly. A month ago Spectrum Development and Design had been facing bankruptcy, but at the last minute James had put a vast amount of money into the company to save it from collapse. Bruno knew for a fact that James's financial advisors had been strongly against the deal, but James had refused to listen.

Sexual attraction could make a fool of even the most astute man, Bruno acknowledged bitterly. His father had proved that when he had married a woman half his age. Miranda had caused Stefano Di Cesare's downfall, both professionally and personally, and—even worse—the vacuous actress with her surgically enhanced figure had engineered a rift between Bruno and his father that had not been resolved before Stefano's death.

He had been in his early twenties when his father had remarried. Old enough and mature enough to want Stefano to be happy, but still grieving for his mother, who had died less than a year earlier. *Dio*, he had tried his best to like Miranda, even though his instincts had warned him she was an avaricious slut. But his instincts had proved right, he thought grimly, and now they were warning him that Tamsin Stewart was another Miranda, playing on the emotions of a vulnerable older man.

Bruno had huge respect for James, and over the years they had done business together they had become close friends. But the similarity between the Earl's and his own father's situation could not be ignored. Stefano had also been a lonely widower, flattered by the attention of a pretty young woman— surely James Grainger had more sense than to lose his head to a blonde sex-pot?

Across the room, Tamsin Stewart was laughing with James, her lovely face animated and her eyes sparkling as they shared a private joke, seeming oblivious to the other dancers around them.

Annabel stared at them for a moment, scowling. 'She was married to the brother of one of my friends, you know,' she muttered. 'Caroline told me how she blatantly targeted Neil once she knew that he was a successful businessman earning a fortune in the city. Apparently Neil realised he'd made a mistake soon after they married—when Tamsin moaned about his long working hours but was happy to spend his money. But when he tried to end their relationship, she told him she was pregnant—presumably to make him stay with her.'

'So she has a child?' Bruno queried sharply.

'Oh, no,' Annabel replied. 'Neil divorced her, and I don't know what happened about the baby. Caroline thinks Tamsin may have made up the story about being pregnant, but it didn't work. As I said, Neil insisted on a divorce, and Caro thinks he's well shot of her.

'Daddy's latest idea is to have Ditton Hall completely refurbished,' she said dully. 'Even though Mummy loved it the way it is. And he's going to ask Tamsin to design it. Daddy says that we have to accept Mummy's gone and move on, but I couldn't bear it if Tamsin moved into Ditton Hall. I'd have to move out and live on the streets or something.'

The idea of spoilt, pampered Annabel living rough was laughable, but Bruno caught the note of real misery in her voice and his anger intensified. The young girl had been devastated by her mother's death, and was understandably hurt and dismayed by her father's relationship with Tamsin Stewart.

His mouth compressed into a hard line as he moved lithely towards the dance floor, tugging Annabel after him. 'Your father would never do anything to upset you, and he certainly wouldn't want you to leave Ditton Hall,' he reassured her. 'Now I think it's time you introduced me to the lovely Miss Stewart.'

Tamsin glanced at James Grainger and frowned when she noted the greyish tinge to his skin. He looked drained, she thought worriedly. 'After this dance I think you should sit down and rest. You must have been on your feet for most of the day, and you know what the doctor said about getting too tired,' she told him firmly.

James chuckled, but did not argue with her. 'Yes, Nurse. You sound as bossy as my wife—and that's saying something.' His smile faded and a flash of pain crossed his face. 'Lorna would have been in her element today, organising everything. She'd have loved it.'

'I know,' Tamsin said softly. 'But you've done a wonderful job with this wedding. Davina looks so happy, and I'm sure that neither of the girls has guessed.' She bit her lip and then murmured, 'But, James, I really think you should tell them— if not now, then after Davina and Hugo get back from their honeymoon.'

'No.' James Grainger shook his head fiercely. 'Eighteen months ago they lost their mother to cancer. There's no way I'm going to tell them I've been diagnosed with the same disease. Not yet anyway,' he added, when Tamsin opened her mouth to argue. 'Not until I've seen the specialist again and discussed my prognosis. I don't want to worry them unnecessarily. Annabel is only eighteen, and she's too young to have to deal with any more traumas. Promise me you won't say anything to the girls or anyone else?' he pleaded.

Tamsin nodded reluctantly. 'Of course I won't, if that's what you want. But I'm coming to the hospital with you on Friday. The chemotherapy made you so sick last time.' She paused before adding hesitantly, 'I could be wrong, but I get the feeling that Annabel isn't happy about us meeting—especially now you can no longer pretend we're discussing my designs for Davina's flat. If she knew your trips to London are to the hospital…'

'No,' James insisted again. 'She'd be scared witless. Anyway,' he added cheerfully, 'I've told her I'm meeting you to discuss ideas for refurbishing Ditton Hall.'

'Yes,' Tamsin said slowly, 'I'm afraid that's what's upset her.'

But what could she do about the situation? Tamsin fretted. She had first met James Grainger when she had been commissioned to design Davina and Hugo's flat, and had quickly realised that beneath James's friendly charm was a man teetering on the edge of despair at the loss of his wife.

Tamsin had sympathised with James, and understood his reluctance to burden his daughters with his misery when they were grieving for their mother. And so she had taken time to chat to him whenever they had met at the flat, and had gently encouraged him to talk about Lorna Grainger.

A deep friendship had developed between them, and James had confided in her when he'd gone for tests to determine if he had prostate cancer. Since the diagnosis she had faithfully kept his secret, but she had been unable to persuade him to reveal the truth to Davina and Annabel. And now she had a feeling that Annabel resented her friendship with James.

Sighing, she let her fingers stray to her neck, nervously checking the diamond necklace that hung like a heavy weight around her throat.

'Stop fiddling with it. It's fine,' James chided her.

'I'm terrified I'll lose it. I really think I should take it off and return it to you.'

'I've told you, I don't want it back. It's a present.'

'And I told you I can't accept it,' Tamsin told him firmly.

'Please understand. It must be worth a fortune, and it wouldn't be…appropriate for me to keep it.'

'I just wanted to thank you for your support these past few months by giving you something special for your birthday,' James said stubbornly. 'I don't know what I would have done without you. Lorna would have liked you,' he added gruffly.

The sadness in his eyes brought a lump to Tamsin's throat, and on impulse she leaned up and kissed him lightly on the cheek. 'I help because we're friends, and I certainly don't want you to repay me with expensive jewellery.' She gave the older man a rueful look, knowing that he would be deeply hurt if she insisted on returning the necklace. 'But thank you—the necklace is beautiful and I'll treasure it.'

'Daddy, you haven't danced with me once this evening.'

At the sound of the faintly petulant voice, Tamsin glanced round. Her heart sank when she saw Annabel Grainger staring sulkily at her. She quickly stepped away from James, feeling guilty that she had monopolised his attention. But as she swung round to walk off the dance floor she cannoned into a hard wall of muscle encased in silk—and when she lifted her head her eyes meshed with the midnight-dark gaze of Annabel's partner.

Her first thought was that she had never in her life seen a man like him. His stunning looks stole the breath from her body, and as his eyes locked with hers she stood stock-still and simply stared at him, absorbing the impact of his perfectly sculpted bone structure and the dark olive skin stretched taut over his high cheekbones. His jaw was square, and hinted at an implacable determination to always get his own way, but his mouth was wide and sensual, and Tamsin felt a curious longing to trace the full curve of his upper lip with her fingers.

Awareness seeped through her veins until her body throbbed with a slow, deep yearning that began in the pit of her stomach and radiated out, weakening her limbs with a desire that was shockingly fierce and utterly unexpected. The gleam in his ebony eyes warned her that he knew what she was thinking, and her face burned. Hopefully not *exactly* what she was thinking, she prayed fervently, and she hastily banished the fantasy of him carrying her off to the nearest empty room and making passionate love to her.

Tension coiled in the pit of her stomach, and heat suffused her whole body so that she was sure her face must be scarlet. He was exceptionally tall, sheathed in an expertly cut dark grey suit that emphasised his height and the width of his shoulders, and even when she stepped away from him, mumbling an apology, she felt overwhelmed by his powerful masculinity.

'Forgive me, pumpkin, but I thought you were enjoying yourself with your friends,' James apologised to his daughter. 'Have you been taking care of my little girl, Bruno?'

'Of course,' the man replied smoothly. 'But you know, James, now that Davina is married, and about to leave Ditton Hall, I think Annabel feels in need of her *papà*.' His accent was unmistakably Italian, his voice as rich and thick as clotted cream, but Tamsin caught his faintly reproving tone and James must have detected it too.

'Come and dance with me, then, darling,' he said jovially. 'Tamsin, do you mind if we swap partners? I have it on good authority that Bruno is an excellent dancer.'

An awkward silence followed, and Tamsin stiffened, unable to bring herself to meet the man's gaze. His close proximity was actually making her tremble, and she was terrified that if she danced with him he would realise the effect he had on her. 'I think I'll sit this one out,' she mumbled, keeping her eyes on James. 'You go ahead.'

James shook his head. 'For heaven's sake, where are my

manners? I haven't even introduced you. Tamsin, this is Bruno Di Cesare—head of the House of Di Cesare fashion empire, and a very good friend. Bruno, may I introduce you to Tamsin Stewart? Tamsin is an amazingly talented interior designer.'

Annabel made an impatient noise and tugged her father's arm. 'Come on, Daddy. I want a drink,' she said loudly, but Tamsin barely heard her, or noticed when James escorted his daughter over to the bar. The music and the other guests on the dance floor faded to the periphery of her mind, and she felt as though only she and Bruno Di Cesare existed.

'Miss Stewart.'

His voice seemed to have dropped several degrees, and his coolness sent an involuntary shiver down Tamsin's spine. Perhaps it was his height that made him seem so intimidating, or maybe it was the hardness of his features and the slightly cynical curl of his lip that made her feel uneasy. She gasped when he suddenly extended his hand and enfolded her fingers in his firm grasp.

'Or may I call you Tamsin?'

He rolled her name on his tongue as if he was savouring a fine wine, and lifted her hand to graze his lips across her knuckles, causing an electrical current to shoot from her fingers along every nerve-ending to her toes. His eyes glinted with amusement when she blushed, and she hated the fact that he clearly knew how much he affected her.

'I hope I can persuade you to dance with me,' he murmured in his sinfully sexy accent, and there was no hint of coolness in his voice now, making her wonder if she had imagined it.

Tamsin had a feeling that he could persuade her to do anything he liked. His smile did strange things to her insides and she felt hot and flustered. He was beautiful, she thought helplessly. She hadn't felt like this since…ever. Not even when she had met her husband.

She'd been attracted to Neil, of course, and as their court-ship had progressed she had fallen in love with him. But she had never experienced this incredible, almost primal sexual awareness that was now pounding through her veins.

At school she'd always been too engrossed in her studies to suffer the same teenage crushes on pop stars or boys in the sixth form which had affected her friends. Her life had been mapped out: qualifications, a career, marriage and babies. But her dreams had been shattered by Neil's infidelity. Her personal life had imploded, and she no longer knew what she wanted, but she suddenly found that she wanted to do something utterly crazy—like fling herself into the arms of this sexy stranger and press her lips against the sensual curve of his mouth.

With a jolt she realised that she was staring at Bruno Di Cesare, and she blushed. She was acting like a teenager on her first date, she told herself irritably, and with a huge effort she returned his smile and strove to sound cool as she murmured, 'Thank you—I'd love to dance.'

She followed him onto the dance floor and a quiver ran through her when he retained his hold on her hand and slid his other arm around her waist, drawing her against the solid muscles of his thighs. She could feel the heat that emanated from his body, and the exotic, musky scent of his cologne swamped her senses. Each of her nerve-endings seemed acutely sensitive, and to her horror she felt a tingling in her breasts as her nipples hardened and strained against the silky material of her dress.

Bruno felt the signals Tamsin's body was sending out and his eyes narrowed on her flushed face. A few moments ago, before James had introduced them, she had been coolly dis-missive of him. But now that she knew he headed a globally successful business empire she was no longer dismissive, but soft and pliant in his arms, with the tip of her pink tongue tracing the shape of her bottom lip in a deliberate invitation that triggered an instant response low in his pelvis.

Money was a powerful aphrodisiac, he thought sardonically. He acknowledged his good-looks without conceit, but knew that even without his classical bone structure and athletic build his wealth ensured that, where women were concerned, he never had to try very hard. Sometimes he wondered if life would be more exciting if he did. He dismissed the thought with a faint shrug and watched Tamsin Stewart's pupils dilate when he smiled at her. It was a clever trick, and he guessed that behind the façade of wide-eyed *ingénue* she was a clever lady.

She was beautiful, but flawed, he reminded himself grimly. A gold-digger with her greedy eyes focused on James Grainger's fortune. He was convinced that she was a woman like his stepmother—a parasite who hoped to worm her way into the heart of a grieving older man and no doubt bleed him dry. But although his brain felt nothing but contempt for her, his body was not so fussy, and he felt an unmistakable tightening in his gut as he imagined crushing her soft pink lips beneath his and removing her dress to tease her tight, swollen nipples with his tongue.

His desire for her was an irritating complication, but it seemed that Tamsin Stewart was equally aware of the chemistry between them. Bruno's jaw tightened and his lips curled into a cruel line. He had been unable to save his father from Miranda's grasping clutches, but no way would he stand back and watch James make the same mistake, he vowed grimly.

Cold, contemptuous anger solidified in his chest as he stared at the array of diamonds around Tamsin's neck and assessed how much the necklace James had given her was worth. He could not believe that the beautiful blonde was interested in a man old enough to be her father for any other reason than that

James was extremely rich. But her undisguised awareness of him provided him with an ideal weapon to foil her plans—and he would have no compunction in using it.

CHAPTER TWO

'So you are an interior designer? Annabel told me you recently completed work on Davina and Hugo's flat,' Bruno said, dipping his head so close to Tamsin's that his warm breath fanned her cheek.

'Yes,' she murmured distractedly, as she attempted to ease away from him a fraction. She felt his hand tighten on her hip so his pelvis rubbed sinuously against hers. Her thought process seemed to have deserted her, and she regretted drinking the glass of champagne she had been presented with when she had first arrived at the reception. Surely it was the alcohol that was making her head swim, rather than the intoxicating presence of the man who was holding her against his broad, muscular chest?

She wondered with a sinking feeling what else Annabel had said about her. Davina's sister had never been particularly friendly towards her—but that was hardly surprising when she was a close friend of Tamsin's ex-sister-in-law, Caroline Harper. Caroline had disliked her on sight, and had bitterly resented Tamsin's presence in Neil Harper's life. Tamsin had understood that Caroline's fractured childhood and her parents' acrimonious divorce had led her to cling to her older brother, but her jealousy had been one of many factors that had driven Neil and Tamsin apart.

'I was honoured when James appointed me to design the flat,' she explained, lifting clear blue eyes to Bruno and smiling at him. 'It's Davina and Hugo's first home as a married couple, and I wanted it to be special.'

And, of course, it had given her an opportunity to ingratiate herself with an extremely wealthy man, Bruno mused cynically, irritated to discover that Tamsin's eyes reminded him of the cobalt Tuscan sky on a summer's day. James Grainger inhabited the rarefied world of the aristocracy, and spent most of his time at his country estate or his gentlemen's club. If it had not been for the commission Tamsin would never have met James, and she had obviously made the most of her luck.

'So, have you only known the Graingers since you won the commission?' he queried.

His sexy smile made it hard for Tamsin to think straight, but she detected a slight nuance in his voice that puzzled her, and she wondered why he was so interested in her relationship with the family.

'Yes. As you can imagine, I worked very closely with Davina and Hugo, and I'm pleased so say they loved my designs. We became friends, and they asked me to their reception tonight.'

'And I understand from Annabel that you are also friendly with James?'

Bruno's expression was bland, but once again Tamsin detected the faint note of censure in his tone. She decided she'd had enough of playing twenty questions. 'James Grainger is charming, and I would like to think we are friends.' She flushed guiltily as she remembered her promise to James that she would not reveal his secret to anyone. She guessed that Bruno was unaware of James's health problems, and it was not her place to tell him. 'We met a few times when he came up to inspect my work on the flat, and on a couple of occasions we had lunch.' She faltered when Bruno regarded her steadily with his unfathomable dark eyes. 'I think James is lonely since he lost his wife,' she added. 'He seemed to want to talk about her.'

'And I'm sure you offered a sympathetic shoulder for him to cry on,' Bruno drawled softly.

While Tamsin was trying to work out quite what he meant by that statement, or if he had even meant anything at all, he trailed a long, tanned finger down her cheek and rested it lightly on the diamond necklace around her throat.

'This is almost as exquisite as the woman wearing it,' he murmured, the sensual gleam in his dark eyes causing Tamsin to catch her breath. 'You have superb taste, *bella,* to have chosen such a beautifully crafted piece of jewellery.'

'Oh, I didn't buy it…it was a present.' Tamsin hesitated; there was no reason why she should not say that the necklace had been a birthday present from James, but she had a strange feeling that Bruno would question why the Earl had given her such an expensive gift. It would be impossible to explain that James had wanted to thank her for the hours she'd sat in the hospital waiting room with him without revealing his secret.

Was it her imagination, or had the stunning Italian's face hardened fractionally behind his smile? Although once again his voice was as seductive as molten syrup as he queried mildly, 'A present from your lover, I suppose?'

He had to be teasing her, didn't he? The look of disappointment on his face couldn't be real. But the warmth of his body pressed close up against hers and the strength of his arms as they tightened round her waist were very real, and Tamsin shook her head dazedly. Common sense told her that a man as gorgeous as Bruno Di Cesare could not really be interested in her. But she remembered how their eyes had locked when she had first stumbled against him on the dance floor, and she recalled her instant and overwhelming feeling that she had known him for eternity. Was it possible that he had been overwhelmed too?

'I don't have a lover,' she whispered, unable to tear her eyes from the sensual curve of his mouth.

'I find that hard to believe, *cara*.' Bruno's velvety voice caressed her and he moved his head even closer to hers, so that his jaw brushed against her cheek. 'But perhaps whoever gave you the necklace hopes to be your lover?'

'No,' she denied sharply, jerking her head back. James was a dear friend who was still grieving the loss of his wife, and the idea that he had given her the necklace for any other reason than friendship was horrible. She didn't understand why Bruno was so interested in the wretched necklace anyway.

When she tried to step away from him he drew her inexorably closer, so that she could feel the hardness of his thighs pressed against hers. 'I'm not involved with anyone right now. Does that satisfy your curiosity?' He unsettled her, but before she could demand that he release her, he tightened his arms around her.

'Absolutely,' he growled, in a low, intense tone that made the hairs on the back of her neck stand on end. 'And I am relieved that you are not involved with another man, Tamsin, because it means that you are free to become involved with me.'

'Wh...what?' she said, stunned. 'We don't know one another. We only met five minutes ago.'

'But the attraction between us was instant,' Bruno stated coolly, the glint in his eyes daring her to deny it. 'Sexual alchemy at its most potent.'

As if to prove his point, he slid his hand down her back until it rested at the very base of her spine, and then exerted pressure so she was forced into even closer contact with his blatantly aroused body. His action should have appalled her, but to Tamsin's shame all she could think was that their clothes were an unwelcome barrier, and that she longed to feel his warm, naked flesh pressed against hers.

'Lust is such an honest sentiment, don't you think?' he murmured, in his deep, sexy voice that alone had the power to bring her skin out in goosebumps. 'The chemistry that exists between a man and a woman. I want you and you want me—what could be simpler or more honest than that?'

It would be very easy to be swept away by Bruno Di Cesare's sultry charm, Tamsin acknowledged. If she was honest, part of her longed to succumb to his magnetism and follow blindly wherever he led—which, from the sexual heat in his gaze, would, she guessed, be straight to his bed. But some deeply ingrained instinct for self-protection warned her that she would be way out of her depth. She had never met a man like Bruno before. In the two years since her divorce she hadn't even been on a date, and although she could not deny that she was attracted to him, experience had taught her to be cautious.

Fortunately there was a lull in the music, and she stepped firmly out of his arms. Across the room she saw James walking into the adjoining banqueting suite, and she gave Bruno a cool smile. 'I think I'm going to investigate the buffet, *signor*,' she said steadily. 'The sandwiches I bought at the service station on the way down were inedible, and I'm starving. I'm sure you'll have no trouble in finding another dance partner,' she added dryly. She had been aware of numerous pairs of female eyes following Bruno around the dance floor, and knew that the moment she walked away from him there would be a scramble for his attention.

He glanced across the room, following her gaze over to James before his eyes settled once more on her face, and for a split second she thought she glimpsed a look of icy contempt in the dark depths. But then he smiled, and she guessed she must have imagined it. He released her, but remained close by her side as she walked through into the banqueting suite, where a buffet table ran the length of one wall.

'Forgive my impatience, Tamsin,' he apologised huskily, when she frowned at him. 'I'm afraid I've offended you. But my only excuse is that your loveliness takes my breath away.' He handed her a plate and glanced at the wonderful variety of canapés and finger foods displayed in front of them. 'I hope you will allow me to join you?' he begged with exquisite politeness, but his eyes gleamed wickedly when he added dulcetly, 'I suddenly find that I too am starving, *bella.*'

Tamsin's lips twitched. He was an incorrigible flirt who could charm the birds from the trees, but common sense told her that his flattery was all part of a game he was playing. She was reasonably attractive, but there were other, far more beautiful women here tonight, and she could not believe he was seriously interested in her. She helped herself to a couple of blinis topped with cream cheese and smoked salmon, and glanced at him, her pulse-rate quickening when she found his eyes on her. Electricity fizzed between them, shockingly fierce, and she quickly looked away and stared blindly at the food on the table, discovering that her appetite had deserted her.

Bruno Di Cesare was a playboy, she reminded herself as she recalled what she knew of him. She preferred the business section of the newspapers to the gossip columns, but the president of The House of Di Cesare frequently featured in both. She'd read that the company had been created eighty years ago by Antonio Di Cesare, to produce expertly crafted leather goods. Over the years it had diversified to become an iconic fashion house, and had also cornered a worldwide market in top-quality household goods—everything from exquisitely designed sofas and dining tables to the china and glassware that graced the tables of those wealthy enough to afford them. The main outlet for the Di Cesare brand in the UK was Grainger's department store in Knightsbridge, which would explain Bruno's friendship with James Grainger.

Bruno inhabited a different world from hers. He was a billionaire—admired by his peers for his ruthlessness in the boardroom, and by his numerous lovers for his prowess in the bedroom. He was used to having whatever he wanted, whether it involved business or a woman, but if he thought he could simply click his fingers and have her, he was going to be disappointed, Tamsin vowed firmly.

James Grainger was sitting at one of the tables arranged around the room, and once Tamsin had selected her food she started to make her way towards him. But Bruno was instantly at her side, steering her determinedly over to an empty table in a secluded corner. Before she could remonstrate, he took her plate, set it down on the table, and drew out a chair for her to sit down. A waiter materialised with a bottle of champagne in an ice bucket. Bruno filled two glasses, handed her one, then raised his own, his smile revealing a set of perfect teeth that gleamed white against his olive skin. For some reason Tamsin was reminded of a wolf preparing to devour its prey, and a faint prickle of unease feathered down her spine.

'What shall we drink to Tamsin? To us, as we set out on a journey to see where this sexual awareness between us might lead?'

'Certainly not,' Tamsin replied quickly. 'We ought to toast the bride and groom and wish them a long and happy marriage.' Her voice faltered a fraction as she thought of her own failed marriage. Davina and Hugo were so in love that it seemed to radiate from them—but would it last?

Her brief marriage had been a salutary life lesson that had left her heart bruised and her pride in tatters. She had been an impressionable twenty-one-year-old when Neil Harper had swept into her life. She'd fallen in love with the good-looking, ambitious banker, and been overjoyed when he proposed six months later. But the fairy tale had ended a year after their wedding, when he'd left her for a glamorous city trader called Jacqueline.

On her wedding day she had thought that her love for Neil would last a lifetime—and that he loved her with the same intensity, Tamsin remembered sadly. She had believed that her hopes and expectations had been his dreams too, and it had only been afterwards, after he'd moved out on Christmas Eve and told her he was filing for a divorce, that she'd learned he had been sleeping with Jacqueline even before the wedding, and that their affair had continued when he and Tamsin had returned from honeymoon. Her marriage had been a sham from the beginning, she acknowledged bleakly, unaware that Bruno was watching the play of emotions on her face.

'Why the frown, *bella*?' he queried. 'Don't you think Davina and Hugo's marriage will last?'

'Oh, I'm sure it will. I certainly hope so, anyway. I'm sure they really love each other.' Tamsin murmured. 'And that's the most important thing, isn't it?'

The sudden huskiness in her voice aroused Bruno's curiosity. 'Is it? I'm afraid I'm not an expert on love and marriage—having experienced neither,' he drawled. 'But experience has taught me that many women regard getting married as a convenient route to financial security—either within the marriage or after, with a hefty divorce settlement.'

Tamsin put down her spinach tartlet, sure that she would choke if she bit into it. 'How horribly cynical you are. I can't believe any woman would marry for financial security. I'm quite sure Davina didn't marry Hugo for his money—and I married because I was in love with my husband, not because of the size of his bank balance.' She stared at him, wondering what he would think if she revealed that her ex-husband was a wealthy banker. Would he refuse to believe she hadn't married Neil for his money?

Bruno glanced at her speculatively. 'Ah, yes, Annabel mentioned you'd been married. But I understand you are now divorced?'

'Yes,' Tamsin said flatly, lowering her gaze and ignoring his querying look. The reasons why her marriage had ended were still painful, and she had no intention of discussing them with a stranger.

Bruno shrugged laconically. 'And yet you are still optimistic that Davina and Hugo's marriage will be successful. I would have thought that after your own failed attempt at marriage you would see the pitfalls in such an outdated institution. Do you really believe it is possible to remain faithful to one person for a lifetime?'

It was clear that he regarded the idea of love and lifelong fidelity as ridiculous, but Tamsin met his gaze steadily and nodded her head. 'Yes, I do. Despite what happened to me, I think marriage is a wonderful institution. I hope that one day I'll meet a man who I can share my life with. And I won't care if he's rich or poor,' she added fiercely, remembering his outrageous statement that most women married for financial gain.

'An admirable sentiment, *bella,*' Bruno said silkily.

Tamsin sounded convincing, but he was still deeply suspicious of her relationship with James Grainger. Annabel had said that Tamsin had received a generous divorce settlement from her ex-husband, so it was little wonder she was such an enthusiastic supporter of marriage. Miranda Maughn had deliberately targeted his father and used all her feminine wiles to tempt him up the aisle. Had Tamsin decided that marrying and divorcing rich men was a viable career option? He could think of no other reason why she had engineered a friendship with a vulnerable man almost forty years older than her.

For the past ten years James had welcomed him into his home and treated him like a son, Bruno mused. Now it was time he repaid the older man's kindness and saved him from the greedy clutches of a callous gold-digger.

He refilled Tamsin's glass with champagne, and dismissed her small protest with a stunning smile that had the desired effect of making her blush. 'You're not driving, are you?' he queried when she lifted the glass to her lips with fingers that noticeably shook. He frowned as a thought suddenly occurred to him. 'Are you staying here, or at Ditton Hall?'

'Oh, here—James did invite me to stay at the Hall,' Tamsin explained, 'but he has a house full of relatives staying for the weekend, and I thought it would be easier if I booked a room here in the hotel. Where are you staying?'

'I also have a room here.' There was no mistaking the sultry gleam in Bruno's eyes as he added, 'Who knows? Perhaps we'll have breakfast together.'

'I think that's extremely unlikely.' Tamsin strove to sound cool, hoping to hide the fact that she was thoroughly flustered that he anticipated them spending the hours before breakfast together—in his bed. He had a nerve, she thought crossly, but she could not repress the tremor that ran through her at the idea of his olive-toned naked limbs entwined with her own paler body as he made love to her.

Bruno sat back in his chair and studied her speculatively over the rim of his glass. She was blushing again, and he watched in fascination as her creamy skin became tinged with pink. The sophisticated women he usually associated with never blushed—but it was a useful trick, he conceded. With her wide eyes and rosy cheeks Tamsin Stewart looked innocent and unworldly, but he doubted she was either. He dropped his gaze deliberately to her breasts, a cynical smile curving his lips as he noted the provocative peaks of her nipples jutting beneath her dress.

Persuading her that he was a better and richer option than the Earl promised to have its compensations, he decided as he shifted in his seat, attempting to ease the ache in his loins.

'Tell me about yourself,' he invited Tamsin when she pushed her plate away, her food barely touched. 'Do you have a family? Brothers and sisters?'

Tamsin wondered why he had asked, as she seriously doubted he was interested in the boring details of her life, but at least making small talk might help her to ignore the smouldering chemical reaction between them that was in danger of combusting. 'I have two sisters, both happily married to my lovely but not very well-off brothers-in-law,' she told him pointedly. 'And one brother, Daniel, who I work for.'

'Ah, yes—Spectrum Development and Design,' Bruno murmured, and once again Tamsin thought she detected a slight nuance in his voice that puzzled her. 'How is business? I understand the property market in England is struggling at the moment?'

'I really only concentrate on the interior design side of the company, while my brother deals with actually buying and selling the properties, but everything seems to be going well,' she replied with a smile. 'Daniel has just bought a penthouse flat in Chelsea that we intend to renovate and sell, and the profit margins are predicted to be good.'

'He must need a large amount of capital for that kind of venture,' Bruno commented. 'Do you have a sympathetic bank? Or help from private investors?'

'Well, we do borrow money from the bank, of course. Though I'm not really sure about private investors,' Tamsin mumbled, her cheeks turning pink. She had only joined

Spectrum a year ago, after gaining valuable experience at another bigger design company. She was concentrating all her efforts on building up the interior design side, and had little to do with the overall running of things.

Bruno was watching her. His dark, unfathomable gaze made her feel uncomfortable, and she quickly changed the subject. 'How about you—do you have a family?'

'My parents are both dead,' Bruno replied. 'I have one sister, who is a couple of years older than Annabel Grainger.'

His jaw tightened as he remembered Jocasta's unhappiness when his father had married Miranda. His stepmother had torn his family apart, he remembered bitterly, his eyes narrowing when Tamsin put her hand to her throat and stroked the diamonds that sparkled against her skin. Stefano had been besotted by his young wife and had given her many pieces of Bruno's mother's jewellery that should have been passed on to Jocasta. Indeed, Bruno had recently paid his stepmother five times the valued price of a ruby necklace and earrings that his mother had worn on her wedding day. He was sure his father had not given away jewels that had a priceless sentimental value to Miranda, but Stefano had died without leaving a will, so his second wife had inherited everything.

Bruno had not cared about the palatial house in Florence, but he had been determined to reclaim his mother's jewellery. Fortunately Miranda needed money to maintain her lavish lifestyle, and had been willing to sell—at a price. His stepmother's greed sickened him, and as he watched Tamsin lovingly caress the necklace James Grainger had given her the bile in his throat threatened to choke him.

'Is something wrong?' Tamsin asked uncertainly. A moment ago Bruno had been smiling at her, but now his mouth was compressed into a thin line and his eyes were hard and cold. He seemed to be lost in his own world and, once again she felt a prickle of unease run through her.

Her voice seemed to drag him back to the present, and he visibly forced himself to relax. But although he smiled warmly at her, Tamsin shivered.

'Everything is fine, *bella*. Would you like more champagne?'

'No, thank you.' She quickly grabbed her glass before he could refill it. She rarely drank alcohol, and her head felt as though it was spinning after the two glasses she had consumed. She glanced over to where James had been sitting, hoping that he wasn't too tired, but he had gone. When she glanced back she found that Bruno was watching her impassively.

'Shall we return to the ballroom?' he said, standing up and drawing her to her feet.

'Please don't feel that you have to remain with me,' Tamsin said, suddenly desperate to escape him. His potent masculinity disturbed her more than she cared to admit, and she needed time to collect her thoughts and control her body's wayward response to him. 'I'm sure you must want to mingle with the other guests.'

'On the contrary, *cara*, there is only one woman I wish to mingle with,' Bruno assured her throatily as they entered the ballroom, and before she could object he drew her into his arms and brought her body into intimate contact with his.

From then on the evening took on a dreamlike quality, with Bruno holding her close, his eyes blazing with undisguised hunger as they drifted slowly around the room. Several times Tamsin caught sight of James Grainger, but when she attempted to step away from Bruno he tightened his hold around her waist and teasingly informed her that he had claimed her for the rest of the night.

'I'd really like a word with James,' she remonstrated. 'I've hardly spoken to him all evening.'

'I think you should leave him to spend time with Annabel,' Bruno replied, a hard edge to his voice. 'She misses her mother terribly, and now that Davina is moving away she is going to need her father more than ever.'

Tamsin thought that Annabel looked perfectly happy, surrounded by a group of her friends, but Bruno was stroking his hand lightly up and down her spine, and she found it difficult to think of anything but the sensuous glide of his fingers. She knew she should stop this madness and demand that he release her, but her tongue seemed to have tied itself in knots and her body had developed a will of its own. Desire unfurled deep within her like the petals of a flower slowly opening, and instead of pushing him away she relaxed and melted into him, so that her pelvis came into direct contact with his. The solid ridge of his arousal was so shockingly hard that she stumbled, and he tightened his arms around her, bringing her into even closer contact with him, his eyes gleaming mockingly from beneath heavy lids when he noted her flushed face.

'Trust me, you're not the only one to be embarrassed,' he muttered self-derisively. 'We need to get out of here—now, *bella*.'

Without another word he gripped her hand, tugging her after him out onto the wide terrace that ran the length of the ballroom. He drew her into a shadowed recess where a profusion of roses and clematis grew against the wall to form a bower. The night air was cool on Tamsin's heated skin and her head spun. That last glass of champagne had been a bad idea, she thought numbly when Bruno turned her to face him. Yet she wasn't drunk on alcohol, but on the heady feeling that she was a desirable woman. After two years of feeling a failure, the scorching sexual hunger in Bruno's gaze restored a little of the pride that Neil had stripped away.

She stared at him, unaware that the half-hopeful, half-uncertain expression in her eyes and the slight tremor of her lower lip made her impossible for him to resist. He muttered something in Italian as he reached for her and hauled her against the hard wall of his chest. Tamsin made no effort to resist him. She seemed to be rooted to the spot, her heart thumping painfully beneath her ribs as he slowly lowered his head.

His lips were warm and firm, demanding a response she was powerless to deny as he slid one hand to her nape, gently tugging her head back so that she was angled to his satisfaction while his mouth continued a sensual assault that left her trembling. He stroked his tongue persuasively against the tremulous line of her lips, insisting she allow him access, until with a little gasp she capitulated and opened her mouth, so that he could thrust deep into her moist inner warmth.

Heat surged through her veins and her breasts felt heavy and ultra-sensitive as the swollen peaks of her nipples jutted to attention, straining against the silky material of her dress. She lost all notion of time and place; she was only aware of the warmth of his skin as she lifted her fingers to trace his jaw, the musky scent of his cologne that swamped her senses. She wanted the kiss to last for ever—wanted him to continue his wicked exploration with his tongue—and needed with an almost desperate urgency to feel his hands on her body. When she leaned into him he curved his fingers possessively around one breast and she moaned softly, but seconds later he drew back and stared down into her desire-darkened eyes, breathing raggedly.

'*Dio bella*, you are a sorceress,' he rasped. He sounded stunned, almost angry, and he gripped her shoulders as if he wanted to thrust her from him.

'Bruno?' Tamsin whispered his name fearfully, wondering why he suddenly looked so furious—wondering if she had done something wrong.

She wasn't very good at this, she acknowledged bleakly. Neil's repeated infidelity throughout their marriage was proof that she did not know how to please a man. Mortified, she tried to jerk away from him, but Bruno tightened his hold and slammed her hard up against him, so that she could feel the erratic thud of his heart beneath her palm.

'This is madness,' he growled in a raw tone. He seemed to be waging a battle with himself, and he was breathing hard as he stared at her upturned face before he lowered his head once more. Their mouths met, fusing with a wildfire passion that was fierce and hot and shockingly primitive. His tongue forced entry between her lips and proceeded to explore her with a thoroughness that left her trembling, her limbs so weak that she clung to his shoulders and anchored her fingers in the silky dark hair at his nape.

Nothing had prepared her for the bolt of white-hot need that ripped through her, scalding her flesh and tossing her doubts and inhibitions aside as if they were flotsam on the tide. She was burning up in the blazing heat of his passion. At last Bruno eased the pressure of his mouth a fraction, and the kiss became a long, unhurried tasting that drugged her senses and stoked her desire, so that her breasts felt full and heavy and ached for his touch.

'My room or yours?' he demanded, barely lifting his mouth from hers.

His harsh, grating voice splintered the soft night air and shattered the spell he had woven around her. Reality reared its unwelcome head, and she stared at him dazedly.

'I...'

'I have to have you, *bella*—tonight.' He had never known such fierce hunger for a woman, and such was his desperation to possess her that he was tempted to carry her into the shadowed grounds and make love to her on the grass.

Somewhere in the recesses of his mind Bruno knew that he had an ulterior motive for persuading Tamsin into his bed. His intention was to persuade her to transfer her attention from James to him—secure in the knowledge that, whilst James might be tempted to fall in love with her, he, Bruno, never would.

But right now nothing seemed more important than assuaging the throbbing ache that consumed him.

'The other guests are starting to leave. No one will notice if we slip away to my suite,' he muttered hoarsely, staring at Tamsin in disbelief when she shook her head and stepped away from him.

'I can't,' she whispered. 'I'm sorry.'

'*Madre de Dio!* Tamsin—'

Bruno's furious voice followed Tamsin as she flew along the terrace and through the doors to the ballroom, her heart beating so hard she was sure it would burst out of her chest.

He was right. Many of the guests were leaving, and only a few couples remained on the dance floor. They would not have been missed. If she had said yes to Bruno's husky request they would already be in his room, and he would be kissing her with the same hungry passion that had overwhelmed them both a few moments ago.

Why hadn't she agreed to go with him? she asked herself angrily. Why hadn't she for once in her life followed the dictates of her body rather than her brain? Bruno had aroused her to such a fever-pitch of desire that every muscle seemed to be screaming with sexual frustration. But the sound of his voice, his confident assumption that she would fall into his bed as readily as she had responded to his kisses, had halted her wanton response to him.

After her disastrous marriage her self-confidence was at rock-bottom, she acknowledged miserably, hurrying out of the ballroom and across the hotel foyer. She had been flattered by Bruno's attention and shocked by the feelings he aroused in her. But she was well aware of his reputation as a womaniser. He was a billionaire playboy who was used to women throwing themselves at him, and her pride refused to allow her to be just another notch on his bedpost.

'Tamsin, my dear, is everything all right?' James Grainger emerged from the hotel lounge and Tamsin skidded to a halt in front of him. 'You look rather flushed.'

'Oh…it was hot in the ballroom, and I think I've had a little too much champagne,' she said quickly, casting a nervous glance over her shoulder to see if Bruno had followed her. 'I'm going up to my room now, James—' She broke off and caught hold of his arm as he swayed unsteadily. 'You don't look at all well.'

'I'm just tired. It's been a long and emotional day—but a successful one, I think,' James murmured, giving her a weary smile. 'Davina and Hugo are on their way to the airport, and Annabel is still in the bar with her friends. But I'm going back to the Hall now. Hargreaves is waiting out front with the car.'

'Let me help you.' Without waiting for James to reply, Tamsin tightened her hold on his arm and urged him to lean on her as they walked slowly across the foyer. At the top of the steps he stumbled, and she was glad when his chauffeur hurried to offer his assistance. 'I'll come and see you tomorrow,' she promised gently, and James nodded.

'I'd like that. I want to discuss ideas for the house.' He hesitated, and then added in a voice tinged with embarrassment, 'Tamsin, I couldn't help but notice that you seemed rather taken with Bruno tonight. And there's nothing at all wrong with that,' he continued swiftly, when she blushed scarlet. 'I've known Bruno for years, and he is a fine, honourable man—but a man, nevertheless, who has a deserved reputation as a playboy. Just be careful, hmm?' he said softly as he climbed into the car. 'Goodnight, my dear.'

Bruno walked to the end of the terrace, breathing hard as he sought to bring his body under control. He could think of several words to describe Tamsin Stewart, and none of them pleasant, he thought savagely. Her passionate response to him had stoked his hunger until it was a raging furnace, and her cool rejection had left him in agony. Why had she stopped? Did she take pleasure in teasing men and taking them to the edge? Or had there been another reason why she had walked away from him?

And then, illuminated in the light spilling from the hotel entrance, he saw her with James Grainger—saw James get into his car and realised that Tamsin was about to join him. So that was her game. That was the reason she had refused to go to his room—she was going back to Ditton Hall with James.

With a furious curse Bruno swung round and strode back along the terrace, his body rigid with anger as he heard the car pull away. Davina's wedding must have been an emotive day for James, and he was clearly missing his dead wife, he thought grimly. Tamsin had obviously decided that this was a perfect time to make a move on the Earl—and there wasn't a damn thing he could do to stop her.

CHAPTER THREE

THE following morning Bruno's temper was still simmering dangerously, and his body was aching with the sexual frustration that had kept him awake until the early hours. Failure and rejection were not words he was familiar with, but last night he had experienced both—and he was incensed. Not only had he failed to keep Tamsin away from James Grainger, but she had responded to him with a passion that he had believed matched his own and then turned it off as easily as flicking a light switch, leaving him racked with unfulfilled desire.

His plan to rescue the Earl from her greedy clutches by enticing her into his bed was not proving as easy as he had expected. He was furious that he had not prevented her from accompanying James back to Ditton Hall—and the idea that she might even have spent the night in James's bed made him want to hit something.

Breathing hard, he strode into the dining room—and halted abruptly at the sight of Tamsin sitting alone at a table overlooking the hotel gardens.

In a pink tee shirt and white jeans, with her blonde hair falling around her shoulders like a curtain of silk, she looked young and innocent and at the same time incredibly sexy. The hungry beast that had clawed in Bruno's gut all night stirred

into life once more, and his body reacted with irritating pre-
dictability as he walked towards her.

'*Buongiorno*. May I join you?'

Tamsin had been watching a sparrow hopping along the
terrace, and the sound of Bruno's deep, sexy drawl made her
heart plummet. She turned her head and eyed him warily,
sure that he must be furious with her for the way she had run
from him last night.

'Yes, of course,' she murmured, wondering why he had
bothered to ask when he had already sat down at her table. She
didn't know what to say to him, and her face burned as she
recalled in stark detail the passionate kisses they had exchanged
on the moonlit terrace. At the time it had seemed like a dream,
but now it was more like a nightmare—especially when she remembered how fervently she had responded to him.

She wondered if he was going to demand to know why she
had led him on and then fled. She had behaved appallingly,
she thought miserably, but he did not look angry, and when
his beautiful mouth curved into a slow smile her heart-rate
quickened. Last night he had looked stunning in a formal suit,
but this morning—in jeans and a cream shirt open at the throat
to reveal a glimpse of dark chest hair—he was raw, masculine perfection, and she could not take her eyes from him.

'Did you sleep well, Tamsin?' he queried, transferring his
smile briefly to the flustered-looking waitress who was
pouring his coffee.

He seemed to have a devastating effect on all women,
Tamsin noted sourly when the girl knocked over the milk jug
and apologised profusely as she mopped up the mess.

'Yes, thank you,'

Bruno seemed unconvinced by her reply. 'Your room here
at the hotel is comfortable?' he persisted.

'Yes—it's a bit small, but it's fine.' Perhaps he was hoping to taunt her that she would have been more comfortable sharing his room, not to mention his bed? she thought darkly. She met his gaze and smiled sweetly. 'How about you—did you have a good night?'

'Unfortunately not. I spent a very restless night. But we both know the reason for that, don't we, *bella*?' he said dulcetly, his dark eyes glinting with amusement when she blushed. 'Sexual frustration is not a comfortable bedmate, I find.'

She was surprised that he was teasing her with no sign of anger, and her feeling of guilt doubled. 'I'm sorry about last night. I realise I gave you the impression that I…that I was…'

'That you shared my urgent need to make love?' Bruno suggested, and the way his voice caressed the words 'make love' sent a quiver down Tamsin's spine. 'It is a woman's prerogative to change her mind,' he said lightly, reaching across the table and tilting her chin with one lean, tanned finger when she refused to look at him. 'Patience is not one of my finer virtues. I rushed you, but I understand that you did not feel ready to explore this fiery attraction that burns between us,' he murmured softly.

Tamsin stared at him wordlessly, fascinated by the specks of gold in his dark eyes. Tiger's eyes, she thought, as she dropped her gaze to his mouth and remembered how good it had felt when he had kissed her. She wished he would do it again, and gasped when he traced his thumb over her lower lip in a sensuous caress. She wondered if he knew how badly she wanted him to replace his thumb with his mouth… The sultry gleam in his eyes warned that he did, and it took all her will-power to sit back in her seat.

'I suppose you will be going back to Italy soon?' she said breathlessly. He would return to his billionaire lifestyle and she would never see him again, she accepted, wondering why she felt so ridiculously disappointed when he nodded.

'And now that the wedding is over, I assume you will return to London?'

'Yes, but not immediately. My sister lives just north of here, and I'm going to visit her. But this part of Kent is so beautiful, and I want to visit Hever Castle—I don't know if you've ever been, but the Italian Garden is stunning. And I promised James I'd go to Ditton Hall and discuss his plans for the house.'

'Don't you think he'll be busy?' Bruno demanded shortly. 'I understand several of his relatives are staying at the Hall.'

'Oh, they're leaving today, and Annabel is going to stay with friends in Cornwall,' Tamsin explained cheerfully. 'James will be on his own, and I thought he might like some company.'

Bruno stiffened as anger surged through him. It seemed that Tamsin had not spent the previous night with James Grainger after all, but she was still trying to worm her way into his life. He forced himself to smile, satisfied to see the soft flush of colour that stained her cheeks. She might have set her sights on the wealthy Earl, but she was not as immune to *him* as she would like him to believe.

'I do not know this part of England well, but it is, as you say, very beautiful, and I am intrigued by this Italian Garden. Let's do a deal, Tamsin,' he suggested in his rich, sensuous voice. 'You will show me the castle, and in return I will take you to dinner tonight.'

'But I thought you had to return to Italy?' Tamsin faltered, desperately trying to dampen her excitement at the idea of spending the day with him. After her behaviour last night, she was amazed that he wanted to have anything more to do with her, but his dark eyes were warm and he seemed genuinely eager for her company.

'That was my intention,' he agreed, 'but something has happened to cause me to change my plans—or perhaps I should say someone.'

'I see.' Tamsin strove to sound cool and failed abysmally. The sexual tension that had simmered since he had joined her at the table now blazed between them, and Bruno stared intently into her eyes, as if defying her to deny that she wanted to be with him. He was an inveterate womanizer, and she must be out of her mind to even consider spending five minutes with him, Tamsin thought ruefully. But he was also the most gorgeous man she had ever met, and she couldn't resist him. 'Well, in that case,' she said, 'I'd love to be your guide.'

Hours later, Tamsin flopped onto her bed and stared up at the ceiling, a soft smile on her lips. Bruno filled her mind to the exclusion of anything else, and when she closed her eyes she could picture every detail of his sculpted handsome face. Last night she had been sure of her decision not to sleep with a man she did not know. But after spending all day in his company her certainty and resolve were wavering.

It had been a magical day. Hever Castle, once the home of Anne Boleyn, was a romantic idyll surrounded by a wide moat and magnificent gardens. Bruno had been on a charm offensive from the moment he had assisted her into his low-slung sports car—although he had terrified the life out of her when he had raced along the narrow, winding country lanes at breakneck speed.

'Relax, *bella,* I'm a good driver,' he'd told her with his irrepressible arrogance, grinning when she clutched the edge of her seat and closed her eyes.

She had no doubt that he was right. He brimmed with self-confidence, and she guessed that he excelled at everything he did. Failure wasn't an option as far as Bruno Di Cesare was concerned. He was a man who always got what he wanted—she just wondered what exactly he wanted from her.

But from the moment he'd tugged her into his arms in a

secluded corner of the rose garden and kissed her she'd forgotten everything but her desire to be with him. He was a witty and amusing companion, fiercely intelligent, and so utterly charismatic that she gradually forgot her natural reserve and chatted to him unselfconsciously.

She was in serious danger of losing her head, not to mention her heart she acknowledged ruefully as she dragged her mind back to the present. She had showered and blowdried her hair, and had wasted the last twenty minutes dithering over her make-up. Fortunately she had packed her faithful little black dress, and teamed with high-heeled sandals it looked elegant and sexy—so at least she had something to wear. The problem of Bruno, and the realisation that she was falling for him, was not so simple to resolve.

She was not in his league, she reminded herself as she checked her reflection in the mirror. He was a billionaire Italian playboy who had absolutely no intention of settling down. Even if by some miracle he decided that he wanted a relationship with her, she did not see how it would be possible when he spent most of his time in Italy, or travelling around the world on various business ventures. She craved the security of a loving relationship, and he was determined to retain his freedom. The idea was hopeless—and yet being with him felt so right. She felt as though she was drawn to him by an invisible thread, that she had known him for ever. But that was ridiculous, she told herself firmly. Four years ago she had believed that Neil was the right man for her, but instead he had broken her heart and severely damaged her self-confidence.

She had arranged to meet Bruno in the bar at seven o'clock, and after glancing at the clock she checked her make-up once more, and on impulse took the diamond necklace that James had given her from its box. She fastened it around her neck. It lifted her dress from elegant to stunning—and, after all, she would not have many opportunities to wear such expensive jewellery.

Bruno was waiting for her when she entered the bar, tall, dark and impossibly handsome, in a dark suit and white silk shirt. He was standing by the open French windows, staring out at the gardens, but swung round as she approached him, an indefinable expression on his face when he first saw her. Something blazed in his eyes—male appreciation mixed with another curious emotion that caused Tamsin to hesitate several feet from him. It was the same look she thought she had glimpsed the previous night, a look of contempt and disgust that caused a trickle of ice to slither down her spine. His gaze seemed to be locked on the diamonds at her throat—but then he smiled and moved towards her, and she told herself that his unsettling expression had been a trick of the light.

'Tamsin, *bella*, you look gorgeous.' In two lithe strides he was at her side, but instead of taking her hand and lifting it to his lips, as he had greeted her before, he slid his arm around her shoulders, lowered his head and claimed her mouth.

Tamsin gasped at the first butterfly-soft brush of his mouth on hers, and he took advantage of her parted lips, his tongue delving between them as he deepened the kiss in a sensual exploration that left her shaken and longing for more.

All day he had been so charming and attentive that he had made her feel like a princess, and now, when he finally lifted his mouth and stared deeply into her eyes, she felt as though she had fallen into the pages of a fairytale and she never wanted to leave.

'I've booked a table at a French restaurant in the village. It's not far to walk, or would you prefer to go by car?' he murmured, glancing at her high heels.

'Oh, we'll walk,' Tamsin replied quickly, shuddering at the thought of travelling anywhere by car with him again.

'Coward.' He grinned.

His eyes crinkled at the corners when he smiled and Tamsin's insides melted. He was so beautiful, she thought dazedly. So funny, sexy, clever— He was everything she looked for in a man, and it was no good reminding herself that she might never see him again after tonight, no good telling herself that it was impossible to fall in love with a man she'd only known for twenty-four hours. Whatever this feeling was—lust, love, she couldn't put a name to it—she just knew that she had never felt this way before. Her body ached for his touch, and she couldn't fight the sexual attraction that shimmered between them.

She knew from the hunger blazing in Bruno's eyes that he wanted her, and she had half expected him to have arranged for them to dine in the privacy of his suite—but it seemed that he was not going to try and bulldoze her into anything, and that made her respect him even more.

The sound of her mobile phone made her start, and she hastily fumbled in her purse to switch it off. 'Oh, it's James,' she said, reading the caller display. 'Do you mind if I answer it?'

'Of course not,' Bruno replied smoothly, but his smile faded the moment Tamsin stepped out onto the terrace to take the call. He had ensured that there had been no time for her to visit Ditton Hall all day, and he intended to keep her mind focused exclusively on him tonight, but it infuriated him that he could not prevent her from having any contact with the Earl.

Tamsin had perfected flirting to an art form, he thought grimly as he watched her laughing and talking animatedly into her mobile. To his intense annoyance he had enjoyed the day with her far more than he had expected. Much to his surprise, she had been an intelligent and interesting companion, and it had struck him halfway through the day that if circumstances had been different his pursuit of her would have been genuine.

But circumstances were *not* different, and beneath her façade of unworldly innocence Tamsin Stewart was a manipulative woman, playing on James's emotional vulnerability. She had to be stopped—and he intended that her undisguised sexual awareness of him would be her downfall.

The restaurant Bruno had chosen was small and intimate, with stone floors and a low-beamed ceiling that added to its rustic charm, but the food was French cuisine at its very best— each course an exquisite temptation that was out of this world.

'Thank you for a wonderful evening,' Tamsin said quietly when they strolled back through the village to the hotel later that night, her hand firmly clasped in his. The long days of mid June meant that dusk was only just falling, and in the soft, fading light Bruno's eyes gleamed with an unspoken invitation that made her heart skip a beat.

'My pleasure, *bella*,' he murmured in his rich velvet voice that caressed her senses. 'Would you like to go back to the bar for a nightcap—or come up to my suite?' He saw the flare of uncertainty mixed with excitement in her eyes, and was confident that she would go with him. All his life he had been able to charm women with the minimum of effort on his part, and Tamsin had proved no exception. She hadn't taken her eyes off him throughout dinner, and he knew from the tremor that shook her body now that she was close to capitulating. To tempt her further, he dipped his head and captured her mouth, heat coursing through his veins when he felt her soft, moist lips part tentatively beneath his as she responded to the kiss with an intensity that inflamed his hunger. It would be no hardship taking her to his bed, he thought caustically. Rarely had duty been so pleasurable.

When Bruno finally broke the kiss, Tamsin swayed slightly, her heart beating so fast that she was sure he must feel it thudding against his chest. She barely knew him, the sensible voice in her head reminded her. But her heart and her body had formed an alliance and did not want to listen. She did not speak—couldn't, because her throat seemed to have closed up—but his gentle smile told her that he understood, and wordlessly he clasped her hand once more and led her into the hotel.

He kissed her again in the lift, a slow, drugging kiss that inflamed her senses, and once they had made the short journey along the corridor, and he had opened the door to his suite, she followed him inside and went willingly into his arms.

She was under no illusion that he was offering anything more than sex, but she couldn't resist him. She believed in love and long-term relationships, and he wanted neither, but something about this man urged her to dismiss her principles and for the first time in her life follow the yearnings of her body.

'Can I get you a drink?'

The rough edge of barely contained sexual hunger in Bruno's tone made Tamsin shiver, but where last night the sound of his voice had brought her crashing back to reality, now it barely impinged on the sensual haze that cocooned her. She did not want to think; it was easier not to. But something that felt this right could surely not be wrong? she thought fiercely. Silently she shook her head, watching him, waiting, and with a low groan he fastened his mouth on hers and initiated a slow, sensual tasting that stirred emotions in her she'd believed were long buried.

Her eyelashes drifted down and she focused on the feel of his warm, firm lips easing hers apart, and the determined thrust of his tongue as he suddenly took the kiss to another level that was flagrantly erotic. It was good—so good that she murmured a protest when he eased the pressure a fraction. 'Don't stop.'

Was that throaty, seductive whisper really her voice? She

was startled to see streaks of dull colour wing along his cheek-bones, and felt a quiver of feminine triumph when his eyes blazed with unconcealed hunger.

'I have no intention of stopping, *cara*,' he growled against her throat as he swung her into his arms and strode towards the bedroom.

Tamsin gasped and clung to him, but somehow her fingers became entangled with his shirt buttons. She freed them one by one to push the material aside and reveal his broad, muscular chest—gleaming bronze in the lamplight, and overlaid with a covering of wiry black hairs that felt abrasive against her palms.

Bruno set her on her feet and, without lifting his mouth from hers, found the zip of her dress with unerring fingers and drew it down her spine. Still kissing her, he slipped the material over her shoulders and groaned his approval when he revealed her breasts, barely concealed by her black lacy bra. Her dress bunched around her waist and he released her stinging, swollen lips so that he could concentrate on un-dressing her, tugging the skirt over her hips until the dress pooled at her feet and she stood before him in her bra and a tiny black lace thong—and the diamond necklace that had been a gift from James Grainger.

'Let's get rid of this, shall we?' he said, sliding his hands beneath her hair to undo the clasp before placing the necklace on the bedside table. 'I'm sure you don't want to risk damaging such a valuable trinket,' he remarked silkily, his heavy lids hiding the flare of distain in his dark eyes.

Bruno's olive-gold skin seemed to be stretched tight over his prominent cheekbones, giving him a predatory look that filled Tamsin with a mixture of excitement and trepidation. She couldn't quite believe she was here, in his bedroom, about to join him on a very big bed. The thought that he was going to touch her, caress her, caused her to shiver, and each of her nerve-endings seemed to be acutely sensitive as she waited to feel his hands on her skin.

There was still a small part of her brain that insisted she had taken leave of her senses—and perhaps tomorrow she would regret the moment of madness that had seen her go willingly into his arms. But right now all she could think of was the dull, throbbing ache that started low in her pelvis and radiated out, so that every inch of her body seemed to be clamouring for him to possess her. She had never felt a need like this before. Her sex-life with Neil had been good—or at least she'd believed it had. He had obviously had other ideas. But if she was honest she had enjoyed the cuddling afterwards and the feeling of security as much as the act itself. She didn't want to feel safe or secure with Bruno. She wanted, she realised with a jolt of shock, him to throw her on the bed, spread her legs, and take her with all the primitive hunger she could sense he was struggling to control.

'You are exquisite,' Bruno told her raggedly, and her breath hitched in her throat when he unfastened her bra and tossed it aside, before cupping her breasts in his big, warm palms, rubbing his thumb-pads across her nipples so that they hardened into tight peaks that begged for the possession of his mouth.

Bruno felt a surge of satisfaction at her muffled gasp when he trailed his lips down over the creamy swell of her breast and stroked his tongue back and forth over her nipple. Oh, yes, she liked that—liked it so much that she arched her back so that her dusky pink crests pushed forward provocatively. He moved from one breast to the other, laving each peak in turn until her legs buckled and she clung to him for support.

He could feel her trembling when he hauled her up hard against his thighs and she felt the unmistakable ridge of his erection nudge impatiently between her legs. His plan for a long, unhurried exploration of her body would have to be shelved. His reasons for seducing her suddenly seemed unimportant compared to the hunger that consumed him. He wanted her *now,* with an urgency that shook him as it demolished his self-control. He liked to be in control, always, but he was so turned on that if he didn't act fast he seriously doubted they would even make it onto the bed.

With a muttered oath he lifted her and deposited her on the plush bedspread. There was no time to even pull back the sheets. He needed to be inside her *now,* to bury his shaft deep and feel her muscles close around him. Jaw rigid with tension, he stripped out of his clothes and watched her pupils dilate as he stepped out of his boxers and revealed the full length of his throbbing penis. He glimpsed her faint apprehension and forced himself to slow the pace, exerting an iron will over his eager, hungry body as he stretched out on the bed beside her and leaned over to take her mouth in a deep, sensual caress.

Tamsin kissed him back, her panic receding when she realised that Bruno was in no hurry, and intended to arouse her fully before he expected her to accommodate the awesome length of his manhood, which had sent the breath rushing from her lungs when she'd first seen him naked. His hands were stroking her breasts again, rolling her nipples between his thumb and forefinger until the pleasure was unbearable, and she twisted her hips restlessly, needing him to assuage the ache that was dominating her mind and body.

She felt him tug her lacy thong down her legs before he parted her thighs with a firm intent that increased her excitement. There was no going back now. His fingers were already threading through the triangle of blonde curls and stroking insistently up and down, before pushing gently between her velvet folds to find the slick, wet heat that told him she was ready for him.

Caught up in the swirling mist of sexual anticipation, Tamsin barely registered the noise at first. But it sounded again—louder, infiltrating her mind—until she realised that someone was knocking on the door of Bruno's suite.

'Bruno.' With an effort she tore her mouth from his and pushed against his shoulders. For a few seconds he seemed determined to ignore the noise, and when she denied him her mouth he moved lower, trailing his lips down her throat to the hollow between her breasts.

'It's nothing *bella*. Probably just Room Service or something,' he muttered. 'Forget it and concentrate on me,' he demanded, with a flash of the supreme arrogance that was so much a part of him.

But the knocking sounded again, and with a savage curse he rolled away from her and reached for his trousers. 'Stay there and don't move. I'll be two seconds,' he promised, his eyes blazing as he stared down at her naked body stretched out on the bed.

He disappeared into the sitting room, and seconds later she heard him open the door of his suite. The muffled sound of voices was barely audible in the bedroom, but the interruption had brought with it doubt and uncertainty—and given Tamsin crucial time to think while her heated flesh quickly cooled.

What was she doing? Shivering, she sat up and stared into the dressing table mirror. The reflection showed a woman she did not recognize—a temptress with dishevelled blonde hair falling around her shoulders and cherry-stained, swollen lips. The woman's eyes were glazed and heavy-lidded, but desire was rapidly draining, and now the eyes that stared back at her were wide and troubled.

This woman wasn't *her*, Tamsin thought, shock jolting through her. What had happened to her deeply held belief that sex and love were inextricably linked? Or her vow that she would only give her body to the man she loved? She could not love a man she barely knew. And even though she felt drawn to Bruno in a way she did not understand, that was not love—it was lust.

He was going to hate her, she acknowledged despairingly as she scrambled off the bed and into her clothes. This morning he had seemed to understand her reasons for rejecting him the previous night, but this was so much worse. Only minutes ago she had matched his passion touch for touch, kiss for kiss, and he fully expected to come back to bed and find her ready and eager for his full possession. But she couldn't do it. She didn't love him, and he certainly didn't love her, and although her body longed for him to possess her, she knew in her heart that a few moments of pleasure were not worth the sacrifice of her self-respect.

The voices from the sitting room had faded; presumably whoever had been knocking on Bruno's door had gone, so why hadn't he come back to the bedroom? Perhaps he had decided to fix himself a drink? There was no way she could avoid him, Tamsin acknowledged, her heart lurching at the thought of his understandable fury when she told him she had changed her mind for the second time.

Taking a deep breath, she opened the door and stepped into the sitting room. And stopped dead as her stunned gaze swung from Bruno to James Grainger.

CHAPTER FOUR

'TAMSIN!'

James seemed as shocked by Tamsin's appearance as she was to see him sitting comfortably on the sofa, leafing through a sheaf of documents.

'Hello, James.' She forced the reply, although embarrassment seemed to have robbed her of her voice.

But if she felt embarrassed, James clearly felt ten times worse. His eyes skittered away from her and the view of Bruno's bedroom, and the rumpled bed beyond the door, and he jumped to his feet, the back of his neck brick-red as he bent to collect his papers.

'Right, of course—bad timing, obviously,' he mumbled in his cultured aristocratic accent. 'My apologies to both of you. Bruno, you should have said something when I arrived. I know we arranged to meet tonight, but I quite understand that...other things—' he stared down at the floor, as if wishing a hole would appear at his feet '—take precedence.'

'The fault is entirely mine,' Bruno replied smoothly, not glancing in Tamsin's direction. 'Tamsin and I had dinner together tonight and—well...' He shrugged his shoulders laconically and smiled at James, seemingly unabashed. 'One thing led to another, and I completely forgot we'd arranged to meet. Perhaps we can reschedule for tomorrow?'

'Absolutely.' James practically sprinted over to the door. 'I'll wait to hear from you, Bruno. Goodnight, Tamsin,' he called in a strangled voice over his shoulder, before he shot into the corridor and Bruno closed the door after him.

In the minutes that followed James's abrupt departure Tamsin did not know where to look—although anywhere but at Bruno seemed good. It was ridiculous to feel so embarrassed, she told herself sternly. But only last night James had gently warned her that Bruno was a notorious womanizer, and instead of heeding that warning she had acted completely out of character and been prepared to sleep with him barely twenty-four hours after she'd met him. If James had not interrupted them she would have made love with Bruno—would probably *still* be making love with him, she acknowledged. A tremor ran through her when she looked at him, and her body reacted instantly to the fierce tug of sexual awareness that still held her in its grip.

'Don't look so stricken, *bella*,' Bruno drawled as he strolled across the room towards her.

Something in his voice sent a prickle of unease through her, and she stared at him, shocked by his harsh expression.

'Who knows? If you please me, I might buy you an even more expensive necklace than the one James gave you.'

'I don't understand.' Tamsin shivered. How could she ever have thought his eyes warm? They were as black as midnight, cold and pitiless, and the contempt in their depths was definitely not a figment of her imagination. 'What has my necklace got to do with anything?' She shook her head slowly, trying to collate the thoughts swirling in her brain. 'You *knew* James would come to your suite tonight—you'd arranged a meeting with him.' She paused, trying to understand the message that was hovering at the edge of her mind. 'But then—in the heat of the moment you forgot he was coming?'

Bruno's mouth curved into a parody of a smile. 'I didn't forget,' he told her coolly.

Although that was not quite true, he acknowledged silently. His hunger for Tamsin had been so intense that by the time he had laid her naked body on his bed his only aim had been to assuage his desperate need to possess her. It hadn't been until James had knocked on the door that he had remembered his reason for inviting her to his room, and for a few moments he'd still wanted to forget everything but the exquisite feel of her skin beneath his fingertips, and the sweet, damp heat between her legs that told him she was ready for him.

'But why did you ask James to come tonight when you'd already invited me to dinner?' Tamsin persisted in a shaken voice.

Her eyes were huge in her pale face, but the vulnerable, little-girl-lost-look was all part of her act, Bruno told himself darkly.

'It's quite simple,' he said in a bored tone, crossing to the bar and sloshing a liberal amount of whisky into a glass. 'Do you want a drink?'

'No!'

He shrugged and tipped half the contents of the glass down his throat. 'I set you up, *bella*. I invited you to my room with the deliberate intention of seducing you, knowing that at some point James would turn up and find us together.' He moved towards her and trailed his forefinger down to the vee between her breasts. The delicate floral fragrance of her skin teased his senses, and he realised that his heart was slamming painfully in his chest. 'I have to say you made it very easy for me,' he taunted softly.

'I see.' Something was very wrong. Nausea rolled over Tamsin, and she jerked away from him as if his touch defiled her. 'Do you want to tell me why you would do such a thing?'

'I wanted to end your involvement with James,' Bruno stated bluntly. 'He may be temporarily blinded by your not inconsiderable charms and your pseudo-sympathy, but he's a shy, conservative man, and now that he thinks we're sleeping together he'll forget any romantic ideas he may have had about you.'

'What romantic ideas?' Tamsin demanded in a stunned voice. 'James and I are friends. He doesn't see me in…that way.' She shook her head in angry disbelief as Bruno's words slowly made sense. 'He's the same age as my father, and he's still grieving for his dead wife.'

'Yes—James is lonely and unhappy. What an ideal time for an attractive, *sympathetic* young woman to engineer a relationship with him,' Bruno drawled softly.

'I don't believe this. What sort of a relationship do you think I hoped to *engineer* with him?'

'I think you saw the benefits that could come from having an affair with a rich, older man,' Bruno said, in a hard, cold voice that sounded the death knell to the stupid fantasies she had woven in her head throughout the day. 'You saw that James craves companionship. His daughters are growing up and moving away, and soon he will be alone in his great ancestral home. Perhaps you even saw yourself as the next Lady Grainger,' he continued in that same icy tone. 'And if you grew bored with being tied to a man forty years older than you, a divorce could be extremely profitable.'

He gave a harsh laugh, remembering his stepmother's unforgivable treatment of his father once she had secured his ring on her finger. Miranda was a greedy, conniving cow, and he was certain that Tamsin had been cast from the same mould. 'Meeting a lonely widower who also happens to be a hugely wealthy landowner must have been like finding gold at the end of the rainbow,' he murmured, his lip curling contemptuously.

For a moment the room actually swayed beneath Tamsin's feet, and she gripped the doorframe to steady herself. 'I don't believe this,' she said again, her voice shaking with emotion. 'My relationship—my *friendship* with James is completely innocent. He doesn't have romantic feelings for me, and I have certainly never tried to encourage anything like that.'

'So why does he regularly travel to London to see you? He told Annabel his visits are business-related, but he stepped down from his position as chief executive at the Grainger's store when Lorna first became ill. He has no reason to make trips to the city every Friday—apart from to meet you for lunch. Was it during one of those meetings that you persuaded him to buy you the diamond necklace?' he queried scathingly.

'I didn't persuade him to buy me anything.' Tamsin defended herself furiously, but she could not deny that she *did* meet James on Fridays, and she crossed her arms defensively in front of her.

On one occasion they'd had lunch at a restaurant near to the hospital and for once had had quite a bit to drink—Dutch courage, James had said a shade grimly—before his appointment with the consultant who'd had the results of his tests. But once his cancer had been confirmed he had started an immediate course of chemotherapy that made him feel too sick to eat.

For a few seconds she contemplated telling Bruno the real reason for James's visits to London. Bruno was his friend. Would it be wrong to tell him the truth—as long as he swore to keep the news from Davina and Annabel? But it was not her secret to tell. James was adamant that he did not want anyone to know about his illness—perhaps because he wanted to come to terms with it privately. She had promised James she would say nothing, and she could not betray his trust.

Bruno was watching her intently. 'Nothing to say, *bella*?' he queried silkily.

'My meetings with James are none of your business,' she muttered, feeling a pain like a knife being inserted between her ribs when Bruno's mouth curled in disgust. 'But obviously there were occasions when James wanted to discuss Davina and Hugo's flat.'

'Annabel said the flat was finished weeks ago.'

Annabel said... Suddenly a lot of things made sense—in a twisted sort of way, Tamsin thought numbly. James's younger daughter was a spoilt and self-obsessed young woman, but surely she couldn't really believe that her father was involved with his interior designer?

'What concerns me more,' Bruno continued, 'is that James has invested a considerable amount of money in Spectrum Development and Design—against the advice of his accountant. I understand that your brother's company was close to bankruptcy, and I assume you persuaded James to bail him out. It doesn't sound like the wise sort of business decision I'd expect from James,' Bruno added harshly.

His own father had been revered for his sharp business brain, but his obsession with Miranda had made him careless, and he had been blind to the sharks circling ever closer until the House of Di Cesare had been on the verge of collapse. He would not allow James to follow the same destructive path.

Tamsin was staring at him with wide, stunned eyes. 'What money?' she demanded shakily. 'I don't know about any investment, and I've certainly never asked James to put money into Spectrum. The company *isn't* facing bankruptcy. Daniel would have told me,' she said desperately, when Bruno gave her a scathing look.

'Two months ago the bank was ready to retract its support unless Spectrum repaid its debts,' Bruno said coldly. 'Curiously enough, the figure owed matched the amount of James's investment.'

'But I didn't know anything about it—' Tamsin broke off, her mind whirling. Spectrum was Daniel's company, and she was simply one of his employees. But he was also her brother—he wouldn't have kept something as serious as the threat of bankruptcy from her, would he? she wondered sickly. And how had James become involved?

She stared at Bruno and saw the contempt etched onto his hard features. It was clear that he really believed she was money-hungry and had latched onto James, and the realisation made her want to crawl away and hide.

Another thought struck her. 'You say that James is your friend—but if you really believe he has developed romantic feelings for me, why did you arrange for him to find us together? Didn't you think he might be upset?'

'Sometimes it is necessary to be cruel to be kind,' Bruno informed her, with such haughty arrogance that Tamsin forgot her misery and trembled with rage. 'I felt it was better for James to realise what kind of woman you are now than to be disillusioned later.'

'And what kind of woman am I?' she whispered, her throat hurting as if she had swallowed glass.

'A gold-digger,' Bruno replied flatly. 'Before you knew who I was, you couldn't even be bothered to look at me. But the moment you learned I was a billionaire you abandoned James and fell into my arms. I'm not sure what last night was about,' he went on relentlessly, ignoring her muffled gasp at his decimation of her character, 'but I imagine it was to whet my appetite and inflame my desire for you.'

He moved suddenly, taking her by surprise as he snaked his arm around her waist, gripping her chin with his other hand to tilt her face to his. 'I have to admit, your tactics were successful,' he said, in a low voice that throbbed with a mixture of sexual hunger and self-disgust. 'I still want you, Tamsin, and although I'm sure you'll deny it, you want me too.'

He slid his hand down to her breast, and to her abject shame Tamsin felt her body betray her. The memory of how he had stroked her naked breasts and laved each sensitive crest with his tongue tormented her, but the cynical expression in his eyes ripped her emotions to shreds.

'So today,' she whispered, her voice barely audible, 'you deliberately set out to charm me?' She remembered how they had walked hand in hand through the gardens of Hever Castle, talking, laughing, enjoying each other's company—or so she had believed. It had been a magical day, one that she knew she would never forget, but now she wanted to weep with mortification as she recalled how she had trusted him and believed that he was as drawn to her as she was to him. 'And dinner tonight? That was all part of your grand plan to win my trust and entice me to your room? You made love to me—' her voice cracked '—simply to end my so called "relationship" with James?'

Bruno stared at her white face. She was good, he acknowledged, feeling some indefinable emotion twist in his gut when he caught the shimmer of tears in her eyes. She looked shattered. But no doubt that was because he had wrecked her plans to ingratiate herself with her wealthy Earl, not because he had genuinely hurt her. His stepmother had been an accomplished actress too, with an inexhaustible supply of tears that had fooled his father every time.

But tears did nothing for him, and his eyes narrowed as he stared down at the outline of her full, rounded breasts, clearly visible beneath the clingy material of her dress. The first part of his plan had been accomplished. Now that James believed he and Tamsin were lovers, the older man would step back and realise that his future did not lie with the beautiful blonde. But Tamsin did not have to lose out completely, and neither did he.

With slow deliberation he began to stroke her breast, gently brushing his thumb across its centre, and heat surged through him when he felt her nipple harden beneath his touch.

'Don't!' Appalled as much by her body's treacherous response to him as his damnable arrogance, Tamsin gasped and tried to draw away, but he felt the tremor that ran through her body and laughed.

'Why not, *bella*? You know we're good together,' he taunted softly. 'Half an hour ago you could not disguise your desire for me any more than I can deny my hunger to possess you. Forget James,' he urged, his voice suddenly fierce and feral with sexual tension. 'I can give you what you want.'

Before she could think of a reply to his arrogant statement, he swooped and claimed her mouth in a searing kiss—hot, hard, forcing her head back as he thrust his tongue between her lips. The chemistry between them was a potent force she could not deny. Her body remembered his touch and trembled with renewed desire, but her pride fought a desperate battle and she tore her mouth from his, breathing as if she had run a marathon as she pushed against his chest.

'How can you want me? You think I'm a...a gold-digger capable of duping a vulnerable man,' she cried wildly.

'True, but I am not a vulnerable man, *bella*—far from it. I know what you are, and to be frank I don't care. I want you naked and willing in my bed. As I am sure you are aware,' he added mockingly, as he slid his hand to her bottom and pulled her up against his hard, aroused body. 'I want you now Tamsin—in the same way that you want me.'

The gleam in his eyes, coupled with the note of supreme confidence in his voice that said she would be unable to resist him, compounded Tamsin's humiliation, and she shuddered and gagged on the corrosive bile that filled her throat.

'Get your hands off me,' she hissed, and a strength she hadn't known she possessed empowered her to thrust him away from her. 'I would rather die than share your bed.' She sped across the room, terrified that he would come after her—terrified that if he touched her, her body would betray her once more.

But when she reached the door she could not help but turn her head to look at him, absorbing his masculine beauty for one last time. How had she not noticed the inherent cruelty in the curve of his lips, or the hard, unforgiving coldness of his eyes? She had seen what she wanted to see, she thought bitterly. Once again her judgement had failed her. She had married a man who had had no intention of remaining faithful to her, and now she had been drawn to another who had let her believe he was genuinely interested in her while secretly planning to humiliate her.

She had to get away from him before she gave him the pleasure of seeing her fall apart, but she forced herself to speak. 'James told me that you are an honourable man,' she said with quiet dignity as she opened the door. 'But clearly he was wrong. I hope and pray that you rot in hell Bruno Di Cesare,' she added fiercely, her voice shaking with emotion. 'Because that's where you belong.'

CHAPTER FIVE

TAMSIN arrived back at her North London flat late on Thursday evening, and was immediately greeted by her flatmate Jess.

'I was expecting you back from your sister's two days ago,' Jess said cheerfully as she padded into the kitchen in her pyjamas and filled the kettle. 'I was beginning to think you'd eloped with a handsome stranger.' She took one look at Tamsin's shuttered expression and sighed. 'But you're here, so obviously not.'

'Obviously.' Tamsin dropped her case and gathered up the pile of letters from the kitchen worktop. 'Vicky wasn't feeling well, so I took a few more days off work.'

'Oh, dear—what's wrong with her? Nothing serious, I hope.'

'She's pregnant,' Tamsin said, in a voice carefully devoid of all emotion, 'and this time round she's suffering from terrible morning sickness. I stayed on so that I could take the twins to nursery in the mornings and give Vicky a break.'

She felt Jess's eyes on her and sighed. Her best friend had an uncanny knack of reading her mind, but right now Tamsin didn't want to share her thoughts with anyone—or discuss the events of the previous weekend. Within twenty minutes of fleeing from Bruno's room she had flung her belongings in her case, checked out of the hotel and raced out to her car, hurtling along the winding country lanes as fast as he had done earlier that day. Less than an hour later she had arrived at her sister's house and invented an excuse about an uncomfortable hotel bed as she'd apologised for turning up on Vicky's doorstep at midnight.

'Well, that's brilliant news,' Jess murmured, glancing speculatively at Tamsin's pale face and the purple smudges beneath her eyes. 'But I suppose a little part of you wishes it was you expecting a baby?'

'Tricky—unless I've developed the ability to reproduce without any help from a man,' Tamsin drawled. She didn't want to go there, or dwell on the hateful feeling of envy that had speared her when Vicky had announced her news. She loved both her sisters to bits and adored her little nephews and niece, but Jess was right. She *had* wished that she was happily married to a devoted husband, with a baby on the way.

'So how was the wedding reception?'

'Okay.' Tamsin made a show of reading the gas bill, and her voice was deliberately non-committal, but Jess wasn't fooled.

'Just okay, hmm?' she mused. 'You didn't meet any gorgeous men—or even one particular gorgeous man? Like the one who called here on Tuesday night?'

'What man?' Tamsin dropped the letters, her expression so haunted that Jess instantly dismissed the idea of teasing her friend.

'Tall, dark, handsome—if you'll forgive the cliché,' Jess said quietly. 'Italian, I think. He didn't give his name, but he left this.' She withdrew the diamond necklace from her dressing gown pocket and dropped it into Tamsin's hand. 'He said he was sure you wouldn't want to lose it. Oh, and he left a business card.' She took a small card from the kitchen drawer. 'He wrote a message on it, and I've been very good and haven't read it.' She made a vain attempt at humour, but her smile quickly faded. 'Tamsin, what's happened? Who is he?'

'He's no one.' The necklace felt cold and hard in Tamsin's palm. Almost as cold as the lump of ice around her heart. She glanced at the business card and despised herself for the way even the sight of Bruno's name caused a fluttering feeling in her stomach. His message was brief.

You know we could be good together bella. *I promise you will find me a generous lover. Call me.*

The word *generous* made Tamsin want to scream. She could visualise him scrawling the message, could picture the haughty arrogance on his face and his confident, cynical smile that once she had finished sulking she would jump at the chance of an affair with a billionaire. How could she have been so *stupid*, so *trusting,* and so criminally *naïve* as to think he had actually fallen for her?

Ignoring Jess's bemused expression, she tore the card in half and repeated the action again and again, before dropping the pieces into the bin. 'He doesn't exist,' she told Jess coolly. 'Have you made that tea yet?'

The London traffic was teeming, and despite his chauffeur knowing all the short cuts, Bruno's car was making slow progress back to his hotel. He had spent the day with his legal team, working on a takeover bid for one of the House of Di Cesare's rivals, and negotiations had been tense. Usually he relished the cut and thrust of business, the tactics and manoeuvres of boardroom warfare, and the sense of satisfaction when he emerged the victor. But today, for some reason, his mind had not been as focused as usual, and several times throughout the day he had checked his messages on his

mobile, annoyance mingling with faint disbelief that Tamsin
Stewart hadn't rung.

Of course he expected her to. Not immediately—he'd
allowed for a couple of days while she raged and sulked
before she accepted that James Grainger was not going to be
her sugar-daddy. And then she would read his message again
and realise that a virile billionaire was not such a bad
exchange for an elderly millionaire. Assuming that she was
like all the other women Bruno had known, her finger would
dial his number faster than you could say diamond necklace—
but not yet, it seemed. She was cleverer than he'd thought.

The memory of the way she had rejected him on the night
of the wedding reception taunted him and his jaw hardened.
But she was not that clever, and she was in danger of over-
playing her hand. He was returning to Italy next week, and
he had no intention of phoning her before he left.

If he wanted female company there were several women
he could have phoned who would immediately have accepted
an invitation to dinner. But he chose to dine alone and spent
the evening working. It was past eleven p.m. when he
switched off his laptop and phoned James Grainger's London
residence—out of curiosity rather than any expectation of
talking to the Earl. Annabel had said her father regularly spent
Friday nights in town, after his meetings with Tamsin, but he
already knew that Tamsin was away—visiting relatives, her
flatmate had explained—so presumably James had remained
at Ditton Hall.

The phone rang five or six times, and Bruno was about to
cut the call when a breathless female voice answered.

'Hello—can I help you? Who's calling, please?'

Tamsin waited impatiently for the caller to reply. It was
probably a sales call, and she was tempted to slam down the
receiver. Unsolicited calls were annoying enough during the

day, but it was late at night, and if she hadn't still been here James would have struggled out of bed to answer it.

'Miss Stewart—what a surprise,' a familiar accented voice drawled sarcastically. 'Although perhaps I should not be surprised by your tenacity, *bella*. James is a very wealthy man.'

'Bruno.' Tamsin's heart leapt into her throat, and to her disgust her hands shook and she had to grip the phone. 'Um…I suppose you want to talk to James—but he's in bed, and I'd rather not disturb him.'

'Have you worn him out, then, *bella?* Spare me the details, please.'

The hateful mockery in Bruno's voice ignited Tamsin's anger, and she coiled the telephone cord around her fingers and briefly imagined wrapping it around his neck.

'You are disgusting,' she hissed. 'The only reason I haven't told James about your despicable treatment of me and your foul accusations is because I know it would upset him.' And James had enough to deal with right now.

'Really? I thought it was because you're worried he might realise the truth.'

'The truth being that I'm a greedy gold-digger, I take it?' Tamsin said coolly, while her insides boiled. 'James is tired because we've had a busy day. I'll ask him to return your call tomorrow.'

Bruno's eyes narrowed at the dismissive note in her voice. He wasn't used to being dismissed—especially by a hoity-toity English miss whom he had good evidence to prove was a conniving bitch. He couldn't believe she was with James, and white-hot anger jabbed his gut as he closed his mind to the image of her in James's bed.

'I'm intrigued, *bella*,' he murmured. 'A busy day doing what, exactly?'

Tamsin thought of the hours she had spent with James in the

hospital. He had needed blood tests, some of his notes had gone astray, and they'd had a long wait in the oncology unit before he'd received the cocktail of drugs that were fighting his cancer. He had been sick on the way home; fortunately his chauffeur, Hargreaves, had managed to pull over in time, and once back at his flat he had gone straight to bed, dismissing her plea that he really must tell Davina and Annabel about his illness with the assertion that he was determined to fight it on his own.

'We went window shopping,' she lied to Bruno. 'James is thinking about redecorating Ditton Hall, and we looked at fabrics and things, putting some ideas together.'

Bruno gave a harsh laugh that grated in her ear. 'And I suppose your next step will be to suggest staying at Ditton Hall while you draw up plans for its renovation? You think you're clever, Tamsin,' he grated in a low, cold tone that sent ice slithering down her spine. 'But I warn you, I'm one step ahead of you, and I will do everything in my power to prevent you from hooking your claws into James.'

Tamsin urgently tried to contact her brother over the weekend, but he was away fishing, and her calls to his mobile went unanswered. She spent most of Monday at one of her project sites, chivvying contractors who had fallen behind schedule and trying to track down a consignment of silk wallpaper that had disappeared seemingly from the planet, and her temper was at boiling point when she finally marched into the offices of Spectrum Development and Design.

'Why didn't you tell me about Spectrum's financial problems?' she launched an attack on her brother the moment she saw him. 'I had a right to know. You asked me to join the company,' she said angrily, 'and you were the one who said you wanted to involve me in the decision making.'

'I do,' Daniel muttered, tapping the end of his pen on the desk and not quite meeting her gaze. 'But I didn't want to worry you. Moving from an established, successful design company like Carter and Coults to Spectrum was a big leap of faith for you. How could I tell you six months after you'd joined me that I'd mucked up big-time? I should have known that turning the house in Mountfield Square into flats would go over budget, but I couldn't foresee that the rise in interest rates would deaden the housing market so that the flats didn't sell.'

'But we were close to *bankruptcy!*' Tamsin cried. 'Don't you think I would have noticed when the administrators moved in?'

'It wasn't as bad as that,' Daniel insisted.

'No, because James Grainger bailed us out.' Tamsin felt the familiar sickness in the pit of her stomach that had been with her since she'd learned that Bruno had been right. James's investment in Spectrum *had* saved it from collapse, and it was little wonder that Bruno was suspicious of her friendship with the wealthy Earl. 'I wish you'd told me,' she muttered miserably.

'One of the reasons I didn't was because James thought you might feel awkward,' Daniel explained. 'I admit that I used your friendship with him...'

'*Oh, Daniel!*'

'...when I approached him and asked him to put money into the company. But I didn't really expect him to agree—and I made it clear that I didn't. To my surprise he was really interested. He offered to put up the money to keep the bank happy until the Mountfield flats are sold—and he'll get a good return on his investment now that property prices are picking up again.'

Tamsin's face mirrored her doubts, and Daniel sighed. 'Stop fretting, Tam; everything's going to be fine. We just need a couple more good deals and we'll be in the black again. The interiors side of the company is doing great, thanks to you. Oh, and you're seeing a prospective new client tomorrow. You're meeting him at the Haighton Hotel at twelve, so don't be late. I need you to make a good impression.' He grinned and pushed his over-long hair out of his eyes. 'I'm counting on you, sis.'

With Daniel's words in mind, Tamsin dressed to impress the following day. Her self-confidence had been crushed by her divorce, and for many months afterwards she had dressed with the sole aim of fading into the background. But gradually, with Jess's badgering, she had begun to take a renewed interest in the way she looked.

Interior design was about making a statement, and she accepted that clients would judge her appearance while they debated hiring her to design their homes. A bold red and white patterned skirt, a crisp white jacket and matching accessories certainly made a statement, and as she ran up the steps of the Haighton Hotel and glimpsed her reflection in the glass doors, the heavy cloud that had sat over her since her last conversation with Bruno lifted a little.

Why should she care about his opinion of her? She knew she wasn't a gold-digger with her eye on James's fortune—and so, more importantly, did James. Bruno was bitter and cynical—although she couldn't understand why, when he appeared to have everything life and money had to offer. But he was gone—back to Italy, or jetting around the globe—and with luck she would never see him again.

At the reception desk she gave her name, and explained that she had a meeting with Alistair Collins. The clerk made a brief phone call, and a few moments later a pleasant-faced, fair-haired man walked across the foyer to greet her.

'Miss Stewart—it's a pleasure to meet you.' He shook her hand briefly as she returned his greeting. 'If you would like to come up to the suite? I think we'll be more comfortable than in the guest lounge.'

Alistair Collins smiled as he ushered her over to the lift, and after a brief hesitation Tamsin stepped inside and they were whisked up to the top floor. The Haighton was one of London's top hotels, and its décor of muted shades and plush pale carpets exuded discreet elegance. Her client led the way along the corridor to the Ambassador Suite, and she glanced around, admiring the gracious, airy sitting room with its huge windows that allowed sunlight to spill into the room.

A figure was silhouetted against the light. His height and the width of his shoulders were impressive, but it was the arrogant tilt of his head that triggered Tamsin's unease. She glanced questioningly at Alistair Collins, and frowned when he indicated that she should step further into the room while he retreated to the door.

'Miss Stewart's here, Bruno. Will there be anything else?'

'No. *Grazie*, Alistair.'

Bruno swung round to face her at the same time as Tamsin heard the snick of the door, indicating that Alistair Collins had left the room. For a few seconds her muscles froze, and her brain seemed to have deserted her, but her eyes locked on Bruno and greedily drank in the perfection of his face: the planes and hollows formed by his sharp cheekbones, the heavy brows and strong nose, the hair the exact colour of a raven's wing that gleamed blue-black in the sunlight, and the cruel beauty of his sensual mouth.

Her first thought, when her brain reconnected, was that once again her hopes had been raised and dashed by this man. She had come today expecting to discuss a possible commission, and although Daniel hadn't said as much, she knew how important any new business venture was to Spectrum's ailing finances. She had no idea why Bruno had gone to such lengths to bring her here; she just wanted to leave—*pronto*.

Bruno was watching her, his dark eyes trailing over her

in a lazy appraisal that ignited her temper and sent fire surging through her veins. Suddenly it was imperative that she spoke first.

'It was rather juvenile to trick me into coming here, don't you think?' she said coolly, lifting her chin and meeting his gaze steadily, although her heart was jerking painfully beneath her ribs. 'I'm sure your staff have better things to do with their time—as I do with mine.' She turned on her heels and headed for the door. 'I'll see myself out.'

'Sit down, Tamsin.' The command was softly spoken, but it was a command nevertheless, and she turned her head and glared at him.

'Why?'

'Because I haven't given you my permission to leave,' he drawled, still in that quiet, controlled voice that disturbed her more than if he had shouted.

'I don't need your permission, Bruno.'

His smile slashed his face, but it did not reach his eyes, Tamsin noted when he moved away from the window and strolled towards her. 'I expect all my employees to carry out my requests without argument.'

'Then I consider myself fortunate that I am not one of them.'

Nervous, but determined not to be cowed, Bruno acknowledged, feeling the faintest hint of admiration for her. His eyes raked her slender figure, noting how her slim-fitting skirt hugged her hips and the cut of her jacket emphasised her tiny waist, while the top button was at a point that revealed a tempting but decorous amount of cleavage. Power-dressing, smart and yet undeniably sexy—but she hadn't known she was meeting him, and had dressed to please another man. Rage fired inside him, surprising him with its intensity, and the temptation to claim her sassy scarlet-glossed lips with his mouth and kiss her into submission was so strong that his muscles clenched.

'Since I have decided to employ your services, *bella*, you are under my control—so sit while we discuss my requirements.'

The gleam in his eyes was unmistakable: raw sexual hunger that made Tamsin tremble with a mixture of outrage and excitement that she tried desperately to deny. In what way did he want her services—and what exactly were his requirements? The connotation in his words sickened her—did he expect her to be his *whore?*

His mouth twitched with amusement as he read her mind, and Tamsin tightened her grip on her laptop case and held it in front of her like a shield.

'I'd sooner work for the devil than you.'

'Try my patience much more, and you'll find him infinitely preferable.' Bruno swung away from her, sat down on a sofa and indicated that she should join him.

Something about his expression warned Tamsin that the only way she could retain any dignity was to comply and, taking a deep breath, she walked over to the sofa and perched as far away from him as possible.

'This is my villa in Tuscany.'

She glanced down at the coffee table and saw several photographs strewn across it.

'It is in the heart of the Chianti region, about an hour's drive from Florence. The house was built in the seventeenth century and has been in my family for many years, but since my father died ten years ago it has fallen into a state of disrepair. Extensive structural work is now complete, and I wish to concentrate on the interior decoration so that I can use the villa as a weekend retreat.'

Bruno sat back and surveyed her coolly. 'That's where you come in. It's an enormous project, but one that your brother assures me you are capable of. In our preliminary discussions he agreed that in order to devote all your attention to the Villa Rosala you will have to relocate to Italy until the work is complete.'

Relocate to Italy—with him! Tamsin shuddered and tore her gaze from the temptation of his wide, sensual mouth. She would rather relocate to the bowels of the earth. A number of responses came to her mind, but she opted for the most succinct.

'You must be joking.'

His hard stare filled her with trepidation. 'I assure you I'm not. And the amount I'm prepared to pay for your expertise isn't a joke either.' He paused, and then added silkily, 'At least your brother does not seem to think so. In fact I gained the impression when I spoke to him yesterday that he's desperate to win this commission.'

'When you spoke to him…' Tamsin felt as though a net was closing around her, trapping her. 'I assume you somehow persuaded Daniel to withhold your identity?' she said bitterly.

'I simply suggested that it would be good if you saw the photos of my villa without any preconceived ideas.'

Tiny beads of sweat formed on Tamsin's upper lip as desperation edged closer. She hated him. There was no doubt about that when she had spent every night for the past week cringing with mortification at the way she had melted in his arms, unaware that he had set out to deliberately seduce her. But although her mind was strong, her body was playing traitor, and she was agonisingly aware of him. The subtle musk of his cologne filled her senses, and the memory of his bronzed, naked, muscle-packed body taunted her subconscious.

'Spectrum employs two other interior designers besides me. Both are highly qualified, and respected for their flair and innovation. I'm sure they would jump at the chance of *relocating* to Tuscany,' she added, her voice as dry as a desert.

'But I want you, Tamsin.'

The words hung in the air. Since the moment she had

stepped into the room and faced him sexual tension had simmered between them. Now the atmosphere altered subtly, and Tamsin could hear her blood thundering in her ears as her breathing quickened.

'No.'

She moved swiftly, but not fast enough. He caught hold of her shoulder as she jerked to her feet and hauled her back down onto his thighs. His hand moved to her nape, tugged her head back, and for a split second she stared into his eyes, shocked by the raw hunger in their depths, before he lowered his head and captured her mouth in a fierce, possessive kiss.

She fought him furiously. Her pride demanded that she keep her lips tightly closed, and every muscle in her body locked in rejection, but he did not seem to care. His tongue probed with wicked intent, insisting that she open her mouth to him, while his hand moved upwards and his clever fingers dealt with the pins that secured her chignon. Her hair tumbled onto her shoulders, soft as silk, and his low groan of approval quivered with such feral, sensual need that she could not fight him any more.

Sensing her capitulation, he altered the tenure of the kiss, deepened it, and thrust his tongue deep into her mouth to explore her with an eroticism that drove everything but her desire for him from her mind. Her hands, which had been bunched into fists on his shoulders, uncurled and drifted around his neck, but as she buried her fingers in his thick black hair he lifted his mouth from hers, set her back from him, and with cool deliberation gripped her arms and forced them into her lap.

'Can I take it that you will offer no further objections to accepting my commission?'

The mockery in his eyes seared her, and with a low cry she scrambled to her feet, snatched up her case and flew over to the door. 'I wouldn't work for you if you paid me a million pounds. I know what all this is about,' she threw at him, her voice shaking with anger and shame that once again she had been unable to resist him. 'The commission to design your villa is just a ploy to keep me away from James.'

'It's certainly one reason,' Bruno said coldly, violent anger surging through him when he recalled that she had been at James's flat late on Friday night. Had she stayed all night? The idea filled him with revulsion, and another emotion that made him question his true motivation for wanting to end her relationship with his old friend. Surely it wasn't jealousy that burned in his gut? 'I am utterly determined to stop you making a fool of James,' he warned. 'But I have studied the portfolio of your work on your website, and although your morals are questionable, your talent is not. You are a gifted designer and I genuinely admire your work. My private jet will take us to Italy on Friday,' he informed her, his hard stare daring her to argue.

It was obvious to Tamsin he had chosen the day deliberately, aware that she usually met James on Fridays. Of course he did not know that James had received his last course of chemotherapy for a few weeks.

'A car will come for you at ten.'

He opened the door, indicating that their meeting was over, but Tamsin wasn't finished. She hadn't even started.

'Forget it,' she snapped, eyes flashing fire. 'You can't make me go to Italy with you.'

'I agree that I can't physically bundle you aboard my plane,' Bruno conceded with a mocking smile. 'But I'm confident I can persuade you. The simple truth is that you need me, *bella*. Think about it,' he continued silkily, when she appeared to be struck dumb at his arrogance. 'This commission is a fantastic opportunity for your career, and for Spectrum. I am the billionaire head of a globally successful fashion empire. I could call on the world's top designers to decorate my house, but I've chosen you.'

He paused for a moment to allow his words to sink in, and then added, 'I have already told Daniel that I'm willing to allow Spectrum to use my name on future advertising. This commission could raise Spectrum from being a small company to a major player in the world of interior design, and your brother knows it.'

Bruno's eyes narrowed as he watched Tamsin's tongue dart out to moisten her lips. He fought the urge to taste her again, to kiss her until she was soft and pliant in his arms and he could do what he had wanted to do from the moment he had first seen her at Davina's wedding reception—take her to his bed.

'I can't force you to work for me, Tamsin,' he drawled, 'but who would believe that you refused the chance of a lifetime? I would only have to make the odd comment at a party to start the rumours flying. Word would get around that I was disappointed with your ideas and decided not to employ you—hardly the endorsement your brother is hoping for. I fear that would be the end of Spectrum,' he taunted in his soft, mocking voice. 'So, unless you want that to happen, I suggest you are ready and waiting at ten o'clock on Friday.'

CHAPTER SIX

BRUNO'S plane touched down in Florence early on Friday afternoon. Apart from enquiring if Tamsin was comfortable, he had ignored her for the entire flight, his laptop open in front of him and his mobile phone clamped to his ear. But once they were whisked through Customs and had climbed into his waiting limousine, he seemed to visibly relax.

'Home,' he murmured in a satisfied tone, as he sat back and stretched his arm along the seat. 'I have travelled all around the globe, but for me Florence is the most beautiful city in the world. Have you visited here before, Tamsin?'

'I've been to Italy, but not Florence—I spent my honeymoon in Rome. It was beautiful,' Tamsin said quietly, a faint, wistful note in her voice.

She'd been so happy, she remembered sadly, and so in love. She had believed that those two wonderful weeks with Neil were a prelude to the rest of their lives. But her marriage had ended in heartbreak less than a year later, and the memories were forever tainted with the knowledge that her husband had never had any intention of remaining faithful to her.

What a trusting fool she had been, she brooded, as she glanced at Bruno's stern profile. He turned his head, and his eyes were hard and dismissive as he flicked them briefly over her. The perfect symmetry of his features could have been chiselled by one of the Old Masters, and although she told herself that she hated him, her heart lurched as she absorbed his masculine beauty. She obviously had a fatal attraction to heartless bastards, but she would not be foolish again. Bruno stirred her in a way no man had ever done, but she was determined to fight her awareness of him.

She had known from the minute she had walked into Daniel's office and seen his eager, hopeful expression that she had no choice but to agree to accept Bruno's commission. Her brother had put his heart and soul into creating his company, and she couldn't offer a valid reason why she should turn down a deal that—in his words—would put Spectrum on the map.

But although Bruno had forced her to come to Italy with him, she was determined that their relationship would be on a professional level only—and fortunately he must have decided the same thing. The desire that had burned in his eyes a few days ago had disappeared, and when he looked at her now his expression was one of cool contempt.

The roads through Florence were busy, but eventually the car drew up outside a gracious apartment building beside the River Arno and Bruno ushered her inside.

'I have to attend a meeting this afternoon, so we'll drive on to the villa this evening,' he explained, while Tamsin glanced curiously around his home.

The elegant lounge was huge, with a high ceiling and pale walls. Full-length curtains framed windows that looked down on the river and commanded a wonderful view of the Ponte Vecchio. Bruno's tastes were eclectic and expensive—the artwork on the walls were original pieces by modern artists and Old Masters, and the furnishings comprised beautiful silk covered sofas in neutral shades, dotted with brightly coloured cushions.

'This is stunning,' she murmured.

He gave her a cool smile. '*Grazie*. I would like to recreate the feeling of light and space at the Villa Rosala—but, as you will see later, there is much work to do.' He glanced at his watch and walked over to the door. 'I will be at my office for the rest of the day. If you wish to go shopping, one of my bodyguards, Tomasso, will escort you.'

'I don't need a bodyguard,' Tamsin objected. The only thing that had lifted her spirits for the past few days was the thought of exploring Florence's rich cultural history. But she preferred to do so alone, not with one of the henchmen whose brooding presence in the front of the car that had brought them from the airport had put her off trying to talk to Bruno.

'Nevertheless, Tomasso will remain with you at all times. While you are working for me, your safety is my responsibility,' Bruno told her in a tone that brooked further argument, before he swung on his heels and strode out of the door.

It was stupid to wish that he really cared about her, Tamsin told herself later, as she strolled through the busy city streets, the stocky, unsmiling Tomasso at her side. It was more likely that Bruno believed she was a shoplifter, as well as a gold-digger who preyed on rich elderly men, and that was why he had insisted that the bodyguard should accompany her.

But sunshine and blue skies made it hard to feel miserable for long. Florence's history and rich culture as the birthplace of the Renaissance meant that it was a popular place for tourists, and the hour she queued for entry to the Galleria dell'Accademia was worth it when she finally stood before Michelangelo's *David* and felt over-awed by its beauty. The Uffizi Gallery was equally stunning, and to her surprise Tomasso proved to be a charming and knowledgeable guide, who was clearly pleased by her admiration of his city and was eager to show her as much as possible.

Dusk was falling by the time they returned to Bruno's apartment. Tamsin was hot and tired, but happy after an enjoyable day. Tomasso spoke little English, and she spoke no Italian, but they had communicated in sign language and gestures, and they were both laughing as they staggered through the door. Their smiles quickly faded when a grim-faced Bruno strode out to meet them. He grated something in Italian to Tomasso, who flushed uncomfortably and left without another glance at Tamsin, and her heart sank when he turned and glowered at her.

'It appears that no man between the ages of sixteen and sixty-five is safe from you, *bella,*' he drawled sardonically, 'but I would be grateful if you could restrain yourself from flirting with members of my staff.'

'I wasn't flirting with him. I was just being friendly,' Tamsin defended herself hotly, her cheeks flaming when Bruno's brows arched upwards.

'As *friendly* as you are with James Grainger?'

'Oh, for heaven's sake!' Tamsin's happiness instantly dissolved, and her shoulders slumped dejectedly.

She was an accomplished performer, Bruno thought darkly, hardening his heart when he caught the glimmer of tears in her eyes. She knew just how to pull the right strings. She'd spent one afternoon with Tomasso and already he was eating out of her hand—and it was easy to see why, Bruno conceded irritably. In a lemon-yellow skirt and white sleeveless blouse, she looked young and innocent—and at the same time incredibly sexy. Her hair was caught up in a loose knot on top of her head, but stray tendrils curled around her face, and his fingers itched to release her hairclip and bury his face in the silky golden strands.

While Tamsin had been out enjoying herself with his body-guard he had spent several hours in a strategy meeting with his board. To his furious disbelief he had struggled to concentrate on what was being said because he had found himself thinking about her, rather than ways to increase company profits in the Far East. His usually sharp and decisive mind had deserted him, and as his senior staff had seemed surprised at his inattention he'd been incredulous. Business was his top priority—always—and he'd been shocked by his impatience to end the meeting and spend the rest of the day with a woman he despised, but who intrigued him more than any woman had ever done.

Muttering a savage imprecation beneath his breath, he tore his gaze from the temptation of her mouth, hovered briefly on the firm swell of her breasts outlined beneath her thin top, and jerked away from her, his nostrils flaring as he sought to bring his hormones under control. It was no good reminding himself that she was a woman like his stepmother, or that his father had sacrificed his company, the respect of his peers and his relationship with his only son because of his obsession with a woman who had married him for his money. Even knowing those things, he still wanted her.

But there was no chance he would become obsessed with her. He was sure his interest in her was so intense because of her unexpected determination to resist him and the wildfire chemistry that smouldered between them. The sooner he took her to bed the better, he mused. He would be in control, and as with all his affairs the beginning would spell the end. His lovers never held his interest for very long, and he had no expectations that this pale skinned English rose would be any different.

He spared her another glance and saw that she looked tired and fragile, her eyes huge in her pale face. 'There has been a change of plan,' he informed her abruptly. 'It's getting late, so I have decided that we'll stay here tonight and go to the villa tomorrow.' His mouth tightened when she frowned. 'Is there a problem?'

Yes—him! Tamsin thought viciously, still smarting from his accusation that she had been flirting with Tomasso. 'I hoped to go the villa today. The sooner I start work, the sooner I can leave—which I'm sure suits both of us,' she snapped.

Bruno swore succinctly. 'Tell me, *bella,* do you intend to sulk indefinitely because I've wrecked your chance of securing yourself a wealthy sugar-daddy? Or is there a chance you could behave like an adult so that we can establish a reasonable working relationship?'

'I never regarded James as a *sugar-daddy.*' Tamsin threw her hands in the air. 'I am not after his money.'

Bruno gave a disbelieving snort. 'I find that hard to believe when you lead such an expensive lifestyle. You drive a new top-of-the-range car, and your designer clothes will not have come cheap. How can you afford to shop in Bond Street on the salary a small company such as Spectrum must pay you? Someone must have been supplementing your income, and my guess is that you encouraged James to buy you those things you craved but were out of your price range,' he accused her scathingly.

'I did not.' Twin spots of colour appeared on Tamsin's cheeks. 'James has never bought me *anything.*'

'What about a diamond necklace worth several thousand pounds?'

'That was different—it was my birthday present.' Tamsin's face burned hotter. 'It didn't really cost thousands, did it?' she faltered. 'I know I should have refused to accept it, but I didn't want to hurt James's feelings.'

'That was most thoughtful of you, *bella.*'

The mockery in Bruno's tone made Tamsin want to hit him. 'I bought my car and my clothes with some money I inherited,' she told him furiously. 'It wasn't a fortune, but it was a sizeable sum. The sensible thing would have been to invest,' she admitted. 'But the last couple of years since my divorce haven't been much fun and when the money came through my family encouraged me to go mad for once—which I did,' she added defiantly, lifting her chin to meet his sceptical gaze. 'I have never asked James for anything, and I certainly didn't appeal to him to put money into Spectrum. My brother told me that James offered to help—but trust you and your horrible, twisted mind to think the worst.'

She blinked hard to banish the angry tears that stung her eyes. Bruno was looking at her as if she was something unpleasant on the bottom of his shoe, and she was angry with herself for caring what he thought of her. But for some stupid reason she *did* care, and she could not drag her gaze from him.

In his black designer suit he looked every inch the powerful, billionaire businessman, but as well as supreme confidence, he exuded a raw sexual magnetism that triggered a response in her she was powerless to control. She hated the effect he had on her—and, even worse, the mocking gleam in his eyes that told her he knew exactly how he made her feel.

'Did something happen in your past to make you so bitter and mistrustful?' she demanded. She guessed that being a billionaire had its downside. Had he fallen in love with a woman and later discovered she had only been interested in his money? It was impossible to imagine the hard, ruthless Bruno she knew in love, but perhaps when he had been younger…?

Bruno was silent for so long that she thought he would not answer, but then he glanced at her, his face shuttered. 'Oh, yes, something happened,' he murmured derisively, and his tone made her blood run cold. He paused, and then continued in a hard tone, 'I grew up at the Villa Rosala—an idyllic childhood, with parents who adored each other as much as they adored their children. When my mother died, at about the same age as Lorna Grainger when she lost her life, my father was devastated. After thirty blissful years of marriage he was lost and lonely, despite the efforts of my sister and I to comfort him. But then he met a young woman.'

Bruno's face hardened, and Tamsin was shocked by the note of undisguised loathing in his voice.

'Miranda was an actress, with a complete lack of talent but a willingness to sleep with anyone who might further her pathetic career. When she met my father she was in her twenties, and he was over sixty with a heart condition. My mother had died less than a year before, and as soon as Miranda learned that my father was the president of the House of Di Cesare she attached herself to him like a leach. They married a few weeks before the first anniversary of my mother's death,' he revealed bitterly, 'and Miranda immediately insisted that they move to a huge house in the city— more in keeping with her position as the wife of a billionaire.'

'So, did you stay on at the Villa Rosala?' Tamsin queried.

'No. I was a young man, in my early twenties, and in my last year at college. My father wanted us all to live as a family.' Bruno gave a harsh laugh. 'I loved him, and I wanted to be with my sister, Jocasta, so I gave in to his pleas and moved to his new house, knowing that it was big enough for me to be able to avoid Miranda most of the time. Unfortunately, she had other ideas.'

His face darkened, and Tamsin shivered at the fury glinting in his eyes. 'What do you mean?'

'I mean that my dear stepmother quickly grew bored with having an invalid husband more than twice her age, and thought that I would provide her with the active sex-life she presumably wasn't getting with my father.' He saw the shocked expression on Tamsin's face, and his mouth curved into another grim smile. 'When I refused to play ball she was furious, and determined to pay me back for rejecting her. She engineered a situation. I can't even remember now the exact reason she made up to lure me to her bedroom—suffice to say that when I arrived she was naked, and flung herself at me just in time for my father to walk in and find me—as he believed—making love to his wife.'

Tamsin could not restrain her shocked cry. 'But he believed you, didn't he? I mean, however bad it looked, your father must have eventually calmed down and listened to you? You were his son.'

Bruno shook his head. 'Unfortunately I underestimated Miranda's acting skills. She gave a performance worthy of an Oscar, insisting that I had pursued her relentlessly and badgered her for sex, culminating in my bursting into her room and trying to take her by force.'

'She accused you of attempting to rape her?'

Tamsin could not disguise the horror in her voice, but Bruno must have misinterpreted the look of disgust on her face, because he grated harshly, 'I didn't touch her.'

He didn't need to defend himself. Tamsin could see the truth stamped on his face. And she knew instinctively that it *was* the truth. He would never attempt to force a woman against her will. Despite the way he had treated her, she was certain that he was an honourable man with a strong protective streak—arranging for his bodyguard to watch over her this afternoon was evidence of that. She also knew without him telling her that he had loved his father and been desperately hurt by his refusal to believe his word over his new wife's.

'So, what happened?' she asked softly.

'My father threw me out and said he hoped never to see me or speak to me again,' Bruno revealed unemotionally. 'And his wish came true. I understand that after a few years he finally came to his senses and realised how conniving Miranda was—helped when he discovered that she had numerous lovers. But by then it was too late. He had lost the respect of his friends and his peers, and the trust of his board. In-fighting and a series of ill-advised business decisions had brought the House of Di Cesare to its knees. I had moved to the US to live with my father's cousin Fabio, and we were building up the household goods side of the company. I heard rumours that my father regretted the past, and his mistrust of me, but he died before we were reconciled.'

'Oh, that's terrible,' Tamsin whispered.

'No, *bella,* that's the destructive power of love,' Bruno told her harshly. 'My father was blinded by his feelings for Miranda and couldn't see that she was a cold-hearted bitch who was only interested in his wallet. If he'd had any sense he'd have just taken her to bed until his fascination for her died. But instead *love* made a fool of him and he sacrificed everything—including his relationship with me.'

With a muttered oath he pushed open the glass doors and strode out onto the balcony, gripping the railings so hard that his skin was in danger of splitting across his knuckles. After a few moments Tamsin followed him and stood hesitantly in the doorway, her eyes drawn to the tense line of his shoulders.

'I vowed on the day he banished me from his life that I would never mistake lust for a deeper emotion,' he grated. 'Love weakens and destroys. I have no intention of allowing it to weaken me.' He suddenly swung round and moved toward her, his hand shooting out to capture her chin between his long, strong fingers. '*This* is the only truth that exists between a man and a woman, *bella mia*—the mutual exchange of sexual pleasure that does not require messy emotions or ridiculous protestations of everlasting love.'

His eyes glittered like polished jet beneath his hooded lids, and his face was shadowed and unreadable as he swiftly lowered his head and claimed her lips in a hard, stinging kiss that sought to dominate.

Shocked at the unexpectedness of his actions, she had no time to think or muster her defences. Every instinct warned her not to respond to him when his mood was so dark and dangerous, but while she fought to keep her lips clamped together her body was already softening, eagerly welcoming the stroke of his hands over her hips and bottom as he hauled her against the solid strength of his thighs. His tongue pushed insistently between her lips, forcing entry, and Tamsin's will-power deserted her. With a low moan she opened her mouth so that he could explore her moist inner warmth with a thoroughness that left her shaking so badly that she was forced to cling to him for support.

Her weakness for him was humiliating, but she couldn't fight him. She curled her arms around his neck, tipping her head back so that he could deepen the kiss and take it to another level that was flagrantly erotic. She felt his fingers tug impatiently at the buttons of her blouse and heard his muttered curse before he simply wrenched the material apart, sending the tiny pearls pinging in all directions. He dragged her lacy bra cup aside with the same barely suppressed savagery, and for a few seconds Tamsin felt cool air on her bare flesh—until he tore his mouth from hers and bent his head lower, stroking his tongue backwards and forwards over her tight nipple and then closing his lips fully around the rosy crest.

Sensation ripped through her, so that she cried out and arched her back, lost to everything but her urgent need for him to continue sucking her while his wickedly clever fingers captured her other nipple and rolled it between his finger and thumb. It was like gorging on a feast after the past weeks when her body had been starved of him. But it couldn't last.

'Much as I despise myself—I want you, Tamsin,' he grated, his voice laced with self-disgust as he tore his mouth from her flesh and stared down at her. 'I watched you with James Grainger and I knew you were a woman like my stepmother. But unfortunately that knowledge does nothing to lessen my hunger for you.'

His words hit her like icy water, and she gasped and tried to draw away from him.

'You want me with the same urgency,' he told her harshly, daring her to deny it. 'But if you're waiting for me to dress it up with fancy words and promises that are impossible to keep, then you'll be waiting a long time—and we're both going to be hellishly frustrated.' He placed his hand back on her breast, but to her surprise he eased her bra back into place and drew the edges of her blouse together, his eyes gleaming in derision at her obvious confusion. 'We both recognised the chemistry that burns between us the moment we met. Why fight it, *bella?* You know we could be good together, but you resent the fact that I'm not fooled by your innocent smile. You'll come to me eventually,' he mocked. 'And you'd better not make me wait too long.'

The softly spoken taunt brought Tamsin to her senses, and she shuddered with shame and self-disgust. 'I'm afraid you'll be waiting for ever,' she told him, her teeth clenched to prevent them from chattering as reaction turned her blood to ice. 'I admit that you push all the right buttons, Bruno—I award you ten out of ten for technique. But I'm not looking for a stud. All I want to do is to be left in peace to get on with the job you've brought me to Italy to do. So do us both a favour and go and relieve your sexual frustrations with someone else.'

CHAPTER SEVEN

FOUR weeks later Tamsin took refuge from the midday sun beneath the shade of the cypress trees and stared out at the view from the rear of the Villa Rosala. The air was still and heavy, and sunlight shimmered on the patchwork of green olive groves and golden wheat fields, while in the distance the dense forest gave way to towering mountains.

Tuscany in the height of summer was simply breathtaking. She had landed a dream job, designing the eight bedrooms and numerous living rooms of a house that she had fallen in love with at first sight—so why did she feel so restless?

It was because Bruno hadn't come this weekend, she acknowledged heavily, hating herself for her weakness where he was concerned. Since he had brought her to Italy he had spent every week in Florence and each weekend at the Villa Rosala, arriving on Friday evenings and leaving again early on Monday morning, and, although she despised herself for admitting it, she looked forward to his visits with increasing eagerness.

Although their conversations were mainly about her designs for the villa, an unspoken truce seemed to have settled between them—which was not a situation she could have envisaged after their explosive confrontation on the balcony of his Florence apartment, when she had vowed that she hated him—and hated herself more for her complete inability to resist him.

During the drive to the villa the following morning she had avoided speaking to him or even looking at him, but once they'd been alone in the big, beautiful old house she'd been unable to ignore the wildfire chemistry that burned between them. She was aware of the undisguised desire in Bruno's eyes, and knew it was mirrored in her own, but a gut instinct for self-protection warned her that she could not give in to the dictates of her body while he held such a low opinion of her morals.

'I swear I have no ulterior motive for my friendship with James, and I wouldn't have allowed him to buy me things even if he'd offered,' she had insisted during Bruno's last visit, when he had made yet more disparaging comments about avaricious women and rich old men.

They had been sitting on the terrace enjoying the late afternoon sunshine, Bruno looking like a bronzed demi-god in cream chinos and shirt, his hair gleaming like black silk and his dark eyes shaded by designer sunglasses. His sinfully sexy body would tempt a saint, Tamsin had thought despairingly, let alone a woman who hadn't had sex for years and whose libido had suddenly stirred into urgent life.

She had searched desperately for a way in which she could prove to Bruno that she wasn't the gold-digger he believed, and once again she had been tempted to tell him about James's illness. But James had entrusted her with his secret and she owed him her loyalty.

'Instead you shopped for designer dresses using money you had been bequeathed in a will?' Bruno drawled silkily.

'That's right.'

'But the story of your inheritance isn't quite so straightforward, is it, *bella*?' he continued. 'You were not left a small fortune by a grandparent or a close relative. For several years you befriended an elderly gentleman—a neighbour who had lived alone since his wife's death and had no other family.'

Tamsin wondered how Bruno knew so much about her, but finally nodded her head in agreement. 'Yes, Edward Abbot—Ted—had been on his own for years. He was a wonderful, fascinating man; he flew Spitfires during the War, and was shot down over France. His arthritis meant that he couldn't walk very well, but he was determined not to go into a care home. I used to get bits of shopping for him, and help him with his housework, although really I think he just liked having company. When he died, I couldn't believe that he had named me as his only beneficiary.'

'No, it must have been a shock—a very pleasant one,' Bruno commented softly, and this time there was no mistaking the mocking note in his voice.

'What is that supposed to mean? What exactly are you suggesting?' Tamsin demanded angrily.

'I was merely pointing out that you seem to make a habit of making friends with wealthy, lonely men.'

The realisation that Bruno believed her friendships with Ted and James were all part of a Machiavellian plot to get her hands on their money made Tamsin feel physically sick, and she swung away from him before he saw her angry, humiliated tears.

'You can't go through life thinking that every woman is like your stepmother,' she snapped.

But of course that was exactly what Bruno had done, since the day his father had remarried and given his loyalty to his new wife rather than his son. Tamsin understood the reasons for Bruno's bitterness, what she didn't understand was why she felt so hurt by his insistence that she was no better than Stefano Di Cesare's second wife.

Bruno had returned to Florence soon after that argument,

speeding down the drive with tyres squealing, throwing up clouds of red dust, indicating his impatience to be gone. The days after he had left had dragged past, and although she hated herself for it Tamsin had counted the hours until Friday evening. But Bruno hadn't arrived then, or over the weekend, and now it was Monday and she had resigned herself to the fact that she would not see him for another week.

Clearly other interests had kept him in Florence, she thought dismally, recalling the image of the stunning dark-haired beauty he had been photographed with in the newspapers. The sight of the woman clinging possessively to his arm had caused a sick feeling in the pit of Tamsin's stomach, which had added to her irritation with herself. Of course he had a mistress, she'd told herself angrily. He was a handsome billionaire playboy and he was hardly going to live like a monk.

Cursing her stupidity, she stretched out on the grass and closed her eyes. She hadn't slept well all week, and had lost her appetite despite the wonderful meals the housekeeper and cook Battista plied her with.

Her emotions were a mess, she conceded disgustedly, and her pride seemed to have deserted her, because despite knowing that Bruno despised her—she could not stop thinking about him, or fantasising about him making love to her.

A dark shape was shading the sun. Tamsin frowned and stirred before she slowly opened her eyes and stared at Bruno's hard profile. He was lying beside her on the grass, propped up on one elbow. Silhouetted against the hazy apricot light, he reminded her of an exquisite sculpture. But when he turned his head towards her she was achingly aware that his golden skin was *not* hewn from marble, and knew that it would feel warm and sensual beneath her fingertips.

Shocked by his unexpected appearance, she could not

disguise the flare of desire in her eyes. The boundaries between dreams and reality blurred. She didn't know if he was real, or a figment of her imagination but it no longer mattered, and she lifted her hand to him in unspoken invitation.

'Do you often cry in your sleep?'

His voice dispelled the lingering cobwebs in her mind and she quickly dropped her hand and sat up. Her cheeks were wet, but when she went to brush her fingers over her face he forestalled her and caught a stray tear with his thumb-pad.

'It's just a dream I have sometimes—it's nothing,' she said shakily. It was months since she'd had that dream, and the fact that it had returned was an indication of her unsettled state of mind. She shifted beneath Bruno's speculative stare, feeling the familiar tug of awareness at the sight of him in faded denims that moulded his thighs and a black tee shirt through which she could see the delineation of his powerful abdominal muscles.

'You were calling for Neil. I heard you from down by the pool,' he said brusquely. 'That was your husband's name, wasn't it? Do you often dream about him?'

Tamsin frowned. 'No, never,' she replied tersely. 'You must have been mistaken. He's the last person I would dream about.' She could not hide the faint bitterness in her voice, and she flushed when Bruno gave her a curious glance.

'Why did you split up? You were only married for a year, I understand. Love's young dream did not last very long, did it?' he murmured mockingly, reminding Tamsin of his scathing opinion of marriage.

Bruno did not believe in love or fidelity. He would never understand the devastation she'd felt when she had learned that Neil had been unfaithful, and she had no intention of confiding in him. 'We realised that we wanted different things,' she said shortly. 'It seemed sensible to end our relationship sooner rather than later.'

Her face was shuttered, but Bruno caught the note of regret in her voice and was irritated by it. She sounded as though she was genuinely sad that her marriage had failed, and he wondered why he disliked the idea that she might still have feelings for her ex-husband. 'I'm sure the sizeable divorce settlement offered some consolation,' he drawled laconically. 'I understand your husband was a wealthy banker?'

Tamsin drew a sharp breath and jumped to her feet. 'I won't even try to dignify that statement with a reply,' she hissed. 'Think what you like, Bruno. I really don't care. Why are you here, anyway?' she snapped. 'I assumed you were busy with your girlfriend.'

'Which one?' Bruno queried lazily, following her across the lawn.

'The one you're pictured with in this morning's newspaper,' Tamsin spat.

She marched back towards the villa, but he easily caught up with her, plainly amused by her simmering anger. 'You mean Donata.'

'Do I?' Even her name was exotic, Tamsin thought miserably. 'I'm afraid I don't have a list of the names of all your lovers.'

'It's a long list, *cara*.' Bruno's sudden, unexpected grin caused her heart to flip, and an emotion that felt horribly like jealousy burned inside her when she noted the wickedly sensual gleam in his eyes 'But actually Donata isn't one of them. She's my second cousin, and the only other great-grandchild of Antonio Di Cesare.'

Tamsin shrugged her shoulders, feigning disinterest, but Bruno continued. 'Actually, I dated two beautiful women last night.'

'Bully for you.'

'It was my sister's birthday, and I always spend it with her. Jocasta was deeply affected by the rift between me and my father.' Bruno's brief spurt of good humour quickly faded and his face darkened. 'She was five years old when my mother died. Her birth had taken my parents by surprise, but she was a very welcome addition to the family. After my mother's death Jocasta clung to me, her big brother, and when my father remarried she needed me more than ever. Miranda did not like children,' he added grimly. 'And when my father banished me he refused to allow Jocasta to see me. We were only reunited after my father died, when I returned to Italy and cared for her for the remainder of her childhood. We remain close, and I took her and our cousin to one of Florence's finest restaurants to celebrate her birthday.'

Bruno fell silent as they crossed the courtyard and entered the villa. From his expression it was clear he was thinking about the past, and his hatred for the woman he blamed for destroying his relationship with his father. Tamsin sighed; Bruno seemed determined to believe she was a woman like his stepmother, and she didn't know how she could convince him otherwise.

'The work on the villa is really coming on,' she said when they stepped into the hall. 'The new terracotta floor tiles are down, and most of the paintwork in the lower floor rooms is finished.' She nodded to the workmen, who were busy applying paint in a subtle shade of gold to the walls of the wide, airy hall. She had established a good relationship with all the contractors and smiled at the men, unaware that their gazes lingered on her long, tanned legs and the way her denim shorts moulded her pert derrière.

But Bruno noticed, and was surprised by the intensity of the urge that made him want to grab the workmen by their necks and boot them out of his house. He did not pay them to leer at his woman, he thought furiously, and snarled at them to get back to work before he followed Tamsin into the lounge, his frown deepening. When the hell had he begun to think of her as *his woman?*

But she soon would be, he decided fiercely. All his attempts to dismiss her from his mind had failed—four weeks of agonising frustration was testament to that, he acknowledged derisively. His only alternative was to face the problem head-on and seduce her into his bed.

He was furious that Tamsin seemed to have some sort of hold over him. Despite her protestations of innocence, he was still convinced that she had deliberately forged a friendship with James Grainger for financial gain, and the realisation that she had previously done the same thing with elderly war hero Edward Abbot reinforced his view that although she had the face of an angel she did not have the heart to match.

But this knowledge made no difference to his hunger for her. Night and day he couldn't stop thinking about her, and he was determined to take steps to control the situation. His father's obsession with an avaricious slut had caused him to make a series of business blunders that had severely damaged the House of Di Cesare—but he was not obsessed with Tamsin, Bruno reassured himself. He simply wanted to take her to bed and expurgate his inconvenient desire for her.

'I've made up a workboard of fabrics and colour schemes for the dining room, but I don't know if you've time to look at it now,' Tamsin said, while Bruno glanced around the sitting room that looked bright and stylish now that the dark walls had been painted in shades of cream and peach. 'Are you going back to Florence tonight or in the morning?'

'I shall be here for the next few days at least. I don't have any meetings scheduled, and I can just as easily work here as at my office.'

'I see.' Tamsin's heart lurched, and she immediately decided that she would avoid him as much as possible. She was terrified that she might unwittingly reveal how much she longed for him to take her in his arms and kiss her. 'Well, I'll do my best not disturb you,' she murmured.

She made to walk past him, but he stepped closer, blocking her path. 'But you do disturb me, Tamsin,' he said softly. 'You've disturbed me since the moment we first met.'

His eyes glittered with unmistakable invitation, but from somewhere Tamsin found the strength of will to fight the insidious warmth that flooded through her veins. 'When you decided that I was planning to con a vulnerable widower out of his money, you mean?' she snapped coldly.

Bruno was too close. She could feel the warmth of his body, and her senses flared when she caught the subtle musk of the cologne he favoured. She needed to move away from him *now*, while she could still think straight, but he reached out and ran a finger lightly over her cheek before cupping her chin in his palm.

'I have been thinking about that,' he murmured, his voice as soft and sensuous as crushed velvet. 'And maybe I was wrong.'

'You don't really believe that,' Tamsin whispered, even while hope flared in her chest. 'You think I'm a woman like your stepmother.'

Bruno had moved closer still, and now his arm snaked around her waist, drawing her body into intimate contact with his. His eyes were hooded and slumberous, but Tamsin could feel his tension, and knew he was exerting his formidable will over his body, to prevent himself from lowering his head and ravishing her mouth with hot, hungry kisses. But she *wanted* him to kiss her, she acknowledged as a tremor ran through her. She wanted it more than she had ever wanted anything in her life.

'I'm not what you think I am. I'm really not,' she told him huskily, her eyes locked with his by some invisible force. 'Now I know about your family history I understand why you assumed the worst of me, but I swear that I have no hidden agenda for my friendship with James.'

She couldn't bear him to think she was unscrupulous, but as his head lowered slowly towards her everything but her frantic need to feel his lips on hers faded from her mind.

The last time he had kissed her, on the balcony of his apartment, he had sought to dominate and punish her. This time he was no less dominant, and his lips were firm as he determinedly parted hers, but the underlying gentleness of the kiss tore down her fragile defences, and she responded to him with all the pent-up need that had been building since she had arrived in Italy.

Bruno slid his hand into Tamsin's hair and angled her head so that he could deepen the kiss. Her mouth felt soft and moist beneath his, and the tentative stroke of her tongue sent blood thundering through his veins.

'You are like a fever in my blood,' he growled. He hated himself for his weakness, but he had fantasised about making love to her for weeks, and now that she was in his arms he couldn't fight the temptation of her silk-soft skin beneath his fingertips. With a muttered oath he caught hold of the hem of her tee shirt and dragged it over her head. She made no attempt to stop him, and when he reached round and unfastened her bra she shivered and stared up at him with undisguised excitement in her eyes.

She gave a little gasp when he cupped her breasts in his hands. He knew what she wanted, and his body hardened and strained uncomfortably against his jeans as he trailed his mouth down her throat and then lower. Her nipples had already swollen to tight, hard peaks, and he laved first one and then the other with his tongue, before closing his mouth around one crest and sucking until she whimpered with pleasure.

'I'm prepared to accept that I may have misjudged you,

bella,' he murmured, as he lifted his mouth from her breast. He moved up to claim her lips once more in a slow, drugging kiss that stoked the fire burning inside him. He frowned, startled to realise that it wasn't just a line to coerce her into his bed. Maybe he *had* been wrong about her? he brooded, his eyes narrowing as he studied the delicate beauty of her face.

But right at this moment he didn't care. The contrast of her pale creamy skin against his darker flesh was an irresistible temptation. He wanted to see and feel her naked body beneath his, and his fingers deftly released the button of her shorts and slid down the zip before he lifted her and laid her down on the sofa.

In his haste to join her he knocked into a low wooden table, scattering Tamsin's design magazines and a pile of postcards over the floor. He had already settled his body on top of her, and he cursed and stretched out an arm to gather up her things, rubbing his hips sinuously between her thighs and thinking of nothing but his urgency to remove the rest of their clothing and sink his aroused shaft deep into her.

'You must have written to half of England,' he muttered as he retrieved several postcards depicting famous sights of Florence.

He threw them onto the table and stared at Tamsin, tempted by her softly swollen lips and her dusky pink nipples that strained provocatively towards him. *Dio,* he was desperate for her—but whilst his body was clamouring for sexual fulfilment his brain had registered something that made him hesitate, and glance again at the postcard on the top of the pile.

'Why are you writing to James?'

'I…' Tamsin licked suddenly dry lips. Her heart was beating in frantic jerks, and her chest rose and fell in time with her swift, shallow breaths. Seconds ago Bruno's eyes had reminded her of warm molasses, but now they were as hard and cold as polished jet. 'It's just a postcard, that's all, telling him about how the villa is coming on, and what the weather is like here. Why shouldn't I write to him?' she demanded angrily, her desire fading to be replaced with fury as Bruno's lip curled contemptuously. 'He's all alone at Ditton Hall while Davina and Annabel are away.'

She also knew that James had been advised by his doctors to rest as much as possible and keep visitors to a minimum during this break from chemotherapy, but she couldn't explain that to Bruno—and from the look of rage on his hard face she doubted he would listen or believe her anyway.

'How annoying for you that you're stuck here in Tuscany, *bella*,' Bruno drawled, in a voice that sent ice slithering down her spine. 'Given the chance, I'm sure you'd hurry straight to Ditton Hall to ease James's loneliness.'

He slid his eyes insolently over Tamsin's breasts. Her nipples were still hard, begging for the possession of his mouth, and when he trailed his finger across one rosy peak he heard her muffled gasp, saw her eyes darken with desire.

'Bruno...don't!' She brought her hands up to cover her breasts and he gave a harsh, unpleasant laugh.

Madre de Dio! How could he be such a fool? When she'd looked at him with her huge blue eyes and given him that shy, innocent smile, he'd actually started to trust her. But she was a clever little actress—like his stepmother—and he was no better than his father. The thought burned in his brain and fury surged through him, made even worse by the knowledge that his anger was mixed with a primitive sexual hunger that he seemed unable to control.

'I could take you here and now, Tamsin, and we both know you wouldn't stop me,' he taunted cruelly. 'I even admit I'm tempted. I'm as frustrated as hell, and it would be so easy to sate my hunger within your delectable body. But I suddenly find I am fastidious,' he hissed, and he rolled off her and stood staring down at her semi-naked body with such searing contempt in his eyes that Tamsin felt sick with humiliation.

'No!' She gave a sharp cry when he snatched up the postcard she had written to James and ripped it in two. 'How dare you? You had no right to do that. This is ridiculous,' she grated, temper giving her the necessary impetus to scramble off the sofa and drag her tee shirt over her head. 'I'll write to who I damn well like. Either that or I'll leave the villa, terminate my contract and go home. You can't *make* me stay here,' she said, faint desperation edging into her voice when Bruno stood, towering over her, his dark eyes mocking her.

'Oh, but I can, *bella*,' he murmured silkily. 'You will remain here until your work on the villa is complete, and after that I'll decide what I'm going to do with you. But you won't be visiting Ditton Hall any time soon,' he promised in a hard voice.

And after awarding her a look of blistering disgust he strode from the room, leaving Tamsin shaking with rage and misery that yet again she had fallen into his arms, only for him to humiliate her.

CHAPTER EIGHT

A STORM was brewing. The night air was hot and heavy and although the air conditioning was working flat out Bruno felt stifled inside the villa.

He couldn't sleep—but what was new about that? he thought bitterly as he strode through the dark garden down to the pool. If he'd learned anything over the past few weeks it was that sexual frustration was not conducive to a restful night.

He had driven back to Florence at the beginning of the week—only hours after he had arrived at the villa—not trusting himself to remain under the same roof as Tamsin without wringing her neck or giving in to the hunger clawing in his gut and carrying her off to his bed. Common sense told him to forget her, get on with his life and, if necessary, sleep with as many women as it took to eject her permanently from his mind.

But to his disgust his common sense seemed to be in short supply—along with his customary needle-sharp business brain and the ruthless ambition that had earned him the respect of his company board members and the fear of his enemies. It had been a hellish week, and his secretary had been unable to disguise her relief when he had sent her home at six o'clock, telling her that he would be spending the weekend at the Villa Rosala should she need to contact him.

Muttering a profanity, he dived into the pool. The water was blessedly cool on his hot skin, and he swam until his muscles ached but were no longer knotted with tension. How could his cool, logical brain accept his initial suspicions about Tamsin and yet his body still crave hers with a carnal, shaming hunger? And how could it be that, despite knowing her for what she was, he missed her company? During their discussions about her designs for the villa he had found her to be intelligent and interesting, and every week he had secretly found himself looking forward to the weekends so that he could spend time with her.

So Tamsin was different from his usual diet of airhead socialites, he conceded, flipping over to float on his back while he stared up at the starless night sky. But she was no different from every other grasping, eye-on-the-main-chance woman who was attracted to his wealth as much as to him. Women like his father's second wife.

Miranda had seen his father coming, he thought bitterly. She'd understood the vulnerability of a grieving widower and ruthlessly exploited his father's loneliness—and he had been flattered by the interest of a beautiful woman so many years his junior, and fallen for her so hard that he'd been blinded to the glaring fact that she was only in love with his bank balance.

Every instinct Bruno possessed warned him that Tamsin was another Miranda. But he would *not* be another Stefano, he vowed. Tension gripped him once more and he began to slice through the water, completing lap after lap as he fought to exorcise her from his mind.

It was hot, stiflingly hot, and Tamsin felt as though she was in a furnace. She could feel the pain building until it seemed to rip through her, tearing at the fragile threads of life within her. With an agonised cry she fought against the sheet that imprisoned her body like a shroud and sat bolt upright, her chest heaving as she opened her eyes and realised that she was in her bedroom at the Villa Rosala.

She had been dreaming. The old, familiar dream that even after all this time was still shockingly real. The human mind was an amazing thing, her GP had explained gently when she'd visited him, convinced that she was going mad. The stomach cramps and the terrible dragging sensations low in her pelvis were as real as they had been when she'd miscarried her baby, but now that she was awake they were fading, whereas on that day the pain had been unendurable.

She didn't want to think about it. Her body had long since healed, but the pain in her heart was still raw, and she certainly couldn't risk lying down and going back to sleep knowing that she would return to the dream, where she was running along endless hospital corridors looking for her baby. Her room felt like an oven, and she felt a sudden desperate need for fresh air. When she crept through the dark, silent house and stepped into the garden the air prickled with static electricity that warned a storm was coming closer. A low rumble of thunder from the distant hills confirmed it, but she couldn't face going back inside.

For the second week in a row, sleep had eluded her for most hours of each night. Even when exhaustion did finally claim her, towards dawn, she was tormented by images of Bruno's hands caressing her, his lips brushing softly against her skin, until she awoke burning up with desperate, shaming, sexual frustration and an overwhelming desire to burst into tears.

She didn't know why she had dreamed about the miscarriage tonight. She was rapidly turning into an emotional wreck, she thought dismally. And it was no good telling herself that the only reason she thought about Bruno constantly was because her body was fixated with his. She had been drawn to him from the moment she'd first met him—had felt that her soul was joined with his by invisible twine—and despite his cruel, scathing contempt of her, she was terrified that she was falling in love with him.

Thunder sounded again, ominously close, and raindrops as big as pennies spattered onto the stone steps that led down to the pool. Clouds obliterated the moon, and the darkness seemed as cloying as a heavy cloak, but a sudden streak of lightning lit up the sky and illuminated a statue of such breathtaking beauty that she stopped dead, unable to tear her eyes from its perfect form.

'Bruno.'

The sudden dark after the lightning blinded her, but seconds later another bolt zigzagged above and threw his naked body into stark relief as he hauled himself out of the pool.

Her brain was struggling to comprehend that he was really here, and not just a figment of her imagination. He hadn't arrived at the villa before she had gone to bed and, recalling his fury with her the last time she had seen him, she'd told herself that he would probably remain in Florence for the weekend.

But he was here, alive and real, and so utterly beautiful that her breath caught in her throat as she moved slowly, as if in a trance, down the steps towards him.

'Go back to bed, Tamsin,' Bruno's voice sounded harsh, slicing through the cloying night air. 'The storm's nearly on us and you shouldn't be out here.'

Tamsin heard his words but did not heed them as she continued down the steps. The lightning had faded, but not before her eyes had glimpsed the rippling muscles of his chest and abdomen and the awesome power of his erection.

Bruno was here, and she needed him. She needed to blot out the pain of losing her baby—a pain that was as raw now as it had been years ago—and she craved the warmth and the strength and the exquisite pleasure only his body could give. She wanted a re-affirmation of life—proof that she could still experience happiness, however fleeting—and without pausing to examine her actions she walked towards him.

The slow patter of lazy raindrops suddenly became a deluge; thunder echoed around them and lightning split the sky in two.

'Tamsin—go.' He was feet from her, and she heard his sharp intake of breath when she lifted the hem of her night-gown and drew it over her head. Her naked body was milky pale against the darkness, but he could see that her breasts were swollen and ripe for him, her nipples jutting provoca-tively, begging for the stroke of his tongue and the hungry caress of his mouth.

They stood facing each other, so close that electricity seared between them, making the tiny hairs on Tamsin's body stand on end. Close enough to touch, but not touching—not yet. Two people bound by an invisible force as pagan and powerful as the lightning that rent the sky. Nothing existed but the fierce, primal hunger that made them both tremble. Time and place faded and they were simply a man and a woman, naked beneath the heavens, waiting for that finite moment when passion exploded and swept them up in its storm force.

Bruno was breathing hard, his chest heaving as he sought to control the dictates of his body and failed. 'You have one last chance, *bella*,' he ground out roughly. 'If I touch you I won't be able to stop. Not this time.'

'I don't want you to stop.' Tamsin's eyes were slowly growing accustomed to the dark, but although she could not see him clearly her other senses were so acute that she could feel the heat emanating from him, and hear each harsh, jerky breath he took. 'I can't fight you—*this*—any more,' she whis-pered. The chemistry between them was a potent force she could no longer deny, and she needed him as she needed oxygen to breathe.

His control snapped suddenly, violently. 'Tamsin,' he reached for her like a man in a dream who fully expected her to disappear beneath his touch. He ran his hands up her arms and pushed her wet hair back from her face with fingers that shook slightly. Thunder sounded directly above their heads, a harsh, primitive growl, as he hauled her up against his rain-slicked chest and captured her mouth in a hungry, desperate kiss.

One hand tangled in her hair, holding her fast, while his mouth crushed her lips with an urgent passion that matched hers. It was as if the restraint he had enforced over his body for the past weeks had suddenly burst, and his hunger was a seething torrent that smashed everything in its path. Tamsin clung to his shoulders and matched him kiss for savage, yearning kiss, parting her lips and welcoming the erotic thrust of his tongue. The storm raged around them, but she was conscious of nothing but her clamouring need to feel him deep inside her, for his body to join with hers in a pagan ritual as old as man so that they became one.

'*Dio*, what are you doing to me?' he muttered harshly as he swept her into his arms and laid her down on the sodden grass, immediately covering her body with his own. 'I knew you were a sorceress, *bella*. You make me feel like I'm the strongest, most powerful man in the world, and yet at the same time you weaken me.'

This last accusation was barely audible, and the words seemed to be wrenched from his throat, clawing at Tamsin's heart. She understood him—understood how he must resent this wildfire passion and his shocking level of need, as she did. And yet, like her, he could not fight it.

It was even worse for him, because he despised and mistrusted her, believed she was like the stepmother he hated.

How he must hate himself for his inability to resist the chemistry that bound them together. Tenderness swept over her and she slid her fingers into his hair as he lowered his head to her breast. The rain was falling so hard that it felt like needles piercing her skin, enervating each nerve-ending so that her entire body felt acutely sensitive. She could smell the wet earth mingled with the primitive perfume of male pheromones, and when he drew one pointed, throbbing nipple into his mouth she arched her back and gave a thin, animal cry that was swallowed up by the noise of the storm.

Her body had been created for his touch, she thought when he slid his hand down and pushed her thighs apart, with a rough impatience that made her tremble with anticipation. Despite his urgency she knew instinctively that he would never hurt her, and when he parted her his fingers were gently persuasive, teasing her with butterfly-soft caresses before slipping inside her, one and then two digits, tenderly stretching her in readiness for his full possession.

'Bruno, please—now.'

She dug her nails into his rain-wet shoulders and anchored there as she tried to urge him down onto her. She couldn't wait. Every muscle in her body ached, and she twisted her hips as the subtle movements of his fingers created a spiralling knot of tension low in her pelvis. With shaking hands she pushed his soaking hair back from his brow and caught the feral glitter in his dark eyes as he slowly lowered himself. She could feel the solid ridge of his erection push into the soft flesh of her belly, and then nudge insistently between her legs as she stretched them wide and lifted her hips to welcome him.

The savagery of his first thrust startled her, and her audible gasp caused Bruno to still, his shoulder muscles bunched and his breath shallow and rasping in his throat.

'Tamsin?'

She heard the questioning note in his voice, and as she felt him slowly withdraw she frantically wrapped her arms around his neck, pulling him down so that he gave a muffled groan and thrust again, deep and fierce, as he took her with a primitive force that was shocking and wonderful. Tamsin felt her vaginal muscles close around him, and she smiled a secret smile of feminine triumph when the last vestiges of his control splintered and he drove into her in a pagan rhythm that sent them both spiraling higher and higher towards the edge of heaven.

Her last conscious thought as waves of intense sensation closed over her was that this was where she was meant to be—in his arms, her body joined with his in the most fundamental way.

He was still driving into her with strong, hard strokes, but his pace had increased, become more urgent, and suddenly she was there, her body suspended for timeless seconds, before rapture devoured her and she sobbed his name over and over in the intensity of her climax. As she writhed beneath him, he paused and snatched air into his lungs. She could feel the thunderous beat of his heart echoing in unison with hers, and she opened her eyes to see his face, shadowed and mysterious in the enveloping dark.

A thin sliver of moonlight spilt from behind the clouds and settled on the hollows and planes formed by his sharp cheekbones as he threw his head back and muttered a savage imprecation in his native tongue. She knew he was trying to prolong the moment of release, but then he surged into her one final time, his harsh groan of ecstasy muffled against her lips as he claimed her mouth in a searing kiss. His big body shook, and she wrapped her arms around him and held him close, loving the feel of his weight pushing her into the damp earth.

She could have remained there for ever, beneath the wild night sky while the torrential rain lashed their bodies, but eventually Bruno lifted his head from the hollow at the base of her throat and stared down at her, his expression unfathomable.

'You certainly choose your moments, *bella*,' he growled. Another flash lit up the sky and he rolled off her and tugged her to her feet. 'We'd better get inside before we drown or we're electrocuted—although the lightning is nothing compared to the sexual energy generated between us.'

With her hand imprisoned in his they raced through the rain, back to the house. Tamsin could only imagine what they looked like, naked and so wet that their hair was slicked to their heads, and she prayed that Battista was not awake and watching the storm from the window of the staff cottage.

Bereft of the heat of Bruno's body, her skin quickly chilled, and she was shivering by the time he led her into the master bedroom. The subtle shades of silvery grey and duck-egg-blue worked brilliantly, she mused as she glanced around his room, which was the first in the villa she had completed. The bedside lamps she had chosen to complement the décor looked perfect, but the glow they emitted seemed blinding after the dark, and she blushed when Bruno's dark eyes settled on her.

'You can't be embarrassed now,' he said, plainly amused when she crossed her arms over her breasts. 'Not after what we just shared. Or are you only a wildcat on dark and stormy nights?'

'Don't!' She shuddered at the memory of her wanton response to him, but he caught hold of her wrists and tugged her arms down, naked desire burning in his gaze as he cupped her breasts in his palms.

'You are incredible Tamsin,' he muttered raggedly. 'I have never felt such hunger for a woman, or known such fierce passion. And I am greedy for you again.' The last was uttered on a raw note, as if he was ashamed of his need for her.

Colour winged along his cheekbones as her startled gaze

rested on the jutting length of his arousal. Oh, God—again, and so soon. She was conscious of an answering heat flooding through her veins and pooling between her thighs as he stroked his thumb-pads gently over her nipples. She stared at him wordlessly, hopefully, and with a muttered oath he lifted her into his arms.

'Next time we'll enjoy the comfort of my bed, rather than making love in a mud bath. And, talking of baths…' He shouldered the door to the *en suite* bathroom and carried her into the shower, where he activated the spray and proceeded to soap every inch of her until she was panting and mindless with wanting him.

He shampooed her hair, and when they were both free of all traces of mud, he wrapped her in a towel and rubbed her dry. He took his time, and was clearly amused when her patience snapped and she flung the towel to one side before curving her arms around his neck.

'Now, Bruno—please, *now*.'

Her husky plea shattered his restraint and made a mockery of the idea that he should wait a while before making love to her again, to give her body time to adjust to the power of his possession. Muttering something in his own language, he lifted her and strode back into the bedroom, tumbling them both onto the bed and lifting her so that she straddled his hips.

'Oh, yes—now, *bella*,' he growled, his eyes glinting at her shocked expression when he guided her onto his swollen shaft. 'Have you never done it like this before?'

She flushed at the note of faint surprise in his voice and shook her head, her eyes widening as she absorbed him deep into her, and then gasped when he clasped her hips and began to rock her up and down. It was exquisite, and when she fell forward and he captured first one nipple and then its twin in his mouth she was sure she would die of pleasure. But instead the sensations kept on building as he taught her to ride him. The last of her inhibitions dissolved beneath his murmurs of encouragement, and their mutual climax was so intense that she almost blacked out. It was only the sound of him groaning her name that kept her anchored to consciousness.

She did not know how long she lay on top of him, their bodies still joined, the silence fractured by the sound of their ragged breathing, but at last he rolled her onto her back, stretched out beside her and tucked his hands beneath his head. Without the comfort of his arms holding her close the warmth quickly drained from her body, and doubts and re-criminations assembled in droves. The silence shredded her nerves, and as last she sat up and swung her legs over the side of the bed—only to find herself trapped when he snaked his arm around her waist and hauled her back.

'Don't even think of leaving.' His voice was cool and con-trolled, no hint of the fire that had blazed between them minutes before.

The underlying note of mockery hurt, even though she had mentally prepared herself for it, and Tamsin shivered, her eyes wide and wary when she turned her head to look at him.

'I think we have proved conclusively that, whatever else we might think of each other, neither of us can deny that the passion between us is wilder and more elemental than anything nature cares to dole out,' he said dispassionately. 'From now until the villa is finished you'll spend the nights here with me, *bella mia*, and that's not negotiable—*lo capite*?'

'How can you bear to make love to me, thinking of me as you do?' she asked, shaken by the hardness in his eyes. 'I thought you were too *fastidious?*'

With one swift movement he tugged her down so that she was flat on the mattress and rolled on top of her, trapping her beneath him. He was fully aroused, and Tamsin drew a sharp breath when he slid his hands beneath her bottom, lifted her, and entered her with one powerful thrust that took him deep within her. His eyes locked with hers and his mouth curved into self-derisive smile.

'Clearly not *too* fastidious,' he murmured, and then captured her mouth in a brutal kiss that cut off her angry response and drove everything but the exquisite sensation of his possession from her mind.

When Tamsin opened her eyes next morning it was to the sight of a blue and cloudless sky revealed through the open curtains. The storm of the previous night might have been a dream, but her aching muscles and the feeling of drowsy contentment served as a reminder of her enthralling sex session with Bruno—both in the garden and then throughout the rest of the night that she had spent in his bed.

'Fool,' she berated herself as she padded over to the window and stared out at the sun-soaked garden, where scarlet geraniums had already recovered from their battering by the rain and vibrated with exuberant colour.

The pool glinted aquamarine at the far end of the terrace, and the sight of it made her groan as she recalled how she had stripped and offered herself to Bruno like a sacrificial virgin. She was hardly virginal, she thought derisively. Not after a night in which he had seemed intent on expanding her sex education. Caught up in a flaming vortex of passion, she had proved a willing pupil—and she had been tutored by a patient and wickedly inventive master.

She would never be able to look Bruno in the face again, she thought despairingly, covering her hot cheeks with her hands. Where was her pride when she needed it? Buried, along with her self-respect, her brain replied caustically. When she was away from him she could think logically, but the moment he held her and looked at her with that hungry gleam in his eyes she was lost.

He had told her that he wanted her in his bed while she remained working at the villa, and although she should refuse him she knew she would not. He was offering nothing but sex. Even though they had shared the most wondrous, incredible pleasure in each other's arms, his attitude towards her had not softened. He despised her, but he wanted her, and she would not deny him when it would be denying herself too.

She had no idea where he had gone, or whether he expected her to wait for him, but it was a working day, and the minuscule dribble of pride she still retained insisted that she should get on with the job he had brought her to Tuscany to do. As she emerged from his room, clutching his robe around her, she heard his voice floating up the stairs. She guessed from the one-sided conversation that he was speaking on the phone, and her few words of Italian meant that she could not have eavesdropped even if she had wanted to. But something in his tone made her pause on the landing.

He sounded as though he was having an argument with whoever was on the other end of the line. Not a furious row; his short, staccato phrases reminded her of a bickering lover—now angry, now cajoling—as if he was trying to make someone see his point of view.

It was a familiar scenario, she thought grimly, remembering the occasions when she had caught Neil muttering secretively into his mobile phone. His explanation had invariably been that he'd been speaking to someone from the golf club—or work, or the gym. And she'd believed him. In her trusting, Pollyanna optimism that their marriage was working, she'd never doubted her ex-husband's word or his loyalty.

It was only after Neil had gone that she'd realised those calls had been from Jacqueline. Now, as she pushed open her bedroom door and heard Bruno's voice again, this time catching a name, she wondered what was so important that he'd risen early to talk to his beautiful cousin Donata.

CHAPTER NINE

AUGUST slipped lazily into September, and the view from the Villa Rosala became a tapestry of reds and burnished golds as the leaves on the trees turned from green to russet. Tamsin spent the days overseeing the completion of her designs for the house and her nights in Bruno's bed, where their fierce passion showed no sign of fading.

This was possibly the closest place on earth to heaven, she mused one morning, as she stood in the huge, rustic kitchen, looking out at the mist that lay like a silver cloak over the distant fields. Tuscany was impossibly beautiful, and she was falling more deeply in love with each passing day—and not simply with the countryside, the voice in her head warned.

Bruno filled her mind as he filled her body—utterly and completely. She could think of nothing but the exquisite pleasure of his warm skin sliding on hers, and the sound of his gorgeous, sexy accent when he teased her or murmured softly in Italian as they lay together in the afterglow of making love.

If she wasn't careful he might become her reason for living— and that would be a dangerous situation. It was hard to believe that they had been lovers for over a month, but now the villa was very nearly finished, and it was time she went home.

Somehow—incredibly—their relationship had evolved

over the days and weeks from a bitter, resentful passion to something that was softer, occasionally even gentle, and anger had been replaced with tentative friendship. She knew that Bruno still mistrusted her, but he no longer accused her of being like his stepmother. She had even thought briefly of trying to discuss her friendship with James Grainger, but the same problem remained. James had specifically asked her not to tell anyone about his cancer, and she still could not give Bruno a viable reason for her regular meetings with the Earl.

Even if she did break James's trust, and Bruno believed her, he still thought she had deliberately befriended her elderly neighbour and persuaded him to make her a beneficiary in his will. On balance it seemed safer not to upset the fragile peace between them for the short time that she had left at the villa.

Lost in her silent reverie, she jumped at the sound of his voice. 'The bathroom suppliers have just phoned.' Bruno strode into the kitchen and Tamsin spun round, the sight of him in his grey suit and pale blue silk shirt causing a familiar weakness in her lower limbs. 'The taps and other fittings that were delayed are now in stock. I told them you would phone back to arrange delivery.'

'Great,' Tamsin replied, desperately trying to inject enthusiasm into her voice. Completion of the *en suite* bathroom attached to one of the guest bedrooms had been delayed because of a problem with the suppliers, but once the fittings were in place she only had to choose towels and a few accessories to match the apple-green decor and the last room in the villa would be finished. 'Hopefully they'll deliver in the next couple of days, and then I'm all done here,' she said brightly. 'I'd better start packing.'

Bruno stiffened in the act of pouring a glass of fruit juice and frowned. 'I didn't realise you were in such a rush to leave,' he murmured, his eyes narrowing when she carefully avoided his gaze.

'I've been here for over two months,' Tamsin pointed out. 'When I spoke to Daniel last week he wanted to know if the villa was nearly finished as he has another commission lined up for me. It seems I'm quite in demand.' She faltered when Bruno's mouth tightened ominously.

'Why do you sound so surprised, *bella*? You have great talent, and the work you have done on the Villa Rosala exceeds all my expectations.'

'I'm glad you like it.' Why on earth did his words of praise cause tears to fill her eyes? Tamsin thought impatiently as she picked up a teatowel and dried a dish draining on the rack so thoroughly that she was in danger of rubbing off the pattern around the edge.

A tense silence fell while Bruno gulped down the juice and poured himself a cup of strong black coffee. He had woken that morning, as he had every other morning for the past month, feeling energised from a night of incredible sex. He was shocked by Tamsin's reminder that she had been staying at the villa for two months. He could hardly warrant that time had passed so quickly—particularly this last month that they had been sleeping together. Without him being conscious of it, they had settled into a routine of domestic bliss that should have set alarm bells ringing in his head, and the realisation that he was in no hurry to change the situation caused him to frown.

When had he begun to view her as his mistress rather than simply another blonde who was temporarily sharing his bed? he wondered. And why was he so irritated by her seemingly happy acceptance that he would want her to leave as soon as her work on the villa was complete? But what was the alternative?

With an angry shrug of his shoulders he drained his coffee cup and snatched up his briefcase, hardly able to believe that he was contemplating asking her to remain at the villa. There would have to be some sort of timescale, he brooded. And rules would have to be drawn up and fully understood by Tamsin before he could issue such an invitation, so that when he wanted to end the affair he could do so without suffering the annoyance of recriminations or tears.

'We'll talk about it when I get back,' he grated as he moved towards her and dropped a brief, hard kiss on her mouth. Her lips instantly softened and parted, and he could not resist the temptation to deepen the kiss, his body stirring when he felt her tongue slide into his mouth to tangle erotically with his. 'Why don't you stay on a while?' The words had left his lips before he'd had time to consider them, and once again he felt a jolt of shock that he did not want her to leave. Not yet, anyway. 'You must be owed some holiday from Spectrum. Spend it here with me, *bella*.'

The throaty invitation sent a quiver along Tamsin's spine, and she gave a silent groan of despair when her body sprang to urgent life. Only this morning Bruno had teased her that she was insatiable, when she had followed him into the shower, boldly encircled his shaft with her hands and stroked him, until he'd growled something in Italian and lifted her onto him, cupping her bottom while he thrust into her.

'I could take a week's leave, but with this new commission pending I can't stay for ever.'

Bruno forced himself to step away from the temptation of Tamsin's delectable body and tried to dismiss the fantasy of removing her clothes and spreading her beneath him on the enormous kitchen table. 'Who said anything about for ever?' he queried idly. 'You should know by now that I don't do eternity, *cara*, but you can't deny it would be more convenient if you continued to live here for a while. Once you're back in London we won't be able to meet up so often. My diary is pretty full for the next few months, and I can't rearrange my schedule to include overnight stops in London.'

He paused in the doorway and glanced back at her, noting how two months in the Tuscan sun had lightened her hair, so that it swung on her shoulders in a curtain of platinum blonde silk. 'Perhaps you should think about resigning from Spectrum?' he suggested, in a casual tone that masked his surprise as the unbidden words left his lips.

'Resign…? And do what exactly?' Tamsin demanded, confounded by the idea.

'I promise I can think of numerous ways to keep you occupied,' Bruno murmured coolly, seemingly unaware of the storm brewing on the other side of the kitchen.

'But this is my *career* we're talking about. I can't give it up just so that we can have a regular sex-life.' She was still reeling from his implication that he wanted their relationship to continue after she returned to England, and the idea that he wanted her to sacrifice her career so that she could stay with him was simply beyond belief.

Bruno glanced at his watch and gave an impatient shrug. 'So get a job here in Italy. I have a lot of influence in Florence, and I don't doubt I could secure you a position with any design company you choose.'

Twin spots of colour stained Tamsin's cheeks, and she put her hands on her hips to prevent them from seizing one of the heavy copper saucepans hanging from the ceiling beams and hurling it at his head. 'You don't think that my honours university degree in Design and several years' experience would count for much, then?' Her voice rose a notch, and Bruno's expression darkened. 'You're saying that even if I was totally useless companies would still offer me a job if I traded on the fact that I'm sleeping with you? Wow! That makes me feel good,' she hissed sarcastically.

'*Madre de Dio!* It's typical of a woman to make—how do you say?—a mountain out of a molehill,' Bruno growled. 'It was just a suggestion, *bella*. If you want to rush back to England, then go. We'll have to put up with the inconvenience of a long-distance affair and meet when I can allocate you time in my diary,' he added nastily, wondering why he suddenly felt the urge to be so unpleasant.

'Always supposing that the slot is equally convenient in mine,' Tamsin said through gritted teeth. How had she ever thought that his arrogance was an endearing trait?

Bruno's mouth tightened and he dipped his head. 'Of course. But I fear that two busy careers are not conducive to a smooth-running affair.'

Tamsin gave a tight smile. 'Well, instead of expecting me to sacrifice my job, you could always give up yours.'

His astounded expression was almost comical, and he stared at her as if she had suddenly grown another head. 'Don't be ridiculous. I am the president of a billion dollar global business empire. My position as head of the House of Di Cesare is my birthright, and soaring profits are proof that I have earned my place at the top,' he added proudly. 'You are blessed with great artistic flair, but—' He broke off and threw his hands in the air in a typically Latin gesture.

'But I'm just a lowly designer?' Tamsin finished grimly.

'I didn't say that,' Bruno exploded, as the last of his patience evaporated. 'I asked you to live with me. I did not expect the invitation to trigger a third World War.' He had confidently assumed that she would jump at the chance to stay on at the villa. He did not ask women to be his mistress every day of the week, and he wondered if she realised how many of his self-imposed rules he was breaking. 'I have to go. I'm late for a meeting,' he snapped, another glance at his watch revealing that he was going to have to phone his secretary and ask her to delay his meeting with a conglomerate of Japanese businessmen.

The day that had started so well with a wild sex session in the shower was rapidly deteriorating, he thought grimly. And it was all Tamsin's fault. He hated being late—and why the hell had she decided to discuss their future relationship now, when she knew he had to get to work? She trailed into the hall after him, and as he opened the front door he caught a glimpse of undisguised misery in her eyes and felt a curious tightening in his chest.

'We'll continue this discussion tonight,' he promised in a softer voice, but another surge of irritation that she hadn't immediately agreed to stay on at the villa with him prompted him to add, 'May I remind you that *you* instigated this morning's sex session, *cara?* I'm not knocking your eagerness,' he drawled. 'The passion between us has always been mutual, and we're both going to suffer the frustration of the damned if we're living a thousand miles apart.' As if to emphasise the point, he skimmed his hand lazily over her breasts and smiled when her nipples instantly hardened and jutted provocatively beneath her thin cotton shirt. 'Think about it,' he advised, his stinging kiss forcing her angry retort back into her mouth.

And while she was still debating which succinct phrase best expressed her fury, he slid into his car, fired up the engine and sped off down the drive.

Bruno was the most arrogant, egotistical...Tamsin ran out of adjectives as her temper simmered. He had made her sound like some sort of nymphomaniac—but the truth was she couldn't have enough of him, she acknowledged dismally, and the thought of going back to England and only seeing him occasionally was unbearable. But could she really give up her position with Spectrum in order to enjoy a few more weeks, at most, with a man who had always made it clear that he did not want a long-term relationship—especially one with a woman he still believed was a gold-digger?

She watched the contractors' van pull up in the front court-yard and four elderly-looking workmen slowly emerge. They should finish the tiling in the guest bathroom today, and she would not need them again—which was probably a good thing, she mused as she waved to the men. The housekeeper, Battista had told her that one of them—Luigi—was over seventy. They worked well, and were clearly master-crafts-men, but every task took twice as long as Tamsin had allowed for. She couldn't understand why Bruno had dismissed all the younger workmen…

His suggestion that she should give up her job and remain in Tuscany with him tormented her for the rest of the day. He had said they would discuss the future of their affair when he came home that night, and she didn't know what she was going to say to him, but she was reprieved from having to make a decision when he phoned late in the afternoon and ex-plained that problems in the New York office meant that he had to make an unexpected trip across the Atlantic. He was flying out the following morning, and had decided to spend the night at his apartment in Florence.

'I'll be back at the weekend,' he promised, when Tamsin could not hide the disappointment in her voice. 'It's only five nights, *bella*. If you decide to go back to England after the villa is finished we'll spend most of our time apart.'

'It will only be four nights if you come back here tonight,' she pointed out, trying not to sound as though she was des-perate to see him, and failing badly.

Bruno laughed, and the low, sexy rumble curled around her aching heart. 'I wish I could, *bella,* but something's come up. I'll see you soon.'

With a heavy heart Tamsin cut the call and wandered dismally around the empty villa. Every room looked stunning, but she found no pleasure in her finished designs, and the house seemed soulless without Bruno's vibrant presence. She could not bear the thought of sleeping alone in his bed, and spent a restless night back in the room she had occupied when she had first arrived at the Villa Rosala.

Finally, in the hour before dawn, she gave up. Bruno hadn't even gone to the US yet, and she missed him so much that she ached. She was under no illusion that continuing her affair with him would lead to happy-ever-after—and after her failed marriage she wasn't even sure it existed—but she'd settle for happy-right-now. And, having made the decision to remain in Tuscany for as long as he wanted her, she was eager to tell him before he left Florence.

Bruno had told her she could borrow the little car that the groundsman, Guido, used whenever she wanted, and she had often driven to the surrounding villages, but never as far as Florence. The sky was still pearly grey, streaked with pale pink, as she sped away from the villa, and she didn't see another vehicle on the road as it snaked through the country-side. An hour later she reached the outskirts of the city. Fortunately it was still so early that the traffic hadn't built up, and with the aid of her road map she managed to find Bruno's apartment without too much difficulty.

By the time she entered the lift her heart was pounding. She must be mad, she told herself. Bruno would have to leave for the airport soon, and she would only be able to see him for a few minutes. Would he be pleased when he learned of her decision to stay on at the villa as his mistress? Or would he already have had second thoughts? Her stomach clenched. What if he had changed his mind and no longer wanted her?

She had a vivid mental image of how he had lifted her into

his arms and made love to her with raw, primitive passion in the shower the previous morning and her nervousness lessened. He hadn't tired of her yet—and who could say, the little voice of optimism in her head whispered, how long his hunger for her would last?

'Signorina Stewart!' Bruno's butler, looking as smartly dressed as ever, despite the early hour, could not hide his surprise when he opened the door.

'Hello, Salvatore.' Tamsin followed him down the hall, her heart sinking at the oppressive silence of the apartment. 'I hoped to catch Signor Di Cesare before he left.'

The butler shook his head. 'He has already gone to the airport.' His usually impassive features softened slightly at her obvious disappointment. 'Sit down and I will bring you a cup of tea, *signorina*.'

Tamsin gave him a weak smile, but as soon as he had gone she stared bleakly out over the river and felt silly tears sting her eyes. Bruno would be back at the weekend, she tried to console herself. But part of the reason for her mad rush to Florence was because she had wanted to tell him she would stay with him before her nerve failed. They would have to make up for lost time when he returned, she decided firmly, a smile curving her lips as she considered on how five nights of abstinence would sharpen their hunger for each other, and how they would probably spend the entire weekend in bed.

It seemed pointless to linger in the empty apartment, but as she stepped into the hall, on her way to tell Salvatore not to bother with the tea, Bruno's bedroom door opened and a woman emerged.

'*Chi sono voi?* Who are you?' she demanded haughtily, in Italian and then in English.

Tamsin stared at the woman, wondering why she seemed

familiar. And then realisation dawned. She was the woman from the newspaper—Bruno's cousin Donata.

'My name is Tamsin Stewart. I…work for Signor Di Cesare,' she explained quietly.

'Is that so?' Donata's perfectly shaped eyebrows arched upwards.

The newspaper photograph had not done Donata justice, Tamsin conceded, studying the young Italian woman's glossy black hair, which tumbled around her shoulders, and her slanting dark eyes. She was seriously beautiful, and Tamsin felt a flicker of unease when she strolled into the hall, fastening her robe as she moved—but not before Tamsin glimpsed the skimpy black lace negligee she was wearing. It was obvious from her sexily tousled hair and the sleepy yawn she hastily hid behind her hand that she had spent the night in the apartment. But why was she coming out of Bruno's bedroom, looking like a smug sex-kitten who had gorged on cream?

'Tamsin Stewart?' Donata shrugged her shoulders uninterestedly. 'Are you a new maid? I'm sure you weren't here on my last visit. And shouldn't you be wearing a uniform?' she demanded, glancing at Tamsin's colourful cotton skirt and strap top. 'Just because Signor Di Cesare isn't here, it is not an excuse for standards to drop. You can run my bath and then get changed.'

'I'm not a maid. I'm an interior designer and I'm currently working on Bruno's villa.' Tamsin struggled to ignore the woman's rudeness, dredging up a smile that wasn't returned. 'I…need to go over a few things with him regarding some of my designs.' She invented a valid reason to explain her visit.

Donata's eyes had narrowed when Tamsin had used Bruno's Christian name rather than the more formal Signor Di Cesare, and she said mockingly, 'This early in the morning? You're very keen, Miss Stewart.'

Tamsin felt the betraying flare of heat scorch her cheeks, but ploughed on. 'I thought I might catch him before he left for his trip.'

'Well, you're too late. Bruno left twenty minutes ago, and he was running late then. I'm afraid we overslept…' The woman's mouth curved into a coy smile. 'After an energetic night.' She paused, her brilliant gaze noting how the colour leached from Tamsin's face. 'Oh, dear—you're not another of Bruno's little girlfriends, are you? I really must learn to be more discreet.'

Nausea slopped in Tamsin's stomach and made a mockery of her determination to remain calm. 'What do you mean? I know who you are,' she said, more strongly. 'You're Bruno's cousin.'

'Second cousin,' Donata corrected her softly. 'My father and Bruno's father were cousins, and I am a Carerra, but I am Antonio Di Cesare's great-granddaughter, and eventually, of course, I will take the Di Cesare name—when Bruno and I marry.'

'When you marry?' Tamsin parroted. 'Are you saying you are engaged to Bruno?'

Tamsin felt a curious buzzing sensation in her ears and she gripped the edge of the bureau. Years ago, when her ex-husband had admitted he was having an affair, she'd been sure she would never again feel such a raw sense of betrayal. But this was much worse. The idea that Bruno could be planning to marry his stunning olive-skinned cousin, with her knowing eyes and cruel smile, made her feel physically sick.

Donata shook back her silky curls and stretched languorously. 'It's not a formal arrangement at the moment, but there has been an understanding between us for years. I'm not sure if you know anything of Bruno's history,' she continued, glancing speculatively at Tamsin, 'but after his father banished him he moved to the US and stayed with my family. My father, Fabio, has never made any secret that he would love to have Bruno as his son-in-law,' she continued, 'and Bruno is very close to Fabio, so…' She shrugged her shoulders and smiled maliciously at Tamsin. 'I'm not sure Papà would be so pleased if he knew I actually share Bruno's bed on my regular visits to Florence, so we keep that a secret,' she said in a mock whisper, placing one long, scarlet-painted finger-nail across her lips.

Tamsin's stomach twisted, and she shook her head disgust-edly. 'It sounds like a marriage made in heaven,' she said tightly. 'But what about love?'

Donata looked at her incredulously, and then threw back her head and laughed. 'What *about* love, Miss Stewart? As far as I'm concerned it's not a vital commodity to a success-ful marriage, and Bruno shares my view.'

She stepped closer and stared intently into Tamsin's face. 'Don't tell me you've fallen for him? You fool,' she said spite-fully. 'Bruno isn't interested in *love*; he saw how it destroyed his father and he vowed when he was a young man that he would never repeat Stefano's mistakes. We're ideally suited, he and I,' she stated confidently. 'We both have something to gain from marrying—for me, money and power, and for Bruno, the strengthening of the Di Cesare bloodline, because I am a direct descendant of Antonio Di Cesare. Much as I loathe the idea of pregnancy, I'm prepared to give Bruno a child. You don't think he'd sacrifice all that for you, do you?'

She saw the confusion in Tamsin's eyes and gave another cold smile. 'Until we formalise our relationship, Bruno is free to indulge his predilection for attractive blondes. You're not the first, Miss Stewart, and I doubt you'll be the last. But ultimately Bruno is mine, and I'm prepared to wait for him for as long as it takes.'

Tamsin was saved from having to try and formulate a reply when the butler appeared, bearing a tray. 'Your tea, *signorina*,' he murmured, his bland features not flickering as he glanced from Tamsin to Donata.

'That won't be necessary, Salvatore. Miss Stewart is just leaving,' Donata said coolly. 'I'll let you show her out.'

She pushed past Tamsin, into the lounge, and Tamsin followed Salvatore dazedly down the hall, feeling as though her legs would give way at any second. When the butler opened the front door, she managed a faint, ironic smile.

'Thanks for the tea, Salvatore.'

He nodded gravely, and his stern expression softened imperceptibly. 'Sometimes situations are not always as they seem, *signorina*. I will inform Signor Di Cesare of your visit.'

'*No!*' Tamsin shook her head wildly. She had a feeling that Donata would not mention her visit to Bruno, and it would be the ultimate humiliation if he should ever find out that she had rushed to the apartment after only one night apart and come face to face with his lover and future wife. 'Please, Salvatore, don't say a word,' she begged, and after several moments' hesitation he slowly nodded and closed the door.

CHAPTER TEN

LONDON in early November was unremittingly grey and wet. The leaden skies were as heavy as Tamsin's spirits, and she shivered when she emerged from the Underground station and was hit by a blast of icy wind.

Christmas was over a month away, but the shop windows had been festooned with festive decorations for weeks, and Oxford Street was teeming with frantic shoppers.

It was a far cry from the hot, still days of summer in Tuscany. The two months she had spent at the Villa Rosala belonged to another time, another world, she thought bleakly. It had been a time of fleeting happiness that she had always known could not last, and it had ended abruptly when she had fled from Bruno's apartment in Florence with his cousin Donata's mocking laughter ringing in her ears.

Back at the Villa Rosala, she had written him a brief note, explaining that she had decided to return to England to continue with her career, and then she'd left and caught the next flight back to London, where she had spent the weeks since in a state of numb misery that had caused her flatmate Jess serious concern.

Bruno hadn't contacted her, and she hadn't expected him to. For him, their relationship had been a brief interlude of amazing sex with a woman he mistrusted. She suspected that he had resented the sizzling sexual chemistry that held them both in its thrall, and although he had asked her to remain at the villa with him for an unspecified time, he had known all along that he was going to marry Donata.

If nothing else, it proved that she had diabolical taste in men, Tamsin conceded with a grim smile. The only difference was that she had been married to Neil, and he must have known that his infidelity would break her heart. Bruno had never made any promises, but the image of him making love to his beautiful, sultry-eyed cousin hurt a hundred times more than when she had read a text message on her ex-husband's phone and realised that his work colleague Jacqueline was also his mistress.

She had returned to England determined to pick up the threads of her life, but as the weeks had passed a new concern had supplanted her misery and caused her to study the calendar with a growing feeling of dread. A home pregnancy test had confirmed her fears, and she had been even more shocked when her GP had sent her for an ultrasound scan to determine her dates, and she'd learned that she was eleven weeks pregnant.

'I can't believe it,' Jess had said, when Tamsin had confided in her. 'I thought pregnancy was supposed to make you put *on* weight, not lose it. You've been fading away since you came back from Italy. I assume it is Bruno's baby?' she'd added darkly. 'What are you going to do?'

'I don't know.' Tamsin had laid her hand on her flat stomach and tried to assimilate the range of emotions swirling inside her. Elation, joy—fear.

She still could not get her head around the fact that she was expecting Bruno's child. He had always been scrupulous about using protection, apart from one time—the night of the storm. Even now the memory of the explosive passion they had shared that night made her blush. Their loving had been as wild and elemental as the lightning that had ripped the sky apart, and in a strange way it seemed fitting that their child had been conceived at the apex of a thunderstorm.

'You're going to tell him, aren't you?' Jess had insisted. 'You can't do this on your own, Tamsin. I mean, I'll help out as much as I can, but you have to consider your financial situation. You won't be able to work when you're caring for a newborn baby, and Bruno is a billionaire, for heaven's sake. It's only right he should support his child.'

A shudder had run through Tamsin at Jess's words. She could just picture Bruno's fury if she went to him demanding money. 'I suppose I'll have to tell him. He has a right to know. But I don't want anything from him,' she told Jess fiercely. 'This is my baby and I'll take care of him—or her.' Her voice had faltered. 'But it's still early days,' she'd said, her throat constricting as the agonising memory of losing her first baby filled her with fear. 'Anything could happen.'

It wouldn't happen again, she tried to reassure herself now. Her miscarriage had been brought on by the stress of discovering that Neil had been cheating on her throughout their marriage. This time she would not allow anything to upset her, or cause her to risk losing another baby.

But the knowledge that she would at some point have to tell Bruno that she was carrying his child hung over her like a heavy cloud, and the sight of his stunningly handsome face smiling from the front cover of a celebrity gossip magazine had been the last straw. The woman in the picture looked as though she was intent on climbing inside his jacket with him, Tamsin had noted sourly. She was an internationally famous model, and as Tamsin had stared at her she recalled Donata's words that she was happy for Bruno to indulge in his predilection for beautiful blondes until they married.

The sooner she told him about the baby, the sooner she could put him out of her mind and her life, she decided, as she turned down a side street close to Hyde Park. She knew from the magazine article that he was currently in London, and now seemed an ideal time. She was absolutely certain he would not want to have anything to do with her or their child, but her heart was racing with nervous apprehension when she walked into the London offices of the House of Di Cesare.

Bruno got up from his desk and strolled over to the window of his office to stare out at the rain-lashed streets. Usually he exerted such supreme control over his life that nothing ever happened to surprise him. He did not like surprises, he conceded, and nothing had prepared him for the news imparted by his secretary that a Miss Tamsin Stewart was waiting in Reception and wanted to see him.

Why had she suddenly reappeared in his life, almost two months after he had returned to the Villa Rosala—his tiredness from a hellish few days evaporating at the anticipation of taking her to bed—and found that she had gone?

His mouth tightened at the memory. He'd read her pithy little note, explaining that she was returning to her job in London and didn't want the distraction of continuing their affair, with a mixture of anger and disbelief. Being dumped was a new experience for him, and he didn't like it.

Not that he was heartbroken, he thought caustically. Since the day his father had believed his stepmother's lies and told him he no longer considered Bruno his son he had built a concrete wall around his heart that he was confident was impenetrable.

He had cynically wondered if Tamsin was playing a game. Perhaps she believed that his unabated desire for her meant that he was actually falling for her? It was certainly no coincidence that she had walked out on him *after* he had asked her to remain in Italy as his mistress. But if she'd hoped that he would chase after her, she had been doomed to be disappointed. He'd missed her—he would admit that much—but he could live quite happily without her, and the only reason he had instructed his secretary to send her into him in five minutes was because he was curious to know what she was playing at now.

His office door opened and his secretary appeared.

'Miss Stewart's here.'

'*Grazie*, Michelle.' He forced himself to remain at the window for several more seconds before he turned and glanced across the room, and he was irritated to find that his heart was beating uncomfortably fast as he stared at Tamsin.

She had lost weight, was his first thought. Her golden tan had faded, and she looked pale and drawn but no less beautiful. Her incredible blue eyes seemed too big for her face, but he dismissed the idea that she looked fragile with a shrug of his shoulders.

'Please sit down.' He indicated a chair and noted that her hands were shaking when she immediately sat and pushed her hair over her shoulders. He wondered why she was nervous, and why he liked the idea that he disturbed her, but his face was impassive as he resumed his seat and studied her coolly across his desk. 'I'm afraid I'm not quite sure why you are here. Is this a social visit?' he murmured.

'No, not really.' Tamsin licked her parched lips and dropped her gaze to the desk in front of her.

She had been mentally preparing for this for days, but the moment she had walked into his office and seen him—tall and dominant and achingly beautiful—her brain had seized up and she could think of nothing but the memory of the wildfire passion they had once shared. She glanced at him fleetingly and then quickly looked away, her heart hammering painfully in her chest.

'There is a reason why I'm here.' She wished he would say something, rather than continue to stare at her dispassionately, and she wondered if his eyes had ever really been warm during the weeks that they had been lovers, or if she had imagined it. There was no easy way to say what she had to say, and in the end she just said it. 'I'm pregnant.'

'Ah.' Bruno leaned back in his chair and put the tips of his fingers together. 'Of course you are. Why didn't I think you would come up with something like this?'

His sardonic smile stirred her temper. 'I haven't come up with anything. I'm simply here to tell you that I am carrying your child,' she snapped. 'And before you say another word, yes, it's yours—no question. Although actually I really don't care if you believe me.'

Tears burned her eyes. His reaction was pretty much as she had expected, so why did she feel as though he had knifed her in the ribs? She remembered her ex-husband's fury less than a year into their marriage, when she had told him she was pregnant—his disbelief followed by his angry accusations that it was her fault and she must have deliberately missed her contraceptive pill. She had been devastated by Neil's reaction, and distraught at his hints that it was still early days and she didn't have to continue with the pregnancy. She wondered if Bruno was about to make the same suggestion, and a cold slab of anger settled in her chest. He might not want their baby but she did, and she would love and protect the fragile life within her.

Bruno stared at her as if he was determined to see inside her head. 'Forgive me for sounding suspicious, *bella*,' he said softly, 'but I understand that you attempted to persuade your husband to stay with you by telling him you were pregnant.

It didn't work then, and I can assure you that if your announcement that you are carrying my child is a ploy to restart our relationship it's not going to work now either.'

It was amazing how much pain the human body could withstand, Tamsin mused, feeling strangely detached from herself. She even managed to give Bruno a cool smile as she stood up. 'Right—I've done my duty and told you,' she said briskly, picking up her handbag and heading for the door. 'Your reaction is entirely as I predicted, Bruno. I knew you would want nothing to do with your child, and that suits me fine…because I really don't want anything to do with you. Goodbye.'

Her hand was on the doorknob. She was actually going to walk out. Bruno's eyes narrowed. Was she playing another game and gambling on him calling her back? Or was she telling the truth about the pregnancy?

'You've had your pregnancy confirmed I assume?' he growled, his tension rising when she opened the door.

She paused fractionally, her foot over the threshold. 'Yes.'

'How far?'

'Twelve weeks.' Tamsin's pride insisted that she should walk through the door and keep on walking, but she could not resist looking at him one last time.

Bruno's black brows were drawn into a slashing frown as he made a mental calculation. 'The night of the storm,' he said harshly. 'But if you've known all this time, why did you leave the villa? And why wait until now to tell me?'

'I didn't know then. I had an unusually light period a couple of weeks after that night and I assumed everything was all right.' She flushed, embarrassed at having to explain the technicalities. 'I only found out a week ago, and I was shocked when the scan showed my pregnancy was so well established. I could have told you the moment I found out, but—' she gave a faint shrug to hide the bolt of pain that shot through her

'—there is a higher risk of miscarriage in the first three months of pregnancy, and I decided to wait until I was sure I had something to tell you.'

Her voice shook, and Bruno glanced at her speculatively. She looked small and vulnerable, and he had to fight the urge to take her in his arms and simply hold her. His shock at her stark announcement was slowly receding, and he was certain now that she wasn't lying. She really was expecting his baby. He stared at her, searching for signs of her pregnancy. Concealed beneath the folds of that thick woollen coat was a tiny spark of humanity—his son or daughter—and he was shocked by the feeling of possessive pride that surged through him

He had assumed that he would one day have children, although he had never visualised actually settling down and spending his life with one woman. He had taken scrupulous care to prevent any of his mistresses claiming that they had conceived his child. He was cynical enough to realise that many women would consider nine months of pregnancy a small price to pay to secure a regular maintenance agreement from a billionaire—certainly enough to employ a full-time nanny to care for the resulting offspring.

The news that Tamsin was pregnant with his child had initially angered him. How could he have been so stupid as to fall into the age-old trap? But honesty forced him admit that it had been *his* mistake. On the night of the storm his hunger for her had been so urgent that he hadn't even thought about contraception. It was ironic that the first and only time he had ever had unprotected sex he had given Tamsin a child, he thought grimly. But, despite what she thought, he had no intention of shirking his duty.

'Don't look so shattered, Bruno.' Her voice mocked him. 'I don't want anything from you—certainly not your money,' she said bitterly. 'I have no expectations that you'll want a relationship with this baby, but there will come a time when our child will ask questions about his or her father, and I won't lie. I'll have to reveal your identity and make up some story... I don't know—that we loved each other but couldn't be together or something. But you have to accept that your child might want to contact you some time in the future.'

'My child will be able to contact me whenever he or she likes,' Bruno grated. 'Because my child will live with me in Italy and will never be in any doubt that I am its father.' He stared down at her with such haughty arrogance that Tamsin shivered with a mixture of confusion and unease. 'You are carrying the Di Cesare heir. I will not allow him to be born illegitimately.'

'What do you mean?' she whispered, unable to tear her eyes from the stark beauty of his chiselled features.

'I mean that for the child's sake I am prepared to marry you.'

Tamsin did not know what kind of reaction Bruno had envisaged at this astounding statement, but from his thunderous frown it was clear he had not expected her to burst into hysterical laughter.

'Do share the joke, *bella*,' he snapped, when she subsided into hiccups and wiped her eyes with fingers that for some reason were trembling. 'Although I can't say I find the future welfare of our child a laughing matter.'

'I'm sorry.' She gulped for air and found that her emotions had see-sawed and she now wanted to cry. 'It's just that there's a certain irony to this situation that you wouldn't understand.' Years ago, when she'd told her husband she was pregnant, he had promptly divorced her. Now she was pregnant by a man who believed her to be an unscrupulous gold-digger and he was *prepared to marry her*. Big deal, she thought furiously.

'It's kind of you to offer, Bruno,' she hissed sarcastically, ignoring his glowering stare, 'but I have no intention of marrying again—ever. And anyway,' she added before he could speak, 'bigamy is illegal.'

'I thought you were divorced—' he began heatedly.

'I am. But you are engaged to your cousin Donata, and you can't marry both of us.'

'Which trashy gossip magazine did you get that from? Some of the rubbish they print is amazing.'

The look of surprised incomprehension on his face was so good she could almost believe it was genuine, Tamsin thought bleakly. But she knew the truth. She had seen Donata coming out of his bedroom at his apartment in Florence—although she would rather die than admit she had gone there herself to tell him she had decided to stay on at the Villa Rosala as his mistress.

'Well—whatever, I still don't want to marry you,' she said coldly. She was standing in the doorway, but when she tried to step into the corridor he gripped her arm and tugged her back into his office.

'Trust me, *bella,* you're not the kind of woman I would have chosen for my wife,' he drawled sardonically, ignoring her outraged gasp. 'But what we want is no longer important. We have a duty towards our child, and it is a duty I intend to fulfil to the best of my abilities.'

'Even if that means marrying a woman you believe is a conniving bitch, like your stepmother was?' Tamsin queried tightly.

Bruno's eyes gleamed like chips of obsidian—hard and cold and utterly remorseless. 'Even then,' he agreed harshly.

For a moment despair threatened to overwhelm Tamsin, and she gripped the doorframe for support. 'You must know it would be a marriage made in hell,' she whispered. 'How could we live together, make a life together, when there is so much mistrust between us?'

'We managed when you were living at the villa. In fact I recall that we had a very successful relationship.'

'We had a lot of sex,' Tamsin snapped, aware from the sudden prickling of her skin that the atmosphere had subtly altered.

From the moment she had stepped into his office an undercurrent of sexual energy had smouldered between them. Since she had fled from Italy she had only felt half alive, but within seconds of seeing him fire had surged through her veins once more, and each of her nerve endings felt acutely sensitive as her body responded blindly to his magnetism.

His eyes were half hidden beneath his heavy lids, but she caught the glint of feral hunger and she stood, paralysed, as he slid his hand into her hair and tugged her head back so that she was held prisoner.

'Sex cannot be the basis of marriage,' she said tremulously, her eyes locked on his mouth as he lowered his head towards her.

He laughed. 'It's a better basis than love,' he taunted. 'Which is such an overrated emotion—don't you think, *bella*?'

'I believe that love is the only reason for two people to get married.'

His mouth was so close to hers that she could feel his warm breath on her lips. She could not respond to him— must not. But her whole body was shaking, and she would surely die if he did not kiss her. She gave a little moan, half-pleasure, half-despair, when he traced the contours of her mouth with his tongue, and she could not help but part her lips in readiness.

'If you are hoping for love, then I'm afraid you're going to be disappointed,' Bruno murmured. 'But think of the consolations—not only do you get an explosive sex-life, but you've managed to catch yourself a billionaire husband after all.'

His mouth cut off her furious retort and he ground his lips on hers, demanding a response her traitorous body was shamefully willing to give. He crushed her to him, and through the thickness of her coat she could feel his hard, aroused body, feel the answering heat pool between her thighs, and she gave a sob of wretched despair. The weeks without him had been hell, and now that she was in his arms once more she accepted that he was her reason for living. But he didn't love her and he never would, and the knowledge was tearing her apart.

From somewhere she found the strength to tear her mouth from his and push against his chest. 'All the riches in the world wouldn't persuade me to marry you,' she choked. 'I won't do it, Bruno, and you can't make me.'

His mouth curved into a smile totally devoid of warmth as he promised, 'You will, *bella*, and I can.'

CHAPTER ELEVEN

'ARE you okay Tamsin? It's not too late to change your mind, you know.'

Tamsin glanced around the packed register office, filled with friends and family, and in every conceivable space vases of flowers, and gave her brother a rueful smile. 'I think it is. Mum would kill me—and you too, for suggesting it. She's fretting enough as it is because the registrar has been held up by the snow.'

Daniel Stewart grinned, but his voice was serious when he said, 'She and Dad wouldn't mind. They're worried you're rushing into this marriage. I mean, they like Bruno, and so do I. He seems a good bloke—not like that last git you married,' he muttered caustically. 'I know Bruno will take care of you and the baby. But you haven't seemed happy since you set the date for the wedding, and we all want you to be sure you're doing the right thing.'

'I am,' Tamsin replied steadily, with no hesitation in her voice to betray the doubts that had plagued her for the last six weeks. She was done with worrying, she decided, her eyes straying across the room to where Bruno—looking stunningly handsome in a dark grey suit and blue silk shirt—was chatting to her father. During the many sleepless nights she'd endured since she had told him she was carrying his child she had fought a bitter battle in her head—unwilling to marry a man who would never love her, but desperate to give her unborn baby a secure and stable upbringing with both its parents. And, inevitably, the needs of her baby came first.

When Bruno had first made his shocking announcement that his child would not be born illegitimate, she had been adamant that she would not marry him. She had wrenched free of his arms and hurtled along the corridor in a frantic bid to escape him. But a sharp pain had made her seek the bathrooms, and the discovery that she was bleeding had sent her stumbling back to him, sheer terror and despair in her eyes as she sobbed that she was losing their baby.

To give Bruno his due, he had taken charge of the situation with the decisive determination of a military chief, lifting her into his arms and carrying her into the lift, then bundling her into the car that was already waiting out front and whisking her off to a private hospital.

The consultant she'd seen had tried to reassure her that occasional spotting in the first few months of pregnancy was not unusual, and that as Tamsin had no more pain everything was probably fine. An ultrasound scan had confirmed that their baby was developing normally, but as memories of her miscarriage had flooded back, Tamsin's tenuous hold on her emotions had given way and she'd wept—as much for the baby she had lost as the one she'd feared she was about to lose.

From that moment on Bruno had taken charge of her life. And, although she despised herself for her weakness, Tamsin had let him. She had not even argued when he'd insisted that she move into the apartment he had recently leased. The doctor had suggested bed-rest for a few days, and Bruno had taken the suggestion so seriously that he'd only allowed her out of bed so that he could carry her to the bathroom.

His concern had had a bittersweet poignancy that had made Tamsin cry still more—because she'd known that it was for their baby rather than her.

Living with him day by day, loving him as she did, had been hell on earth, and she wept each night after he bade her goodnight, burying her face in her pillows to muffle the sound of her crying.

The days leading up to the fifteen-week mark, when she had suffered her first miscarriage, had been the worst of her life. But when the date had passed, and her pregnancy had continued normally, a sense of calm had settled over her, and for the first time she'd begun to look to the future and believe that she might carry this baby full-term.

Their child deserved to grow up in a secure family environment, Bruno had argued stubbornly, when she had once again voiced her doubts that marriage between them could not possibly work. She had never heard him sound so passionate. It had been clear that now he was over his shock Bruno wanted their baby as much as she did, and was utterly determined that his child would not be born out of wedlock.

'Well, if this registrar doesn't hurry up, you may not have the wedding today anyway.' Daniel's voice broke into her thoughts. 'Bruno's looking decidedly tense. Hold up—who's just arrived?' he murmured, glancing over to the door.

But it was not the registrar who had just entered the room, and Tamsin gave a shocked gasp at the sight of a familiar grey-haired figure.

'James!'

For a man who had recently had treatment for a life-threatening disease, James Grainger looked remarkably well, and Tamsin told him so when she flew across the room to greet him.

'You're so tanned—and you've gained a bit of weight, thank goodness. How are you?'

'Pretty good.' James smiled. 'A month on St Lucia with my sister and her husband did me the world of good. I haven't got the all-clear yet, but I've got my fingers crossed,' he told her cheerfully. 'Now, tell me, how did you pin this man down?' he chuckled, and Tamsin quickly turned her head, her heart sinking when she met Bruno's unfathomable gaze. 'Congratulations, Bruno. You couldn't have found yourself a more wonderful, generous-hearted young woman than Tamsin.'

'I agree—I'm a lucky man,' Bruno replied quietly.

Something in his tone made Tamsin glance at him, sure she would see the familiar mockery in his gaze, but instead he looked—she frowned—*shattered,* and for a few seconds the expression in his eyes made her heart stop. But then his lashes fell, and she had the distinct impression that he did not want to meet her gaze. Perhaps he believed she had invited James to their wedding and was angry with her, she thought heavily.

But there was no time to explain that James's appearance today was a complete surprise to her, because one of the officials announced that the registrar had arrived and invited everyone to take a seat.

And suddenly this was it—in a few minutes' time she would be Bruno's wife. The strange trance-like calm that had cocooned her since she had slipped into her cream wool wedding dress and matching coat that morning fractured, and her heart began to jerk painfully beneath her ribcage.

Memories of her marriage to Neil came tumbling back. She had been so full of hope and expectations that day, but a year later her dreams had been cruelly destroyed—and, even worse, she had lost her baby. Now she had no hopes and no expectations, she thought sadly as she took her place next to Bruno. All she had was a deep and abiding love for a man who had made it clear he would never love her in return.

For a few seconds panic threatened to overwhelm her. She

couldn't go through with it. Instinctively she placed her hand over her stomach. The tiny fluttering sensation beneath her fingers as the baby moved made her heart leap, and the tension drained from her body. For her baby's sake she could do anything.

The ceremony passed in a blur and her hands were visibly shaking when Bruno slipped a plain gold band on her finger. She could not bring herself to look at him, but she could feel the tension emanating from him, and she wondered if he too was besieged with doubts.

Did he wish that he was marrying Donata rather than a woman he believed was as unscrupulous as his stepmother? He had made no further reference to Donata, and although his sister Jocasta was attending the wedding, there was no sign of his beautiful cousin. But Tamsin could not forget the triumphant gleam in Donata's eyes when she had emerged from Bruno's bedroom in Florence, and was certain that she and Bruno had been lovers.

The thought was agony, and she blinked hard to dispel her tears as the registrar pronounced them man and wife and Bruno turned towards her, brushing his mouth briefly over hers in a kiss that held neither passion or warmth. It was a fitting beginning to a marriage that was based on convenience rather than love, Tamsin thought dismally. Her heart ached, but pride came to her rescue and she pinned a bright smile on her face and turned to receive the congratulations of their guests.

It was many hours later before Bruno's plane landed in Florence and he settled Tamsin in his car for the last leg of their journey to the Villa Rosala. In the dim interior she looked pale and incredibly fragile, her long eyelashes making dark crescents on her cheeks.

His mouth tightened. He had feared that the journey to the

villa would be too much. They should have stayed in Florence tonight and travelled on to the house in the morning, but for some reason Tamsin had adamantly refused to stay at the Florence apartment, and had seemed so upset at the idea that he had reluctantly given in.

It seemed irrational to him, but he'd blamed her sudden dislike of the apartment on the pregnancy hormones that had turned her from the cool, level-headed woman he had first met into an emotionally fragile mass of insecurities. She had experienced no more bleeding, thank God, but no amount of reassurance from medical experts had calmed her fears of suffering a miscarriage.

Perhaps it was natural for pregnant women to worry endlessly, he brooded, frustrated by his inability to help her and her refusal to confide her concerns to him. Instead she spent a lot of time in her bedroom, clearly wanting to avoid him. Usually he had no patience for tears, but the sound of her weeping caused a peculiar pain in his gut. She hadn't smiled once since he had made the arrangements for their wedding, and he guessed her tears were because she hadn't wanted to marry him—but in that she had had no choice, he thought grimly. Because no child of his would be born illegitimate.

He swore beneath his breath and forced himself to concentrate on the narrow, twisting road that snaked though the dark Tuscan countryside. 'Not much further now,' he murmured when he felt Tamsin's eyes on him. 'You must be tired. It's been a long day.'

'Mmm.' But an unexpectedly lovely day, Tamsin mused, thinking back to the short but moving wedding ceremony, and the celebratory lunch afterwards at a nearby hotel.

All her family had been there—her sister Vicky looking heavily pregnant—and Jess had been her maid of honour, and spent most of her time bickering with Daniel, as usual. It was amazing how two intelligent people could be so blind, Tamsin thought sleepily. She liked the idea of having Jess for a sister-in-law; she just wished the two of them would stop fighting and recognise that they were attracted to each other.

'I loved the flowers,' she said to Bruno, recalling the profusion of pink and cream roses and lilies whose exquisite perfume had filled the register office. 'I thought Mum must have ordered them, but she was as surprised as me.'

'I'm glad you liked them, *cara*.' The amusement in Bruno's voice caused her heart to skip a beat.

'You mean…you? Why?' she faltered. 'I mean, thank you—they were beautiful… But you didn't have to. I didn't expect anything.'

'No,' Bruno said in a curiously, dry tone. 'I have come to realise that you have very few expectations.'

Any other woman would have demanded that the wedding take place at some grand location, followed by a lavish reception as befitted his billion-pound fortune. Tamsin had asked for nothing other than the attendance of her family and close friends, and he had even had to bully her into choosing a wedding ring from a top Hatton Garden jewellers. After considerable arguing she had eventually settled for a narrow plain gold band, and he was sure she had chosen it because it was one of the least expensive rings in the shop.

As if she could read his mind, she suddenly said, 'You don't have to wear your ring. I wasn't sure if you would want one or not. I mean…' she shifted restlessly in her seat, sounding as if she wished she had never started the conversation '…it's not as though ours is a normal marriage, and you might not want to advertise the fact that you have a wife.'

Tamsin had a stark image in her head of him chatting up gorgeous women at the nightclubs in Florence, his ringless finger advertising that he was a free agent, and a heavy weight settled in her chest. Bruno had a reputation as a playboy. He was hardly likely to curtail his socialising because he had acted honourably and married the woman who was expecting his child.

'I am quite happy for the world to know I am married,' he murmured coolly, 'and I will be honoured to wear my wedding ring.'

He swung the car through the gates of the Villa Rosala, his mind dwelling on Tamsin's assertion that their marriage was not a 'normal' one, and wondering why he wanted to smash his fist into the thick stone walls of the villa.

The house looked warm and inviting, with golden lamplight spilling from the downstairs windows. It had been his childhood home—a place of love and happiness before the bitter dispute that had divided him and his father. But now it was going to be a family home again—if he had not completely wrecked his marriage before it had even begun, he thought grimly.

He pulled up on the drive and cut the engine, but instead of getting out of the car he turned his head to Tamsin, unable to hold back the question that had been eating away at him ever since his conversation with James Grainger shortly before the wedding.

'Why didn't you tell me about James?'

Beside him, Tamsin stiffened. 'Tell you what about James?'

'That he has cancer. That the reason he went to London every week was to attend hospital and receive treatment. And that his chemotherapy left him feeling so weak that he relied on your help,' Bruno finished tensely.

'How do you know all this? Do Annabel and Davina know about James's illness?' Tamsin queried sharply.

'I assume so. He told me that Davina went with him on his recent visit to the specialist.'

'Thank goodness,' Tamsin murmured. 'I begged him to tell them before, but he was determined to deal with it without worrying them, and he didn't want anyone to know he had cancer.'

'Apart from you,' Bruno said quietly.

'Yes, but it's not what you think,' Tamsin replied quickly, her heart sinking at Bruno's grim expression. He already believed she had befriended James because he was a wealthy widower—what would he think of her now he knew James was suffering from a potentially life-threatening disease? 'James and I became friends when he hired me to design Davina and Hugo's flat,' she explained. 'I think he confided in me because he had no one else he could talk to. He was desperate to save his daughters from more worry when they were still grieving for their mother, but he could discuss his fears with me, confident that I would never betray his secret.'

Bruno's jaw tightened. 'Your loyalty is commendable, *bella*. You allowed me to think the worst of you, to accuse you of being a gold-digger like my step-mother, and you never attempted to defend yourself by explaining the real reason for your meetings with James in London.'

'I couldn't,' Tamsin said simply. 'I promised James.' She hesitated, and then muttered, 'Even if I had told you, I don't think you would have believed me. From the outset you were determined to think the worst of me. When you looked at me you saw your stepmother, and because you couldn't punish her for wrecking your relationship with your father, you punished me.'

'That's not true,' Bruno growled angrily. 'There were many pointers that proved you were like Miranda, and I don't deny I was determined to save James from making the same mistakes my father made. The old man who made you the beneficiary of his will—' Bruno broke off and raked his hand through his hair. 'Your father told me today that you put most of the money you inherited into a charity that organises care for the elderly, to enable them to live in their own homes.'

Tamsin shrugged awkwardly. 'I spent some of it on me. I paid for Jess and I to go on holiday—she stuck by me through my darkest days after my marriage ended and I wanted to thank her—and I bought some new clothes. My confidence took a battering when Neil left me, and I suppose I was trying to re-invent myself. I didn't marry him for his money, you know. I married him because I loved him. But I have no idea why he married me,' she said bitterly, 'because he was unfaithful from the day we returned from our honeymoon until the day he walked out and moved in with his mistress.'

She opened the car door and stepped onto the drive, drawing her coat around her to shield her from the rain that had been falling since they had arrived in Italy. 'I'm glad James told you the truth. He still faces an uncertain future, and he needs the support of his friends. I swear I'm not like your stepmother, Bruno. I've never wanted anything from you.' Apart from your love, she thought silently. But his face was a hard, arrogant mask, and even though he now knew that she hadn't planned to fleece a vulnerable widower, she could detect no softening in his attitude towards her. Suddenly she felt desperately tired and dejected, and her shoulders slumped. 'We're married now, and I suppose we'll just have to get on with it,' she muttered.

Bruno gave her a sharp stare as he rounded the car. 'As you say, we'll just have to get on with it,' he drawled sardonically, lifting her effortlessly into his arms and ignoring her murmured protest that she weighed a ton as he carried her through the front door. 'This is where you belong now, Tamsin. You and my son. It's true that the only reason we married is for our baby's sake, but I swear I will do everything in my power to make you and our child happy.'

Bruno's dark eyes burned into hers, and his vow seemed to echo around the hall of the villa, but his words enveloped Tamsin in a black cloak of despair. She was well aware that he had only married her because of the baby, but she didn't need to have him spell it out quite so brutally.

Would he have been so determined to marry her if she was expecting a girl? Of course he would, she acknowledged heavily. He had not even asked to know the sex of their child—but, having safely passed the fifteen-week landmark, she had begun to believe that she would carry this baby full-term, and had been eager to know as much as possible about the child she was carrying inside her.

Bruno was undoubtedly delighted that they were going to have a son. He had gone rather quiet and given her an odd look when she had shyly suggested that he might want to name the baby after his father, but little Stefano was the only reason she was here in the house she had designed and fallen in love with almost as much as she loved its master. And she would be happy, she told herself fiercely.

But as she stared into Bruno's beautiful sculpted face it was hard to see how—because there was always going to be something missing.

She swallowed the lump that had formed in her throat and gave a theatrical yawn. 'If you don't mind, I think I'll go straight to bed. I'm exhausted—what with travelling and everything,' she finished lamely, when Bruno's mouth thinned.

'You were the one who insisted on driving down to the villa. I would have been quite happy to stay at the apartment tonight, *bella*.'

Tamsin said nothing, but paled at the memory of how she had met his cousin emerging from the master bedroom of his bachelor pad. She stroked her hand over the firm swell of her stomach, as if to reassure herself of the presence of her baby, and Bruno's eyes followed her movements. The atmosphere in the hall changed imperceptibly, and as his eyes became slumberous beneath his heavy lids, she felt a quiver low in her pelvis.

It felt strangely surreal to be back at the villa. The last time she had been here they had spent practically every waking hour making wild, tempestuous love. Now she was over four months pregnant, and they were married, but it was not a conventional marriage and she didn't know if Bruno expected to consummate their unconventional relationship.

His expression was unreadable as his eyes moved from her rounded belly to her breasts, which were now full and heavy. She looked very different from when she had last shared his bed, she thought on a wave of fear. What if he took her to bed and was revolted by her pregnant body? Or compared her curvaceous breasts and hips with Donatella's model-thin figure? The thought was unbearable, and when he moved towards her she took a jerky step backwards.

'I really am tired,' she said in a thin, sharp voice. 'I thought perhaps I could have the room I slept in when I first came to work here?' Bruno's silent, narrow-eyed scrutiny unnerved her, and when he lifted a hand to her she visibly flinched, and admitted in a panic-filled tone, 'I don't know what you expect from me. I know at my last antenatal appointment, the doctor said that my pregnancy is progressing fine,' she continued shakily, 'and that there is no reason for us not to…well, you know…' She tailed to a halt, her face burning as she recalled the doctor's blunt statement that it was perfectly safe for them to have sex. Bruno had been sitting next to her, and when they'd left the surgery she had wanted to die of embarrassment, but to her relief he had not mentioned the subject, or attempted to make love to her.

It wasn't that she didn't want him to. Now that her sickness had stopped she was feeling incredibly fit and energetic—and shockingly turned on. He had told her that the amazing sex they enjoyed was as good a basis as any for marriage, and if his body was the only thing he would share with her, she would take it.

Her nights were tormented by fantasies of Bruno exploring every sensitive dip and curve of her body, before moving over her and entering her with deep, powerful thrusts. She longed for him to take her in his arms and lead her along that wickedly pleasurable path to sexual ecstasy, and sometimes she caught him looking at her in a way that made her think he wanted her too. But then she would remember Donata's exotic beauty and stunning body, and her doubts would return.

Bruno dropped his hand to his side and snatched up Tamsin's travel bag, determined to control the shaft of blinding anger that surged through him. 'I don't expect anything from you,' he informed her in a clipped tone. 'Certainly nothing that you are not willing to give, *bella*. But I'm afraid you'll have to share my bed tonight. Your clothes and belongings arrived here a couple of days ago, and Battista has put them all in the master bedroom. I fear she has a romantic streak, and believes that as we are now man and wife we will be sleeping in the same room. I'll leave you to disabuse her of the notion,' he said tightly as he shepherded her up the stairs. 'In the meantime, fortunately my bed is so big that if you keep to your side of the mattress you can pretend that I am not even there.'

The open sarcasm in his voice scraped Tamsin's already raw nerves, and when they reached the landing she spun away from him. 'I would still prefer to sleep in my own room. I tend to wriggle around a lot during the night, and I might disturb you,' she added, trying to prove to him how sensible it would be for them to have separate rooms.

'I think that's entirely likely, *cara*,' Bruno drawled in that same hatefully sardonic tone. 'But that is my problem. None of the guest beds are made up,' he told her firmly, gripping her arm and literally frogmarching her into the master bedroom.

His mouth tightened at the flare of panic in her eyes, and he dropped her travel bag onto the bed and strode back over to the door.

'Stop looking at me as though you're terrified I might murder you while you sleep,' he grated harshly. 'I have never taken a woman by force in my life, and I certainly don't intend to start with my pregnant wife. I have to make a couple of phone calls,' he continued in the same icy tone. 'I suggest you hurry up and get into bed. And for both our sakes let's hope you are asleep when I come back.'

Brilliant. They had only been married for a few hours, and already they weren't speaking, Tamsin brooded miserably as she trailed into the *en suite* bathroom. She was tempted to defy him and sleep in another room, but the thought of finding sheets and bedding and making up a bed was too much. It had been a long and emotionally draining day, and her body ached with exhaustion. She unzipped her travel bag, and frowned when she lifted out a flat package wrapped in tissue paper.

'Your wedding present is in your overnight bag,' Jess had whispered in her ear, when she and Bruno had taken leave of their guests after the celebratory wedding lunch.

Tamsin had assumed the gift was perfume or, knowing Jess's quirky sense of humour, a musical toothbrush, and tears filled her eyes when she unfolded a gossamer-fine ivory silk nightgown. Further searching in her bag revealed that Jess had removed the oversized tee shirt she had packed and, cursing and loving her friend in equal measures, she slipped the nightgown over her head.

At four and a half months pregnant, she had not expected to look sexy, but the diaphanous material skimmed her bump, while the lacy bodice plunged low to reveal the new fullness of her breasts. Jess had clearly bought it with seduction in mind, but all that was in Tamsin's mind was racing into bed and ensuring she was hidden beneath the covers before Bruno returned.

She was too late. When she walked back into the bedroom and saw him sprawled indolently on the vast bed, her heart jerked painfully in her chest. He had removed his tie and unfastened his shirt buttons to the waist, revealing his muscular olive-skinned chest, covered with a mass of wiry, black hairs that arrowed down beneath the waistband of his trousers. Who had he needed to speak to on his wedding night? Tamsin wondered, feeling the familiar sick jealousy burn like acid in her stomach. Had he phoned Donata? Or did he have another mistress in Florence? He was so gorgeous it was impossible to believe he had been celibate in the weeks between her departure from Tuscany and meeting him at his London office to tell him she was pregnant.

Tamsin hovered uncertainly in the doorway, and Bruno's eyes narrowed as he stared at her gorgeous, lush curves and felt his body's instant, throbbing response. He longed to tug her down onto the bed and remove the tantalising wisp of transparent silk that brushed against her thighs and cupped her breasts, displaying them like plump, ripe peaches. He wanted to discover every inch of her voluptuous body and bury his face against her satin soft, delicately scented flesh—but he knew that he had no right to touch her, and the guilt that had been steadily intensifying inside him since his conversation with James Grainger rose up and threatened to choke him.

'Come and get into bed,' he said quietly, drawing back the covers. 'You look exhausted, *cara,* and that's not good for the baby.'

And of course the baby was all he was interested in— which was just as it should be, Tamsin told herself as she slid into bed and tugged the sheet up to her chin. Clearly the sexy nightdress had failed to disguise the fact that she looked fat and tired. She really didn't know why she cared, or why tears were burning her eyes. She squeezed them shut, praying that Bruno would think she was already asleep when he emerged from the bathroom.

Several minutes later the mattress dipped, and she heard the dry amusement in his voice as he leaned over her and dropped a brief, tantalising kiss on her lips. 'Asleep so soon? You *were* tired. Sweet dreams, *bella mia.*'

With about an acre of mattress between them, she had no idea what, if anything, he was wearing in bed, but the idea that he could be lying naked next to her caused liquid heat to flood through her veins, and it seemed impossible that sleep would ever relieve her of the restless desire that made her muscles ache. Her mind re-ran their wedding ceremony at the register office until her thoughts became fuzzy and sleep claimed her.

Suddenly she wasn't in the register office, but a church. Bruno was striding down the aisle, away from the altar, and she was running after him, sobbing his name as she begged him not to leave her. But as she reached him he swung round, and it wasn't Bruno—it was…

'Neil!'

'*Madre de Dio*, Tamsin. Wake up. You can't keep getting upset like this—it can't be good for the baby.'

Slowly Tamsin opened her eyes and stared up at Bruno's grim face. Her cheeks were wet, and her throat felt as though she had swallowed glass, but her mind was clouded and she didn't know why she had been crying. 'I was dreaming,' she whispered, frowning as she tried to recall what about. It must have been the old recurring dream about losing her baby, she decided, scrubbing her eyes with the back of her hand. 'I'm sorry I disturbed you.' She had never seen Bruno look so furious, and she bit her lip. 'I told you I should have slept in another room.'

To her dismay, he did not argue. 'I'll have Battista prepare a room tomorrow,' he snapped. 'Go back to sleep now.'

Bruno rolled onto his side and switched off the bedside lamp, so that the room was plunged into a darkness that was as black and heavy as his mood. He felt a bitter, burning sensation in his gullet, as if he had drunk poison. Why the hell did it matter that she still dreamed of her ex-husband? he asked himself angrily. He had heard the pain in her voice earlier, when she'd told him how she had loved Neil Harper, and it was clear that his infidelity had broken her heart. Did she still have feelings for her ex, despite the despicable way he had treated her? Was that the reason her eyes had shimmered with tears when he had kissed her at the end of their wedding ceremony? She'd been wishing that it was Neil she had just promised to spend the rest of her life with rather than him?

But she had married *him*, Bruno thought savagely. She was expecting his child, and the health and well-being of his unborn son was the only thing he cared about. With that settled, he rolled onto his back and stared up at the ceiling, waiting for sleep. But it didn't come, and by dawn his eyes felt gritty and a lead weight seemed to have settled in his chest.

CHAPTER TWELVE

WHEN Tamsin opened her eyes the next morning she found she was alone, and the only sign that Bruno had slept beside her all night was a faint indentation on his pillow. She wondered if he was still annoyed with her for waking him in the night. She couldn't even remember the dream that had left her sobbing. It had certainly been a traumatic wedding night—but for all the wrong reasons, she acknowledged dismally, recalling his tight-lipped expression when he had shaken her awake.

She could hear rain hammering against the window, and when she pulled back the curtains the Tuscan countryside was hidden behind a veil of grey mist. The river that usually gurgled gently at the side of the house was fuller than she had ever seen it, and white frothy waves danced across the surface as it hurtled down into the valley.

Bruno was in the kitchen when she went downstairs. He looked remote and forbidding, in black jeans and a matching jumper, but heart-stoppingly sexy, with his hair falling onto his brow and faint dark stubble shading his jaw. Tamsin was immediately conscious that her loose-fitting trousers and tunic top were hardly a turn-on, and she quickly subsided into a chair opposite him at the table, so that he couldn't see her swollen stomach.

'You're going to be twice the size you are now,' her mother had laughingly informed her when they had been shopping for her wedding outfit.

Tamsin felt quite happy about the visible sign that her little son was growing bigger, but from Bruno's expression she was sure he found her lack of waistline unattractive, and she wished he would stop looking at her.

'You'd better decide which room you want,' he said tersely, while he poured her a glass of fruit juice and buttered one of the still-warm rolls that the housekeeper must have baked that morning. 'I'll leave you to explain to Battista why you are moving into your own room, and she can carry your things. You are not to get over-tired,' he warned her as he handed her the roll and passed her the cherry jam that he knew was her favourite. 'Anyway, there's no rush. I'm going back to Florence. I have an early meeting tomorrow morning,' he continued at her obvious surprise, 'and I have some paperwork to catch on first. After that I'm flying to Paris, and then Amsterdam, and I won't be back until the end of the week. So you'll be quite safe to sleep in my bed for the next few nights.'

She flushed at the mockery in his tone and put down the roll after one bite, as the image of him rushing back to meet Donata at his apartment destroyed her appetite. 'I'll move my things into another room as soon as you've gone,' she said stonily. 'I want my own space.'

'As you wish.' Bruno scraped back his chair and stood up. 'I'll go now, and then you'll have all the space you could possibly wish for.' He thrust his arms into his leather jacket and stood towering over her, so impossibly beautiful that Tamsin longed to throw herself into his arms and beg him to stay with her. Their marriage had got off to a truly terrible start, and she had no idea how to retrieve the situation.

'It's lucky we didn't arrange a honeymoon if you're so busy

at work,' she muttered, knowing she sounded like a petulant teenager, but unable to stop herself.

Bruno turned in the doorway and glared at her. 'A honeymoon is the usual way to start normal married life, I agree. But, as you pointed out, *bella,* our marriage is far from normal. Our wedding night was evidence of that.'

'You mean because we didn't have sex?' Tamsin flung at him, stung by his implied accusation that she hadn't delivered the goods on their wedding night.

'I mean because you spent the night dreaming about your ex-husband,' Bruno replied icily, before he strode out and slammed the front door so hard that the villa trembled on its foundations.

What on earth did he mean? Tamsin moved to the window and watched listlessly as he hurtled down the drive so fast that the car's tyres squealed on the wet gravel. Neil was the last person she would ever dream about—although he had featured in a few of her nightmares. She could almost believe that Bruno had sounded jealous, but now she really was entering the realms of fantasy, she acknowledged as she headed back upstairs. She didn't know if he really had an early business meeting tomorrow, or whether he was racing off to see his mistress, and although she told herself she didn't care, she could not hold back her tears as she buried her face on his pillow and wept for everything that their marriage could have been if only he had loved her.

After a couple of hours she pulled herself together and wandered aimlessly around the empty house, before picking out a room along the corridor from the master bedroom that had an *en suite* bathroom and an additional dressing room that she decided would make an ideal nursery for Stefano. She already had a few ideas about a soft blue colour scheme and a hand-painted border, but after another fruitless hour she gave up trying to sketch her plans.

Back in the kitchen, Battista looked unusually harassed, and Tamsin immediately decided to postpone asking the housekeeper to help her move her belongings out of Bruno's room until another day.

'This rain is bad,' Battista said worriedly, wringing her hands when Tamsin asked what was wrong. 'Down in the valley the river is close to spilling out,' she explained in her broken English. 'If it does it will flood the village, and my daughter's house is right in its path.' The older woman wiped her eyes on her apron. 'I'm scared for Carissa and the *bambini.* Carlo is only a few months old, and the little girls will be so frightened. Guido would go for them, but he has hurt his back and has to lie still.' More tears slid down her wrinkled face, and Tamsin instinctively hugged her.

'I'll go and get your daughter and her family and bring them back here. The Villa Rosala is on a hill, and I imagine we're safe from flooding here,' she added as she stared out at the torrential rain. She prayed that Bruno had reached Florence safely. Maybe she would ring him later. And if Donata answered, well—her heart lurched at the thought—at least she would know why Bruno had driven off in such a hurry.

She pushed the familiar pang of jealousy to one side and smiled reassuringly at Battista, who was shaking her head.

'You can't go. Signor Di Cesare would never allow it.'

'Well, he isn't here, so he won't know, will he? Please don't worry, Battista. I'll take Guido's car, and I'll be back with Carissa and the children in no time.'

Bruno stared blankly at his computer screen and realised that he had read the same paragraph of legal jargon three times. He seemed incapable of concentrating on the finer details of the exciting new business deal that he had spent months setting up and which he was now close to completing. Even worse, he couldn't care less if the House of Di Cesare opened a new flagship store on the Avenue des Champs-Elysées in the heart of Paris.

He didn't care about anything, he acknowledged heavily. At least he didn't care about any of the things that had previously been important to him—predominantly work, the company, and his determination to atone for his father's failures in the last years of his life and make the House of Di Cesare a world market leader. Under his leadership the company was already enjoying phenomenal success, but he felt weary and defeated—as if he had fallen into a deep well of despair and could not summon the energy to climb out.

In another few months his son would be born, he reminded himself. He would be a father to little Stefano, and he was determined to be a good father—like his father had been to him. But, unlike his father, he would never allow anyone to come between him and his son.

His child would be the most important thing in his life. That was the reason he had married Tamsin—the only reason, he told himself fiercely. But as he got to his feet and stared out over the dark, rain-lashed city he knew he was lying to himself.

The knowledge that he had misjudged her was eating away at him. He had been wrong about her. He had leapt to conclusions based on his past rather than logical thought, and he had treated her so badly that it was little wonder she had spent the weeks running up to their wedding weeping and trying to avoid him.

Was there any possibility of salvaging their marriage? When he had driven her down to the villa he had been cautiously optimistic that he would be able to make his peace with her, apologise for the way he had treated her and re-establish the tenuous friendship that had developed between them while they had been lovers. But that was before he'd discovered that she still dreamed about her ex-husband.

Why should he care if Tamsin was still in love with Neil Harper? he brooded as he paced the floor of his study and raked his hand through his hair until it stood on end. At least it negated any possibility that she might fall in love with *him*.

The knock on his study door dragged him from his bitter thoughts, and he forced a smile for his butler. 'Salvatore, how are you? I am sorry to hear about your mother. Did all your family return to Sicily for the funeral?'

'*Si*—it went well. My mother would have been pleased at the turn-out,' Salvatore replied gravely. '*Signor*, I have not seen you since your trip to the US—I went back to Sicily before you returned—but…' The butler hesitated, and then said, 'There is something I must tell you.'

Two hours later Bruno screeched to a halt in front of the Villa Rosala and leapt out of the car. Rain lashed his face as he ran towards the house, and above the noise of the wind he could hear the angry sounds of the river as it crashed down the hillside. Thank God his ancestors had built the villa here at the top of the valley, away from danger if the river burst its banks. Lights from the windows made the villa glow like a beacon of warmth in the gathering dusk, and some of his tension left him as he thought of Tamsin curled up safe and warm in front of the fire in the sitting room.

He would have been here sooner if he had not wasted precious minutes on the phone, furiously warning his cousin Donata that if she ever lied to, or even spoke to his wife again he would cut off the monthly allowance that she received from the Di Cesare fortune. He had no idea why Donata had made up her fantastic tale that they were engaged. He'd never given any indication that he wanted a relationship with her, let alone marry her, but she had always been a spoilt bitch. He did not care if she was the only other great-grandchild of Antonio Di Cesare—he would be quite happy if he never set eyes on her again.

But Tamsin did not know that Donata's claim had been pure fantasy. He had been mildly irritated when Donata had turned up at his apartment the night before he had flown to the US, with some story about a broken love-affair, and had pleaded with him to allow her to stay. He had left at dawn the following day to catch his flight. But according to his butler Donata had gone to his room in the early hours, dressed—as Salvatore had so delicately put it—like a woman of the streets, and been furious when she'd discovered that he had already gone. When Tamsin arrived at the apartment a short while later, Salvatore had said, Donata had clearly implied that she had spent the night with Bruno, and Tamsin had looked—in Salvatore's words—heartbroken.

Why had Tamsin gone to the apartment? Bruno wondered curiously. Had she intended to tell him to his face that she was returning to England and her career? Or had there been another reason for her visit? Suddenly it seemed imperative that he know the truth, and he strode into the villa, unable to control his urgent need to see her.

He frowned when his housekeeper, Battista, hurried into the hall. She had clearly been crying, and at his terse, 'Where is Signora Di Cesare?' more tears poured down her cheeks. It took endless moments and all of his patience before he finally learned that Tamsin had driven down to the village in search of Battista's daughter, and as he recalled the wild night, and the angry, churning river, an icy feeling of dread filled him.

'I don't know what has happened.' Battista stumbled after him as he turned back towards the front door. 'The telephone is not working, and the *signora*, she left hours ago.'

Bruno did not hear his housekeeper's sobs. He was already behind the wheel of his car and driving as fast as the dire conditions would allow along the steep, narrow road leading down to the village. The gleam from the headlights cut through the dark, and as he turned a corner and saw Guido's familiar little car, upended and partially submerged in the river, his blood turned cold.

'*Madre de Dio,* Tamsin, where are you?' He shouted her name over and over, his stomach churning as terror unlike anything he had ever felt in his life gripped him. She did not answer and, slipping and sliding on the mud, he scoured the banks with his torch until the ever-rising waters of the swollen river forced him back to his car, before it too was swept away.

Why had she come out in the storm when she must have realised that the river was dangerously close to bursting its banks? It was sheer madness. But as soon as she had heard that Battista's grandchildren were at risk she would have been determined to help, Bruno acknowledged grimly. Far from being the callous, unscrupulous woman he had believed, she possessed—as James Grainger had stated—the most generous heart of anyone he had ever met. It was a pity he had not realised it sooner, he thought savagely, because there was no sign of her by the river, and sick fear gagged his throat as he faced the knowledge that he might be too late.

Somehow he managed to drive on into the village, heading for the town hall where lights and voices indicated that many of the villagers had taken refuge there.

'Have you seen my wife? Signora Di Cesare—she is English, blonde hair…' He pushed his way through the throng of frightened people into the hall, his heart pounding. She *had* to be here. They *had not* drowned in the river—Tamsin and his unborn son. His life would not be worth living without them—without her.

He acknowledged the blinding truth on a wave of sheer, agonised fear as he scanned the packed room. *'Tamsin! Where the hell are you?'*

'Bruno—I'm here.'

The small, hesitant voice sounded from behind him, and he spun round and stared at her—covered from head to toe in mud, so it was not surprising he hadn't recognised her.

She was sitting with Battista's daughter and her children, smiling at Carissa's baby. *Smiling,* he noted savagely, as he swallowed the constriction in his throat and felt an unfamiliar burning sensation behind his eyelids. She was smiling while he had been going out of his mind.

'Tesoro…' He reached for her blindly. His vision seemed to be blurred, and as he drew her small, muddy form into his arms and held her close to his heart, the dam that had held back his emotions for so long broke, and he buried his face in her hair, his chest heaving.

'Bruno…darling—don't.' Tamsin's voice cracked. 'Stefano is fine; he's been kicking like mad. Here.' She guided his hand to her stomach. 'Can you feel him? I'm sorry,' she whispered, visibly shocked by the betraying wetness on his face. 'I know you must have been terrified to think you had lost him.'

'I thought I had lost both of you,' Bruno admitted harshly.

Relief surged through him, robbing him of his voice, and he did not add that if she had been swept away in the river he would thrown himself in after her. He claimed her lips in a gentle, evocative kiss that tasted of mud and tears, although he did not know if they were hers or his. Tamsin was staring up at him as if he had lost his mind. And perhaps he had, he thought as he lifted her into his arms and began to make his way out of the hall. What other explanation could there be for the madness that filled him with a wild euphoria? He did not believe in love, but everything that was dear to him was here in his arms, and he would never, ever let her go.

Afterwards Tamsin could not remember much about the journey back to the Villa Rosala, but the sight of Guido's car in the river brought back those terrible moments when she had feared for her life and that of her baby.

'It's over now, *cara*, and you are safe—thank God,' Bruno grated harshly, when he heard her murmur of distress, and then they were home, and he was carrying her up the stairs while Battista clung to her daughter and grandchildren, who had travelled up to the villa with them in the back of Bruno's car.

He said nothing as he stripped her out of her sodden, muddy clothes before removing his own, but his eyes flared with answering hunger when he caught her unguarded look of desire. 'Later, *cara mia*,' he promised softly as he joined her in the shower. 'But first we need to get you clean. You don't smell too good, *bella*,' he teased, and watched her eyes darken as he smoothed the soap over her breasts and the firm swell of her stomach.

'Don't—I look fat,' Tamsin whispered in an agony of embarrassment, but Bruno drew her hands down from where she had tried to hide her shape from him and stared at her, dull colour streaking along his cheekbones as the hard length of his arousal nudged her thighs.

'You are pregnant with my son,' he said rawly, 'and you have never looked more beautiful than you do now.'

'Bruno—kiss me, please.' Tonight she had thought that her life was over, but by some miracle she had managed to squeeze out of the window before the car was sucked beneath the water, and swim against the ferocious current to the shore. She had been given a second chance at life, and pride had no place in it

When he reached for her she opened her arms and slid them around his waist, while he moved his mouth on hers in a shattering kiss of pure possession. It was bliss when she had been starved of him for so long, and she melted against him, uncaring that her fevered response to him revealed the secrets of her heart. She opened her mouth, eagerly welcoming the bold thrust of his tongue as he deepened the kiss to another level, but then, despite the fact that they were both shaking with need, he stepped out of the shower, enfolded her in a towel and carried her into the bedroom.

He placed her on the bed as carefully as if she was made of delicate porcelain, but to Tamsin's disappointment, instead of joining her, he donned his robe and moved towards the door.

'I'll leave you to get dry, *cara,* while I make you some tea. You must be in shock after tonight,' he explained, a curious note in his voice as he added, 'I need to take care of you.'

She didn't want him to take care of her. She wanted him to make wild, passionate love to her, Tamsin thought dismally. But of course what Bruno really meant was that he wanted to take care of his baby—although Stefano seemed none the worse for the trauma she had put him through, and from his energetic kicking definitely had a future career with the Italian football team.

She dried her hair, so that it fell in a curtain of gold silk around her shoulders, and slipped the nightgown that Jess had bought her over her head before she climbed into bed. She wondered if Bruno expected her to have moved into her own room—as she had told him she would during their last bitter exchange before he had driven back to Florence. If so, he was going to be disappointed, because she was his wife and she belonged in his bed—and even the spectre of his beautiful cousin would not detract her from her determination to fight for him.

Her eyes flew to his face when he returned a few minutes

later, bearing a tea tray, and her heartbeat quickened when he stretched out on the bed next to her. Her senses flared at his closeness, and she took a gulp of the hot, sweet tea and tried not to imagine his naked body hidden beneath his robe.

Now that she was safe she kept re-running everything that had happened down in the village, but for some reason her mind locked on the expression she had seen on his face when he had first spotted her in the village town hall. His patent relief had been mixed with another, indefinable emotion that had made her hope… But then she had reminded herself that his concern was for their child. Now that look was back in his eyes, and she was shaking so much that she had to put down her tea before she spilt it.

'There is something I have to know Tamsin,' he said quietly as he lifted her hand and stroked his thumb-pad over the pulse jerking frantically in her wrist. 'Why did you go to the apartment on the morning that I flew to the States?'

'How did you—?' She broke off and bit her lip. 'Salvatore told you, I suppose?'

Bruno nodded. 'He told me that you met my cousin.' When she made no reply he tipped her chin and stared into her eyes, an emotion she did not recognise blazing in his midnight-dark gaze. 'Donata lied to you, *cara*. I did not sleep with her that night, or any other night. There has never been anything between us.'

'But she said you intended to marry her to strengthen the Di Cesare bloodline,' Tamsin faltered. 'She also said that you had a weakness for blondes, and I was just another in a long line of women who had graced your bed and meant nothing to you. But of course I already knew that,' she added thickly.

Bruno made a harsh sound low in his throat and sprang up from the bed, moving jerkily instead of with his usual lithe grace. He paced the room restlessly for several moments, before he swung back to face her, his expression so tortured that Tamsin caught her breath.

'You were right when you said I was determined to think the worst of you,' he said abruptly. 'I had suspicions about the reason for your friendship with James Grainger. But if I had been behaving logically I would have had you properly investigated, spoken to people who knew you—maybe even spoken to James about my concerns,' he added with a humourless smile. 'But I took one look at you at Davina's wedding and I knew you were trouble. Not for James,' he continued relentlessly when she opened her mouth to protest, 'but for me.'

He walked back over to the bed and stood staring down at her, his eyes narrowed on her face.

'Did you go to Florence because you hoped to see me?' he demanded, his eyes burning into hers as if he was determined to read her mind.

A few moments ago she had vowed to forgo her pride, but now her courage seemed to be deserting her. She hesitated, and then lifted her chin. 'Yes. I wanted…I was going to tell you that I had decided to stay on at the villa with you. I had no expectations that we had any sort of future together—not when you mistrusted me as you did,' she said huskily. 'But I wanted to be with you and nothing else seemed to matter.'

'But instead you met Donata, and believed her lies,' Bruno said flatly.

'She was very convincing.' Tamsin swallowed hard. 'And it seemed entirely likely that you had another mistress. Neil was repeatedly unfaithful when I was married to him. And you and I—well, you had never made any promises,' she added quietly. 'Neil destroyed my self-respect with his lies, and I…I thought you were the same as him.'

'I am nothing like your ex-husband,' Bruno grated impatiently. 'And after what you've told me about him, I can't believe you're still in love with him.'

Tamsin stared at him in astonishment. 'I don't love Neil.'

'Then why do you still dream of him? Why did you call his name in the middle of the night and weep when it was me who tried to comfort you, not him? *Dio,* you cried every day before our wedding because you wished you were still with him, rather than about to marry me.' He threw her a furious look. 'I have even wondered if you wish you were carrying his child rather than mine.'

He was breathing hard, and abruptly swung away from her, but not before Tamsin glimpsed the flash of raw pain in his eyes. She shook her head slowly, trying to make sense of his words.

'You're wrong, Bruno, I don't dream about Neil. I remember now that when I said his name last night I had been dreaming that you were leaving me. I was crying, but when I reached you, it was Neil, and I realised that I had never loved him at all. As for carrying his child—I did once—for fifteen weeks,' she whispered. 'I was devastated when I discovered that Neil was having an affair. I already knew that he wouldn't be pleased about the baby, and I'd been worried about telling him. We'd agreed to wait a couple of years before thinking about a family and my pregnancy was an accident. But I still hoped...'

Her voice faltered. 'I hoped that he would end his affair and stay with me and the baby. Instead he was furious—told me he didn't want our child, that fatherhood didn't fit in with his career plans, and he was going to file for a divorce.' She closed her eyes briefly. 'He then suggested that I should abort our child. I moved out that day—I couldn't bear to remain in the house we had shared. I rented a flat, and a few weeks later I suffered a miscarriage.' Her fatalistic shrug masked the pain that had never left her. 'So in a way Neil got his wish—there was no baby. I know you must have found my constant crying irritating,' she murmured, flushing beneath his hard stare. 'But being pregnant again brought back all the feelings I'd had when I lost my first baby, and I was so scared I would lose this little one too. I certainly wasn't crying over Neil,' she added sharply, and then queried in a puzzled voice, 'But even if I did dream of him, why would you care?'

For a moment it seemed that Bruno would not answer. He had moved over to the window, and stood staring out at the wild night, his shoulders rigid with tension. But suddenly he jerked his head round, his dark eyes blazing and the same tortured expression he had worn earlier making deep grooves on either side of his mouth.

'Because I love you, *tesoro*.' The words were deep and low, and shaking with such emotion that Tamsin felt as though her heart had stopped. 'Although, God forgive me, I did not want to,' he admitted rawly. 'I experienced first-hand the destructive power of love. I watched my father's obsession with Miranda destroy him, and I was determined that no woman would ever have such a hold over me.' He walked back over to the bed, his eyes never leaving hers, and with every step he took Tamsin's heart beat a little faster. 'And then I met you.'

'And immediately decided I was a gold-digger, like your stepmother,' Tamsin said on a shaken voice.

'I think I knew almost from the beginning that you were nothing like Miranda,' he said sombrely. 'But I had to believe it. It was like a talisman—if I believed you were like Miranda, I couldn't love you. I refused to be a weak fool like my father, and I fought my feelings for you—convinced myself that what we shared was just blindingly good sex.' His mouth curved into a rueful smile, and for the first time Tamsin felt a faint, tremulous hope that this was real and not some cruel practical joke. 'I should have known that it was only that good because when I made love to you it was with my heart as well as my body,' Bruno added fiercely.

Oh, God! He seemed to be waiting for her to say something, but the words were trapped inside her, and she tore her eyes from him and nervously pleated the bedspread between her fingers.

With a muttered imprecation he whipped the covers back and sat down next to her. The month that we lived here together as lovers—you were happy,' he said gruffly. 'I can make you happy again, Tamsin.' He reached out and traced his finger down her cheek before cupping her jaw in his palm. 'When you left me I told myself I was glad, and I was determined to forget you. But you dominated my thoughts and haunted my dreams, and when you came to me in London and announced that you were carrying my child, it gave me the excuse I needed to force you back into my life—this time for good.'

'Bruno…' She still could not comprehend that he loved her. 'You married me because you wanted your son.'

'No, I married you because I wanted you—*want* you—will always want you,' he said, in the same harsh tone that she suddenly realised masked the fierce storm-force of emotions he was battling to control. He brought his other hand up to smooth her hair back from her face and she saw that his fingers were shaking. 'Give me one more chance,' he said, and now his voice was urgent, desperate, and it tore at her heart. 'I know you've been hurt in the past, and that you never deserved my appalling treatment of you. But I love you more than life, *tesoro*, and if you let me, I will teach you to love me.'

Even when he was trying to be humble he sounded arrogantly sure of himself, and of his ability to bend her to his will, but the faint wariness in his eyes and the rigid set of his jaw spoke of a vulnerability that broke through the last of Tamsin's defences.

'Darling Bruno…' She traced the shape of his mouth as she

had longed to do all that time ago, when they had met at Davina Grainger's wedding. It seemed incredible that this proud, uncompromising, awesome man was actually begging for the chance to persuade her to love him, but the raw emotion in his eyes was real, and she knew with a certainty that shook her that he would love her for ever.

'I don't need you to teach me to love you. I fell in love with you when I fell into your arms at Davina's wedding. And although there have been many times when I've hated you,' she said ruefully, 'I never stopped loving you and I never will. You are my life,' she told him fiercely, her voice suddenly strong as she sought to convince him that he was her reason for living. 'Love me, Bruno…'

She cradled his face in her hands and kissed him with all the pent-up love and passion that burned inside her, and he needed no second bidding as he ran his hands feverishly over her body.

'*Cara mia,* I don't deserve your love,' he said thickly. 'But I will cherish you and our son for the rest of my life. *Ti amo,* Tamsin. You don't know how many nights I have lain awake dreaming of this,' he growled in a low tone that throbbed with desire as he drew the straps of her nightgown down her arms so that her breasts spilled into his palms. 'I could *die* with wanting you.'

His tongue laved her sensitive swollen nipples, first one and then the other, until she arched beneath him and sobbed his name. When he stripped her completely some of her doubts returned, but he dealt with them by pressing hungry kisses over the firm mound of her stomach, telling her over and over how much he loved the fact that she was full and ripe with his child.

And then he moved lower, and Tamsin lost all sense of time and place as he gently pushed her thighs apart and stroked his tongue across her acutely sensitive clitoris, before probing deeper into the moist warmth of her vagina. When he moved over her and entered her with one firm, yet exquisitely tender thrust, he groaned her name and cupped her bottom as he set a rhythm that sent them spinning higher and higher towards heaven on earth.

Their loving was achingly familiar and yet wonderfully new as they finally spoke the words of love that had been locked away for so long. But then there was no time for words, just soft cries and deeper groans as Bruno's control shattered and he drove into her hard and fast, and Tamsin clung to him as wave after wave of incredible pleasure swept through her.

'Don't cry, *tesoro*,' he pleaded, when the last shudders of spent passion finally left him. He rolled onto his back, taking her with him so that she rested her head on his chest, and he felt her tears anoint his skin. 'Tonight I faced the utter desolation of thinking I had lost you for ever, but fate has given me a second chance and I will never let you go.' He brushed his lips over hers in a gentle benediction and said quietly, 'You have my heart, *cara*.'

Tamsin gave him a dazzling smile and wondered how it was possible to feel such happiness. 'And you have mine, my darling—for ever.'

EPILOGUE

STEFANO GIANCOMO DI CESARE entered the world on a beautiful spring day, after a short, uncomplicated labour, and promptly demonstrated that he had inherited his father's stubborn determination to have his own way, as well as a healthy set of lungs. Tamsin fell in love with him as instantly and as irrevocably as she had fallen in love with her husband, and was overjoyed when she and Bruno took their son home to the Villa Rosala.

'How do you like the idea of spending six weeks in the Bahamas?' Bruno queried, when Stefano had been settled in his crib and he was able to have Tamsin to himself for a couple of hours. 'I thought we could combine a honeymoon with our first family holiday—seeing that neither of us wants to be away from our son for more than five minutes,' he added with a wry smile.

He was happy to admit that he was as besotted with his baby son as he was with Tamsin, and he felt the familiar tug on his heart when she stretched up and pressed her mouth on his.

'It sounds wonderful. But I don't mind where we go as long as we're together,' she said seriously. She took one last peep into the crib and followed Bruno over to the bed. 'Stefano is so gorgeous, isn't he? In a year or so I'd really like to give him a little brother or sister. What do you think?'

Bruno was busy unbuttoning her blouse, and he gave her a wolfish smile as he tugged it from her shoulders before he unfastened her bra. 'Stefano is perfect. But I think we should put in plenty of practice in making babies, *cara*—starting right now.'

And as he drew her into the loving circle of his arms, Tamsin had to agree.

* * * * *

THE PREGNANT MIDWIFE

FIONA McARTHUR

A mother to five sons, **Fiona McArthur** is an Australian midwife who loves to write. Medical Romance™ gives Fiona the scope to write about all the wonderful aspects of adventure, romance, medicine and midwifery that she feels so passionate about—as well as an excuse to travel! Now that her boys are older, Fiona and her husband Ian are off to meet new people, see new places and have wonderful adventures. Fiona's website is at www.fionamcarthur.com.

To Carol,
Gone to a gentler place but never forgotten.
The best bits are for you, my friend.
Love, Fiona

PROLOGUE

Dubai—United Arab Emirates

THE crack of the starter gun echoed across the desert and silenced the noisy crowd for a heartbeat as the annual doctors versus nurses camel race began.

Hunter Morgan, paediatrician and contestant for the doctors' side of the neonatal nursery, kicked his camel into a gallop as the crowd roared. Ex-patriot medical staff can't get out much, he thought with a wry grin, though he noticed even some black-robed Arabs were among the throng. He wondered fleetingly what the attraction was in the hospital games for them.

To be honest, he wouldn't have been here if Kirsten Wilson hadn't dared him. She was a determined woman. She'd cornered him in the neonatal unit and he could still remember her enchanting tenacity as she'd ensured his participation. She'd promised to pound on his door in the dark if he didn't show, to let the tyres of his car down, to tell everyone she was pregnant with his baby, and he stifled a laugh at what a frenzy of gossip that would have caused.

It was his own fault people took bets on any sign that his immunity to women was failing—he'd never weakened before.

Still, Kirsten had made him laugh more in the last few months than he had in the last five years.

5

She was an amazing woman. Hunter clamped his lips shut to stop the flying sand from coating his tongue. He pulled his scarf more closely into his face, despite the early heat, and wiped his eyes so he could focus on the delicate shoulders of the woman riding in front.

Kirsten was tall for a woman, he knew that. When she was standing in front of him in the unit, he could just see over her head. He used that trick to keep the mental distance between them. He'd discovered if he spent too long looking into her wonderfully expressive face he'd lose track of what she was saying and just enjoy the show.

He really didn't think she was aware that she threatened his peace of mind.

The first marker was coming up and she still sat lightly, and delightfully, on her throne-like seat as if she'd grown up there. He wasn't quite as comfortable but that didn't mean he couldn't win.

Dormant competitiveness surfaced where it had been lacking. 'Second really isn't good enough,' he said to himself as he urged his camel on, tapping with his crop to let the beast know.

Kirsten was only winning because of her lighter weight and those strange encouraging noises she was making to her camel, but he had to admit she could ride. Her white burnoose billowed out behind her and the sun glinted off the flying cloud of red hair which she usually kept confined. He realised she was attracting the attention of the raucous local contingent.

The corner barrel appeared and he almost checked the gait of his animal until he saw she wasn't going to slow her beast. She skidded around full pelt and he watched in trepidation. Her camel swayed unsteadily and she hauled on the reins to direct it into the turn. The woman was mad—and scared the bejesus out of him when she was like this—but he felt his own blood begin to pound.

Incredibly, still mounted, she flashed back past him towards the winning post and, as usual, her eyes were wild with exhilaration and the joy that seemed to shine on everything she did. In that instant, the barrier he'd erected against the entire female race five years ago finally splintered into a thousand pieces of flying sand and he woke up to life again.

Which was even more reason why he couldn't let her win. If she could send the safety factors to hell, so could he.

Hunter and his camel rounded the barrel at a gravity-defying angle and for a moment he thought he was going down with his mount, but his camel strained to keep its feet. Swaying high above the sand, Hunter urged his mount to greater speed. The beast responded to the command in his voice. This wasn't a charity race day any more. This was a personal struggle for supremacy between him and that alluring woman.

He charged her down with sand flying and the other contestants left far behind. The cheers from the hospital crowd were a distant buzz in his ears.

'Come on,' he growled, and the camel flicked its ears as if to tell him to go to hell. The ground was a blur below him but he could see nothing but the red hair in front which was drawing closer. Inch by inch he gained on her until he passed her camel's tail and then its bony rump and finally he was level with Kirsten's shoulder.

She laughed at him, tucked in her chin and slapped her camel on the rump with her tiny crop, and pulled away for a moment. But her camel was tiring, finally, and Hunter edged back level so that right at the end they crossed the finish line together.

Both camels slowed to a trot and then finally stopped, their hairy sides heaving and breath snorting from their huge nostrils. 'Well ridden, Sister Wilson,' Hunter had to concede, as they pulled up.

'Well ridden yourself, Dr Morgan.' She laughed back at him, barely breathless. Then she slid lightly down the great height from her camel without waiting for the boy who was running towards her. Kirsten moved to the camel's face, stroked the giant's neck and whispered something in its ear. For a horrible moment there, Hunter thought she was going to kiss the disgusting beast.

His own camel turned and nipped at his leg as if to say, I've given you all I've got—now get off!

He tapped behind its knobbly knee with his crop and the camel knelt down to allow him to slide off.

The other riders began to dismount around them and he shook hands with the contestants. Hunter drew a deep breath and smiled. He felt terrific.

The flags fluttered in the morning air and the colours of the barrackers suddenly seemed brighter than he'd noticed earlier. It really was the most beautiful day and he couldn't remember the last time he'd noticed something mundane like the weather. His eyes were drawn to Kirsten, surrounded by her fellow nurses, and he forgot the weather to appreciate the woman.

Later, on the winner's dais, when Kirsten stood beside him to share the trophy, Hunter frowned down the calls of their fellow medical staff to kiss her. Unexpectedly, she stretched up and kissed his cheek before he realised what she was doing.

Kirsten's hair smelled of some herbal shampoo and a whiff of camel, and the feather-light feel of her lips against his cheek was more delightful than he was prepared for. His hand lifted of its own accord and caught her chin as she started to turn away, and he tilted her face back towards him. When he swooped to steal his own kiss, he wasn't sure who was the most surprised—him or her.

Hunter hadn't realised how much he'd wanted to do this. She felt right in his arms, as if she belonged there. It had been so long since he'd held any woman and now he knew why. He'd been waiting for Kirsten.

The feel of her lips against his was magic and when he released her, he could see the surprised recognition of something special mirrored in her beautiful green eyes. Then she was swept away by an admiring crowd of mostly male hospital staff. This time he followed.

And so it had started—eight weeks of magic. Silly, inconsequential conversations about stars and myths and unlikely scenarios that made him laugh in the cool of the evening after their shifts. Rendezvous at breakfast, eating fruit and rolls out under a tree in the courtyard while she fed the birds, hilarious trips into the bazaars where she would haggle fiercely with wizened street vendors as he watched in almost embarrassed awe until she'd won her bargain. Gradually they came to spend most of their off duty time together.

At work, they concentrated on their jobs and she

remained Sister Wilson, Nursing Unit Manager of Neonatal Intensive Care, and he Dr Morgan, Paediatrician, because that was how Hunter wanted it.

He was terrified to rush or be sidetracked by the fierce ache to possess her, a trap that had snared him into foolishness and disaster in his first marriage. The simmering sexual tension between them only added to the intoxication of Kirsten. Hunter finally began to trust again.

Until that morning when his world shattered and he saw Kirsten in the arms of Jack Cosgrove, the senior consultant—and he realised that the woman he loved was just like his ex-wife. The darkness surrounded him again and he couldn't believe he'd been such a fool. But he wouldn't be one again.

CHAPTER ONE

Sydney—late September

MIRA! Kirsten Wilson stood outside the familiar three-storey headquarters of Mobile Infant Retrieval Australia and sighed with contentment at the sign. It was a relief to be back, both at MIRA and in Sydney.

Six years ago she'd watched the stabilisation and retrieval of a premature infant from Gladstone, her home town in northern New South Wales, and Kirsten had known MIRA was where she wanted to be. Before her stint in Dubai, she'd spent a year here at MIRA headquarters learning the ropes. It would be great to be back in the team.

Kirsten had moved her focus from the birthing suites favoured by her two older sisters, who still lived and worked in the tiny hospital at Gladstone, to the more specialised medical area of neonatal intensive care. But she would always share the Wilson family love for birth and holistic midwifery.

Kirsten adored tiny babies and revelled in the methodology of protocols in an emergency, which was why she'd gained as much experience as possible before her return to MIRA. Eagerly Kirsten swung open the door and stepped confidently into the foyer.

The receptionist jumped up to welcome her and

11

Kirsten felt instantly at home. It was going to be a wonderful day.

'Hi, Maggie.' Kirsten couldn't contain her grin. Maggie and Jim Rumble were childless and ran MIRA headquarters and the dynamic staff like the parents of a large family. Their unobtrusive guidance worked well in the often highly stressful situations.

Maggie, thinner and aged a little since last Kirsten had seen her, bustled out from behind the desk and hugged the much taller flight sister. 'Kirsten. It's wonderful to see you. Welcome back. I'll take you through because I want to watch Jim's face when he greets you.'

She pulled Kirsten to walk beside her, effervescent with excitement. 'So when did you get back to Australia?'

Kirsten looked down at Maggie and slipped in a quick hug of her own. 'I've only been back in Australia about two months. My older sister—you know Bella, she visited me here a few times—married one of the locums in Gladstone. I filled in on the wards up there while she was on her honeymoon.' Her face softened. 'And I've been learning to be an auntie to my eldest sister Abbey's baby.'

She refocussed on the familiar corridors with approval. 'Now I'm back in Sydney for a while and I'm so glad there was a vacancy here.'

'There would always be a place for you here, you know that. For as long as your feet can stay in one place, that is.' Maggie winked up at her. 'Did you meet our current paediatrician, Dr Morgan, over in

Dubai? He's only worked here for a couple of months.'

Kirsten's fingers tightened on her shoulder-bag strap and she forced them to relax their death grip. Not Hunter Morgan? Of all people! She kept her face expressionless but it wasn't easy. She swallowed to moisten the sudden dryness in her throat. 'It's a big place, but his name does ring a bell.'

Kirsten tried to contain the familiar sting of pain and disappointment that came when she thought of Hunter, but it washed over her like a shore-dumping wave at Manly Beach and the force of it left her so cold she shivered.

From an oasis of sharing and caring and joy in her relationship with Hunter, something she'd never planned on, she'd been evicted from his life with a shattering suddenness that had left her reeling in an emotional desert more barren than any sand outside the hospital compound. Hug a married man in sympathy a couple of times and lectures on morality was where she landed! She'd tried to make him see how ridiculous his accusations were but he'd doggedly avoided her. Then anger had come to her rescue and at least straightened her spine. Piously, he'd even warned her of the penalties of adultery in Arab countries before he'd left. She gritted her teeth at the memory.

The urge to just walk out of MIRA now and think about this before she got in too deep was tempting. Maggie was looking up at her, puzzled by something she heard in Kirsten's voice, and Kirsten forced herself to smile.

It was too late already. She'd so looked forward

to being part of the team again. Now this. There'd be no freedom from tension if she had to fly with that man.

In the control room, three other people were waiting and Kirsten tilted her chin with a determined smile.

Hunter Morgan dominated the room even with his back towards her and his concentration directed to a phone conversation. Her heart sank in a shivering mess. Kirsten knew the thick dark hair and square set of his shoulders intimately. Her eyes had drilled holes between those massive shoulders many a time in those last few weeks as he'd walked away from her. He swivelled slowly to face her, still talking into the phone, and Kirsten looked away to Jim.

'Welcome back, my dear.' Jim was the senior paediatric consultant, control room supervisor and occasional flight doctor. A short, round man, Jim had the kindest face in the world. His eyes crinkled with years of good humour and he bounced across the room when Maggie announced Kirsten's arrival. He shook her hand so hard Kirsten could feel her head wobble and she suppressed a smile. The warmth in his face almost brought tears to Kirsten's eyes as she suddenly longed for the safety and shelter of her own family.

He presented her to the other woman in the room as if she were a major prize. 'Kirsten Wilson, Ellen! This is our senior flight nurse, Ellen Gardner, who I think started just after you left.' The other nurse inclined her head in acknowledgement. She was three or four years younger than Kirsten's twenty-eight and if she felt any anticipation at Kirsten's arrival she hid it well beneath a smooth make-up mask.

They shook hands and Kirsten offered a friendly smile, and then, for Kirsten, the other woman's presence faded away as Hunter replaced the telephone receiver and turned fully to face her.

'Kirsten, meet Dr Hunter Morgan. Hunter comes to us fully qualified and plans to move into emergency paediatric care after his stint with us.' Jim completed his sentence as if he had just given Kirsten a huge present.

Great, Kirsten thought. I'd rather have herpes. There was something in Hunter's face that made Kirsten raise her chin even higher. The man had an aura that ensured women were aware of his presence, and few could resist falling at least a little under his spell. Kirsten vowed to be one of those few if it killed her.

His chiselled features matched the fierce intelligence behind his insolent grey eyes and that unexpected sensuality in the tilt of his lips still packed a punch that landed somewhere below Kirsten's midriff.

She felt like stamping her foot. Hunter Morgan must be her nemesis. Just when things promised to go to plan, he intruded into her carefully ordered world and threw her into chaos.

Hunter met Kirsten's glare and memories of their last battles hung between them. Neither blinked and the moment froze for an extended few seconds until they both looked away.

Oblivious to the tension between his two newest staff members, Jim rubbed his hands together. 'Well, let's hope you two don't run off to get married, like the last lot.' The older man laughed with a slow, deep resonance that seemed to reverberate in his rounded stomach. Jim's idea was bitterly humorous and his rolling laugh helped. Kirsten's usual good humour asserted itself. Dr Rumble, indeed.

'I don't think there's much chance of that,' she said, and hung onto her calm smile as if meeting the man who had caused the only professional problem in her career wasn't in front of her. So what was she going to do?

MIRA was her vocation and an environment in which she knew she could make a difference. And only Hunter stood in her way. She'd gone to Dubai to set herself up financially and gain more experience to be better at this job. How ironic that a man she'd met there could ruin it for her when she came back.

But he could only ruin it for her if she allowed herself to be brought down by his negative attitude. The good news had to be that most doctors only stayed at MIRA for a six-month term. With luck she'd have just a few months of discomfort. She began to feel better.

Kirsten held out her hand with resolve. 'Hello again, Dr Morgan.'

Hunter couldn't believe her bare-faced gall after what had passed between them. While he'd been devastated at seeing her in the arms of another man, she'd thrown herself into dangerous pursuits as if nothing had been between them. Desert skiing, ballooning, four-wheel-drive safaris—she'd been in the thick of it everywhere he'd looked until he'd stopped watching in those last few weeks. Working with her in the unit had been so icily professional the other staff had avoided the pair of them when they'd had to be together.

He took her slender fingers in his and although the tension was slight, he was aware how she stiffened beneath his touch. Unintentionally, his grip tightened.

Her fingers were warm under his and he remembered when he'd finally accepted he'd been drawn to her as a woman. Her red hair flying straight out behind her head as she'd revelled in the danger of the race. She loved danger all right, he thought cynically. Life of the party, and always on the lookout for some mad new adventure or life experience, Kirsten had been the sun that less exuberant staff had gravitated around yet she had never seemed to favour one person—until him.

Initially, Hunter had blocked that attraction because he'd thought, mistakenly, he'd sensed a core of innocence beneath her bravado that he'd had no right to taint with his cynical distrust of women. But the joy she seemed to find in the everyday had worn his resistance down and he'd finally allowed himself to accept the idea that he'd found the woman he could plan his future with.

Until that morning!

He'd thought the tearoom was empty when he rounded the corner but then he saw them. Cosgrove twisted to protect the woman from his eyes and at first he only realised it wasn't Jack's wife cradled so passionately in the man's arms. And then Kirsten stepped out of the man's embrace to face him. He knew his face mirrored his devastation.

'It's not what you think,' Kirsten whispered. The same words Portia, his wife, had said when he'd confronted her with her lover five years before. It felt as if a stiletto was still lodged under his ribs after all this time and Kirsten was twisting it deeper.

Foolishly, in the last few months at MIRA, he began to believe he was over his shock at Kirsten's behaviour. What a fool he was.

Aware at first hand of the devastation that could be caused by infidelity, both as a child and as a husband, Hunter did the right thing when he ruthlessly severed their relationship. Afterwards, the gap left by Kirsten's friendship in his life warned him how close he'd come to repeating the mistake of his first marriage.

Here she was, threatening his peace of mind again. Typical. Jim's promise of the perfect candidate for the job had been too good to be true. He lifted his own chin, staring down at the top of her colourful red head and not into her magical if devious eyes.

'Kirsten, how nice to see you. Settled back into Australia?' He could feel the tug of her arm as she tried unobtrusively to free her hand. He chose to let her go and she snatched her hand back so fast he smiled.

Interesting. He looked down to see her eyes narrow as she probed behind his smile, and Hunter realised he could make this woman's life hell. That wasn't his style but he couldn't help a little satisfaction that he wasn't the only one feeling discomfort.

Hunter had left for Sydney and stepped straight into this job. He'd never really understood the dramatics Cosgrove or his doctor wife had displayed. He understood less why Kirsten had felt the need to come between a married couple.

Jack had even seen Hunter and tried to explain away his involvement with Kirsten, but Hunter had wanted no bar of it. He'd heard that Jack and his wife had moved on to Canada for a holiday before heading back to Australia so the man must have seen sense. He wondered if Kirsten had been asked to leave Dubai and if she was sad she'd lost her conquest back to his wife. Maybe Jack had been just another diversion—like he'd been, Hunter thought with gritted teeth.

'We must catch up later on how your last few days in Dubai panned out. Do you see much of Jack Cosgrove or Eva?'

'Sure,' Kirsten answered easily enough, but she felt the innuendo in the question. A few months ago, with Hunter, she'd known she'd found the man she wanted to spend her life with and it had certainly seemed as if he'd felt the same way.

Then it had all stopped with his ridiculous accusations. Hunter's lack of faith had shattered her. Obviously his suspicions remained. Kirsten had always prided herself on her honesty and came from a family that had high moral standards. To see that the man she'd loved had no capacity for trust, had shown her a serious flaw in what she'd thought a perfect relationship. Kirsten had forced herself to accept it had been better to find out then, but it hadn't helped her hide her hurt and disillusionment from Hunter. There'd always been an extra tension or double meaning in any communication they'd shared since Jack.

But she was over the brief Technicolor space he'd occupied in her life. Kirsten turned away to ask a question of the senior flight sister. He had the problem, not her, and she'd just have to learn not to let it rankle.

Ellen Gardner wasn't much warmer than Hunter, but she was safer. The two women moved across the room to discuss a map on the wall and Kirsten was glad to increase the distance between her and that man.

The area serviced by MIRA was bounded by the New South Wales border, though sometimes patients were transferred to Canberra in the Australian Capital Territory if beds were scarce. MIRA serviced around one hundred and forty hospitals of varying levels of care by road or air. They transported the critical patients to the closest paediatric or neonatal intensive care facility that had the resources to cope, often using fixed-wing aircraft or helicopters, depending on the ground facilities, weather and condition of the patient. The whole structure worked closely with the NSW Ambulance Service.

'Are the same number of personnel still flying in the aircraft?' Kirsten imagined it would be running in a similar vein from when she'd been here over eighteen months ago. Jim, as supervisor, hadn't changed, but she needed to convey to the other sister that she herself wasn't a threat to Ellen's authority.

'The minimum team consists of one transport doctor, one transport nurse and, of course, the pilot. Your first few flights will be supervised by me—' Ellen smiled without humour '—to ensure you don't require any further orientation on the use of the latest equipment or updates on aviation medicine. I'll also make sure you still have the skills needed for clinical call conferencing. Of course, space is always at a premium, but if there's room, we try to accommodate a parent as well. I'm not sure how many were here in your time...'

Kirsten suppressed a grin at the inference she'd worked at MIRA back with the dinosaurs.

'But now we have ten doctors,' Ellen continued, 'most on a part-time roster, and twenty-five nurses as well as support staff. Plus our very experienced pilots.'

'The pilots were good even back then,' Kirsten murmured, tongue-in-cheek.

'I gather you're not afraid of flying.' Ellen raised pencilled eyebrows.

As if. 'I'm not afraid of much,' Kirsten said quietly as the men came across to join them. Hunter obviously caught the end of the conversation.

'So what *are* you afraid of, Sister Wilson?' Hunter looked down at her with a wicked smile and Kirsten's concentration slipped for a moment. She'd forgotten, or had maybe blocked out the memory, of what it felt like to be on the receiving end of one of his smiles.

When he was amused, Hunter's eyes became flecked with molten silver and he had the ability to thaw her reserve with sudden heat. A heat that wasn't helped by the sensual curve of his lips. The man was too blatantly male and eight weeks of unresolved sexual tension lay buried, sizzling, somewhere deep between them. She flushed and tried to remember the question. She wasn't going to let him do this to her again. She wasn't going to let him tantalise her with possibilities and then refrigerate her with his chilly moral lectures.

Her brain clicked into gear, no thanks to him.

'Afraid? Only of leeches.' She shuddered. 'I discovered that on a survival course. But that's why I'm a midwife and neonatal nurse and not a doctor like you.'

The others laughed and Ellen looked admiringly across at Hunter. 'I'll bet you're not afraid of anything, Hunter.'

Kirsten only just resisted the urge to roll her eyes as she turned back to look at the map again. As she did, she saw that Hunter was watching her and not Ellen. 'I'm a commitment-phobe. I have one other phobia but as it's not flying, it shouldn't worry you,' he quipped, and arched his eyebrows at Kirsten.

Jim called them all to order and the meeting started. They discussed rosters and allocation of calls and the division of labour to ensure the skill mix remained even among the disciplines while integrating the new staff member.

When the meeting was over, Jim took Kirsten's arm. 'Come and look at the latest photos.' He flicked open the album and Kirsten smiled as photos of country hospital nurseries all over the state flipped over.

Dozens of photos were of tiny patients, dwarfed

by mountains of equipment, and the recognisable trousers and shirt of the MIRA team with the reflective stripe below the knees as they hovered over their charges. Kirsten even saw two old snapshots of herself, smiling into the camera. Then there were photographs of the aircraft and grinning pilots, as well as some aerial photos of different airstrips.

Kirsten could feel the thrill stir in her stomach. She was meant to be here. The excitement that had been there before she'd met Hunter Morgan was here again too. The intensity she'd planned to fill the hollow emptiness left from her shattered relationship with Hunter rekindled.

'Glad to be back, my dear?' Jim said as she closed the album.

Kirsten smiled up at him. 'MIRA is something I'll always love.'

'We're lucky to have you. Welcome home, Kirsten.'

Kirsten hugged the older man but her eyes drifted to Hunter, who raised one eyebrow cynically then turned away. Just one annoying fly in the ointment, she thought to herself, and suppressed a sigh.

Hunter left the room as if he were back in the camel race, out of control. Despite the fact he was heading towards the neonatal intensive care unit and his tiny patients. The great thing about babies was they had no ulterior motives. They struggled to survive by sheer tiny heart and determination and the skill of their carers, and you could trust them. Not like women.

As he entered the huge teaching hospital, his

thoughts kept drifting back to that last scene of Jim with his arm around Kirsten. Hunter couldn't believe that Kirsten was here at MIRA and, knowing his luck, no doubt would show up in his NICU. And as before, she'd be blatantly in his face. The hell of it was, he couldn't deny he was still attracted to her.

Nearly six months ago, he'd begun to let her close, until that episode with Jack Cosgrove. Painfully, but almost with relief, his heart had hardened implacably as if pleased to justify that distance. Having been a cuckolded husband once before, Hunter had vowed to stay immune to the power of a woman. But Kirsten had burst into his black-and-white world like a comet and had showered him with so many bright moments and such a zest for life he'd been blasted out of his usual comfort zone. Thank God and good sense he hadn't slept with her. Fantasies of her in his arms were bad enough, without having to contend with real memories.

After the truth had come out, such had been his bitter disappointment at his own stupidity he'd found he could barely speak to the woman and it had become untenable for him to continue working there, though he'd cited other reasons for heading back to Sydney.

Hunter stabbed the elevator button with more force than necessary and he spared a glare at the female orderly who warily shifted a few paces away from him. The last thing he would allow was distraction during neonatal transfers at MIRA. His passion for his work as his tiny patients struggled for life was what had helped him through Portia's deceit. And it would get him through Kirsten's return, he thought as the elevator doors opened. Getting out at his floor, he strode through the swing doors that led towards the neonatal intensive care unit. And he wouldn't be distracted in his unit either.

Kirsten had mapped her life out twelve years ago when her mother had died a year after her father. She'd decided she would be self-sufficient, travel and live the adventurous life she'd read about to escape a fifteen-year-old's reality of her parents' deaths. Until she'd begun, to her surprise, to imagine settling down with Hunter.

Thanks to Hunter Morgan and his icy lectures, she remembered why she didn't need any man, why she was determined to stay focussed on the two-bedroom flat she'd transferred her attention to. All she needed was a home to return to occasionally and the world was an adventure. The extra income for a casual night duty once a week in the NICU would help pay extra off her mortgage and maybe she'd even be able to start saving for her next overseas holiday.

Her interview at NICU was brief and she was swiftly accepted as a casual RN to start immediately. Gloria Westerland, the nursing unit manager of the NICU, introduced her to the other staff.

Hunter, her nemesis, just had to keep popping back into her life. Because she was prepared this time, Kirsten was pleased her reaction didn't register on her face. When Gloria paused at the crib where Hunter examined one of his tiny patients, he barely looked up.

'This is Kirsten Wilson, Hunter. She's a very experienced NICU nurse and will be working Saturday nights here.'

He grunted. 'We've met. Burning the candle at both ends as usual, Kirsten?' He nodded briefly and then went back to work without waiting for an answer. Kirsten stared at a point somewhere over his left shoulder and didn't say anything. She was thankful when the NUM moved on.

'Despite his lack of warmth in this instance...' Gloria glanced curiously at the tall paediatrician and then turned back to Kirsten '...Hunter is a real asset to the unit. He's kind, brilliant with the babies and contactable any time, day or night, for the five days of the fortnight we have him, and I guess you know he works at MIRA for the other five days.' Gloria gazed back to where Hunter leaned over the infant. 'And he's not bad to look at.'

Kirsten couldn't help a glance over her shoulder. His face was chiselled into stern lines as he concentrated and she missed the brilliance of his smile. He'd been able to warm her across the room when he'd smiled at her, and it wasn't only her that was affected. Gloria's understatement drew an answering smile from Kirsten. Not bad to look at indeed. 'We met in Dubai, but we've agreed to disagree. I'm not worried.'

Gloria nodded. 'That explains it. So you're sure you might want some extra shifts, apart from MIRA?'

'I'm sure.' Kirsten glanced at her watch. 'I start at MIRA on Monday and I've just bought the sweetest unit overlooking Randwick Racecourse.

The occasional night shift would work perfectly for me.'

'Well, I'm happy.' Gloria sagged with relief. 'The weekends are always the hardest to fill with experienced staff.' They shook hands. 'We'll see you Saturday night, then. When you have more time, I'd love to hear about your experiences overseas.'

Kirsten rolled her eyes comically. 'Have I got some stories to tell you.' The two women laughed and shook hands, and Kirsten tried not to notice that Hunter was watching her from across the room. She hadn't mentioned to Gloria that she also hoped that on night duty she'd be able to avoid contact with Hunter Morgan more easily.

For her heart's sake, that was a must.

CHAPTER TWO

KIRSTEN'S first shift as a night neonatal nurse started off quietly, if you could call the beep of two dozen heart monitors and the hiss of several ventilators breathing for tiny infants quiet. It was strange but good to be back in an Australian hospital and she glanced around at her workmates. In Dubai, the eclectic mix of nationalities was always fun but she had missed the twangy accent and dry wit of the Australians.

Kirsten was rostered to start at MIRA headquarters on Monday morning, but for tonight it would be good to have a chance to see what had changed on the home front. Around midnight, though, her leisurely check was cut short.

Twenty-eight-week twin girls were rushed in from the delivery suite with very little warning, and Kirsten was actually happy to see Hunter follow them in.

Kirsten took over the care of one child, Kinny Baker, and her coworker, Patricia, took the other sister, Carla. Weighing in at just eight hundred and fifty and nine hundred grams respectively, Kirsten spared a brief thought for the long road the girls and their parents had ahead of them as the tiny infants were placed in the humidicribs to keep warm.

Hunter had already intubated the girls in the delivery suite within a few minutes of birth and the babies had been hand-ventilated with tiny resuscitation bags by delivery-suite staff until they could be transferred to the nursery and connected to the ventilators. Kirsten attached Kinny's three leads to the heart monitor and clipped the pulse oximeter to her tiny foot to check peripheral oxygen saturation. The capillary oxygen saturation in an infant, or sats, was a good indication of how the respiratory system was coping.

Silently, Hunter appeared beside Kirsten and she could feel the warmth from his body beside her as he attended an initial physical examination while Kirsten was establishing baseline observations.

'Hello, little one,' he murmured to Kinny as he moved to listen to her heart and lungs. Then he examined her tiny body for any abnormalities. Kirsten checked the endotracheal tube was secure now she was hooked up to the ventilator.

She tried to ignore the seeping heat that burned into her hip from his nearness and her chest ached with unwilling sadness. She watched Hunter deftly insert a tiny intravenous cannula into Kinny's arm and together they splinted the little girl's tiny forearm to safeguard the line. They'd done this for so many infants in the past. Tonight it was all achieved without speaking.

Kirsten found she could still anticipate Hunter's treatment plan and the thought brought a pang to be shrugged off as she considered what they'd achieved. Airway was secure, breathing was controlled via the ventilator and circulation didn't seem to be a problem. Kinny looked good.

The IV would avoid the need for feeding until Kinny's condition had stabilised and provide immediate access for antibiotics and any other drugs the premature infant would need.

Kinny's arm, smaller than Hunter's little finger, emphasised the extreme fragility of their tiny charge. Next to Kinny's shiny, transparent skin, Hunter's brown hand looked like carved stone. A little like his face whenever he needed to look at her, Kirsten thought dryly.

Kinny's dad, Ken Baker, arrived from the delivery suite and his eyes misted at the sight of his tiny daughters as they lay pink and fragile amidst the technological paraphernalia. Attached to each baby, a network of leads snaked out through a port in the side of the humidicrib and connected to the digital monitor beside Kirsten's and Patricia's work area around the cribs.

Hunter's voice was quiet as he spoke to Kirsten. 'Now that we have them connected, if you want to get the surfactant from the fridge, I'll have a quick word with their dad.'

Kirsten nodded and turned to go, but Hunter stopped her. 'We can use half an amp for each baby down the tube—that will be plenty.' She dashed off and Hunter gently steered the babies' father closer to the cribs so he could watch their progress.

He shook Mr Baker's hand. 'It must look pretty daunting to you but both girls are doing really well.' As an opening line it must have worked, Kirsten thought as she returned, because Ken seemed to sag a little with relief at Hunter's smile.

She carried a tiny feeding tube to help ensure the hormone reached well into the little girl's lungs.

Hunter went on. 'Your daughters are sedated to allow them to rest while the ventilator expands and deflates their lungs for them. The tiny amount of liquid that Sister is squirting into their breathing tubes is a hormone to help stop their lungs from sticking together, which means less pressure is needed by the ventilator to expand their lungs.' Ken nodded that he understood and Hunter went on.

'Less pressure from the ventilator is a good thing because it means less long-term damage and less chance of a hole in the lung occurring.'

Kirsten listened to Hunter explain the humidicribs to the babies' father with a small smile. 'It's like a miniature rainforest in that crib,' he said, and his hands illustrated his point. 'All premature babies around your daughters' gestation are about eighty to ninety per cent fluid and they need moisture or they'll dry out, a bit like chips.'

The father blinked at the graphic image and Kirsten turned away to hide her smile. Hunter was right but a less graphic description might have been better.

Ken shook his head at all the technology. 'So how long do they stay here?'

'This young?' Hunter looked at the girls thoughtfully. 'They stay on average the time it would have taken for them to come to term naturally. So about twelve weeks! If all goes well, we'll wean them off the ventilator in about a week and even start them on maybe a few drops of breast milk every four hours in a few days. But they won't get anything to eat till then.'

The girl's father rubbed his stomach in sympathy. 'But they get what they need out of the drip, right?'

Ken looked as though he couldn't take much more information.

'That's right,' Kirsten said. 'I think you're doing really well with the day you've had. Did you want to get back to your wife? You know you can come back any time.' Ken nodded with relief. She handed him two instant photos of his tiny daughters which she'd taken while she and Patricia had weighed the babies earlier. 'Take these with you. Please, let your wife know she's welcome to come down and see your daughters any time.'

Kirsten showed him how to get back to the delivery suite and when she returned, Hunter was beside Kinny's crib, looking in. 'Dry out like a chip?' she said, and shook her head.

Hunter had the grace to look embarrassed. 'Well, they do dry out.'

'The poor man will worry that his babies will be crinkled when he comes back.' Kirsten laughed and sat back on her stool to do the next round of observations and for the briefest moment they both seemed to forget the past as they shared a smile. Then they both looked away.

It was after three a.m. before Hunter decided he could leave his charges in the NICU staff's hands.

Patricia looked up. 'Do you want a coffee before you go, Hunter?'

Kirsten was surprised when Hunter agreed because the last thing he'd seemed had been eager to stay around. She wondered at his motives.

'Sure. You ladies have done a great job tonight.' By the warm glance that passed over her, Kirsten gathered even she was included in the compliment. He always had been fair with his appreciation. She looked away.

The last thing she needed Hunter to see was her

confusion at approval when he'd been impersonat-
ing the basilisk all night. She knew she was good at
her job, so why should it mean so much for Hunter
to say it?

'Decaffeinated shouldn't keep me awake for
what's left of the night,' he said. 'I almost envy you
girls a night shift if it means you can sleep through
the day.'

'You must get very tired,' Patricia murmured
sympathetically, and Kirsten shifted on her stool
with resignation. And she'd thought Patricia a sensible woman. As if Hunter sensed her distaste at the
drift of the conversation, he turned himself fully to
face her. 'And are you sleeping today, Kirsten?'

'After lunch,' she said shortly, and turned back to
record Kinny's vital signs on her chart. He came to
stand beside the crib and looked down at her as she
sat on the stool. They weren't touching but she was
aware of how close he was. She could have lifted
her fingers a centimetre and she'd have been able to
feel the warmth of his skin. It was strange, the way
she could force herself to ignore these thoughts
while they were working, yet when the tension was
over it was as if the build-up she'd ignored took
over.

'So what's planned for you this morning that's
more important than sleep?'

Kirsten smiled noncommittally and unconsciously
leaned her body slightly away from him. 'My new
unit. I've unpacking to do.' Her tone didn't encourage further questions and he shrugged. Then she
glanced back over her shoulder. 'If you want to grab
coffee, Patricia, I'll stay here and watch both girls
until you and Hunter come back.'

Patricia's pleased smile wasn't reflected in Hunter's face and Kirsten stowed that piece of useless information away for later. The good news was he moved away to follow the younger woman to the tearoom and Kirsten felt the tension ease from her neck.

This was ridiculous. Already she could tell that half the women in NICU were attracted to the man and she knew better than to join the ranks. She'd seen how fickle he could be and how cold he became when he withdrew his favour. A brief glow under the Hunter Morgan sunlamp, despite the memories that could make her smile softly in weak moments of the night, were not worth the chill of being discarded. Now she knew why she preferred a non-threatening platonic friendship with men. She'd get on with her satisfying life as a single woman, and for male companionship she'd stick with those who were no risk to her peace of mind. Maybe she'd tattoo 'Just friends' on her forehead.

As if conjured up, a pair of masculine hands encircled her eyes from behind. 'Boo,' a male voice whispered, and Kirsten spun around under his light hold. Thin and blond, Marcus Gleeson, a young registrar she'd shared some of her MIRA experience with last time, grinned cheekily at her. 'Hey, Wilson, where'd you spring from? You're more gorgeous than ever.'

Kirsten looked him up and down. 'I morphed out of this stool here. Gorgeous, eh? I'm sure three in the morning is my best time.' She looked critically at the bags under the young man's eyes. 'How are you, Marc? Still playing the field?'

His smile wavered for a moment and then he

shrugged. 'I might tell you later, you always were a good listener. But what about you?'

Kirsten tilted her head and noticed his usual mischief was missing. Unable to help herself, she stood up, reached out and drew Marcus into a quick sisterly hug. 'Poor baby. We'll have coffee soon.' When she stepped back she looked up into the cold eyes of Hunter.

Kirsten resisted the ridiculous urge to explain and sat back on her stool and spun to look into crib. Both babies were stable and it wasn't time for more observations so she turned back to find Hunter still staring at her. She raised her eyebrows in a 'what?' gesture and his gaze moved over her dismissively before he turned away without answering.

Marcus watched him walk away. 'What's wrong with the boss?'

Kirsten shrugged and tucked her hands into her pockets to hide the effect Hunter's disdain had had on her.

Hunter glared at the point where the exit light showed the way out and strode faster than usual towards the door. He'd actually felt like lifting Gleeson up by the scruff of his skinny neck and tossing him out the third-floor window. Which was not a normal thought. Up until today he'd quite liked the young chap. Hunter frowned. He supposed Gleeson was only a couple of years younger than he was, but Hunter felt like an old man compared to his registrar.

He'd seen the smile Kirsten had given Gleeson and the way she'd hugged him. Hunter had thought Gleeson was enamoured by Patricia and had spent his coffee-break steering the young woman towards Marc and away from himself. That was probably why he felt so annoyed. The flat of his hand slapped the door open. Lack of sleep could make you intolerant—though he hadn't noticed that problem before tonight. Perhaps he was getting old.

On Kirsten's first shift back at MIRA she started at seven in the morning. It felt strange to be back in the familiar spread of rooms and balconies. She found her old locker with the key sticking out waiting for her, and she had to smile. Maggie would have done that.

Kirsten had brought a bag of things from home to keep on site and there was a feeling of *déjà vu* in packing them back into the locker, having emptied it eighteen months ago. She tucked her bathroom bag, small pillow and quilt at the back for those nights when all the checking and cleaning was finished and they were waiting for a call. If she was going to do extra nights in the nursery she might be glad of an hour's catch-up sleep.

Headquarters had two bedrooms with proper beds, a sofa in the TV room and a fold-up bed that could be erected in the education room. But from past experience she knew there wasn't usually much chance of sleep.

Most days, the MIRA staff averaged two retrievals per ten-hour shift, with each trip taking between three to five hours. Sometimes it was much longer if the infant was difficult to stabilise before transfer.

Hunter came into the room and Kirsten shoved away her box of emergency muesli bars, relieved she'd finished packing her locker. The sudden awkwardness at his presence made her press back to let him past.

The locker room was tiny and he couldn't help brushing against her as she shrank almost inside her locker to keep out of his way. Just that minute contact made her stiffen in denial of an attraction she didn't want to feel.

'Worried about catching germs, Kirsten?' he drawled, but didn't look at her as he put away his jacket. Kirsten gritted her teeth as she backed out of the small space.

'Don't be a pain, Hunter.'

There was silence from behind her as she left the room. Great beginning to the first day, she chided herself, but he'd started it. She sensed him follow her out towards the kitchen. They really needed to get professional here and bury the past. She slid her lunch into the fridge and eyed the new vending machines in the kitchen that hadn't been there last year and grinned. Sweets, chips, Coke and microwave meals—a truly balanced diet for those who wanted it.

One of the male registered nurses from the night shift wandered into the kitchen with an empty coffee-cup, let out a whoop when he saw Kirsten, picked her up and swung her around. 'Kirsten Wilson. How the hell are you?' he said, and gave her a big hug. At the look on Hunter's face Kirsten could either have laughed or cried. She chose the former and hugged Paul Netherby back. Take that, Hunter Morgan, Kirsten thought as the big nurse put her down, but when she turned to see what his reaction was, Hunter had gone.

Suddenly she felt flat, and in denial she became more vivacious.

'It's good to see you, Paul. How's Serena and the baby?'

The man's face fell. 'She left me. Not interested in taking her place, are you?' He looked cautiously hopeful but Kirsten wasn't fooled.

'Nobody could take Serena's place for you. If you've hurt that woman, you have some major sucking up to do and you know it.'

Paul hugged her again. 'I love you, Kirsten Wilson.' Hunter returned with a dirty coffee-mug and his lip curled as if he'd just swallowed a particularly loathsome insect. Kirsten signed. Paul was oblivious and dragged a stern-faced Kirsten out into the other room. 'You know me so well,' he chattered as they left. 'Come and meet my partner from last night, the delectable Nicky.'

Hunter stood at the sink and stared out the window, but he couldn't see anything. Lord, he'd had a lucky escape. That woman attracted men like flies and she seemed to lack all moral judgement. Hunter knew about poor Serena Netherby and the flighty Paul, and he'd thought they were almost back together again. And they even had a baby. Netherby was just the sort of low-life Portia, his ex-wife, would have liked, too.

He couldn't believe Kirsten could be so stupid as to believe anything Netherby said, but obviously they'd had some kind of past relationship to be that friendly.

It was all none of his business and he'd had a lucky escape. It was good to have a calm and safe life again. Now there was no reason he and Kirsten couldn't be professional about this—she'd always maintained that in the unit.

Ellen wandered into the kitchen to find Hunter gripping a cup, white-knuckled, at the sink.

'You OK, Hunter? she asked, and he blinked and smiled a perfunctory greeting.

'Fine.' He glanced down at the cup in his hand and loosened his fingers. 'Looks to be good flying weather out there,' he said, and walked away.

Ellen glanced out the window at the shredded clouds scattered ahead of a thick cumulonimbus front. 'What planet are you on today?' she muttered, as she switched the kettle on.

Paul, Nicky and the other night team members had left and Ellen cornered Kirsten to run through the protocols and check routines. All the time Kirsten nodded that she understood, she was aware of Hunter on the sofa as he pretended to read the newspaper. He kept staring at her over the top of the pages, trying to put her off, and if he didn't stop she'd clock the man with one of the cushions.

She knew he could get up to mischief. It would be just like him to decide to amuse himself at her expense.

Before the battle of wits could escalate, the MIRA phone rang and personal tensions disappeared. Jim took the incoming call from a base hospital on the north coast and they all looked towards the conference phone as Hunter joined in.

A three-hour-old baby boy, Isaac Curtin, had been diagnosed with a large ventricular septal defect (VSD) or hole in the heart. Born in Taree, an hour's flight north of Sydney, baby Isaac needed to be airlifted to a major centre for care and assessment by

a paediatric cardiologist and probable urgent correc-
tive surgery.

Kirsten listened to Jim as he outlined the hospital
doctor's problem, what his needs were and other
possibilities, but she could tell they all agreed retrieval was the best option. Jim conferenced the call
with Hunter, a paediatric cardiologist and a surgeon
in Western Sydney, and Hunter took notes on the
recommended treatment for stabilisation by the
MIRA team after the decision was made to transfer.

Kirsten's heart did a little flip-flop of excitement
and she couldn't help savouring the flush of adren-
alin for her first retrieval in a year and a half despite
the fact she was sharing the trip with Hunter and
Ellen. She shrugged. The baby and parents were the
important people.

The preparation and flight routine emphasised
minimum delay in departure and Kirsten pushed the
equipment out onto the roof ahead of the rest as all
the sequences returned from memory.

The extra-warm greeting Kirsten received from
the tall pilot, Keith, a man not noted for warm greet-
ings, was observed stonily by the two senior staff
members as they followed Kirsten into the helicopter. Kirsten rolled her eyes. Hunter probably thought
she was having an affair with Keith now. She
winked at Keith and watched Hunter's eyebrows
shoot up.

An experienced fixed-wing instructor, as well as
helicopter pilot, Keith had flown many times in the
past with Kirsten. She'd shared several hilarious pic-
nics with Keith and his wife at the Camden Aero
Club before she'd gained her own unrestricted pilot's licence, and she considered them both good

friends. Darned if she'd start feeling uncomfortable around Keith because of Hunter Morgan's hang-ups.

'Looks like it'll be a bumpy ride.' Keith seemed to derive a certain malicious satisfaction from the forecast and Kirsten grinned back. He hadn't been able to make her airsick yet.

Stormclouds accumulated off the starboard wing and Kirsten was glad they were in the sturdy Bell 412 helicopter. At least there was plenty of room for the extra staff member and Kirsten didn't have to stare at Hunter all the way.

Prior to take-off, baby Isaac's weight and birth date had been fed into the computer and the MIRA program-generated drug sheets produced the correct dosage for every conceivable drug they might need on the retrieval. This double-sided printed sheet was a valuable tool in saving time in drug calculations and dramatically cut the chance of medication error. The team prepared the most likely drugs *en route* to save more time at the destination hospital.

Ellen ran through the probable scenario of arrival for Kirsten, as if she'd never been on a retrieval or even an aircraft before, and Kirsten listened and nodded. At least Ellen was a distraction from Hunter who was on the other side of the cabin, watching with his arms folded. She wished he'd recheck the portable crib or something because she found his scrutiny hard to ignore.

At last they arrived and Kirsten heaved a sigh of relief. Next time she'd make sure she had the window seat as a distraction.

CHAPTER THREE

AT THE destination hospital, if there was time, the first step was always to meet the parents, then quickly move to assess the patient.

Baby Isaac would become more tired as his incoordinated heart struggled to achieve what had been so easy inside his mother, and Kirsten knew they'd have to watch out for heart failure.

Isaac's parents looked very young as they hovered anxiously on the periphery of the medical drama, and Kirsten went over and shook their hands.

'Hi, I'm Kirsten Wilson and I'm one of the neonatal nurses from Sydney. This must be pretty frightening for you both.' The young couple nodded and Kirsten smiled. 'We're going to keep you updated as we make Isaac as comfortable as we can for the flight. After that we'll get Isaac and you, Mum, transferred to the major hospital. When you get there, the paediatric cardiologist will talk you through his treatment plan.'

Lily, Isaac's mum, clutched her boyfriend's hand tighter. 'There seems to be so many people here and Isaac looks so small.'

'I know,' Kirsten said. 'But he's getting the best care so he can have the safest trip we can manage for him. About one baby in a hundred has a heart problem so we've done this before.'

Both parents sagged a little with relief at Kirsten's confidence. 'We'll all be with you until we hand

Isaac over to the staff at the city hospital so don't forget to ask questions as you need to.'

Lily nodded and Kirsten rejoined her colleagues. She allowed herself a brief stroke of Isaac's head as she began to record his respiratory rate, heart rate and oxygen saturation as she looked for signs of cardiac failure. Ellen connected the baby to the MIRA monitors as well as the referring hospital's equipment to ensure constant monitoring during change-over, and she offered Kirsten the stethoscope to listen to Isaac's chest. The heart murmur was very clear.

'What's your instinct on this baby?' Hunter spoke quietly in her ear and Kirsten knew he was testing her.

'He's breathing faster than he should be so respiration is affected, and he's sweaty and that's not a good sign. I'd say he has substantial fluid backing up in his lungs and when I listened to his chest he sounded "wet".' She glanced at Hunter. 'The heart murmur is loud and I'd say it's a large VSD.'

Ellen, dressed in a lead apron, held Isaac while X-rays were taken, because it was important to see the quality of Isaac's lungs and any cardiac enlargement. As soon as they were finished, Kirsten did a quick twelve-lead ECG to give Hunter some idea of the electrical conductivity of the sick baby's heart.

Hunter took the chance while the nurses were busy to explain things to the parents and reassure the base hospital staff on the excellent job they'd done in preparation for the retrieval team. She had to admit that when he wanted to use his charm he was a master at putting people at ease, which helped in situations like this.

She watched him put his arm around Isaac's mother and clap his father on the back as he congratulated them on their beautiful son. His obvious empathy with frightened parents had a lot to do with the attraction she'd felt for him when they'd first met.

They couldn't be friends but they should be professional about their differences at least. She could still admire his skill and empathy as a neonatal intensivist.

Hunter returned to the baby and the equipment Kirsten had assembled. He inserted an intravenous cannula in Isaac's hand and when the newborn grasped Hunter's finger, they shared a smile across the humidicrib at the wonder of tiny babies.

This was ludicrous, Kirsten thought, and vowed to establish some 'safe' camaraderie because moments like this were too special to waste on something that was never meant to be.

The finality of that thought stayed with Kirsten as she turned away to document the time of insertion and the start of the minuscule measured amounts of intravenous fluids.

'Let's give him a diuretic to see if we can offload some of this fluid he's accumulating,' Hunter said, and Kirsten handed him the preloaded syringe with the ampoule taped to it.

They checked the dosage together and just as Kirsten started to relax, Hunter had another question for her.

'What else are we looking for?'

Kirsten glanced down at Isaac and the answer came readily. 'Probably signs of any other abnormalities or indications for other syndromes that this condition can run with.' The obvious ones were often identifiable by abnormal facial characteristics. She glanced across at Isaac's dad, and any facial features that might have hinted at a genetic disease were vetoed by the mirror image of father and son. She smiled, and Hunter, following her thoughts, did too. Then they both looked away quickly and Kirsten busied herself by recording what they'd done.

All treatment for the stabilisation of baby Isaac would be diligently recorded, as would any improvement or deterioration in his condition. Later in the week, at the team meetings, all cases would be reviewed and discussed to ensure any improvements in care would be noted and used in the next case.

Within a short while they had achieved the best oxygen saturation and cardiac output they could for Isaac, and all that was left was to fix the cables and tubes, clean up their mess and prepare for transfer.

For Hunter, working with Kirsten was as hard as he'd feared it would be, yet at the same time incredibly easy. The last few months he'd felt he had become adept at completing retrievals with Ellen and the other neonatal nurses, but with Kirsten the clinical component of patient care seemed so much more streamlined.

There was no need to ask for anything. She had either already done it or had what was required ready for him to complete the procedure, as it had always been in Dubai.

And, as it was then, all the time she smiled—at the baby, at the parents, at the referring hospital staff. And at him.

Hunter had forgotten how much joy she shared

with those around her. Even in the midst of tension and fear, she was a reassuring light that parents and staff turned to when things seemed blackest, and suddenly there was hope or at least reason in the chaos.

He'd blocked out how many times he'd witnessed her like that in the past and he did not want to go there now, but it was hard not to remember. How ironic that she was happy and he was miserable.

'Dr Morgan could explain that better,' he heard her say, and bit back the contradictory comment that jumped to mind. She could explain anything but this was part of the 'have faith in the great doctor' theme that he'd noticed she used at times when she didn't feel she was getting through to parents.

He stepped into the breach and smiled. 'Hi, again.'

'I can't get this blue and pink blood thing, Doc.' Isaac's dad, Lionel, shook his head.

Hunter nodded. 'Another way to explain Isaac's hole in the heart is to imagine his heart as a house with four rooms.' Kirsten blinked and stared at him, and that amused Hunter. He'd picked this technique up from the internet.

'Some babies have problems with the doors or one-way valves between the rooms, some have problems with the plumbing or hallways—that's arteries and veins in the house—and Isaac has a problems with his walls. Specifically his septum—the two internal walls of the larger rooms have a big hole between them.

'Pink blood that's come back from the lungs with oxygen on board goes to the left ventricle and blue blood that's had all its oxygen used by the body needs to be pumped to the lungs via the right ventricle.' He paused and Lionel nodded.

Hunter went on. 'His cardiologist will patch the hole and stop the pink blood mixing with the blue blood so that useful oxygen-carrying blood will be pumped around his body.'

'Like a hole in the carburettor of my car that stuffs the mix?' Hunter and Kirsten smiled.

'Exactly like that.'

Lily didn't even try to understand the mechanics and Kirsten noticed she was becoming more agitated as she watched the door. 'Are you waiting for someone, Lily?'

Lily's eyes filled with tears. 'My mother. I hoped she'd come back but my dad is still angry with us for having a baby and he might not let her come. I wanted to see her before we left.' She lowered her voice and Kirsten had to strain to hear her. 'I'm terrified of going in the helicopter but I know Isaac needs me.'

Kirsten flagged down one of the staff from the nursery with a big can-you-help-me-please smile and arranged for them to phone Lily's mum. 'He's a very lucky little boy to have a mum like you,' she reassured Lily. 'We'll try and get onto your mother for you but I'll look after you if she can't make it before we have to leave. You might like the helicopter ride so much you'll be surprised. At least when you and Isaac come home you'll know how brave you were to go in the helicopter. You're doing something no one else can do for him just by being there.'

Lily smiled weakly and nodded. 'I hope so.'

'I won't leave you until someone else is there to

look after you,' Kirsten said, and Lily nodded, relieved.

They were almost ready to go and unhurriedly, Kirsten gave Lionel final directions to streamline his arrival in the city later that morning.

Hunter shook hands with the referring hospital's doctor and glanced across at Kirsten. No wonder Jim had been pleased to see her back. Kirsten was invaluable in this job and Hunter had to rethink any inclination to not make it easy for her.

It wasn't in the interests of MIRA to lose such a valuable staff member. But he wasn't running away this time so he'd better make the effort to establish a more professional relationship with her. They needed some rules and he'd make damn sure she stuck to them.

On the flight back, baby Isaac was as warm and sweet as they could make him before his surgery, and would be in the best condition possible to start his next phase of treatment.

Kirsten spent time with Lily and explained about the tests her son would undergo. Lily shuddered at any turbulence during the flight and Hunter and Kirsten took turns to sit with her and divert her mind with what might be happening for Isaac in the next few days.

'What's an echo?' Lily asked, as her fear of flying lessened and she began to think ahead. 'One of the doctors mentioned it and it sounds very strange.'

Kirsten smiled. 'Echocardiography is what it sounds like. It's a device that detects the sound that is reflected from Isaac's beating heart and echoes the graph it makes onto a computer screen. You can actually see the different colours of the blood as it moves in and out of the heart on the screen so the echocardiogram can show all kinds of heart problems children and grown-ups have.'

Lily clutched Kirsten's hand. 'He'll have lots of needles, won't he?' Lily obviously had a fear of injections, too. 'Will the echo hurt him?'

Kirsten looked across at Isaac as he slept in the crib. 'For the echo, he'll probably cry because babies don't like being without clothes, but it's very similar to the ultrasound you had during pregnancy except it's over his chest instead of your stomach. He will have needles for other tests, but try and take it all one day at a time.'

'Will we know how bad his heart is affected right away?'

Kirsten nodded. 'If your doctor is there for the echo, he'll be able to tell straight away or as soon as you see him afterwards.'

Kirsten noticed Ellen staring at her and she stood up. 'I'll be back in a minute to give you an idea what happens when we get to the hospital.'

She crossed the tiny area to the cribs. 'Did you want me, Ellen?'

'No. Sorry I was staring, I was actually enjoying your explanations.' The senior sister smiled deprecatingly. 'I tend to get bogged down in medical jargon but I can see it's not your problem.'

Kirsten laughed. 'I love this bit. Helping the parents understand what all the procedures mean so that they can project more calmness for their babies. I really think the babies pick it up if the mums or dads are scared.'

Hunter rolled his eyes and Kirsten stared him down. She was sick of his non-verbal innuendos.

'You used to think so, too, Hunter Morgan, so don't roll your eyes at me.'

'It's your hobby-horse.' Hunter raised his hands in surrender and Ellen stared at them both, finally twigging there was a 'past' between them—which explained a lot.

By the time Isaac was transferred into NICU, Lily was composed and determined to stay that way for her son.

The three MIRA personnel saw the infant safely connected to the hospital's monitoring system and then removed their own leads. When hand-over was complete, Hunter saw Kirsten hug Isaac's mother. How many times had he seen her do that?

It looked as though she had a new best friend to promise to visit the next day. With a stab of discomfort his mind shied away from the times she'd done and said some of those same things to him.

Ellen turned to look as well. She grimaced and lowered her voice. 'She's good. I was just about sick of Jim singing her praises, but you can't help but like her. And she's excellent with the parents. One of the girls is off sick for the rest of the week. I'll take her shifts and I'll recommend that Kirsten doesn't need further supervision.' She turned away and Hunter followed her. Great, Hunter thought, so there'd only be the two of them! It would be even harder to ignore her.

Back at headquarters, the window of opportunity for lunch wasn't ignored because MIRA staff never knew when they'd have time for the next meal.

Kirsten pulled her sandwiches from the fridge and glanced out the window at the busy car park below. There had been a few moments of awkwardness but all in all the morning with Hunter had progressed fairly smoothly. If there had been any problems working with him in the clinical situation, she would have had to rethink her position here. But while working with Hunter was a challenge, it was satisfying because he knew what he was doing and together they made a formidable team.

Kirsten heard the chink of money being fed into the machine and turned to see Hunter lift a frozen meal from the slot in the machine.

'I see you're still a mean cook!' The words were out before she could stop them, and she thought he was going to freeze her out, like his pre-packed lunch. To her surprise he took her words in the spirit she'd intended.

'Yep.' He glanced down with a wry grin at the plastic wrapper covering his meal. 'As long as I read the instructions every time, these turn out perfectly for me.'

Their eyes met in mutual memories. Hunter's lack of culinary skills had been the source of amusement between them and some of the more precious times had been when Kirsten had cooked for him in the tiny community kitchen. They both looked away and Kirsten's appetite suddenly deserted her. She pushed her paper bag back into the fridge and walked past him to leave the room.

Hunter raised his hand. 'Just a minute, Kirsten.'

She stopped and the tension in the room went up a notch.

'It looks like we'll be working together often and I'd just like to make several things clear.'

Kirsten raised her eyebrows. 'By all means. As in rules, you mean?'

He stared at a spot over her head. 'Exactly.'

'Good.' Kirsten wasted no time. 'Please, don't sit with your arms folded and stare at me when I'm trying to listen to someone.' She was delighted to see him actually shuffle his feet.

To give him his due, he didn't dispute it. He even smiled. 'Granted. I may have done that and, no, it's not acceptable.' He met her eyes. 'What I meant was that we'd be as professional as I know both of us can be because I think that's the only way this can work.'

'I agree. But what about trust, Hunter?' He froze and she went on. 'Do you trust me when I say I've given a drug or said I haven't? How can you trust me professionally when you can't trust me privately?'

'I trust you professionally and any further discussion of the past is exactly where I want to draw the boundaries. Personal discussions are not on.'

'Surprise me,' she said dryly. 'Any more rules?' When he shook his head she left the room.

He stared after her and sighed. There was so much about the surface Kirsten he really liked. More than liked. Then there was the other side of her that made him wish he'd never met her. Even watching the way she'd greeted the pilot that morning had raised his blood pressure, and he had no right to even notice how she interacted with other men. Yet every time he turned around she seemed to be in some sort of relationship with another attached male.

Apparently, women like Kirsten couldn't help themselves, and that behaviour didn't bode well for the man who would eventually try to tie her down. He had accepted that he could never be that man but he wished he could figure out how she thought for his own clarity of mind. Or was it just that she was an adventurer in the true sense of the word?

He'd over-microwaved his food again. While he chewed he couldn't help remembering the good times they'd shared in Dubai.

The time Kirsten, elbows on table, had frowned earnestly over lunch, and she'd disagreed with his take on the political situation in Australia so vehemently he'd had to agree to disagree, and they'd both ended up laughing.

Kirsten swimming underwater in the compound pool, green eyes open and finning around him like a dolphin, her modest one-piece bathing suit so erotic to him he hadn't been able to leave the water until she'd turned her back.

Her friendships with her tiny patients' families that saw her welcomed into the homes of ordinary Arabs and not just the super-rich, experiences he'd occasionally been privileged to share with her. But it had all been a dream because she wasn't a one-man woman.

He'd barely finished his flavourless lunch when the MIRA phone rang again.

This time a three-year-old girl at Bowral had come down with what the staff there feared was meningococcal meningitis. The little girl needed emergency transfer to a tertiary hospital and time was critical.

Hunter entered the child's weight and age into the computer to generate the drug doses and Kirsten gathered up the paediatric box of medications and resus gear for the situation. The computer printed out the drug sheet and Hunter grabbed the paper on the way out.

'We'll pre-prepare anticonvulsants we could use in case she fits.' Hunter's mind was running through scenarios as they made their way to the helipad.

The referring doctor was conferenced with an infectious disease consultant and they all agreed that time was the most important factor.

Jim authorised a 'hot load' of the helicopter, which was only used for the most time-essential retrievals. It was a decision that lay with the clinical co-ordinator, not the medical staff.

A 'hot load' meant the pilot had the helicopter engine and rotors turning while the team, outfitted with hearing protection, loaded the aircraft under flight crew supervision. This option could shave fifteen minutes from the departure time. A 'hot load' increased the danger to the team significantly and wasn't used lightly.

If they did the same at the other end, they could shave another fifteen minutes off the time, but it meant a parent wasn't allowed to enter the helicopter because of unacceptable danger. Kirsten hoped those few minutes would be critical in saving young Sara Sullivan's life.

When Kirsten arrived at the referring hospital with Hunter she knew instantly the situation was grave. Covered in a fine red rash, Sara was limply unconscious and deathly pale. Ominously, her dimpled limbs would occasional twitch as her cerebral state became more irritated.

'It seems more of a meningitis than a meningococcal septicaemia, which might give us more time,' Hunter said in a low tone to Kirsten.

Her parents, still dressed in the pyjamas they'd come from home in, sat on two chairs at the side of the room, plainly distraught, and Kirsten's heart went out to them.

It must be terrifying, she thought, to see your child so gravely ill in the hands of complete strangers. Already the referring doctor had started the antibiotic treatment ordered by the infectious disease consultant and there wasn't much the MIRA team could do except transfer Sara as quickly as possible to the receiving hospital.

'I'm sorry you can't come in the helicopter with Sara,' Kirsten told Rita, the child's mother, just before they left, 'and I promise to stay with her until she's handed over to the intensive-care staff.'

Rita nodded and her husband put his arm around her. 'We'll be right behind you in the car.'

Kirsten nodded and gave them a card with her personal number. 'If you have any problems, give me a ring and I'll see what I can do.' Both parents nodded and Kirsten squeezed Rita's hand once more and then she had to leave. Hunter was frowning at her and she glared back. Now what was his problem?

He didn't say anything until they were in midflight and Sara was sleeping peacefully for a moment. 'You can't give every parent your number to ring you if they need something.'

She tossed her hair and he remembered all the times she'd done that, especially when he'd said something to annoy her. 'I don't,' she said very quietly, so as not to wake the child. 'Just the ones that I'm not there to settle into the destination ward in case they get lost or can't find accommodation.'

He looked at her raised chin. 'And I suppose you're going to put them up at your place if they can't find anywhere?' he said just as quietly.

She didn't quite meet his eyes. 'Only if they're desperate.'

'If they were desperate, they'd sleep at the hospital.' Hunter silenced an alarm that had been activated by an involuntary movement of Sara's arm. 'New South Wales isn't some big country town where everyone is related, you know.'

'What's that got to do with country towns? Are you one of these people who think those in country towns must be inbred?'

Hunter snorted quietly in disgust. When he regained control he realised Kirsten was waiting for an answer. 'I can't believe you accused me of that.' He shook his head and his voice was barely audible. 'Inbred.' He laughed quietly. 'If you're inbred then I'm all for inbreeding.'

The smile left his face when he realised what he'd said, and changed the subject. 'Just be careful.'

Kirsten looked away from him. Sara was starting to shift uneasily. She held the little girl's hand because Rita couldn't, and when the child began to twitch and shudder with a mild fit Kirsten soothed her while Hunter increased her medication.

'It's OK, sweetheart. The shakes will go away soon.' She watched as Hunter gave more intravenous anticonvulsant and gradually Sara's shaking subsided. It was moments like this that stirred the deep maternal instincts in Kirsten and, as if reading her mind, Hunter's question followed her thoughts.

'Do you ever want children, Kirsten?'

She brushed the damp hair away from the little

girl's forehead. 'Yes. One day. When my parents died I swore I'd never have anyone rely on me like I did on them and decided I'd never have children. Then something happened.' Someone actually. She looked out the window so he couldn't see her face. She'd fallen in love with Hunter and seen that children were an extension of love, not a neatly packaged box you could choose to pick up or not. She turned back to face him and because this was something she'd only recognised recently she went on doggedly. 'I realised I'd been kidding myself all that time. That I was just as maternal as the next woman. But if I ever become a mother, I'll always watch over them. Children are a huge responsibility and I'd do my best to be always there for them.'

Hunter heard the seriousness in her reply and wondered if Kirsten would give up her more hazardous pursuits. 'You might have a couple of adventurous children.'

She looked across at him. 'That's a lovely thought. But you have to be careful because kids need you too much. You know my mother died when I was fifteen, and even though my sisters looked after me wonderfully, I wish Mum had been more careful. I won't do that to my children.'

He couldn't help imagining a young Kirsten, stoically heartbroken as a teenager, and the image moved him more than he wanted to admit to himself. 'Nobody can help accidents.'

'No,' she said, and he could tell the subject was closed. He didn't know why he'd started it when he'd promised himself to maintain his distance, but she'd looked so Madonna-like as she'd soothed the infant that the question had come from somewhere he hadn't expected.

He'd never have kids now. When he'd first married Portia and again when his relationship with Kirsten had blossomed, he'd hoped that one day he would share the joy and fears that he saw every day in his work. That train of thought became too painful and he glanced at his watch. They'd be down in twenty minutes.

Sara was transferred smoothly but Hunter had grave doubts on the child's prognosis because she wasn't improving with all the antibiotics she'd been given. He could see that Kirsten shared his doubts and he knew how she'd worry.

But it wasn't his concern if Kirsten was upset. The little girl was in the best place and they'd done all they could. So why did the thought intrude on his consciousness all day until they finished their shift?

He'd glance across and Kirsten would be staring into space with a frown on her face, and he knew she was worrying about Sara and he wanted to ease her frown away. This side of her was so loyal and caring. When he had a moment to spare, the questions would return and he realised he was spending far too much time thinking about her. All the same, he'd ring the paediatric ICU tonight when he got home and check on Sara's condition.

Hunter unlocked the door to his empty house later that evening and the retrievals he'd done that day with Kirsten loomed large in his mind. Her smile haunted him as he hung his keys on the hook and walked thoughtfully into the kitchen. He found himself trying to imagine what she was doing at this moment.

He made a few calls and then there was a reason to phone her.

When her telephone rang, Kirsten's mind was still with Sara Sullivan.

'Hello.' She glanced at the clock and was surprised to see it was after ten.

'Kirsten?' Her hand froze on the kettle as she recognised Hunter's voice.

'It's Hunter. I'm sorry, I've just realised how late it is. Perhaps I should leave it until tomorrow?'

She kept her voice as expressionless as she could. 'I'm awake. What can I do for you, Hunter?'

He didn't answer for a second, and Kirsten wondered if he'd been cut off, but then he spoke.

'You were great to work with today, Kirsten.'

Kirsten reached into a cupboard and lifted down a cup. 'You sound surprised.'

She heard the laughter in his voice and thought with a pang how long it had been since she'd heard that sound.

'I suppose I shouldn't be,' he said. 'Mainly I want to apologise for any negative impression I may have left you with at your orientation day. I do believe you will be an asset to the service. I just rang to say that I will try to make it as easy as possible for us to work together.'

Patronising pig. 'That sounds sensible to me, Hunter.' Kirsten gripped the phone tighter. 'Was there anything else or shall I see you tomorrow?'

'No, except that Sara Sullivan seems to be holding her own. I just spoke to her paediatrician and I knew you'd been worrying.'

Kirsten bit her lip and remembered all the times she'd seen him watching her that day. He'd been concerned for her—not looking for mistakes, as she'd thought—but that just made him inconsistent. 'How did you know I was worried, Hunter?'

He paused and then she heard the care in his chosen reply. 'Give me credit for some instincts, Kirsten,' he said, and she snorted.

'You have lousy instincts, Hunter Morgan, but it was good of you to ring and let me know.'

'What's that supposed to mean?'

She'd shocked him. Excellent! 'Goodnight, Hunter.' Kirsten put the phone down and sank slowly onto the chair beside the phone and hugged herself. On the surface it had been thoughtful of him to tell her about Sara. Tonight she'd tried to get some information herself, but had been told the unit was too busy to answer her call. Typically, Hunter as a doctor had got through.

But she knew that wasn't why he'd called—it had been to keep her off balance like this. She didn't know what his agenda was but she wasn't going to read anything into it.

Kirsten tried to shake off her agitation as she walked into the bathroom and turned on the bath tap. It wasn't helpful that her sisters where five hundred kilometres away. She needed rational advice and she just wasn't feeling rational. Her older sister Abbey could be relied upon to have the sensible answer and Bella's sympathy was legendary. Kirsten poured too much of Bella's calming oil in the bath and grimaced at the slick on top of the water.

Hopefully, later she'd sleep. She took a sip from the empty cup in her other hand and then sighed at the vagueness of the action. Her brain was fried with trying not to think about Hunter. The chance of falling asleep at all seemed unlikely, and it was Hunter's fault.

CHAPTER FOUR

THE next morning Kirsten tried Paediatric Intensive Care again and managed to speak to Sara's mother, Rita. Apparently the little girl had slightly improved overnight but the doctors were still cautious at raising her parents' hopes.

The young mother's forlorn voice stayed with Kirsten as she rode her pushbike to MIRA headquarters. Despite her reluctance, she would ask Hunter if he could find out any more information on Sara.

Night staff had had a huge night, with three retrievals, and Kirsten's morning began in the same way. They were hurried off to two small outlying hospitals in succession for children in respiratory distress. Both transfers went well and the MIRA staff were back at base just on lunchtime. When they landed on the roof, they could smell the aroma of frying onions drifting up from the east balcony.

'I gather Jim's brandishing a barbecue fork somewhere,' Kirsten said, and Hunter nodded.

'He'll be wearing that spotted apron that does nothing for his figure,' he said. They'd had a good morning, and he was in control. There was no reason they couldn't lighten up just a little.

Coming down in the lift, they came out on the second floor. Through the open-plan room they could see the people out on the balcony.

'Anyone for lunch?' Jim called across at them.

Kirsten started to giggle and Hunter smiled at the staff gathered to cat-call Jim's cooking prowess. Sometimes when the workload eased and several teams were overlapping their shifts, Jim would throw an impromptu cooking experience, and it was no coincidence these occasions often happened after a run of stressful days.

'So it's steak sandwich day, is it?' Kirsten called out, as they pushed their equipment past the gathering. 'We'll be back in a minute—you'd better leave some for us.'

When they'd restocked their equipment and drug box ready for the next case, Kirsten turned back to the balcony. 'Are you in?' The way she said it came across as a you-wouldn't-want-to-join-us message and Hunter bit back his smart why-wouldn't-I comment.

Then he saw Paul Netherby and the pilot, Keith, wave at Kirsten, and there was all the more reason to see what went on. He nodded. 'Sure. Why not? We've had a full couple of shifts and I'm out of here for the next few days.'

Kirsten almost staggered at the wattage beamed her way. He hadn't smiled at her like that since before the fiasco in Dubai. One part of her screamed danger and flight but the other rotated like a rotisseried chicken and basked in the warmth. Maybe she should be the one to give the social occasion a miss. She willed her heart rate to settle and her determination firmed. They had worked well together. Perhaps he was seeing how wrong he'd been. Either way she'd be safe from doing anything foolish with everyone around.

They were welcomed into the group like long-lost

relatives and Kirsten took the proffered sandwich and looked for somewhere to sit down out of Hunter's sight. She smiled at Paul heading her way with his own plate, but before he could sink down next to her, Hunter slid into the vacant chair and waved him off. 'Dip out, buster. I'm here.'

Kirsten nearly choked on her sandwich and couldn't help the startled look she turned on Hunter. He smiled one of those killer smiles at her again and suddenly it was difficult to swallow. What was going on here?

'Since when does sitting next to me improve *your* appetite?' Her question could have been more delicately phrased but at least she'd kept it low enough not to broadcast her dismay to the others.

Hunter pretended to be wounded by her comment and she couldn't help the tiny smile on her own lips in response to the woebegone expression on his face. Then he smiled. 'This is a social occasion and I'm being social. Lighten up, Wilson.' He looked innocent—and she speculated on his agenda as she glanced around to see if there was anywhere else she could sit. No such luck. She would eat her sandwich and then get out of here as fast as she could.

'Fine.' She shrugged one shoulder. 'The weather is interesting today, Dr Morgan.'

'Boring, Sister Wilson.' He shook his head. 'We're being social, not polite.' He glanced at the roof of the balcony as if seeking inspiration for a topic. 'Tell me about your new flat.'

Despite her intentions, Kirsten could feel that breathless anticipation that had trapped her in the past. This was the guy who thought she was an adulteress. She shook her head. 'I don't think so.'

'Let me guess.' He stared thoughtfully at her and Kirsten had to look away because the warmth in his eyes had been absent for so long she'd forgotten how he could make her feel. Drippy, like hot wax in the sun, and she disgusted herself.

'Psst! Over here.' Hunter tapped her shoulder and the warmth from his hand coiled insidiously around her heart. She couldn't ignore him and Kirsten turned back warily. 'Let me see,' he said. 'You're playing house and I'm not invited?'

'Hole in one.' Kirsten pushed her sandwich around on her plate, appetite gone and nerves screaming because she needed to give in to what she had to say to him. If she didn't...

'What about your precious rules? Why this sudden interest? If you want to be friends, you should apologise before we go any further. Admit you were wrong about me, Hunter Morgan!' The words hung in the air between them and Hunter winced.

The smile fell off his face and he was ominously quiet. She stifled the wash of disappointment as the silence dragged on and he didn't respond, and told herself she'd known all along he was toying with her. But that didn't help the feeling that she'd been a fool again. Damn the man.

Finally he answered but he didn't meet her eyes. 'If I was wrong about you, I'm sorry.'

If he was wrong? Big effort, creep. She didn't say it out loud—maybe she should have—but his lack of faith stung anew and she didn't want him to know that. So he still believed she'd had an affair with Jack Cosgrove. What a joke when all she'd done had been to push Jack *back* to his wife.

She should be thankful Hunter hadn't lied about

how he felt. She could go home and call herself a fool for believing he'd realised his mistake for even a minute.

Keith wandered across and Kirsten smiled blindly at him. 'Excuse me,' she said to Hunter, and stood up.

'Keith, I've been meaning to ask you about the new helicopter...' Her voice faded as she took Keith's arm and steered him across to the other side of the balcony.

Hunter stared after her. She'd looked wounded and he felt like a heel, but unfortunately he didn't believe he'd been wrong. He'd seen Kirsten in the man's arms with his own eyes, and Eva had confirmed it. So why did he still want to believe in her? He tensed as he watched Keith pat her hand and dropped his sandwich back onto the plate. He'd begin compiling the statistics he was working on for the study.

The MIRA phone stayed blessedly quiet for the rest of the afternoon and Hunter left as soon as the clock hit five.

The rest of the week was peaceful for Kirsten as Hunter worked his hours in the NICU. Kirsten was paired with Pete Chee, one of the full-time registrars who had almost finished his six months' stint gaining emergency experience with MIRA.

They did a couple of road ambulance transfers for closer hospitals and two fixed-wing retrievals in the west of the state, as well as the usual rotary-wing transfers. By the end of the week, Kirsten felt as if she'd never been away from MIRA.

She kept telling herself how much more relaxing

it was without Hunter there to throw questions at her and keep her off balance, but she couldn't help missing his annoying presence. That was a worry.

She'd been on the road to recovery, she really had, before she'd run into him again at MIRA, and if she was this affected by only a few days of working with him again, maybe this wasn't going to work out.

Hopefully he wouldn't be there in NICU on Saturday night if everything went smoothly, and she clung to that thought because she wasn't ready for the roller-coaster yet again.

Of course, Hunter was the first person she saw as she put her bag away on the ward. 'Good evening, Kirsten,' he said, and Kirsten gritted her teeth.

Kirsten closed her eyes briefly before she turned around and sighed. And she didn't care if he heard it. 'How about you just leave me alone?'

When she turned to face him he took a step backwards from the denial in her face and held up his hands. 'I'm sorry if I upset you the other day.'

'Hunter—get over it. I am.' She brushed past him and Hunter watched her go. He'd had a lot of trouble getting her out of his mind for the last few days and he wasn't sure what was more stressful—being with her and trying to ignore the effect she had on him or being away and trying to block her out of his thoughts. Either way he needed to get a grip on what she was and wasn't going to be in his life.

Though judging by the way she'd brushed him off just then, she knew exactly where he wasn't going to be. Anywhere close to her. Why that attitude on her part should make him even more determined to follow her he had no idea. It was either psychiatric help or find out how Kirsten Wilson ticked. Ignoring her hadn't worked, and if he wanted some control back over his life then this problem needed sorting.

Kirsten shook hands with the evening staff she hadn't met before, and took a seat in the hand-over circle to listen to report, pretending Hunter wasn't leaning on the wall beside the nurses' station. As soon as report was finished the other staff could go home and she could find something to do away from Hunter.

All was reasonably quiet in the unit, it seemed, and Kirsten gladly took over the care of the Baker twins from the previous week. They had been extubated and were breathing well for themselves, and were even having a few mils of expressed breast milk from Mum down tubes into their stomachs.

She introduced herself to Kinny's and Carla's mum, Maxine, who was having a late visit to express her milk. 'Hi, Maxine, I'm Kirsten. Your daughters have come a long way since last week and I see they've started on a little EBM already. That's wonderful.'

Maxine Baker was a small woman with big blue eyes and an air of fragility that, amazingly, reminded Kirsten of the twins. She smiled at Kirsten confidingly. 'It seems a bit useless to see them get two mils down their tubes but I've been told it's the best thing for them.'

Kirsten grinned at Carla's little bottom sticking up into the air as she lay on her tummy in the humidicrib, and then looked at Maxine.

'One of the more recent changes to premature

babies' care has been the earlier introduction of breast milk. Those babies started within a few days, even with only the tiniest quantity of expressed breast milk, had many less problems with their intestinal systems than those who were given nil by mouth for extended periods. So it is very important.'

She smiled. 'The most amazing thing, I think, is that your breasts will be producing exactly the right milk for a twenty-nine-week baby this week, and someone else who had a forty-week baby will be producing milk for a full-term infant.'

'That's incredible.' Maxine shook her head and patted her breasts. 'Clever boobies.'

The two women smiled at each other in mutual mischief.

Maxine peered at Kirsten's name badge again. 'Were you here when they came down here last week, then?'

Before Kirsten could answer, Hunter arrived and joined in the conversation. At least Maxine was happy to see him. 'Kirsten was here all right. She looked after them on their first night.'

Kirsten agreed and wished he'd go away. She turned her shoulder on Hunter. 'I met your husband, too.'

Apparently Maxine didn't hear her as she smiled at Hunter. 'Hello again, Dr Morgan, I thought you said you were going home?'

'I'm just on my way.' He stared at Kirsten but she refused to look at him. He'd upset her at the barbecue and he regretted that, but mostly he remembered her walking away with Keith. Tonight her arms were crossed and she'd turned one shoulder towards him. He doubted she could have made her aversion to his company any clearer.

Maxine turned back to Kirsten. 'So, did you take the photo of the girls that my husband brought up to me?' When Kirsten nodded Maxine smiled and reached into her dressing-gown pocket. She pulled out a 'Mummy's brag book' of photos. 'I keep the photos in my pocket so I can look at them whenever I need to.' Hunter accepted he was superfluous and after one last fleeting look at Kirsten, he took himself off.

Kirsten sighed as she sneaked a glance at his back as he walked away.

'He's a bit of a looker, isn't he?' Maxine smiled knowingly. 'And he's a sweetie.'

Kirsten made some kind of noncommittal sound of semi-agreement then saw that the bigger twin, Carla, was awake. 'Have you had a cuddle yet?'

'I had a nurse of Kinny three days ago but Carla was still too sick then.'

'Well, Carla is awake now—would you like a nurse for a few minutes?'

Maxine's eyes misted. 'I'd love it. I've only stroked her hand so far.'

Kirsten gave Maxine a quick hug. 'I'll just check that no one else will need me for a little while and then we'll do that. Carla needs to snuggle up to you just as much as you need it.'

Kirsten strongly believed in the practice of kangaroo nursing, where the mother of a premature infant tucked her baby down inside her clothes against her skin for a little while. The babies had shown to be more settled and peaceful after skin contact with their mothers but it required a lot of juggling and rearranging of leads and equipment. At least every three days if the infants were stable was a good interval because it didn't tire the babies too much.

Fifteen minutes later, Kirsten felt her own eyes mist as she watched Maxine whisper to her baby daughter as she snuggled her between her breasts. It was moments like these that were for treasuring, and Kirsten took a photo at Maxine's request so the mum could add it to her brag collection.

The rest of the night passed swiftly and Kirsten was busy enough to avoid thinking of Hunter at all. She decided the night shift would be no hardship as long as Hunter stayed away.

By the time she arrived home in the morning, she was so tired she fell into bed and slept dreamlessly, thank goodness, until late Sunday afternoon.

Unfortunately the first person she thought of when she opened her eyes was Hunter Morgan. 'Get out of my head,' she groaned as she opened her eyes. She picked her pillow up and threw it at the wall and then remembered it was Maggie's birthday.

Jim had asked Kirsten to join them for tea if she'd had enough sleep after her night shift, and the idea of a diversion from the dreaded Hunter Morgan ghost sounded a good thing.

She phoned the Rumbles and promised to arrive in due time and Maggie sounded so pleased Kirsten was glad she'd made the effort.

After a shower and dressed in her new pair of stretch jeans that she'd fallen in love with, Kirsten slid the quiche she'd made yesterday out of the fridge and hummed her way to the door.

She picked up the flowering cyclamen she'd chosen as a gift and once outside juggled her load to lock the door behind her.

'Would you like me to take that for you?'

Kirsten jumped, dropped the quiche and then bumped heads with Hunter as they both caught the dish at the same time.

She let go of her half of the dish and used her hand to rub the painful bump on her forehead. She didn't notice the little smear of egg that she wiped into her hair but she was so monumentally angry she wouldn't have cared anyway.

Hunter was oblivious as he admired the way her tight black jeans encased her long legs and he straightened up slowly. The scent of her perfume rang bells he didn't want to hear and she had some low-cut wrap-around top on that looked as though all it would take was a flick of a bow and it would fall to the floor. He swallowed. Her breasts rose and fell with agitation and he turned his head to try and drag his eyes away.

Lord, she had him panting like a teenager, he realised, as he forced his attention back to her face. That was when he realised she was furious.

'What the heck are you doing here?' she practically snarled at him, and he began to see the funny side of it.

'Catching quiches.' He rubbed his own head with his free hand. She wasn't amused and he shrugged at her lack of humour. 'Jim asked me to pick you up in case you wanted to have a glass of wine with dinner. And he said your car was unreliable.'

She spoke through clenched teeth. 'And he gave you my address?'

'Actually, he offered to but I already had it.'

Kirsten dropped her chin and looked at him from under her brows. That little trick was right up there with the hair flick. He remembered how much he used to love it when she did that, but he didn't think it was a good time to mention that.

'Why would you have my address?' She was glaring at him so hard he wondered that he was still standing. He shrugged. 'In case I needed it.'

Kirsten went to answer and then changed her mind and said nothing. She turned her back and checked that her door was locked then walked straight past him.

'I gather you don't want a lift?' He followed her down the stairs and out to the car park, carrying the quiche.

'Not if you were the last man on earth. Goodbye.' She held out her hand to take the pie dish.

He gave it to her and then he grinned because she had to give it back to him to get out her keys. 'I'll wait until you go.'

Darn. Kirsten chewed her lip. She hoped her car would start. She'd been riding her pushbike to work the last few days because her old bush-basher, which she'd picked up from her sister's, was almost beyond it. Both brothers-in-law had suggested she trade Bessy in, and even Abbey and Bella had agreed. But she'd seen a lot of Australia in her old mate and she wasn't ready to say goodbye yet.

'Please, Bessy,' Kirsten muttered as she climbed up into the Land Rover. She held her hand out for the quiche and plant and set them down on the passenger side floor as a gesture of faith that her car would start. Then she shut the door in Hunter's face.

She turned the key. Bessy tried, she really did,

but she just couldn't get up enough enthusiasm to turn over. 'Come on, Bessy. Do it for mama,' Kirsten pleaded under her breath. If only Maggie hadn't sounded so pleased she was coming.

'I think your starter motor is shot,' Hunter was mouthing at her through the windscreen, and she felt like squirting him with the windscreen washers. She took her hand away from the ignition, sank her head down onto the steering-wheel and drew a deep, calming breath.

OK. Fate had conspired against her but that didn't mean she'd be on the back foot for the rest of the evening. She opened her door.

'I was planning on an early night,' she said ungraciously as she handed him the quiche and the pot plant before she got out.

'So was I,' he said, and restrained himself from saying anything else.

CHAPTER FIVE

THE ride over to the Rumbles' was mostly accomplished in silence but just before they found the correct address, Hunter pulled the car over to the side of the road. Kirsten's heart rate jumped but her voice was even when she spoke.

'They live in the next street.'

Hunter glanced at the road sign in front of the car. 'I know. There's something I want to say.'

Kirsten turned her head and looked out the window. 'Say it and then let me be.'

'I guess what I want to say is that I can't leave you alone.' He clasped his hands at the top of the steering-wheel. 'You don't leave me alone.'

Kirsten turned back to him and stared. 'That is so not true. You can't accuse me of that. I barely talk to you unless I have to.' She couldn't believe he was blaming her for chasing him.

He smiled ruefully and she felt the knife twist inside her stomach. There was something she couldn't identify in his face. 'What I mean is,' he said slowly, 'thoughts of you won't leave me alone, and I don't know what to do about it.'

Kirsten felt as if a huge vice was squeezing her heart and she didn't think she could stand it. She couldn't do roller-coasters with Hunter any more. 'So you believe I had an affair with another woman's husband but you still want me?' She didn't think she could have been hurt any more but she found that she could.

'In a nutshell,' he said, and her hand slid down the door until it found the handle and she opened the door.

'You are unbelievable. This is your problem. I'll walk the rest of the way.'

He was out of his door and beside her before she realised he'd moved. His bulk blocked her escape. 'I don't want this either and I just want to try to be friends. Maybe learn to know you again.'

Kirsten blinked back the tears that had sprung up at his words. She'd really loved him and he'd hurt her badly. Now he was asking her to lay herself open to more hurt. 'You can't know someone you don't trust!'

She shook her head, unable to comprehend why he could think that of her. 'Believing lies of your friends is no way to treat people. Not all women are like your first wife, Hunter. I'm not like her but I'm beginning to wonder if she was as bad as you tell yourself she was. Maybe you got that wrong, too?'

He laughed harshly at that and the scorn in the sound was not what she associated with Hunter. 'I heard my mother's lies and I saw my wife in bed, with my boss, in my house.'

Kirsten bit her lip. 'Whoops.' The word accidentally came out a loud but then she regrouped. 'OK. She did it.'

She pointed her finger at his chest and stared up into his face. 'But you saw me hug Jack Cosgrove as I sent him back to his wife. Think about it, Hunter. Do I hug a lot of people? Hug all my friends and the parents of the children I nurse? Did it ever enter your suspicious little mind that maybe you were wrong about me? That you threw away something precious we both had because of your insecurities?'

Hunter shook his head. 'At the time it was plausible. His wife said she'd also caught you together before, and I was swayed.'

'She is jealous and insecure and you believed her over me—when you'd already told me she wasn't your favourite person in the world. It seems strange to me but, then, I'm a fairly straightforward person. Unlike someone else I know, I'm loyal to my friends.'

He tried to tell her he'd begun to change, begun to suspect maybe he'd jumped to conclusions, but she wouldn't listen. It was as if she was afraid to listen and he didn't know what to do.

She pushed him out of the way and walked up the street towards the Rumbles' house. He followed her slowly in the car so that they'd arrive together. They pretended to be civil to each other when Maggie met them at the door. It was going to be a really early night.

By Wednesday, Kirsten knew she had to find some common ground with Hunter because it was just too stressful worrying about when she was working with him next. They'd been avoiding each other since the fiasco at the Rumbles' three nights ago. Although they'd tried to act normally for their hosts' sake, they'd had little success and Kirsten only hoped that they hadn't ruined the night for Maggie. She knew that until Hunter convinced her he'd accepted he'd been wrong, it was too dangerous to allow him any

closer. In fact, she was crazy even considering anything to do with Hunter Morgan on whatever
grounds. But they had to talk if they worked together.

Thankfully the first two days they'd been rostered
on different shifts. Today they'd have to work together and she still wasn't sure what it was that
Hunter wanted. She had a sneaking suspicion he
didn't either.

They began the shift together with an armed truce.

'Good morning, Hunter.'

'Good morning. Kirsten,' he said, and they both
paid minute attention to their lockers. Kirsten
sighed. Hopefully they'd be able to get through the
morning without any personal hiccups. Because that
was what was needed. A firm professional basis to
keep their work and private lives separate.

The first call came two hours into the shift. When
he heard the name of the referring hospital Hunter
couldn't help looking across at Kirsten. He bet she'd
love this.

'We're off to Gladstone for a twenty-eight
weeker,' he said, and as she stood up she tilted her
head at him to see if he was kidding.

Kirsten loaded her kit into the helicopter and
quizzed Hunter as she climbed into the aircraft.
'What do you know about the case?'

'First baby, minimal antenatal care, presented in
second stage of labour and delivered live female infant minutes after arrival,' he said as he loaded his
own resources. 'Therefore no pre-birth steroids
could be given and baby is at high risk of respiratory
problems.'

Kirsten imagined the consternation of her brothers-in-law as they worked with the small amount of equipment they had. 'They'll want to get the baby shipped out before she starts to tire.'

Hunter looked across at her. 'Sounds reasonable to me. She was born at ten a.m. That's twenty minutes ago. Apgars of seven and eight and she's stable at the moment on one hundred per cent oxygen.' He glanced at his watch and chewed his lip.

'It's a shame the other team can't divert and pick this little one up, too. Because we'll have to take the smaller craft, which means we won't be able to bring mum back with us. Jim's coming in to co-ordinate because both teams are out.'

It had started raining lightly earlier in the day and the sleet was miserable as Kirsten tucked her bag under the seat.

The larger Bell 412 was on its way back from a retrieval and the nearest air ambulance fixed-wing aircraft was out the back of Dubbo somewhere. There was always the army aircraft if necessary, but for the moment they'd decided to use the smaller helicopter, even though it would be the first to be grounded in bad weather.

Keith looked grimmer than usual when Kirsten leaned forward to greet him. When he still didn't smile she raised her eyebrows.

'This one on your home turf? Bummer about the rain.' Keith looked across at her. 'Just hope the cloud isn't too thick around Buladelah, or they'll have to wait for the others to get back and unload.'

Kirsten settled herself in her seat as Hunter climbed aboard, but she kept her eyes on Keith. 'Is there much chance of that?'

Keith shrugged. 'I can only try.' And started the rotor.

'What was all that about?' Hunter leaned across and raised his voice so Kirsten could hear the question.

'Could be too cloudy over Buladelah for the small chopper, but Keith said he'd give it a go and wait and see.'

Hunter nodded and handed her the drug sheet printouts then they began to prepare the drugs they'd need for the premature infant. When they'd preprepared what they could, Hunter leaned forward to look out the front windscreen.

It didn't look too bad here, but forty-five minutes up the coast could be a different story. The pilot would have the weather readings. If they had to turn back, they would. MIRA was very careful with its teams. The object was to arrive safely.

'Bella's husband, Scott, is good at cannulating tiny ones, but we just need to get through the weather for them.'

Her words sent a frozen feather of foreboding cross his neck and he sat back in his seat and tried to rationalise where that feeling had come from.

Kirsten knew that if the weather was too dangerous they wouldn't fly. Hunter glanced at Kirsten, something he'd found himself doing with increasing frequency the more he saw of her.

She loved this job so much she was even willing to put up with him. It was as if she couldn't wait to pit herself against the elements for a baby who'd decided to arrive well before it should have. Typical.

He supposed she would be keen to see her brothers-in-law again, although he'd gathered from what he'd overheard her tell Paul Netherby that she'd planned a trip home next week. He wondered what it would be like to be part of an extended family like Kirsten's and then silently laughed at himself for being maudlin.

He remembered a memorable afternoon in Dubai when she'd first talked about her family. They'd lain under a palm tree together, her head in the crook of his arm and her warmth and softness intoxicating next to him as they'd tried to convert cloud formations into recognisable objects—something he'd never done with anyone but Kirsten. But that was the sort of thing he'd found himself doing if he'd been with her. Simple, hard-to-forget things.

The memory bucked in his mind as if he'd hit an internal wind pocket, greater than any sheer outside the aircraft, and he had to clamp down hard on the thought to regain his composure. He couldn't help looking across at her. Her glorious hair was tied back in one of those scrunchie things and she stared out the window as if willing them to go faster.

She looked to be itching to jump out of her seat and do something, and he couldn't remember when he'd ever had that much energy. There'd been a dark time when he would have avoided someone as energetic as Kirsten but he was getting used to her again and he realised with a start that he looked forward to her enthusiasm—and had never really had a chance at being able to ignore her.

He'd been focussed and driven for the last five years since Portia had left him, but he couldn't remember a thirst to live life except for that brief time when he'd first met Kirsten. And she was doing it to him again. Making him look at where he was going and what his grand plan for the future had been since he'd left her. He realised he hadn't had one except to maybe wake up one day and be too old to go to work.

He wondered what her thoughts for the future were, but shied away from the temptation because it was too personal to ask and being personal with Kirsten was just too damn dangerous.

He craned his neck to look out past the pilot through the windscreen. The rain had gone but the cloud looked fairly dense up ahead. The occasional updraught promised an interesting journey home later that afternoon. He noticed the township of Buladelah out the starboard side window and Keith spoke into the cabin mike.

'There's a small storm centre up ahead but the weather bureau reckons we can skirt it and come in from the western side. Might get a bit bumpy but if it gets too silly I'll head back.'

Hunter checked his seat belt and glanced across instinctively to check Kirsten's safety. Her hands were resting lightly in her lap and she was watching Keith with bright-eyed interest. While she was so absorbed he couldn't help his gaze lingering on the curve of her cheek and the pure line of her neck— both silky places he could almost feel under his fingertips. He blinked and stared implacably out the window. She might be untrustworthy, but he was still attracted to her.

He must be some kind of masochist to want to go down that road again. To look wasn't too bad, but when his other senses jumped into the act and he could smell the scent of her skin and hair and hear her breathing against his own face from memory, then he knew his control was shaky. He needed to concentrate on the retrieval, but it was hard when they could do nothing until they landed.

A sudden downdraught slammed him into his seat and then up again against his seat belt, and he looked across at Kirsten. His stomach had given a sickening lurch and he saw her smile across at him. She may as well be at an amusement park, he thought sourly as another sickening sway slewed the whole aircraft sideways.

'Nup. We're outa here!' Hunter heard Keith's exclamation as rain suddenly lashed the windows and he felt the helicopter start to turn back the way they'd come. But it was too late.

As if a large celestial hand was pushing then downward and through the storm centre, the helicopter was sucked into the vortex. Everything started to shake and shudder as Keith tried to fly them out of danger. New lights flashed on the aircraft's dashboard and the beep of warning alarms beat to the increase in Hunter's heart rate.

Hunter looked across at Kirsten and she was fiercely concentrating on what Keith was doing, as if she could help him with her thoughts. The aircraft took a sudden dive to starboard and it felt like they were upside down for a second before it righted itself.

She looked at him and he saw a flicker of uncertainty, and then they heard Keith's voice shouting that he was going to try and put them down.

Kirsten realised this wasn't some drill she'd studied for and that there was a good chance they could die in the next few seconds.

Her eyes filled with regret and their gazes met and

held—the one stable thing in a world suddenly gone mad. He only just heard her words. 'You should have believed in me, Hunter.' And then they hit the trees.

When Hunter regained consciousness he didn't know where he was. There was a canopy of leaves above him and he was dripping wet and strapped into a seat in a tree-house. The side wall of his tree house was gone and if he shifted his left hand he could put it outside the window and wave at the ground ten feet below. Trouble was, when he did that, his tree-house wobbled and the wobbling made his head hurt.

He turned his head carefully and stared across the room and realised it wasn't a room at all—he was sitting in the wreck of a helicopter. As if in slow motion, the last few seconds before the crash came back to him and suddenly his mind was crystal clear and he focussed on the last place he'd seen Kirsten. She was still there but she was as white as snow and not moving. For one awful, gut-wrenching, shattering moment he thought she was dead, but then he saw the minuscule rise and fall of her shoulders as she breathed and he had to sit back and close his eyes for a moment to gain some composure. She was alive. At this moment.

He drew a steadying breath and then forced his gaze to sweep the cockpit but he couldn't see Keith. In fact, he couldn't see the cockpit. The helicopter was sheared off just past the point where the cabin used to meet the back of Keith's seat.

Carefully, Hunter undid his seat belt and shrugged his shoulders. The top half of him worked and it didn't hurt too much. Then he wriggled his toes. More success.

Hunter raised his hand to his forehead and felt the source of nagging pain above his eye and ran his fingers over the sizable egg he found. His fingers came away sticky with blood and he assumed he must have hit his head on the window when they'd crashed. He shifted slowly to the edge of his seat and everything seemed to be fairly reliable so he leaned towards Kirsten, and that was when his luck ran out.

A sudden loud snap heralded the last resistance of the branch holding them in the tree and the cabin of the chopper nose-dived the last ten feet to the ground.

Unstrapped, Hunter was thrown against one of the struts and lost consciousness again.

When Kirsten came to, she was cold. Then she realised she was wet and leaning at a ridiculous angle, strapped to a seat in what would never be a helicopter again. She couldn't believe she was alive. On that thought she remembered Hunter and Keith and wiped her face shakily to clear her mind.

Apparently the chopper wasn't going to explode because she had the feeling she'd drifted in and out of consciousness more than once so some time must have passed since they'd crashed.

She tried to call out but her voice croaked unconvincingly somewhere at the back of her throat without much sound leaving her mouth. She licked her lips and tried again.

'Hello?'

Nobody answered but even hearing her own voice

was reassuring—she was alive. Kirsten concentrated on what would happen if she undid her seat belt. Probably not much as they were on the ground and from the very little she could see, the aircraft appeared to be in the middle of heavy undergrowth that poked through the torn gashes in the aircraft's fuselage.

As she scanned the wreckage inside, she caught a glimpse of pale fingers splayed towards her from behind an unmoored seat and the image of Hunter's hand inside Kinny's crib last week crashed through her mind like a sledgehammer.

'Hunter!' She fumbled with her seat belt, undid the clasp and landed awkwardly on her face in a pile of equipment. Crawling on her hands and knees, Kirsten dragged herself across the littered cabin and levered the seat out of the way and off Hunter's body.

She tried to see if he was breathing but suddenly her vision wasn't working as well as it had been and she couldn't tell—then she realised she was crying.

Kirsten scrubbed at her eyes impatiently and reached for his wrist. At first she couldn't feel a pulse because her own hand shook too much, then she drew a deep breath and steadied herself. It was there, his pulse, it was steady and strong. Hunter was alive. The tears came again, and she let her shoulders sag with relief for a moment before she regathered herself.

She scanned his body and it was impossible to tell how badly he was hurt because he was curled like a rag doll in the corner of the cabin. His forehead oozed blood, some of which had congealed in his hair, and she wiped it away as if to do so would make him feel better. To her relief he stirred under her fingers.

'Hunter?'

He groaned and shifted slightly without opening his eyes and she leant down and spoke in his ear. 'Hunter, can you hear me?'

His eyes flickered open and then he was staring at her. 'We crashed.'

Simple words but indicative of his clarity—Kirsten bit her lip and scrubbed her eyes again. Her throat was thick with relief and she could only nod.

'Are you OK?' His voice was stronger and she felt the weight of total responsibility slide from her shoulders as she accepted he would be fine. Thank God she didn't have to sit by and watch Hunter die.

'I'm fine. Can you move?' She watched anxiously as he wriggled his fingers and then his foot.

'I could last time I tried but got a bit more than I bargained for. We had a stop-over before the final landing.' Kirsten frowned at his words but didn't bother with them as she watched him lever himself to his knees. He swayed for a minute and shut his eyes but then he sat up.

He tried to smile at her and she could tell he was in some pain. 'Do you have a headache to match mine?'

Kirsten smiled back. 'I think yours is worse.' Then she sobered. 'Keith!'

They both looked to where the cockpit should have been, and then back at each other.

'I think the cockpit sheared off earlier. We might find him outside.' Hunter's voice was sober and Kirsten nodded. Neither spoke of their doubts.

It wasn't easy to clamber out of the tangled mess

of the aircraft but finally they stood beside it and stared at the wreckage.

'How on earth did we walk away from that?' Hunter shook his head.

'Keith's skill.' Kirsten shuddered and they both glanced around the crash site at the broken branches and scattered wreckage.

They pushed through a tangle of undergrowth and twisted vines to the other side of the wreck, and the white-painted metal stood out from the surrounding green. 'That looks like the cockpit over there.' Hunter and Kirsten pushed through more broken branches and they both stumbled their way through the scrubby undergrowth until they could kneel down beside the pilot. Keith lay very still on his side strapped to his seat and a large ominous stain of blood had seeped into the leaves and mulch beside him.

Kirsten slid her fingers over the inside of Keith's wrist and felt for his pulse. 'There is a pulse but it's very faint and about a hundred and forty.'

Hunter undid Keith's seat belt and they eased him out of the seat but kept him on his side. The older man didn't stir. His ankle was twisted at an awkward angle and Hunter gently straightened it before he tracked the blood to a huge open gash on Keith's thigh. Kirsten blinked when he dug a folded handkerchief out of his own pocket to staunch the flow.

'I'll get a dressing in a moment.' There was something ludicrous about such laundered whiteness appearing in the wreckage and mud.

For her part, Kirsten did a torchless check of Keith's neurological signs to assess for head injury, but his pupils reacted evenly.

Hunter glanced back at the remains of the helicopter. 'He's almost bled out. He needs fluids. Volume replacement probably won't be enough but hopefully we'll be able to salvage some equipment and get a line going at least as soon as we get some shelter. I'm going back inside the wreck to see what I can find. Can you keep an eye on him as you scout around nearby for something we could rig up for a shelter?'

'I can do that,' Kirsten said quietly, and it all seemed so monstrous that Keith could die here, because if they didn't get rescued soon he *would* die. The chance of rescue earlier than within the next twenty-four hours was pretty slim unless the storm suddenly moved away—and it would be dark soon.

They were on the side of a mountain and a huge fallen bloodwood tree lay beside them on the ground. It must have come down in a previous storm and the gap in the canopy had allowed them to end up nearer to the ground than they would have otherwise. A light drizzle still drifted down from the treetops and they both looked up at the black and purple stormclouds and sheet lightning overhead.

'Not much hope of an aerial search for us until that lot blows over.' Hunter drew her close to his side. 'The emergency beacon will have pinpointed our position. They'll send in ground searchers until the weather clears.'

'It's probably Banda Banda,' she said. 'I remember we flew past Middle Brother but direction got a bit skewed at the end and I'm not sure where we are now.'

Hunter stared at her. 'A bit skewed? That's a diplomatic way of saying we got spat out of a storm.'

He squeezed her shoulder and moved off to see what he could salvage from the chopper.

Kirsten scanned the area for something she could rig up to cover Keith but, barring a full-scale lean-to of wet branches, the wreckage hadn't provided much. What they really needed was a cave.

There were a few boulders higher up the escarpment and a couple of darker areas that promised at least a decent overhang.

The crack of branches underfoot heralded the return of Hunter and she looked up to see what he'd brought. He carried the steel drawer with needles, syringes and emergency drug supplies, and a shoulder-bag of fluid replacement hung off his shoulder. He looked pale against the vivid purpling bruise on his forehead and the egg on his head was oozing blood.

Kirsten hurried to take the drawer from him. 'That little sortie took out more from you than you bargained for,' Kirsten noted dryly. 'I'll do the next trip back inside.'

Hunter didn't comment but he sat heavily when he'd put everything else down. He picked up Keith's wrist and felt for his pulse. 'I'll get less woozy in the next hour. Any change here?'

'No. And I can't see any easy solution to shelter unless I find an overhang we can build a fire under. I'd like to have a quick look up the escarpment because it is cave country.'

Hunter grimaced and then smiled grimly. 'A cave. I'll let you claim home-turf advantage there. You go as soon as we get a line going to replace some of Keith's fluid volume—there's not much else we can do for him until he wakes up. Hypothermia is probably more of a danger at the moment while he's stable, and you won't find anything in the dark.'

Then he really looked at her. Despite the dirty streaks on her face and a red bruise in the middle of her forehead, she looked remarkably calm considering their predicament.

She was incredible. 'You are amazing, Kirsten Wilson. A lot of women would be having hysterics about now.'

'If I thought it would help, I'd provide some for you, but I think we've been remarkably lucky.' She smiled at him and suddenly Hunter was just very thankful she was OK. Things weren't great but they could have been horrific.

He smiled back. 'You're right. Three out of three alive is…incredible. I think fluid replacement will help Keith a lot until we get rescued and can get some blood into him. It could be a lot worse.' That awful frozen moment when he'd first woken and thought that Kirsten was dead flashed into his mind and he closed his eyes as if to block it out. A hell of a lot worse!

When he opened his eyes she was watching him with concern, but she didn't comment. Instead she picked up the red box and started to lay out the cannulas.

'It will have to be the biggest of the small, I'm afraid. At least we have paediatric stuff as well as neonatal or it would take a year to run enough fluid into Keith.'

Within minutes they had two bags of fluid dripping into Keith's veins and more beside him for later.

'I think he's unconscious from loss of blood more

than anything else, but who knows what injuries he sustained when the cockpit sheared off, or how high he was when it happened?' Hunter tucked the extra fluid bags under Keith's legs to raise his feet and then wrapped a space blanket around the pilot and sat back on his heels. 'I'll watch him, you go for your look around.'

CHAPTER SIX

THE orange drug additive labels looked bizarre where Kirsten had fixed them to the nearest tree, but any help to find her way back seemed a good idea. She nodded soberly to Hunter and turned to go.

'Be careful.' Hunter's voice followed her as the bushes closed behind her and she didn't look back because there was something in his voice that warned her that he was having second thoughts about her going. Hunter did not need another invalid, and he would know as well as Kirsten that she couldn't afford to get lost or injured.

Everything was wet and, except for the sound of water running somewhere, incredibly quiet. Where the huge rainforest trees reached up to the sky and sealed the canopy, the side of the mountain wasn't too difficult to traverse. Landmarks were either green or brown, but mostly green. Green moss seemed to cover everything and vivid lime-fronded giant stags and elk horns littered the forest floor where they'd fallen.

Where one of the hundred-year-old giants had crashed to the ground and exposed its roots to the sun, the light had reached the soil and the proliferation of undergrowth made it difficult to go forward. Tangled vines and scrubby bushes blocked her path when that happened and she had to widen the circle around where Keith lay.

The chill in the air was more noticeable now that

the rain had stopped and everything dripped cold water when she touched it. In the back of her brain she knew there must be thousands of leeches in the mulch and the thought raised the hair on the back of her neck. Sensibly, she resisted checking her legs.

She shuddered and forced her mind away from the sudden crawling sensation she could imagine going on under her trousers. It was ridiculous to be scared of leeches but such were phobias. There was no way she was going to look down and see one crawling up her socks. If she did that, Hunter would hear the hysterics he'd expected. She trod doggedly on, curving up towards a darker patch she could see ahead.

Finally she reached the shadow of a crevasse that snaked down the hill in the direction of the wreck. She squeezed between the towering rock faces and the formation split into two sandy bluffs that ran down the mountain as if cleaved by a giant's axe.

She brushed away the spider webs with a stick as she went, and a whisper of excitement suggested she'd found what she'd been looking for. Kirsten had been a member of a caving club a few years back and this type of formation often ran down hills and branched off into caves. There was no roof in the crevasse, so some light reflected down into the corridor, but as a shelter it would only keep out the wind. Water trickled down the walls in places so they would have extra water if they needed it.

Maybe the whole mountain was a honeycomb, she thought as she ran her hand along the back wall. She couldn't see out into the forest now because thick scrub obscured the open wall and she realised she must be near where the huge tree had fallen and exposed the undergrowth. If she peered hard she could see the trees through the covering and she decided to try a little further along.

Suddenly the crevasse ballooned out into a large overhang and a darker area at the back of the overhang promised an interesting excursion later. But this would do if she could find an easy way to reach the forest floor again.

Animal trails in the sand gave clues to previous tenants and she crouched down to see if there was an exit trail nearer the ground. There was a small worn path burrowed through the vegetation about twenty centimetres high and the same wide. Through the gap, about fifty metres away, Kirsten could see the opposite side of the wreck so Hunter and Keith weren't far away.

She couldn't fit through the hole but she could enlarge it if she had some way of cutting or breaking the branches. The beauty was in the closeness of the overhang exit to the wreck and any supplies they wanted to move into cover for the night wouldn't have to be carried far.

Buoyed by excitement of the find, she memorised the angle of the wreck and several odd-looking trees, and headed back the way she'd come until she could ease out of the crevasse. Her bright-orange-stickered tree shone across the forest floor and she picked up the pace, unsure how long she'd been away. By the time she re-entered the clearing she was breathing heavily and she drew a deep breath so she'd be calm when she reached Hunter. She could have saved the effort, though, because he had a scowl on his face.

Hunter had been anxiously scanning the surrounding area for the last half-hour. By the time he'd heard her coming he'd already called himself all kinds of fool for letting her go. Then, when she walked into the clearing as if she'd been for a Sunday stroll, he had to restrain himself from picking her up and crushing her against him because he'd been so worried. Crazy thoughts to have but probably understandable nerves left over from the crash.

'How's Keith?' Kirsten's words prevented any foolishness and he glanced away from her to the pilot.

'He's had four litres of fluid and his blood pressure is coming up. The pad and bandage seem to have stopped the bleeding and I think cerebrally he's lighter.'

'That's wonderful. My good news is that I've found a decent overhang and maybe even a cave, but we need something to cut through the branches or at least protect our hands when we break them. There's another opening not far from the wreck so moving any equipment should be easy, too.'

'Great!' Kirsten missed his irony. 'Let's do it because I'd say we're about fifteen minutes from another downpour and I'd like to get Keith out of the weather if we can. I'll cap the IVs and we'll just have to leave him for a few minutes for the benefit of getting him under cover.' He gestured to the pile of assorted retrievals he'd made and lifted a broken piece of metal with a jagged edge. 'We never fly without one of these.'

She smiled back at his lighter tone and as she brushed past him to head back to the wreck he reached out and held her arm. 'Kirsten.' She stopped and turned to look at him and because they were alone in the wilderness it was nice to even have that contact. 'I was worried while you were away. I'd rather we did things together from now on.'

'OK.' He could tell she didn't get it but he wasn't going through that agony again.

'I mean it. I don't want you going off on your own without telling me. I don't want anything to happen to you.'

'Hunter.' She put her hands on her hips. 'I have done survival courses and gained my Queen's Scout Medal. You and I and Keith have come through a helicopter crash, which puts us right up there beside the luckiest Lotto winners. Somehow I don't think a bush walk is going to kill me.'

He watched her walk away. Of course, he could always strangle her himself. Instead, he followed and watched her pause beside the wreck and glance off into the scrub. Then she walked unerringly to a dense bush and bent down.

As he came closer he could see the small animal trail that seemed to lead into the bush. 'We need to enlarge that trail,' she said.

It only took ten intense minutes as Hunter sawed and ripped the branches from in front of the overhang, and behind him Kirsten had an superb view of just how strong he was as she dragged the broken branches and undergrowth away. The entrance needed to be big enough for Hunter to get through carrying Keith, and they were driven onward by the first few drops of rain. Suddenly they broke into the overhang and Kirsten turned her face toward him, pink-cheeked and exultant.

'That was impressive, Dr Morgan. So you're not just a pretty face.'

He narrowed his eyes at her. 'Flirting is against the rules.'

'I think the rules can go hang,' she said soberly, and turned back toward Keith.

'I think so, too,' he said quietly to her retreating back. He glanced once more into the darkness of the overhang and hoped to heaven he could force himself to go in there. The idea of Kirsten finding out he had a fear of caves wasn't an attractive one, but there was little he could do about it.

He followed her quickly back to where Keith was lying, and Hunter brushed Kirsten away as the rain began to fall more heavily. 'Bring what you can and get out of the rain.'

He picked the pilot up, heaved him over his shoulder and set off doggedly for the overhang. Kirsten frowned after him but couldn't do anything else to help except what he'd asked.

She loaded herself up and followed what was becoming a beaten path to the overhang. When she got there, Keith was lying on his side and Hunter was resting with his eyes shut against the side wall quite close to the entrance.

'Move towards the back, out of the cold,' Kirsten said as she moved past him deeper into the belly of the overhang.

'I'm right here, thanks.' There was something strange about Hunter's voice and she turned back to look at him.

He stayed facing the outside. 'Are you OK, Hunter?'

'I'm fine.' He glared at her. 'And you have a leech on your leg.'

That's when Kirsten lost it. Her eyes met his and

widened and then she looked down at her ankle and
the black skinny worm that was trying to burrow
through her trousers. 'Get it off me.'

She started to shake and Hunter stood up and
inched along the wall towards her. 'Then come out
towards me. I can't go in there.'

'Get it off me.' Her voice was rising and Hunter
edged a little closer. 'Come here, then.'

She picked up her feet and ran towards him. *'Get
it off me.'*

Hunter bent down and scraped the leech off with
his fingernail. It stuck to his finger and wiggled its
tail.

'Oh, my God. Kill it.' Kirsten could barely look
at the insect but she couldn't look away. 'Kill it!'

'Bloodthirsty little woman, aren't you?' Hunter
ground the bug under his heel and pulled her into
his arms and he could feel the shudders that ran
through her body. 'It's OK, Kirsten. It's only a leech
and it's dead.'

'There's probably more under my trousers but I'm
too scared to look.'

He nodded that he understood. 'Turn around and
I'll check you.' He lifted her ponytail and checked
her neck and pulled the damp MIRA T-shirt away
from her skin and looked down her back. Apart from
her bra strap, there was nothing there.

He crouched down. 'I'm going to lift your trouser
legs now. Stand still.' Kirsten stared at Hunter's
dark hair as he lifted her left trouser leg and flinched
when she felt him scrape her shin. 'Now the other
one.' He lifted the other leg and she felt him scrape
her knee-high socks twice more.

He stood up. 'No more. You were lucky.'

Kirsten shuddered again. 'On my survival course I wore full-length pantyhose under my jeans. They can't get through pantyhose, you know.'

'Thank you for that piece of trivia. Next time I go to a rainforest I'll wear full-length pantyhose.'

She knew he was trying to make her laugh and the picture of Hunter in pantyhose, like some larger-than-life male ballet dancer, did draw a weak smile.

'Hold me for a minute, please, then I'll be fine.' It was as if the leeches epitomised all the fears from the day and concentrated them on the fact that she'd had the creatures attached to her as she'd walked around.

Hunter squeezed her against his chest once more and the contact warmed her as nothing else could have, then he put her from him to look into her face. 'We need a fire, and food would be nice but water is more important. We need to make a last trip to the wreck, get the flares and survival kit and anything we can use to keep warm or burn before it gets dark. Are you OK now?'

Kirsten took a deep breath and passed a shaking hand over her face. 'I'm fine,' she said in a small voice. 'Thank you. I hate phobias.'

'Tell me about it,' Hunter said dryly, determined not to go there. He decided he liked the bossy Kirsten better, although there was something adorable about the panicked one. But there wasn't time to dwell on those thoughts.

The light was fading outside. They needed to get settled and find some wood for the night and the next half-hour went quickly.

When they came back to the overhang for the last time, Keith's eyes were open. 'Where are we?'

Keith's voice was weak but they both heard him and knelt down beside him.

'Welcome back, Keith.' Hunter's voice was calm and he met Kirsten's eyes with relief. 'You managed to get us down safely, but you've been out for an hour or two and we were getting worried.'

'The chopper?'

'Not much left, I'm afraid, and the storm is still overhead. Looks like we'll have to stay the night here but they'll probably find us tomorrow morning.'

Keith tried to shake his head but winced and stopped. 'I should have turned back earlier.'

'The storm sucked us in. Easy to say afterwards.' Hunter patted his shoulder. 'You did a great job getting us down.'

Keith opened and shut his eyes a few times as if to clear his vision. 'Where did you say we were?'

Kirsten leaned towards him. 'I think it's Banda Banda mountain. They have trails to the top so a ground crew will come in as soon as they can.'

He lifted his arm to look at the cannula taped there. 'I feel terrible but guess I'm lucky I crashed with medical types.'

'I imagine you'll be black and blue by tomorrow and weak as a kitten. You lost a lot of blood and Hunter's given you fluids until they can replace the blood when they get you back to a hospital.' Kirsten glanced at Hunter. 'We're all feeling pretty lucky. How's your pain?'

'My back hurts and my ankle feels like it's broken but at least I can feel it.' His voice trailed away and his eyes closed.

Kirsten felt Keith's pulse. The beat was definitely

stronger than it had been two hours ago and the rate had dropped to just over a hundred. 'I think he'll be fine.'

'Let's get this fire going.' Hunter held out the box of matches from the aircraft's survival kit. 'You do the honours, Miss Queen Scout, while I get some more wood. If we can get it going we can dry the next lot of wood as we go along.'

Kirsten took the matches and crouched down to the tiny pile of dry kindling and paper they'd salvaged, along with some leaf litter that had blown into the overhang.

Soon tiny flames danced above the sticks and Kirsten fed the fire carefully to make sure it had a solid centre. Hunter came back with more wood to find she'd cut the top off one of the empty plastic IV flask bags and collected water from one of the wall trickles. 'Any ideas what we can use to boil water in over the fire?'

'Shame we don't still carry steel vomit bowls or potties,' he teased, as he began to stack the few blankets rescued from the aircraft before heading back to find anything else that could be useful.

Kirsten pulled a face at his departing back. 'I'll find something.'

'That idea is top-drawer,' Hunter quipped when he came back. He couldn't help but smile at Kirsten's ingenuity. She was leaning over the coals stirring emergency-ration soup from the survival kit in the small steel drawer that had held the needles, as if it were the most normal kitchen appliance in the world.

'My pot even has a handle.' Kirsten grinned up at him and the impact of her smile made him realise again how glad he was that she was alive. It was tragic that it had taken a helicopter disaster to put their relationship into perspective. Kirsten still meant the world to him. And it was unlikely his feelings were going to change.

Keith woke up for half an hour and managed to swallow a little of Kirsten's soup, and they all discussed the rain that poured down outside as the three of them sat huddled together in front of the fire and tried to dry out. The sides of their bodies that faced the fire were warm and Keith drifted off to sleep again. Hunter and Kirsten weren't ready to sleep yet.

Kirsten leaned against Hunter and he draped his arm around her to help her keep warm. To Kirsten his arm felt so right but it wasn't just the heat he radiated, it was the fact that Hunter always made her feel more alive somehow. After today's terror it was good to feel alive and even better to have Hunter's arm around her. It seemed crazy to put up barriers after what they'd come through and she found it easy, too easy, to slip into their old ways. In the past he'd listened as if he hadn't been able to hear enough of her adventures, and her stories had always been more fun when she'd told them to Hunter.

'The cave and the rain makes me remember the time I had to camp out for a week during my survival course.' She grimaced. 'I hated not washing more than anything. Eating strange things didn't bother me but not being able to change my clothes was unpleasant.' She shook her head at the memory.

'Did anyone complain about the smell?' Hunter said, and Kirsten lost her train of thought and stared. Then she saw he was teasing her and she punched him in the arm.

'You rat.'

Hunter chuckled and hugged her briefly against him. Despite the cold, the discomfort and worry about Keith, he was happier than he'd been for several months. Happy to be here with Kirsten tucked under his arm. If it hadn't been for Keith, he'd almost be happy to stay here until they worked out all their differences.

Fancifully he imagined being back in a relationship with Kirsten—no celibacy this time because it hadn't saved him from disaster last time. He'd make sure she was so damn satisfied she'd never leave him. He shifted uncomfortably as his dreaming became more graphic, and he tried to steer the direction of his thoughts into less arousing channels.

'So is this adventurous enough for you, Kirsten?'

She snuggled into him and his heart cracked a little more. 'Maybe too much excitement,' she said, and he could hear the yawn in her voice. 'Especially the leeches...' She softened even more against him as her voice trailed off.

The next morning Hunter woke about an hour after he'd finally gone to sleep. The first rays of sun hit the eastern side of the mountain and burrowed through the scrub to shine directly into his face. He felt as if he'd been rolled down a hill in a barrel of rocks. Everything ached and his head throbbed. His stomach rumbled with emptiness. Keith was snoring healthily and Hunter twisted his neck to see how Kirsten was faring, but her spot by the fire was empty.

He reassured himself that she would be back shortly but his instinct wouldn't allow him to leave anything to chance. He stuffed one of the flares in his pocket and grabbed some kindling and a piece of burning wood. At least if they had a small fire outside as well, they could make smoke constantly to help the searchers.

When he went outside, the forest floor was silent except for the steady drip of water that seemed to be a permanent state of affairs in the forest.

'Kirsten?' His voice disturbed a black and red feathered scrub turkey that had been scratching under a nearby bush and Hunter watched it dart away under the bushes. 'You're lucky I haven't got a bow and arrow, mister. I could go a little barbecued chicken at the moment.' His stomach rumbled again and he kicked a piece of bark out of his way. The bark rolled over and a colourful collection of grubs stared up at him. His stomach heaved and he shuddered.

They'd all assumed the search parties would find them today. If a rescue didn't take place, food could become a crucial issue. They'd emptied Kirsten's flight bag last night and, apart from the soup, they'd shared the two muesli bars and a packet of nuts between the three of them.

He needed to think about some type of trap. Hopefully the survival lady knew which berries they could eat and which they couldn't. He didn't fancy any of the mushrooms, he decided as he cleared a space to build his signal fire. Soon a wisp of smoke was spiralling upwards through the canopy and Hunter began to gather as much drier wood as he could find from under the base of larger trees.

A twig snapped behind him and he turned to see Kirsten bearing another two of the empty IV flasks.

One was filled with small yellow fruit and the other with some form of wrinkled red berry.

'Breakfast is served,' she quipped, and Hunter felt that surge of relief again that she was fine. He frowned at her. 'I thought I said we did things together.'

She did that thing with her lowered chin and under-brow glare. 'And I said a bush walk isn't going to kill me. Besides, you were sleeping.'

He looked dubiously at the berries. 'How do you know we can eat those?'

Good humour restored, she grinned and held up the berries. 'These are native raspberries and grow in clearings—they're perfectly safe.' She popped one in her mouth and chewed it. He could tell she was trying not to screw up her face and he suppressed his own smile.

'I was looking for elderberries but couldn't find any.' She held up the other bag which bulged with the small apple-sized fruit. 'These are cluster figs. They taste similar to strangler figs and have a rich, sweet pulp.'

Hunter shook his head at her enthusiasm and gave up trying not to smile. 'OK, Miss Swiss Family Robinson, you win. All I've done is eye off the scrub turkey.'

'Never mind.' She looked approvingly at his fire and the pile of wood beside it. 'You collect great wood.' On that note she slipped in front of him and disappeared into the cavern. Hunter grimaced and decided against going back inside.

To tell the truth, he'd hated any sort of cave since he'd been trapped in one as a kid. An adventurous ten-year-old, he and a friend had crawled along a tunnel with Hunter in front, and they'd squeezed through the final bend when his friend had become wedged. Unable to move backwards or forwards, they'd been trapped for eight panic-filled hours until Hunter's father had found them.

The memories still brought a sweat to his forehead and sitting close to the entrance had been the only way Hunter had been able to enter the cave last night.

Hopefully, their emergency beacon in the wreck had been pinpointed by satellite by now, and their position marked on some searcher's map.

The storm had disappeared this morning and he wanted to be ready to let off the flares as soon as they heard an aircraft.

'Are you coming in to eat or do you want me to bring you some out there?' Kirsten's voice preceded her eerily out of the cavern and then she reappeared beside him. He thought distastefully of the cramped space.

'I think one of us should stay out here while the cloud cover is clear, in case of searching aircraft.' He glanced towards the cave. 'We probably don't have to stay with Keith all the time as long as we check on him every ten minutes or so.'

Just then the faint drone of a plane drifted to them and they looked up. The plane was very high.

'Should we light the flare?' Neither of them moved and Kirsten looked at Hunter.

Hunter squinted and then shook his head. 'It's a passenger airliner, they wouldn't see it anyway.'

'That's what I thought, too. There should be some local air traffic out hunting for us soon.'

She shook the bag of fruit. 'I'll take the rest of

these back to Keith if you don't want them.' She didn't say it but she was thinking of the cavern at the back of the overhang that she'd wanted to have a quick look in. It sounded like a water source was back there and now that the rain had stopped the rivulets down the walls were harder to milk to keep up their supply. Although any water would be freezing, she wondered if there would be a chance to have a decent wash as well. She'd be able to soak a cloth and give Keith a chance to wash his face at least.

Kirsten didn't intend to go far into the cave but after she'd given Keith a drink, she mentioned her plans to him in case Hunter needed her while she was gone. She had a feeling Hunter would veto the idea if she ran it past him and she just wanted to have a look.

'Are you sure you need to go in there?' Keith shook his head carefully. 'How about you tell Hunter yourself?'

Kirsten didn't quite meet Keith's eyes. 'I won't worry him. I'll be back in a minute.'

CHAPTER SEVEN

KIRSTEN'S tiny penlight was still quite bright and she advanced into the opening of the tunnel with the light ready in her hand. The narrow beam shone around the walls and occasional sparkly crystals embedded in the rock glinted back at her.

It was damp and silent and very dark. Kirsten stretched her hands out and touched both walls and noted that at least the tunnel wasn't narrow. The rock was rough under her fingers and very cold. The roof sloped and the further she went in the more she had to stoop to avoid bumping her head.

. The floor was sandy and, like the roof, it sloped too. Kirsten damped down the excitement she always enjoyed on her caving expeditions. This was no fun day out and she had a good reason for breaking a lot of caving rules. A close water source would be a huge advantage.

A couple of loose rocks bounced away under her foot and she could hear the clear sound of water dripping into a pool. She shone her torch around but couldn't see anything that looked like a water source. She crouched down on her hands and knees to be more balanced should the floor suddenly decide to turn into a shaft, and continued more slowly. It was becoming borderline dangerous and she thought briefly about turning back.

Loose pebbles dug into her knees through her thin trousers and the cold began to eat into her hands. If she didn't get to the pool soon, she would turn back. It wasn't any use if the pool was too far away.

'Kirsten!' Hunter's voice echoed strangely down the shaft and, despite the distance the sound had travelled, she could hear the bite of authority in his voice. She flinched and dropped her torch. The little light rolled to the side of the tunnel and went out.

'Blast.' She glared behind her but Hunter wasn't there to blame so she stifled her annoyance and leaned over quickly to find her torch. Unexpectedly there wasn't a side to the wall of the tunnel any more, and the torch hadn't gone out—it had slid over the edge down a rocky slope. Unable to regain her balance, Kirsten's uneven body weight sent her over the edge to follow her torch down the incline. Unable to grab anything to stop her rolling, she skidded and rolled with some speed during her rocky descent.

The sound of pebbles and larger rocks shifting in front of her warned of the depth of the slope. When the sound of the mini-avalanche in front changed into the plop and splash of stones in water she tried desperately to stop herself from falling any further, ripping her nails and fingers as she frantically grabbed for purchase before she too ended up in the pool—but she couldn't stop. At least the sound gave Kirsten a chance to prepare herself as she bumped over the edge of the pool and into the cold water.

Nothing could have prepared her enough. To say the water was cold was an understatement. The inky water closed over her head like an ice blanket in the dark and the air whooshed from her lungs as she shrieked in shock. For a moment pure panic engulfed her, along with the icy water, and her eyes stung as she widened them as if to allow her to see what was happening.

She thrashed ineffectually for a few moments before she stilled and then it wasn't so cold any more. In fact, it was strangely peaceful if she gave into the sensation of falling slowly into blackness. It was strange to think that Hunter was above her somewhere, standing, oblivious to the fact that she was dying. She almost smiled at the silly thought that Hunter was going to kill her if she died down here.

His face in her mind seemed incredibly sad, and her heart ached fiercely because she knew she'd never be able to tell him she still loved him—and just as she started to sigh out to take a breath she realised she was drowning. Sanity burst into her consciousness and she clamped her mouth shut and fought against the painful urge to breathe underwater. She kicked leadenly upwards until finally she broke the surface. The freezing air was raw in her throat and her gasps seemed thunderous as she tried to fill her lungs with air and tread water at the same time. Maybe the pool wasn't as wide as she'd feared and with the last of her energy she swam heavily to the edge. If she didn't move fast, she'd be too cold and weak to get out.

Kirsten dragged herself over the uneven edge of the bank with her elbows and then painfully pulled the rest of her body up and over the ledge to lie shuddering with great wheezing gasps on the cold stone floor. It was pitch black, freezing, and even Hunter didn't know exactly where she was. Except for her gasping breath, only the sound of trickling water disturbed the silence.

Shivering uncontrollably, Kirsten knew she had

to move. She had to find a way up the slope she'd slid down, get back to the surface and get warm— but it wasn't going to be easy.

The main problem was the dark. The cavern was as black as a moonless night in the forest and she was totally disorientated by her submersion. She had no clue which way the slope faced and all she could do was hope the exit slope was on the side of the pool she'd climbed out on because she wasn't going back in that water.

'Kirsten?' Hunter's voice seemed much fainter than the last time she'd heard it but she had never been so glad to hear his voice in her life. She opened her mouth to call back but her teeth were chattering so much all she made was a clicking noise. She cleared her throat and tried again but Hunter's name would barely have reached the top of the slope let alone up the tunnel to the cavern.

Hunter didn't hear. He'd heard the earlier shriek and was white-faced and grim as he leaned on the entrance to the tunnel. Already he was having palpitations from being this far inside the cavern and his breathing was rapid and shallow.

But he had to go in. His gut feeling told him that Kirsten was in trouble. Heaven only knew why she was in there and he'd probably kill her when they got back to the top. He told himself he'd only have to go a little way, and then he'd come across her on her way back and could give her a piece of his mind as soon as they made it outside again.

Anything else he couldn't think about. In the three minutes since she'd given that cry he'd gathered two candles and two boxes of matches from the survival kit, and had one in his pocket and one in his hand.

One of the millions of long strangler fig vines that had hung down outside the cavern was tied to his foot with a piece of fabric in case he needed rope. But he still didn't really want to go in there.

He had to, however, and in the event they didn't return, he'd shifted Keith to the entrance of the overhang and given him the flare. The outside signal fire had good coals and a heap of green leaves on it to make smoke. He couldn't think of anything else he could do and he didn't want to think about the worst-case scenario.

He cleared his throat. 'I'm going now, Keith.'

Keith's voice was weak. 'I'll be here, waiting.'

The first step was the hardest, although the second wasn't much better. The walls and roof seemed to be closing in on him and it was as if the air was being sucked out of his lungs. When he turned that first corner and the light from the entrance was gone, he had to stop and press himself against the wall for a minute and regroup. It was as if he were ten again.

Every time a rock shifted from beneath his feet his heart rate picked up another two beats and he wondered if he'd hit atrial fibrillation before he found her.

'Kirsten?' His voice seemed to be eaten by the darkness. She didn't answer and the fear of her lying somewhere trapped or injured was far greater than his claustrophobia. He pushed himself off the wall and went on. At about the same place that Kirsten had, he changed to hands and knees which made it hard with the candle. 'Kirsten?' He didn't even notice the hot wax dripping on his hand.

Suddenly he heard the sound of something scraping rock and the rattle of pebbles to his left, and he called again. 'Kirsten?'

'Hunter?' Still from his left, her voice was very faint, considering he could hear her teeth chattering. She must be close and his initial reaction was to crawl to her as fast as he could, but he stopped himself from moving. He held up the candle and tried to see ahead and to the side. That was when he realised there wasn't a side wall to the tunnel he was in.

'Where are you?'

'D-d-d-down here. I fell d-d-down a slope.'

'Can I get down to you?' He felt with his hands and discovered the fall-away at the edge.

'Down's easy. Up is harder.'

The last thing they needed was both of them at the bottom of a slide and no way to get back up again. 'Why are you so cold?'

'Wet.' Her voice was getting fainter and he realised that the effects of hypothermia were setting in. Fear hit him like a fist.

'You need to come out of the cave now, Kirsten. Can you hang onto a vine?'

'My hands are frozen.'

'You have to hang on.'

'I know,' her voice sounded sleepy and Hunter clamped down on the dread that lodged in his throat. 'Think,' he muttered to himself as he weighed up the most sensible action.

Finally he said, 'The vine is coming down now. We'll try that first.' The problem was he couldn't see her and the only estimates of direction he had were the sounds of her voice and movement. 'Clap your hands, Kirsten.'

The slow muffled sound didn't augur well for her strength but he wanted to keep her moving until the vine arrived. He untied the vegetation from his foot and wiped some wax from his finger onto the cloth and tied it to the end of the vine.

'I'm going to light a little piece of rag tied to the end of the vine so I can see you. It shouldn't burn the vine but if it does start to, you have to put the fire out. Do you understand, Kirsten? We need the vine to get you out.'

'OK.' Her voice sounded a little stronger, as if she were determined to use her last strength.

He lit the rag and tossed the vine end over the edge. It didn't slide and just sat, flickering on the edge of the slope.

'Give me a break,' he muttered. He pulled it back quickly and tossed it again before the little fire went out. This time it sailed over the edge and landed beside the pool. He had a brief flash of the picture of the cavern below—water, and at the edge Kirsten, swaying as she knelt on the cavern floor.

Then the flame went out. Inspired by the success of that brief light, he tore another piece of material off his shirt, dipped it in wax and wrapped it around a stone. This one he lit and tossed over the edge too. It spluttered for a moment before it went out but he had enough light to see Kirsten reach for the vine and wrap her hands around it.

Then they were back in the dark except for his candle. 'Stand up, Kirsten. Can you do that?'

'I'm t-t-trying.' He heard the sound of movement and pebbles on rock. 'I'm up.'

'OK. You're going to walk up the slope, slowly, and I'm going to be your handrail. I'll pull, you just have to stay on your feet and keep moving forward. You can lean back on the rope, I will not let it go.'

The next ten minutes were the longest in Hunter's life. For Kirsten, they lasted for ever. She kept her eyes glued to the flickering candlelight shining on the roof above her and kept moving towards it despite the burning pain in her clamped hands which became unbearable. She thought she could feel the warmth of blood running down her wrists but she didn't look and after a while the pain was so sharp she thought she would faint from it. But then she was at the top.

Hunter pulled her over the edge and dragged her against him as he sank against the opposite wall. He wrapped himself around her and it was the most incredible feeling in the world. Then she drifted off to sleep.

After a while Hunter couldn't hold out any longer. 'Kirsten.'

'What now?' She frowned and didn't open her eyes. She was having the best dream!

'Kirsten, wake up!' Hunter's voice was sharp. 'I need you to crawl ahead and get out of the tunnel.'

She drew a shuddering breath and woke up to incredible pain in her hands and the cold and the realisation she did need to move so Hunter could get out of the cave as well.

'I'm sorry.' She shuffled forward and resigned herself to the pain as her hands touched the floor of the tunnel. She made herself move, knee following knee, hand following hand, one after the other with no stopping. After what seemed like hours, she rounded the corner and saw the circle of light at the entrance. She had enough room now to turn around or even stand up, but she just turned her head.

'I see the entrance,' she said, but Hunter wasn't behind her. He wasn't anywhere near her.

'Hunter?' He didn't answer and she realised there had been no sound behind her for a while.

'Hunter?'

He couldn't answer. Once he'd seen that she was going to make it, his phobia had kicked in. The walls of the cave heaved against him and he pressed himself back against the cold rock as if to make more room for his lungs to breathe. He felt like a fool, and useless, but it was bigger than he was. Kirsten was safe and that was the main thing. Maybe he'd always been destined to die in a cave.

When she called his name he willed her to keep going because he knew she didn't have the strength to do it twice.

She called his name again and he moistened his lips and tried to answer. The most he could manage was a whisper to tell her to keep going.

He could feel the roof crushing him, despite the fact that his candle said it wasn't, and he scrunched himself into a ball as if to ward it off. Then something touched him.

'Hunter?'

He opened his eyes and Kirsten was there. He felt her breath on his face. 'Come on, I'm cold!' she said.

He felt the sting of tears in his eyes and he blinked them away. 'I can't move. I'm sorry. Please, go.'

'Claustrophobia?'

'You bet,' he whispered, and he heard her sigh.

Then she snuggled up next to him and took his hand. 'You came in here to save me. That was very brave. And if you can't move then I guess I'll stay, too.'

He blinked. 'Please, go. I can't move but you can. Go!'

'Nope.' She pulled his shirt until his head came down to her level and pressed her icy lips to his. 'I'm cold. Please, come with me.'

He shuddered and shut his eyes and then she pulled his shirt again until he knelt forward. She backed away from him towards the entrance. But her face stayed close to his. 'Kiss me, Hunter.'

His groan came from deep within him as his muscles unlocked and he leaned towards her. His lips touched hers and he savoured the mingling of their breaths and the taste of her against him. He pressed himself against her freezing cold little face. She backed away a little more.

'Again. Kiss me again.'

And he followed her, one knee step and one kiss at a time, until they came to the bend. He could see the light up ahead and he knew they were going to make it. It was all because of her. And then he knew. He would do anything for this woman.

He would enter a hundred caves to find her because she was the one for him. All this confusion and lack of trust and gossip and innuendo was nothing compared to what he felt for Kirsten.

He'd been a fool to trick himself into abandoning her because of his own fears. Fears that he'd never recover if she, too, betrayed him.

When they reached the outside, Keith was still propped against the entrance and Hunter saw him sag back against the wall as if totally exhausted from the tension and unable to believe they were back. Hunter knew how he felt.

Hunter's overwhelming relief at the widening walls of the cavern was cut short when Kirsten sagged onto the floor as she reached the cavern and a fear greater than any he'd had in the cave crashed in on him.

He scooped her up and pressed her cold cheek to his, and she barely moved. She was freezing. He carried her to the fire and kicked the remaining pile of wood onto it to build it up. With fumbling fingers he stripped off her shirt, peeling it away from the deathly pale whiteness of her damp skin, and spread it in front of the fire to dry. Then he pulled off her shoes and wet socks and her trousers until she sagged against him in a tiny pair of pink lacy panties and bra, all cold legs and arms as she shivered.

Quickly unbuttoning his shirt, he pulled it open and then tugged his trousers off and dragged her back against the warmth of his chest and legs in front of the fire. She sighed into him, burying her face in his chest as if to hide from the cold deep within her. He wrapped himself and his shirt around her, closing her inside the cocoon of his own body heat.

'You're so warm,' she murmured. 'Don't leave me.'

'I'll be here as long as you need me.' He hugged her tighter. 'You'll be fine as soon as we get you warmed up.' He cupped her cheek in his hand and dropped a kiss on her lips without even realising he'd done it.

Then he saw Keith's raised eyebrows and Hunter stared him down. Keith made a great show of turning his body away as he manoeuvred himself into a more comfortable position, facing the direction of the clearing.

Kirsten slept against him for an hour as he cleaned her torn hands with his handkerchief dipped in water, and rubbed her feet. Every now and then she'd make a little moaning noise that tore at his heart. He couldn't believe she nearly died inside the cave. If he hadn't come back to the cavern when he had, if he hadn't been able to force himself inside the cave, he'd never have found her in time. What was it with this woman and danger?

Hunter could tell she was finally warming up and he worried that he should have put some IV fluids next to the fire to heat as well so that he could centrally warm her, but he hadn't wanted to leave her to set it all up. Then she opened her eyes and smiled up at him and it was as if the sun had come out in the cavern.

'Hello. Did I go to sleep on you?' She wriggled a little but made no move to leave his arms.

'You were tired.' He smiled down at her and he dared to believe she'd be fine. 'Could you not go into any more caves, please?'

Kirsten decided she could cope with that. She shuddered. 'If that's what you want.'

His shoulders shook with suppressed laughter that was more relief than amusement, and she loved the feeling of being so close to him. His chest hairs prickled against her cheek and she snuggled into his skin. This skin-on-skin stuff was pretty darn good.

'Yes, it's what I want.' He became serious. 'Thank you for coming back for me.'

She didn't want to think about how close he'd

come to staying in there, and couldn't bear to contemplate how much mental anguish she'd caused
him by having to crawl through the cave to rescue
her. 'You wouldn't have been in there if I hadn't
decided to explore.'

'We'll talk about that later. You gave Keith and
me heart failure.'

They both looked across at Keith, where the pilot
was gently snoring, and Kirsten smiled. 'I think he's
over his heart failure.'

Hunter lowered his face to hers. 'I'm not over
mine,' he said, and brushed her lips with his as he
eased her back out of Keith's line of sight. 'I need
much more reassurance.'

When Hunter kissed her this time, there was no
place for regret or fears of later. This was right. Her
exhilaration was tempered by a persistent dread that
suddenly Hunter would remember that he didn't
trust her and pull away. His mouth moved on hers,
as if seeking reassurance that she was fine, and
Kirsten answered his need with her own desperate
hunger and wrapped her arms around his neck. His
hair was thick and springy under her fingers and the
reality of them both being alive and together brought
tears to her eyes. She blinked them away before he
could see her emotion.

Kirsten felt cherished and tiny surrounded by this
big strong man who had faced his deepest fear to
save her from her own foolishness, and finally allowed her to see some of his secrets and insecurities.
He still hadn't said he trusted her but she'd come to
the conclusion that she'd just have to work harder
to convince him. Because she couldn't shut Hunter
out of her life any longer.

She'd take him on his terms, any terms, because they'd been given this chance of living again and there was no way she was going to waste that gift by being too proud or too frightened to show her love. The risk was all her own.

Hunter enticed her mouth open with nudging kisses that promised wonderful things. When his kiss deepened she could do little but answer his heat and fuel the fire between them. She'd waited so long for this feeling of unity, this melding of breath and erotic tango of his tongue with hers, that she felt as if she could die with the tragedy and joy of this moment. This living, breathing, moving mating of their mouths should never end and the moment lengthened into a timeless dream she had no wish to wake from.

Then Hunter's hands trailed softly from where they splayed about her waist up to trace the undersides of her breasts and the circling, sensual movement did nothing to assuage the months of denial and hunger she'd fought within herself for this man. Impatient now for the branding of his touch, she tugged his hand across her skin until his fingers unclipped her bra and slid it out of the way. She sighed with delight as he finally, possessively cupped her breasts and settled her aching nipples deep in his palm. Then he steepled his hand and encircled her flesh between his fingers, kneading and murmuring his delight wickedly in her ear while the slight roughness of his skin sent jagging spirals of heated sensation low in her stomach.

Kirsten slid her hands down from around Hunter's neck and ran them possessively along the solid muscle of his chest, savouring the firmness and planes under her fingers, then travelled around his waist to his back. His skin was so warm and sculpted and she groaned her appreciation against his mouth. When the kiss ended she murmured against his cheek, 'And why have we never done this before?'

Unable to answer at that moment, he groaned deep in his throat, lowered his head further and grazed both nipples with his teeth before circling the aching tips with his mouth and feasting on her. When he lifted his head he stared into her eyes and his voice was ragged with desire. 'Because I knew I'd never stop.'

Exactly what she'd wanted to hear. 'That's reassuring,' she whispered breathlessly, and teased as she arched against him. She had to sink her hands into his hair to press his head more firmly against her breasts, but the flames of his suckling made her ache for a more total possession than this.

Then he returned to kiss her again and they plunged straight into the previous heated hunger that had started this, and she couldn't resist the jerking slide of her hands down his naked back. Driven, her fingers eased further down to cup the firm flesh of his bottom and she raised her hips to grind against him.

Hunter plundered her mouth to answer such a flagrant request. Kirsten swirled in a red mist, only vaguely aware of his body's movements as he shucked his underwear off so that he lay hard against her. Then, with both hands flat against her hips, he slid her lace briefs down until he could hook the elastic in his toe and slide away the last barrier between them. With his nakedness against her, his kiss gentled and she lay drugged against him, trembling with a need that possessed them both.

'This is crazy,' he whispered.

'I know,' she breathed, and he kissed her once more, swiftly. Hunter lifted himself up on his elbows and the veins in his arms stood out as he supported his weight. His corded muscle glinted with firelight and she lay pliant and soft with want, mesmerised by the magnificent male poised above her. The tenderness she saw deep in his eyes stung her throat with tears.

He lowered himself towards her and she closed her eyes, had to, as she welcomed him. And then they slowly and deliberately joined as one. Her indrawn breath whispered his name and sinuously her legs rose up to wrap around his thighs until he was so deep and hard within her she was lost in unfamiliar territory.

He rocked slowly and then withdrew. Bereft, she clutched at his back, urging his return, until he smiled and answered her, deeper and more powerfully. She bit her lip to hold back the throaty moans she couldn't prevent. Gradually the tempo of his thrusts increased until his mouth came down to stifle her gasps and their breath mingled as she clutched at him with stiffened fingers and dared to venture to the edge of the unknown. And then she was falling, her whole body shivering and squeezed with his possession until, for both of them, the cave exploded into a million bolts of molten heat. A sunshine of clenching joy that left her limp in his arms while he held her tightly against him as if he'd never let her go.

Afterwards they lay together, breathless, and gradually the sand beneath their bodies impinged on their consciousness. Both glanced across to the cave entrance and the sound of Keith snoring gently. Kirsten chuckled and Hunter shook his head. 'I can't believe we did that, with Keith just over there,' she whispered, and that was when he saw her hands were bleeding again.

'You're a bad influence on me.' His tone was light and very quiet but Kirsten's stomach sank as she saw the underlying return to reality for Hunter.

Hunter stared at her torn hands and hated himself for not remembering. Lord knew how much pain he'd caused her while his body had taken over. And that hadn't been all he'd forgotten in his lust for this woman who deserved so much more. The supposed disciplined planner realised he'd let Kirsten down in another unforgivable way. Sleeping with Kirsten had been a selfish and irresponsible thing to do but it had changed him for ever. He just prayed she wouldn't regret it. 'I don't suppose you're on the Pill?' He heard himself say it and saw the disappointment in her face.

When she said, 'I can take the morning-after pill,' and reached for her bra without looking at him, he should have been glad that she would take care of that, but he wasn't. Her 'Don't worry about it' made him feel even worse, but the last thing he wanted was to cause Kirsten any pain from an unplanned pregnancy, or complicate a situation that he had a hard time comprehending as it was.

He hugged her shoulders to apologise for shattering the mood with practicality and she rested warm and soft against him for a second, before she turned away to get dressed. He could feel the distance growing between them and he doubted if she realised that he was almost shattered by the revelations of the last hour. So many of his preconceived ideas and plans would now have to be changed. His head was spinning and he fought down the temptation to take her in his arms again. So many ghosts to be laid before he would be free to love Kirsten as she deserved to be loved. But not here. Not now—when Keith's survival still depended on rescue. He dressed quickly and passed her shirt from in front of the fire where it had almost dried, and she turned her back on him again to dress.

Kirsten faced into the darkness of the cave she'd crawled out of—and it felt as if she was back in a darker place. What had she expected? Promises of undying love? Of course he'd thought of the consequences. The lump of tears solidified in her throat and she felt sick. She loved him, and she'd always treasure the beauty of the last hour, but she'd known he feared commitment. To expect anything long term from Hunter was the risk she'd been willing to take, though maybe she should think about it more now that the moment was less heated. At least she had this day of memories—Hunter saving her, weak with relief that she was alive, his tenderness as a lover and holding her as if he'd never let her go. If only she could forget the ending. She shivered and pulled on her damp shirt.

It was then they heard the Chinook.

CHAPTER EIGHT

HUNTER listened to the thump of the rotors for a moment before the enormity of the situation sank in. They had been rescued. He snatched up the flare and ran out into the clearing. This was something positive he could do.

Back to the real world, Kirsten sighed, reminding herself she was glad to be rescued. She brushed an arm across her eyes as the sound of the Chinook grew louder. The rest of her damp clothes went on awkwardly because her hands weren't working properly, and as she finger-combed her tangled hair she realised that her fingers and palms were swelling. How strange she hadn't noticed the pain while making love, or maybe they'd just thawed out now. She went to wake Keith.

The army helicopter swept in from the left at about five hundred feet and Hunter snapped off the cap of the flare to ignite it. Pungent orange smoke poured from the stick and he held it arm's length and moved out towards the wreckage.

He didn't think the personnel on the Chinook could actually see him through the canopy but hopefully they'd see the smoke.

The thump of the rotors vibrated around him and by the time the helicopter hovered over the break in the canopy the wind generated by the rotors was shaking the treetops. Suddenly two ropes unwound from the side door of the Chinook and two men in camouflage snaked down the ropes and landed lightly twenty metres away. They ran towards him, speaking into their microphones as they ran.

'Dr Morgan?'

Hunter threw a thankful prayer skyward at God and the helicopter pilot hovering above and nodded. 'There's an injured man in a cave. Follow me.'

Hunter wouldn't feel rescued until Keith and Kirsten were safely aboard the helicopter. She was still pale and occasionally shivered against him as they watched Keith being winched into the aircraft. He wasn't letting her out of his sight and knew he wouldn't rest until she'd been properly assessed at the hospital. He tried to block out what they'd been doing such a short time ago knowing he loved her— but he wasn't sure how much he could offer. Now wasn't the time to pursue that.

Finally the last soldier had been winched back up into the Chinook and within fifteen minutes they were transported to Port Macquarie Base Hospital where Kirsten was reunited with her sisters.

Keith's wife met them as they stretchered her husband into Emergency. Aware of her distress, Hunter stayed with her to help explain what they'd do for her husband. All the time half of his mind wondered where Kirsten was, even though he knew Abbey and Bella were with her.

When Keith was finally settled into Intensive Care, critical but stable, Hunter left Anna to find Kirsten. He was almost too late.

In Kirsten's room, he barely registered the two other women in the room as his eyes were drawn to Kirsten, the woman he loved, sitting fully dressed in clean clothes on the edge of the bed. She'd showered, her hair was tied back in a damp ponytail and her small hands were heavily bandaged.

After being given warmed intravenous fluids, Kirsten had been pronounced stable, but she refused to stay at the base hospital, opting instead for her sisters' care.

It was all out of his hands and he fought the outrage her discharge left him with because what could he do? She had family, two brother-in-law doctors and two strong-willed midwife sisters, who were keen to take her home, and he was a nobody.

'Hello, Hunter,' she said, and he could tell she was confused about where she stood with him. He wished he could help her but he felt the same. 'These are my sisters, Abbey and Bella,' she said. 'I'm going home with them now.'

He vaguely noticed the family resemblance, but his attention was focussed on Kirsten. 'Are you well enough to go home?' The last thing he wanted was to leave her, but she needed more than he could give her at this moment. The previous twenty-four hours had been traumatic for all of them.

He needed time to come to terms with the past before he could look to the future.

'I'll be well cared for.' She smiled wearily and then looked him up and down. 'What about you?'

He shook his head at her concern. How could she think of him when she'd been through so much? 'I've a few things to sort out. I need to visit my father and I have my own ghosts to lay. Your family is the best place for you.' He stepped across to the bed and kissed her cold cheek. 'The next time I see you, we need to talk.'

She frowned at his ambiguous comment. Talk as

in future or talk as in regret? She hadn't realised his father was still alive and she had no idea what ghosts he was talking about. She was too tired, physically and emotionally, to guess, and damn him for kissing her cheek. 'Goodbye, Hunter.'

'*Au revoir*, Kirsten.'

He watched her leave the room with her sisters, and it felt as if a part of him was torn in two. But leaving her was the most sensible thing. He needed time away from Kirsten to collect his thoughts. How had he reached the stage where even being away from her for a few days would seem a lifetime? Twenty-four hours ago they had barely been on speaking terms, but in that time he'd thought he'd lost her for ever—twice. It was too much, too soon, and this was his last chance for the woman he loved. The happiness of both of them depended on him. She'd come back to MIRA and to him—she had to—and this time he'd get it right.

When Kirsten woke up the next morning her sisters were sitting beside the bed. Her first thought was that she had forty-eight hours, maximum, to take the morning-after pill. Her second thought was she felt too miserably unwell to worry about it today.

Abbey was reading, and Bella was sewing a rip in Kirsten's jacket.

Bella noticed Kirsten was awake first and she smiled. 'Good morning, sleepyhead.'

Abbey put down the book and leaned over to give the invalid a kiss and then tilted her head. 'I thought you'd grown out of giving us heart failure with your adventures.'

'I like to keep you guessing,' Kirsten's voice was

hoarse and it hurt to yawn. Thank goodness she was home, she thought. Her head felt woolly with the beginnings of a thumping cold. She coughed and her throat spasmed and she lay back on the pillows. Great! Just what she needed. Then she wondered how Hunter was.

She hoped her sisters wouldn't jump to conclusions, but Abbey knew everything anyway so there was no point trying to hide.

'How's Keith, and have you heard from Hunter?' she croaked.

Typically, Abbey knew. 'Keith is fine. He has a broken ankle and a haemoglobin of five so is up for more blood transfusions today. Your Dr Morgan flew back to Sydney last night. He rang to ask how you were and I said you were sleeping.'

Both sisters looked at her expectantly and Kirsten couldn't help the heat of colour that brushed her cheeks. 'What?'

Abbey and Bella exchanged looks and then Abbey smiled and changed the subject. 'Hopefully you'll miss out on pneumonia, but you're brewing a decent head cold and you're confined to bed today.'

'After your wash, we'll bring up breakfast,' Bella said. 'Vivie has left Aunt Sophie in charge of her son to come over to make it for you.'

The girls' aunt lived next door with Scott's son, Blake, and his new wife Vivie, and Kirsten glanced out the window at the big house across the yard with a tired smile. Vivie was the best cook in the family.

Normally she would have got up anyway but the thought of hiding in her room for a while was strangely attractive and probably had more to do with realising that Hunter could just fly back to Sydney without a backward glance. She ached all over and her hands hurt. She winced and felt like a baby with mittens.

'I need a long bath with some of your calming oils, Bella. But I don't know if I can wait for breakfast for all of that.'

Abbey lifted a Thermos of hot chocolate from the floor and poured Kirsten a cup. 'Drink this, follow your plan, I'll redress your hands and then we'll bring you a tray in forty-five minutes.'

Kirsten smiled tiredly at her big sister. 'It's great to be home.'

Abbey hugged her gently. 'You have no idea how pleased we are to see you.' Then she turned away to hide the tears in her eyes.

'I'll run the bath.' Bella followed Abbey out of the door and her voice wobbled. It was then that Kirsten realised how hard it must have been for those waiting to hear if any of them were alive.

She stared sadly at the door and wondered if Hunter had anyone waiting to hear that he had made it safely through the ordeal. Obviously she now knew he had at least his father alive, but how strange that she'd had the impression his father was dead from something Hunter had said in Dubai. Obviously some form of estrangement. Kirsten knew at first hand how Hunter could freeze people out if he felt he'd been let down, and she felt a kindred sympathy for Hunter's father.

Thoughts of Hunter's relatives were the tip of the iceberg as far as Hunter was concerned. She really knew nothing about the man. In the cave, things had changed, ground had shifted and new rules had come into play. It was frightening to know those changes had only happened because of the circumstances. Even more frightening was the fact that she didn't want them to go away and she didn't know whether Hunter wished they'd never happened.

She loved Hunter and always would. But that didn't mean they were destined to be together. She was still willing to risk her pride and her heart but she needed some encouragement from Hunter apart from those magic moments in the cave. She would give him one more chance and if he let her down again, she would learn to live in Gladstone.

After Kirsten's bath, Abbey winced at her sister's wounds as she changed the dressings. 'You'll be lucky to be able to go back to work in three weeks, the way you've torn your hands.' Her sister gently rubbed in some salve that seemed to draw the sting from the deep gouges as soon as it touched it.

'What's in that?' Kirsten asked, and Abbey shrugged.

'It's Bella's concoction, and I can smell the lavender, but I'm not sure of the rest. I've found it very effective.'

She placed the last piece of tape on the bandages, and even though they were less bulky, Kirsten knew she would still be awkward with the dressings.

'I hope you're going to cut my food for me.'

Abbey smiled at her. 'We'll look after you.' Abbey paused as if unsure how Kirsten would react to her next statement. 'Everyone would understand if you didn't want to go back to MIRA after the crash. You could stay here after you're healed, and not go back to Sydney.'

To not take the risk, to accept the inevitable without having to stare Hunter in the face... The coward in her admitted the idea was attractive but Kirsten shook her head. 'I have unfinished business in Sydney.'

Abbey nodded. 'I thought you might.' Abbey understood. She always did.

'It may not work out, Abbey. I've been mistaken before with this man. Things weren't real in the emotion of the crash.'

'I'm aware of that. But you've changed, and I don't think it's just the hell you've been through. You know you can talk to me when you're ready. You've been given a few weeks off. Rest, recover and let him stew.'

Hunter wasn't stewing, he was laying the framework for a new life, as well as laying ghosts that had haunted him for longer than he'd known Kirsten. Maybe his emotional denial of his father's existence had helped create the isolated man he had become? After his mother had left and his father had shut him out, Hunter had begun to create his own barriers to emotional damage, with the foundation stone laid by avoiding anyone who could hurt him. He felt surreal, back in Sydney after the crash—suspended somewhere between the isolated rainforest at Banda Banda and the solicitous enquiries from MIRA and the NICU, and the nagging hole where Kirsten should be. He spent the first few days working up to tackle his past and finally he was ready.

Kirsten slept the first few days, while her hands healed more slowly than she'd expected. The lingering head cold left her feeling weak and tearful for most of the week. Or that's what she told herself was making her feel weak and tearful. Hunter left a get-well message with Abbey and sent some roses with an impersonal note the day after he left, he rang twice while she was sleeping but she heard nothing more. He would ring again soon.

The second week Abbey kept her busy, visiting friends and helping out with the baby, and Kirsten soaked in the serenity of a loving home, a delightful nephew and the warmth of her family around her. Her feeling of disquiet grew. Hunter had said he had things to do but surely he could have rung at least once more?

At the end of the first week, Hunter paused outside the stately house and resolutely walked up the stairs to ring the bell.

'Hello, Father,' he said. Hunter shook the old man's hand and he thought how strange it was to follow the tall figure into his childhood home, something he hadn't done for twenty years. Not that he'd spent much of his growing years under the roof. Consigned to boarding schools after his mother had left, Hunter had never breached the walls his father had erected between them until his own bitterness had grown to sour their relationship permanently.

When they were seated, his father looked so frail in the big winged-chair that Hunter was shocked at the passage of years.

'It's good to see you, son. They said you were missing, and I was worried until they rang again.' The old man sighed at the memory and this time Hunter could see the love and concern shining from his father's eyes. Hunter was afraid it had been there all along but he hadn't been able to see it through his own hurt.

He leaned forward and took the frail hand in his and squeezed it. 'We managed to walk away from the wreck. I wondered if I could stay for a few days? Catch up and spend some time together? That experience made me realise I should see you more often.'

His father lifted his shoulder in a painful shrug. 'You're welcome any time. Though why you want to is beyond me. You were right when you accused me of shutting you out. When I finally realised what I'd done to you, it was too late.'

Hunter shook his head and smiled. 'We both should have known better, but maybe we're just too alike to see it.' Hunter took a deep breath and began to let go of the built-up disappointment of years, but it would take time. 'I need to spend time with you.'

The old man's eyes shone suspiciously brightly before he turned away to look across the room. 'I'd like that,' he said gruffly, and then pulled his hand free and gestured to a small table in an alcove. 'Now, enough of this sap and give me a game of chess. I haven't had a good game since my best friend died.' He grinned up as his son towered over him to shift the table. 'You may have grown but I bet you still can't beat me at that.'

Two nights later his father brought up the subject Hunter had been avoiding. 'Your mother has married again.'

Hunter blinked. 'For the fourth time?'

His father's eyes twinkled and Hunter felt his own mouth curve. 'This one's even younger. She was always a difficult woman to please so I don't feel like a failure.'

Hunter looked at the old man he'd come to know more in the last few days than he had in the last thirty-five years. 'So how does that make you feel?'

His father shrugged. 'Sad for her and nothing for me. I got over your mother leaving a hell of a lot quicker than you did.'

Hunter remembered the desolation he'd been left with. 'I used to wish she were dead.' He glanced up. 'Which left me feeling guilty as well as miserable. Terrible, but at least she would have had a reason not to write to me, or send me a card for my birthday, or even pretend that she sometimes thought about me.' He shook his head. 'Pathetic, I know.'

'If you hadn't cared you would have been like her. Thank God you cared.' The old man sighed. 'I pushed her to give me an heir. And she never forgave me. Said it ruined her body, which wasn't true, because it was then she was at her most beautiful.' His father sighed. 'I should never have married her…' He looked under shaggy brows at his son. 'Just like you should never have married Portia.'

Hunter held up his hands. 'Like father, like son.' They both smiled ruefully.

By the time he left a few days later, Hunter knew he and his father would savour the time they had left together. A strong bond had been forged and he was very thankful he'd had the chance. He dreamed of Kirsten and the chance of his own family and how much his father would love being included.

Just one more ghost.

* * *

To say Portia was surprised to see him was an understatement. She opened the door of what had once been his home but was now Portia's fashionable house. After the second ring, his ex-wife answered the door and he could tell that she'd been drinking. It was just after lunch. Funny how he'd forgotten that she often drank too much.

'Well, well,' she said, and gestured him in with a grand sweep of her arm. 'To what do I owe the pleasure of your company, dear man?'

'Hello, Portia.' Hunter ignored her question and followed her. The entry was still grand, with black and white tiles and marble furniture, and he suppressed a shiver at the coldness of the room as he crossed behind her into the formal lounge.

She stopped in front of a huge oil painting of herself and turned to face him. The comparison wasn't kind. 'I'm a widow now. Are you interested, Hunter?' She smiled and a glimpse of the young woman he'd fallen in love with shone briefly from her eyes but faded away with her smile.

'I've just come to make my peace,' he said, and realised that he felt nothing, not even dislike for the woman in front of him. If she hadn't been unfaithful, would he be living in this cold and ostentatious house with the wrong woman? It was a scary thought that he owed Portia a debt for letting him go. What he could have with Kirsten would be so different.

She tilted her head and this time her smile was more genuine. 'You've fallen in love. I'm pleased for you because you weren't destined to be happy with me, Hunter. I never was a one-man woman, though I gave you my best shot.'

She poured herself a drink and then waved the bottle to offer him one. Hunter shook his head and jingled his keys. Suddenly he felt a hundred years younger and he needed to get out and shake the outdated negatives from his brain and focus on the positives for his future.

He had to talk to Kirsten, but it had to be face to face. To wait another week would be agony but this time he would do it right.

By the end of the third week Kirsten was ready to kill Hunter for not ringing. What did his silence mean? It was time to test her future with Hunter or lay other plans. His lack of contact didn't bode well but she was still willing to risk telling him she loved him. Willing to try to start again even with the chance their relationship could be short term.

Maggie rang from Sydney twice and each time when Kirsten heard the long-distance pips on the line she thought it was Hunter. She reconfirmed her return date and assured Maggie she was well. With subtle prompting by Kirsten, Maggie mentioned that Hunter was back at work and looked well and that Keith was progressing steadily.

Finally the morning dawned for Kirsten's return to Sydney and suddenly she didn't want to go. Didn't want to know the answers to the questions she'd been asking herself since the crash.

The nausea hit her as she made to rise and she lay back down in bed and stared at the ceiling. As she turned over in bed the tenderness in her breasts made sudden sense and she sat up slowly as every-thing clicked into place. She never had taken the morning-after pill. Hunter had good reason not to trust her.

Despite the implications she couldn't help the sunbeam of joy that lit her face. Unless she was mistaken, she was carrying Hunter's child and she was fiercely glad.

It was only just daylight and Kirsten rose slowly to slip downstairs to the miniature surgery that Rohan kept for emergencies. Sure enough, at the back of the cupboard she found a pregnancy kit and she slid it into her pocket and climbed back upstairs.

Five minutes later she stared at the distinctive two lines on the test. She was pregnant. She leaned back against the bathroom sink, suddenly faint. The nausea rushed up her throat and she swayed over the toilet. Afterwards, as she washed her face, the question rolled over in her mind like a child's toy. What would Hunter say?

Already Hunter found it difficult to trust her or believe in her, so what would he say about this? She'd told him not to worry and, judging by his lack of communication, he hadn't, she thought with a twist of bitterness.

Suddenly the risks she'd so blithely decided were worth extra heartache were even greater because any relationship with Hunter was no longer just about the two of them. If Hunter couldn't trust her—was too afraid to commit for life to the woman he loved—then their child should never know this. She was no longer the only person taking a risk with Hunter. She risked her child's happiness, too. The stakes were too high to not count the consequences.

At the airport, Kirsten was distracted by the enormity of her discovery and her sudden trepidation at seeing Hunter again.

Abbey watched her sister with some concern, guessing what was on her mind. 'Are you all right?' she asked quietly, and shifted closer, protectively, along the bench.

The news was so recent, so fragile, and Kirsten didn't know whether to tell Abbey or not. Almost as if she'd done something wrong and her pregnancy was her punishment. But she'd done nothing wrong. Just loved a man with all her heart. She knew this was right. She wasn't ready to tell Hunter but Abbey would be a good place to start. Kirsten tested the words in her mind and then took a deep breath. 'I'm pregnant. And I can't believe I'm so happy about it.' Kirsten watched her sister's face anxiously.

Abbey nodded, remarkably unperturbed, and leaned across to hug her. 'If you're happy then we're happy for you. What will Hunter say?'

Kirsten met Abbey's eyes. 'I love the way you know it's Hunter's baby.' She went on. 'I'm not sure I'm going to tell him. There was only the once and I was supposed to take the morning-after pill but I really didn't want to. There was something that smacked of regret if I did and I don't regret what we shared.'

She narrowed her eyes with determination and Abbey was reminded of the strong-willed teenager that Kirsten had been. She shook here head and sat back to listen.

'I was too sick to fight myself for feeling that way and now I'm glad. Does that make me deceitful?'

'It makes you a mother,' Abbey said dryly, and hugged her again. 'It won't be easy if you have to be a single parent, but remember we're all here for you.' She smiled. 'Hunter might surprise you. I hope he does.' She glanced down at her sister's flat stomach. 'And you'll have a job in Gladstone when you start to show if you decide not to tell him. In fact, tell me the whole story from the beginning because all I know is you knew him in Dubai, slept together after a helicopter crash and now you're pregnant by him.'

Kirsten leaned her head on Abbey's shoulder. 'There's no more to tell.'

'Why not?'

'Hunter is divorced. His parents were divorced.' Kirsten sighed and gave the abridged version. 'His wife ran off with the senior consultant five years ago and he doesn't trust women.'

'He can trust you.'

'That's just it. I don't think he can trust anyone. We spent a lot of time together for about eight weeks in Dubai and we became close.'

'I see,' said Abbey, and Kirsten shook her head.

'Not that close—it was almost as if he didn't want sex to cloud the issue.'

'Anyway, he got it into his head I was having an affair with a married man and the man's wife didn't help with her lies. And that was the end of it. He tarred and feathered me in his mind. People shouldn't believe that of those they get close to.'

Abbey frowned. 'Of course you told him it wasn't true?'

Kirsten felt like hugging her sister. Abbey didn't even entertain for a moment the possibility that her sister would have had a liaison with a married man.

It was a shame Hunter couldn't have that sort of faith. 'He didn't believe me!'

Abbey shook her head, confused. 'Why not?'

'I don't think he's used to people being open with their emotions. He saw me hug the guy and put that with the poison from the wife who had another agenda, and that was that.'

The airport loudspeaker crackled to life and the call to board the aircraft made them both look across the tarmac.

'Ring me,' Abbey said, and kissed Kirsten one more time. 'Think about telling him. If you love him—be honest with him.' She shrugged. 'Then it's up to him to be honest back. Your child deserves honesty.'

Abbey could see the shine of tears in Kirsten's eyes and she bit her lip to hold her own back.

'I hear you, big sister.' Kirsten said. She blew a kiss and picked up her bag, and Abbey watched her walk away.

When Maggie met her at Sydney airport, Kirsten stifled the tiny flicker of disappointment that Hunter hadn't even cared enough to meet her after three weeks. But that was what she'd been afraid of.

She tried to infuse enthusiasm into her voice. 'Hi, Maggie. What a great surprise! I thought I'd have to catch a taxi home.'

Maggie looked horrified. 'Oh, we couldn't let you do that.' She hugged Kirsten fiercely. 'We were all so terrified when they couldn't find you all that first day. Welcome back. We've missed you.' She took Kirsten's hands and turned them over, tutting over the dark pink scars of healing. 'Your poor hands.'

Kirsten caught Maggie's fingers in hers and squeezed them to prove her point. 'I'm fine.'

'Hunter was planning to be here but there's an emergency on in the NICU.' Maggie's words made a blush steal up Kirsten's cheeks and she hugged the crumb of hope to herself. Luckily Maggie was steering them both towards her car as she spoke and she didn't notice Kirsten's silence.

Kirsten knew she'd have to bump up her immunity to the mention and sight of Hunter over the next few weeks or everyone would be consoling her on her unrequited love for the man. She would be no object of pity. She'd fight for love but she wouldn't lie down for it. The thought hardened her resolve. 'How's Keith?'

'He's doing well. Back home to convalesce and driving his wife insane.'

Kirsten forced a laugh and they discussed the workload at MIRA as Maggie drove to Kirsten's flat.

Maternal Maggie patted her knee. 'Take it easy for the rest of the day.'

'I'll be fine. I've been lying around for three weeks.'

Maggie looked sideways at her. 'I hope you realise that you and Hunter are celebrities over at the hospital.'

Kirsten shuddered at the thought and climbed out of the car. 'I hope not.' She waved Maggie off. She'd changed, the pregnancy had changed her, and suddenly she didn't want the limelight. That was the last thing she needed while she coped with the idea of a baby—to have her and Hunter under the microscope of the public eye—especially when it was all

one-sided. Limelight was for fun and Kirsten had
finally embraced maturity. She was going to be a
mother.

At the same time, Hunter stood back from the crib
in NICU and watched with satisfaction as baby
Kinny's respirations slowly return to normal. He
turned away to wash his hands. Hopefully, Kinny
would be fine without him now that they'd treated
the pneumonia with antibiotics and reinflated her
lung. He glanced at the clock and realised Kirsten
had landed half an hour ago. She'd be almost home
by now. He resisted the urge to go outside and
phone her, just as he'd been resisting for the last
week. He didn't know what he would do if she regretted the time in the cave. He planned to see her
tonight, before MIRA tomorrow, if Kinny would
stay well enough to let him.

He wondered how Kirsten was coping. People
had asked him about flashbacks from the crash but
his most vivid memories all involved Kirsten—
when he'd thought he'd lost her in the crash and
then later in the cave when he'd thought his life had
ended because he hadn't been able to see how he
could get her out. When she'd collapsed at the tunnel entrance as cold as ice, he'd never been so
frightened. But most frequently he relived when
he'd held her chilled body against his own until
she'd warmed and that magic time when he'd lost
himself in her.

That had been when he'd conquered his fear to
love Kirsten, along with the ridiculous phobia that
he still cringed about. She was the only one who
could have saved him and she'd never leave him in

darkness again. His journey over the last three weeks had shown him how ridiculous his lack of trust had been. No matter what she'd done, Kirsten was nothing like Portia or his mother. She was Kirsten and he trusted her completely—he just hoped she believed him and could forgive him for all the time he'd wasted. He would understand if she was reluctant to believe he'd changed, but he'd never shut her out again. She had to believe that he wouldn't.

Back in the present, he moved over to the desk to write up the infant's medical notes and prayed that Kinny wouldn't have a relapse. That proved to be wishful thinking and he didn't make it to Kirsten's that night—he barely made it to bed before his MIRA shift the next morning.

CHAPTER NINE

KIRSTEN arrived at MIRA half an hour early on Monday morning. She wanted to be well clear of the locker room when Hunter came in because she still didn't know what to expect when she saw him. She couldn't believe he hadn't come to see her last night.

The extra time would also allow her to concentrate on the thought of flying again. There was extra caution to be taken because of her pregnancy, but the flying itself wouldn't harm her baby, although her days of heedless adventures were over.

Kirsten breathed a sigh of relief as she slipped past the door to the stairs undetected. Both nursing teams from the night shift were involved in a noisy discussion in the kitchen and were oblivious to her arrival.

The breeze was cool when she stepped out onto the roof. The sun was struggling to rise above the horizon of tall buildings and the waiting aircraft was in shadow. Her heart rate picked up a little but there was no dread as she walked towards the closed doors of the helicopter.

She peered through the glass and then circled the aircraft, and she saw that it was a new version of the one that had been destroyed in the crash. The thought didn't frighten her. It was good to be back. She heaved a sigh of relief, lifted her head and turned for the stairs.

Her pulse rate jumped again. Hunter was watching her, unsmiling, from the doorway. He looked so tall and handsome in the first rays of sunlight that her heart squeezed as the memories of the last time she'd seen him flooded back. She savoured the sight of him because she'd spent so many hours imagining this meeting that she allowed her feelings to overwhelm her briefly.

For Hunter it was a defining moment. He'd watched Kirsten approach the aircraft warily and he'd thought his heart might explode with pride at her courage. Her sisters had done a good job. She looked a little thinner than he remembered but her eyes were alive with eagerness to start the new day.

And here she was coming across the roof with her hands held out to hold his, no trace of the aversion he was sure she must hold for him.

He bent down and kissed her cheek and suddenly they were back at the cave. 'How are you? How are your poor hands?' he said.

Never could he have imagined the tenderness that welled up inside him now that he allowed himself to touch her. He wanted to kiss each damaged finger and hug her against him and never let her go. The feeling terrified him.

He stared into her face and she looked up at him. But now there was wariness in her greeting. She had the right to be wary.

'Thank you for saving my life in the cave,' she said quietly, and he returned with a thump to a roof-top in Western Sydney.

'Thank you for saving mine,' he quipped, and inwardly cringed at the embarrassment of his claustrophobia. Neither of them mentioned the time that was uppermost in their minds.

They both looked away and the mood was gone. She'd erected a barrier and for the moment he wasn't sorry. Soon he would declare himself but not quite yet. Everything was worth waiting for. He fell into step beside her as she walked back towards the steps.

'How are you?' He thought she looked gorgeous but she seemed a little quieter than her usual self. 'Your sister said you've had a rotten cold.'

She didn't smile. 'I'm fine. Thank you for the flowers.' She went ahead of him down the stairs and he watched her shoulders as she descended. She had such strength beneath those fragile bones. When she opened the door below, the night staff spotted her and crowded around to make a fuss. He eased his way over to the lounge and sat back. As he watched, he realised she was not enjoying the attention and he wondered at the change. There was something missing—maybe a tinge of the exuberance he'd always associated with Kirsten. But, then, why wouldn't there be? She was entitled to a full-scale breakdown after the crash and he wondered if she'd come back to work too soon.

He'd needed to come back to work. After visiting his father and Portia, he'd come back to crowd out his initial desire to grab Kirsten, take her somewhere private and force her to love him. Not fair after the unreal situation they'd found themselves in. He'd promised himself he wouldn't prey on her fragility after the crash. When he next held Kirsten in his arms, it would be with all the trimmings.

Sitting at home, rehashing that magic time in the

cave, he'd accepted he'd have to conquer his petty
jealousy and insecurity if there was to be any future
for them. He'd done more hours in NICU in the last
fortnight than he'd done for a long time as he'd
waited impatiently for her to mend.

The MIRA phone rang and Kirsten was in the
kitchen with the other team. Glad of the distraction
from his thoughts, he snatched the receiver up and
took the call. She was right behind him as they
wheeled the equipment to the aircraft and he
watched her carefully as she strapped herself in as
if it was just another day. He remembered how he'd
been so careful to project the same image as Kirsten
on his own return to MIRA. She didn't need him to
draw attention to it.

Work smoothed over any awkwardness. The
morning started with a six-year-old boy with burns
needing specialised helicopter transport from
Nepean and then a fixed-wing flight from Wagga
Wagga for a two-year-old with epiglottitis. Both
cases required intensive concentration and by the
end of the second case Kirsten and Hunter were
back in professional mode. Something they'd gained
their share of experience with.

They had time for a late lunch back at headquarters before being called out for the retrieval of a
newborn baby with previously undiagnosed gastroschisis.

For Kirsten, this was a first. She'd never seen a
case of gastroschisis—or opening in the abdominal
wall near the umbilicus—meaning the bowel pro-
truded outside the infant's body. She found it hard
to look away.

Kirsten's compassion was fully aroused for baby

Zane Cook and his mother, and she guessed some of her empathy was because of her own newly pregnant condition. Zane's graphic presentation made her realise how devastated she would feel if her and Hunter's baby was born with a blatant defect like Zane's.

Her quick glance at Hunter made him raise his eyebrows as if to say, what? She shook her head and looked away at Zane's parents who were staring across the room at their son in horrified fascination. The membranous mass of bowel that lay on top of their baby's stomach was so unexpected, so bizarre, that Kirsten silently agreed it must be a shock.

Hunter promised to keep the parents updated, and he and Kirsten moved quickly into action beside the local doctor.

'Are you OK?' He barely moved his lips as they crossed the room but his concern was genuine.

'Fine.' Kirsten didn't look at him and they both plastered on smiles as they approached the local doctor.

'You've done a great job, the way you've wrapped the baby's abdomen in clingwrap,' Hunter said approvingly, and Dr Shaney, the hospital doctor, nodded, relieved that help had arrived.

'The last one of these I saw, we were still wrapping in moist packs, but your clinical co-ordinator said to use the clear sandwich wrap.' The men watched as Kirsten took the baby's temperature and blood pressure.

Hunter lifted Zane's little arm and stroked the skin to find a vein. 'They found the problem with the packs over the bowel was that they cooled too rapidly.' Hunter checked Zane's other arm for prominent blood vessels. 'And the babies become cold, which is a huge problem with these kids. We have to keep them warm.'

He shook his head. 'I saw a bowel wrapped in cotton wool once and it was hell trying to get the stuff off the membrane later. Any bits missed can cause peritoneal granulomas.'

Dr Shaney nodded and Kirsten slid the prep swab and cannula in beside Hunter's hand before he could ask for it. She taped the tiny splint in place as soon as he'd secured the line.

Impressed with how easy they made the procedure look, Dr Shaney raised his shaggy white eyebrows. 'Done that a few times together, have you?'

Kirsten and Hunter exchanged a smile and nodded. Hunter drew off a small amount of blood for pathology testing before they connected the baby to the intravenous fluids.

'I'll have FBE, electrolytes, blood culture and group, and hold for cross-match,' he said. Kirsten already had the correct tubes ready and one of the local midwives was labelling them. Hunter injected the required amount in for each test and when he'd finished, Kirsten saved the syringe to check the baby's sugar levels.

'Glucometer reads two point five.'

Hunter pursed his lips, quite satisfied. 'So nil by mouth, IV running at thirty mils per kilo per twenty-four hours. Let me know as soon as the pathology comes back, even if they phone it through when we're in the air. I'm worried about young Zane losing large amounts of colloid fluids into that inflamed gut. He'll need some albumen.'

He looked up and caught the agonised expression

on both parents' faces. 'Pop a nasogastric tube in, Kirsten, and when you get a chance we'll have the usual antibiotic cover for any bugs that think they might want to set up camp. I'll see the parents.' Kirsten waved the NG tube under his nose and Hunter smiled again as he walked away.

It wasn't as awkward to maintain their professionalism as she'd feared it would be, Kirsten thought warily to herself as she finished that procedure. Hunter was making it easy for her and she wasn't sure how long she'd be able to keep up her wall of reserve. Maybe she wouldn't need to. Maybe he had changed since Banda Banda. That thought was very distracting and she sighed and concentrated more intensely. The tube was in the stomach correctly and she taped it to Zane's upper lip and then aspirated any fluid that was in the baby's stomach. Then she checked the clock and smiled at the midwife who hovered to offer help. 'I'll aspirate again before we leave,' she said, and started to tidy her mess.

'You're very efficient.' The midwife helped clear up the last of the disposable equipment.

'Like most things, it gets easier with practice. I'll bet you do many things I'd find stressful until I became used to them again.' She grinned. 'We carry nearly everything in our kit.'

By the time they were ready to leave, everyone was more relaxed. The parents had decided to drive into Sydney together and the staff were so appreciative they'd sent for tea and coffee for the MIRA team.

Tara confided to Kirsten she'd been quietly pleased to have given birth five weeks early because of the nausea she'd suffered for most of the pregnancy. But now she was weighed down with guilt, as if the deformity were somehow her fault.

Kirsten shook her head. 'No one knows why this happens. It's a breakdown in the formation period and it could have been due to a virus or just screwed cell division. You'll never be sure why it happened, but these babies do really well after surgery.' Kirsten smiled. 'It's not something that is the mother's fault.' The whole time she was reassuring Tara, Kirsten knew she'd feel the same way if it had been herself. She couldn't help her protective hand that strayed to her flat stomach or her gaze that drifted to Hunter. When he looked across she turned away guiltily. It was harder than she'd thought it would be to know about her pregnancy without giving it away to Hunter.

Zane's transfer to NICU went smoothly and when they landed on the roof at headquarters, they could smell the aroma of frying onions and the memories of another day did nothing for the growing rapport between Kirsten and Hunter.

Hunter saw Kirsten stiffen and pull back as if she didn't want to get out of the aircraft, and he wondered if it was because of his refusal to believe in her last time. He didn't care what had happened in the past, he loved her and he wouldn't fail her again.

'I gather Jim is cooking in aid of your return,' Hunter said encouragingly as he waited for Kirsten to alight. She grimaced and again he noticed the subtle difference in her usually outgoing personality. 'Are you OK with that?'

Kirsten nodded and followed him down in the lift. They came out on the second floor and the crowd on the balcony cheered and waved a hand-painted banner that read, WELCOME BACK, KIRSTEN, and another that read DYNAMIC DUO.

Kirsten had to laugh and she felt Hunter relax beside her. After the initial babble of conversation she eased herself away from the crowd with her plate and glanced around for somewhere to sit. In the corner, Hunter patted the seat beside him.

Her stomach tightened but not with hunger. How could she ignore the last three weeks of silence? But that was what she was doing. She felt like a fool to even partially believe in fairy-tales but her feet moved across the floor unbidden until she was seated beside him anyway.

He looked searchingly at her. 'How does it feel to be here again?'

Despite her intentions to remain clear-headed, Kirsten was swayed by the warmth in his eyes. 'It's good. I'll always love MIRA but it's been a big day, coming back.'

His statement came without warning and to Kirsten his voice lacked conviction. 'I was wrong to break up with you,' he said. 'We should be together.'

Kirsten blinked and stared at him and he looked away as soon as he'd said it, as if already regretting the words. Was he referring to what she thought he was referring to? Kirsten frowned and realised what had happened. She cautioned herself. Now that he'd slept with her, he felt guilty. The last thing she wanted was for him to lie to her.

'You don't have to say that if you don't mean it, Hunter.' Your baby and I will survive without you, she thought, and her eyes began to sting with unshed tears as she waited for him to reassure her. He didn't say anything else and suddenly she couldn't sit there any more with him.

She put her plate down on the deck, stood up and pushed her way inside past the other MIRA staff and then up the fire-escape stairs to find space on the roof as if the hounds of hell were behind her. Just as she reached the top step her foot skidded on an uneven tread and she fell heavily, striking her stomach on the edge of the step. She gasped with the pain but more with the dreadful fear that she'd hurt her baby, and terror settled over her like a menacing cloud.

She lay against the steps, alone in the semi-dark stairwell, for several minutes and let her tears flow unchecked as she waited for the first cramp to grab her. When it didn't come she shifted until she was half-sitting on the rough concrete and leant her cheek against the cold metal rail and bargained with God. If her baby would be all right then she'd be extra careful, no more heedless flights up stairs or running away. Care and composure would be her middle names and she'd have her baby christened as soon as he or she was born. She closed her eyes and admitted grimly the futility of bargaining, and how stupidly vulnerable she found herself in pregnancy.

She'd been pathetic, again, and she leaned against the cold metal rail and accepted that Hunter wasn't going to be the person she wanted him to be, shouldn't have to be someone she wanted him to be. It wasn't fair to either of them.

Hunter watched Kirsten go. He didn't blame her for not believing him. He was tired from little sleep. His declaration had been on the tip of his tongue all day and he'd blurted it out in a jumble like a five-year-old. He sighed. For an articulate man in a high-powered job he sucked at relationships. He should have seen her early this morning before they'd had to work together, no matter how late it might have been when he'd got away from the unit.

He watched through the balcony window as she disappeared into the fire escape and guessed she was heading for the roof. He'd done that himself a few times in the early days here and suddenly he had to try one more time to make her understand.

He followed via the lift but when he came out onto the roof the area was empty. He glanced behind him to the closed door of the fire escape but there was no entry from the outside. He'd have to go back down the lift and enter from the second floor, although he couldn't imagine what she was doing on the fire escape.

When he saw her sitting on the steps he realised she'd been crying and a deep pain seized his chest because he'd been the one to upset her. She tried to stand as he came closer and he realised she was hurt.

'What happened? Are you all right?' He lowered himself beside her on the step and took her hand. 'How can I help?'

Kirsten didn't say what was on her tongue because if she did she'd burst into tears. She looked up into the concern in his face and wished for the stars. She wished for Hunter to love and trust her—not to feel guilty that they'd made love. Or decide magnanimously that he could forgive her for her past indiscretions.

'I'll be fine,' was what she said, and she winced as she eased herself to her feet. It hadn't been that heavy a fall but the scare she'd given herself had been enormous. Although keeping her fears from Hunter was the hardest part.

He helped her back to the common room and she sat in a lounge chair for a while, shaken and tense as the time passed and she dared to hope no damage had been done.

After work, Kirsten was glad to close the door of her flat and sit down. She'd left her pushbike at the hospital and caught a taxi home because her tummy was still painful. Not cramps as she'd feared but soreness from the fall.

Needing someone to talk to, Kirsten rang a distracted Abbey to ask for advice, but she could hear Lachlan crying in the background and Kirsten reassured her sister that she was fine and would ring the next night.

Too tired to eat, she quickly bathed and changed for bed even though it was still light outside. When her entry buzzer rang, she jumped. She'd almost expected Hunter to call, but still briefly considered pretending to already be asleep. Flushed from the hot water, and droopy with fatigue, she reluctantly opened the door. It *was* Hunter and he carried a Chinese take-away in one hand and a deep purple ceramic pot with a rose bush in the other.

'It's a house-warming present,' he said, but at least he waited for her to ask him in.

The yellow and pink roses were beautiful and she sank her nose into the delicate perfume before she turned the tag to read the label. The rose was called Peace. She had to smile.

'Peace because that's what we have to start between us. May I come in?'

Kirsten could feel the tears scratching behind her eyes again and she cursed the hormones zinging around her body and undermining her composure. When she stepped back, he walked past her and seemed to fill her small flat with his presence. She watched him look around her home with appreciation.

'It's welcoming and vibrant, with a touch of country.' He turned to face her. 'Like you, except when I'm around. Have I ruined everything between us, Kirsten?'

'I'm not sure,' she said sadly, 'but it usually takes two to ruin everything.' She met his eyes. 'Will you tell me the truth if I ask you a question?'

Trapped, he nodded. 'Of course.'

'Do you feel guilty for what happened in the cave when we made love?'

He sighed. 'Of course I do.'

'Thank you for being honest.' She turned away so he wouldn't see her rub the imperceptible bulge above her pubic bone. Never could she regret the baby inside her. But maybe it was time to think about Abbey's offer of work in Gladstone. 'Thank you for the meal and the rose, but I'm tired.' And need time to make sure I'm not going to lose this baby, she thought. If I tell you now, I'll have trapped you into something I don't think you want.

Even if she didn't ask him to be there for their child, she'd never be rid of his shadow hanging over her. But she could get on with her life. She'd struggle through a few more days at MIRA and then decide for good.

Hunter left without a chance to explain.

The next morning at MIRA was slow and Kirsten stayed busy rotating stock on the shelves to keep out of Hunter's way. The first call came just before lunch and when Hunter heard the name of the referring hospital he couldn't help his worried look at Kirsten. If there'd been another crew there he would have suggested they go, but the others were out.

'We're off to Gladstone,' he said, and as she spun her head to look at him he saw her eyes widen. He shrugged and despite their differences they drew strength from each other in shared emotion.

As she helped push the portable neonatal unit to the helicopter, Kirsten admitted that she was glad she was with Hunter because Gladstone wouldn't call them lightly and he was the best they had. 'Who was the referring doctor?'

'Scott Rainford. Isn't he one of the brothers-in-law?'

She nodded. 'So what's the story?'

'Four-month-old baby boy with intussusception. They've started an IV and pain relief but the baby needs transfer down for surgical correction before the bowel necroses.'

Intussusception, when a segment of the bowel telescoped into itself, caused an obstruction in the intestine where the walls of the bowel push in on each other. The blood flow through the bowel becomes impaired, which could lead to significant bleeding, shock and even perforation of the bowel.

'Poor little baby. He must be in agony.' Kirsten winced as she secured the kit. The condition was a painful one and sometimes it was hard to diagnose early. The treatment was to disentangle the baby's bowel by inflating the bowel with barium or an air enema, or if the baby was too sick by surgical correction. If the bowel has been obstructed for too long it could become necessary to remove the section that had been damaged due to lack of blood supply and rejoin the bowel.

'The sooner the better.' She glanced out the window. 'It's better flying weather than last time, thank goodness.' They both thought of Keith, still at home and so fortunate to be alive.

Once the stretcher and equipment were loaded, the aircraft lifted off and turned its nose north. There wasn't much in the way of drugs to prepare *en route* for this trip so there was time to kill on the flight. Hunter glanced across at Kirsten who was watching the terrain below. 'Is this the first time you've done a retrieval in your home town or did you do some before you went to Dubai?'

Kirsten looked across at him. 'Apart from the time we crashed, you mean?'

Hunter grinned back at her. 'I wasn't counting that one because we didn't make it.' He was glad she could talk about it, and hopefully she would be even better after they'd completed this trip today. He knew he'd be glad to get back to Sydney later. 'Do you think we're mad, tempting fate like this?'

She shook her head. 'I like to think I'm a fatalist and I'll be fine until my time comes. Though I might take less risks in the future.' She returned to Hunter's original question about retrievals from Gladstone.

'I've done a couple of retrievals from home. It's always nice to be able to help out.'

He nodded. 'So will the hospital be full of your relatives?'

Kirsten raised her eyebrows. 'Scott is Bella's husband, Rohan will probably be there and maybe Bella. Relatives, friends, school buddies. You'll be surrounded.' She teased him about the comment he'd made a few days ago about country people 'We country folk are related to everyone in town.'

'So, is it a good hospital?' Hunter found he was interested.

'I think so. We have a loyal staff, great doctors and the base hospital isn't too far away if we need to transfer. If we need any extra equipment the townspeople rally around us and raise the money. No complaints.'

She met his eyes. 'Of course, the town's fortunate to have Scott and Rohan because if those guys weren't in town all the women would have to travel fifty kilometres to have their babies at the base hospital. Scott's been here for about fifteen years, and he was doing obstetrics on his own until Rohan came two years ago as a locum. Then Rohan stayed and fell in love with my sister Abbey.'

'That sounds very romantic.' There was a sardonic note to his voice when he added, 'How fortunate for the town.'

Kirsten frowned. 'The town had nothing to do with it. I've never seen anybody more in love than Abbey and Rohan are. It restores your faith in marriage to see them.' She laughed. 'Although Scott and Bella run a close second.'

'So your two midwife sisters married the two obstetric GPs. How come you didn't stick around for the next locum?'

Kirsten didn't like the tone of his voice but she resisted making this personal. 'I did a couple of months when I first came back but MIRA is really what I want to do. Of course, then I didn't know you'd be there or I might have stayed longer.'

He winced but she was smiling. 'Big hit,' he said, and Kirsten laughed and looked out the window.

The flight was uneventful and they landed at the hospital helipad on schedule.

The orderly waiting to help with the equipment clapped Kirsten on the back as she alighted. 'Good to see you, Kirsten,' he said. 'I didn't think they'd send you seeing as it's Abbey's Lachlan.'

Kirsten stopped and stared and Hunter caught the gist of the conversation.

'You go ahead, Kirsten. We'll bring the equipment.'

Kirsten sent one agonised look of thanks Hunter's way and set off up the path towards the hospital rear entrance. When she arrived in Outpatients, Lachlan was in one of the side rooms and her sister Abbey and husband Rohan were holding hands beside the cot, looking down at their son as he moaned in his sleep.

'Kirsten!' Abbey stood up and Kirsten gathered her older sister into her arms.

'You poor things.'

Abbey stepped back and Rohan hugged Kirsten, too. 'We heard the helicopter arrive. Abbey was hoping it would be you.'

Rohan looked more serious than Kirsten had ever seen him. Usually quietly amused by people and life on the whole, Rohan was the type to never get flustered. The joys of having your own family, Kirsten thought as she looked at the two people she'd never seen at a loss in a situation clutching at each other when their son whimpered.

She could hear the sound of the stretcher approaching, so Hunter would be here any moment. 'I didn't know it was Lachlan until I arrived. When did he get sick?'

'During the night,' Abbey said. 'It must have been an incomplete obstruction because between episodes he looked almost well and I thought it was colic.' She looked at her husband and Kirsten could tell Abbey had been beating herself up over this. They all looked at Lachlan as he grunted in his sleep and drew his little legs up.

'Rohan's been on the ward with a prolonged labour for most of the morning and I took Lachlan in to see Scott at morning teatime when I noticed his belly was becoming distended.'

Hunter arrived but because of the size of the room they left the stretcher outside and Kirsten introduced him to her family.

Hunter, this is my sister Abbey and brother-in-law Rohan Roberts. Rohan does obstetrics and the anaesthetics here. Dr Hunter Morgan is our paediatrician.'

They all shook hands and then the referring doctor arrived to meet the team. Hunter's eyes widened as the second tall man crossed the room and dropped a kiss on Kirsten's cheek.

'Hi, Kirsten. Bella hoped you'd be here for Abbey.' He turned to Hunter. 'Scott Rainford. Another brother-in-law of Kirsten's.'

They all turned to look at the baby. 'And this little bloke is Lachlan.' Scott switched the boxed X-ray light on and the illuminated X-ray that was already hanging there showed the blockage clear on the screen. He handed Hunter a sheaf of paper that were photocopies of Lachlan's admission notes, X-ray reports and pathology to take with them to Sydney.

'He became acute this afternoon. He must have been partially obstructed before the full intussusception occurred. As you can see, I've put a line in, nil by mouth and sedated him with some morphine until you arrived. The paediatric surgeon at the Children's Hospital says they'll operate as soon as you get there.'

Hunter nodded and Kirsten had begun to record some observations on the MIRA transfer sheet as Scott was talking. She handed Hunter the stethoscope that he was about to grab from the trolley and their eyes met.

'Beat me again,' he said under his breath, and did a quick examination of Lachlan in the cot. When he palpated the baby's belly he looked up at the parents and grimaced.

'Sausage-shaped mass, textbook stuff. What was the last stool like? Any blood or mucus?'

'Just starting,' Abbey spoke quietly. 'The last one looked like the classic currant jelly.' Then she glanced across at her husband.

He squeezed her shoulder and Rohan murmured, 'Our baby will be fine as soon as they do the operation.'

Abbey nodded but her voice thickened as she struggled to be calm. 'He's been irritable for the last twelve hours or so, and started vomiting late this morning. He's got a temperature now and Scott's given the first dose of antibiotics that the Children's Hospital doctor said to give him.'

Hunter nodded. 'We'll get him down there as soon as we can. You all know that the outcome, when corrected in the first twenty-four hours, is excellent.' He smiled and the tension lightened in the room. 'His analgesia looks sufficient at the moment and while he's covered for pain I won't give him any more. So let's move out of here.' He looked at Abbey and his eyes softened. 'Are you coming with us in the chopper?'

Abbey nodded and Rohan glanced at Scott. 'I'll follow in the car so I can bring them all home. Bella's bringing over a few things for Abbey. She should be here in the next minute or two. We can all come back together in a couple of days when Lachlan can drink and has normal bowel function. By then he'll be able to travel comfortably.'

Kirsten helped Hunter transfer Lachlan and his IV line to the MIRA stretcher. She spoke over her shoulder to Rohan. 'You can stay at my place—I'll make sure Abbey gets a key when she gets down there. It's close to the hospital.'

'Fine. That's settled. Let's go,' Hunter said as they strapped Lachlan in and gathered the paperwork to take with them.

Bella arrived with a small bag and smiled at Kirsten, who was too busy to do more than blow her a kiss. 'I'll ring you later,' Kirsten said, and Bella nodded, relieved.

'Good luck,' she called after them, and Scott put his arm around his wife.

'They're in good hands,' he said as they watched the stretcher disappear.

Lachlan handled the trip well, and Hunter gave another small dose of morphine twenty minutes before they landed to keep the little boy pain-free until he could be transferred to Theatre.

Abbey held his tiny hand all the way and when he was sleeping she spoke quietly with Kirsten about family stuff.

To Hunter, the sisters seemed very close. He supposed they'd have to be if Abbey had been the mother figure for Kirsten from fifteen. Apart from her natural concern for her son, Kirsten's sister was a remarkably restful woman—the complete opposite to her youngest sister, he thought ruefully. The middle sister was different again and even Hunter had to admit she was one of the most beautiful women he'd ever seen, something he hadn't noticed the first time he'd met them. He'd taken more notice this time because he was trying to learn more about Kirsten. In fact, the five of them seemed to epitomise family support and as an only child of divorced parents he couldn't help wondering what that would be like.

Both women were looking at him and Hunter realised that Abbey must have asked him a question. He shook his head to indicate he hadn't heard her and moved over to sit next to them.

Abbey smiled. 'No ill effects from the excitement a few weeks ago?'

Hunter shook his head. 'I managed to get out of it the lightest.'

'Nobody gets off lightly in that situation.' Abbey didn't understand what the problem was between these two. Anyone could see they were in love, and equally confused. She changed the subject. 'Kirsten tells me you two met in Dubai before MIRA?'

He eyed her warily. 'Yes. I came back a couple of months before Kirsten.'

'And you both ended up here.' She watched them as they avoided each other's eyes. They were hopeless. 'I know Kirsten loves it, but do you plan to work for MIRA long?'

Hunter looked out the window and then back at Abbey. 'A few more months. It's a great service and Kirsten is an excellent flight sister. I think she likes the adventure.'

Abbey tilted her head and bit her lip. Obviously you both fancy a bit of adventure, she thought, but she didn't say it. She liked what she'd seen of Hunter and she could see he was no fool. Kirsten's plan to keep the news of his baby from him in case everything didn't work out was doomed. The sooner he knew, the better for Kirsten. 'I see you know her well.'

The twinkle in Abbey's eye made Hunter shift uncomfortably and for a horrible moment there he wondered if Abbey knew about the cave. Before he could think of something to change the subject again, she did it for him.

'So, tell me about Lachlan's surgeon.' She raised her chin and her voice was firm. 'Do you know him?' And then with seeming innocence she added, 'If you had a son, would you let this doctor operate on him?'

Kirsten jumped beside him, and her head snapped around to look at her sister's face. Hunter frowned at her sudden movement, and when he turned back Abbey was watching him. Hunter met Abbey's eyes and answered her question, but he knew that something else was going on. 'Without hesitation,' he said. 'He's the best paediatric surgeon in Australia. Which is the advantage in coming to a research and teaching hospital like this one.'

Abbey sank back in her seat and Kirsten recovered her composure, although she was watching her sister warily. She rubbed her stomach again and he wondered if it still hurt from the fall yesterday.

'Thank you, Hunter.' Abbey glanced at Kirsten, and there was a touch of mischief in her eyes. 'You wait,' Abbey said. 'Having children is magic but very stressful. It fries your brain. I'll be pleased when Rohan gets here to share the worry.' Kirsten frowned at her sister and Hunter had a wild thought that he banished almost immediately. Crazy thought, he told himself, and concentrated on ensuring the paperwork was right. But the idea planted by Abbey refused to go away.

Lachlan's transfer to the hospital went smoothly and Hunter arranged for Kirsten to have the rest of the afternoon off so she could stay with her sister. Lachlan's surgery was scheduled for three o'clock, only an hour away, and Rohan probably wouldn't arrive until at least six that evening.

When they'd handed over their patient and Hunter was about to leave, Kirsten laid her hand on his arm. 'Thank you for suggesting the time off, Hunter.' He squeezed her fingers and it felt so good just to touch her in this tiny way, but he didn't answer her. 'I appreciate it anyway,' she said. 'I'll see you tomorrow.'

He nodded and reluctantly released her hand. 'Good luck.' When he left he had a lot to think about. Meeting her family made his erroneous belief in Kirsten's behaviour even more unforgivable. The bond between the other two sisters and their husbands was strong and obviously Kirsten had developed the same steadiness.

But Kirsten had been different since she'd come back to work and he wondered if she'd decided he wasn't worth the risk. Women fell out of love all the time with the Morgan men. Maybe it was hereditary. He must share that pearl with his father. He crossed the courtyard to MIRA headquarters. He'd promised not to revisit past failures.

That night, after Lachlan's surgery was over, Rohan sent Abbey home to Kirsten's to rest for a few hours while he stayed with Lachlan. The two sisters sipped hot cocoa before going to bed, and it was a relief for both women to relax.

'Thank you for being there for me, Kirsten,' Abbey said. 'I think I'm going soft and seem to need someone now that I'm used to having Rohan look after me.'

Kirsten felt her eyes mist. Even Abbey, whom she'd always thought invincible, could be brought low by fear for her child. 'Any mother would need someone while they were being strong for their baby—and you're a wonderful mother. I just hope I'm as good when my baby is born.'

Abbey shook her head. 'You will be. I see you still haven't told him.'

Kirsten sighed. 'I could have done without your double-edged comments today. You have to have trust before you can have a relationship.' She looked away and Abbey stared at her thoughtfully.

'Well, it's up to you to decide if he's the only man for you.' She patted Kirsten's knee. 'We

Wilson girls seem to be late starters and love doesn't seem to run as easily as we think it should. But I have a lot more faith everything will turn out right for you than I had before I met my Rohan.' Abbey sipped her cocoa and then stroked the side of her mug. 'I like him a lot. I think you both operate on another level from the rest of us. That doesn't happen without reason. Was I imagining it?'

'You never did miss anything.' Kirsten shrugged. 'I couldn't get away with a thing when I was a teenager.'

Abbey smiled at the memory. 'I had a good spy network. So tell me what's happened since you came back.'

'Before the crash I came to accept there was no future in our relationship but then we made love. That was when I realised I still loved him and thought he might love me. I was ready to try again but it doesn't feel like that any more. Now I'm pregnant it just keeps getting more confusing.'

Abbey squeezed her hand. 'Apart from the baby, do you still love him?'

'I'm trying not to.' Kirsten looked at the clock. 'You should get some sleep if you're going to relieve Rohan later.'

Abbey nodded. 'We'll talk about this tomorrow. It's been a big day.'

The next morning, after Abbey left for the hospital, Kirsten decided that she should go home to Gladstone as soon as she'd worked off her two weeks' notice. And she'd see Jim unobtrusively and request not to work with Hunter after today. It was too stressful to see Hunter so often and know her dreams would never come true. She owed it to herself and her baby to get on with planning her life without Hunter's presence. Hearts didn't break, they just ached for a long time, but she'd made the decision.

Hunter noticed there was something distant about her as soon as she came in. She didn't meet his eyes when he enquired about Lachlan and she avoided any chance of them being alone together.

Their first retrieval wasn't until after lunch and the day seemed to drag minute by minute. When the call came, it was to another baby with a heart defect—this time a two-day-old girl.

Considering she wasn't keen to talk to him, Kirsten asked more questions than usual and he wondered why she was suddenly interested in congenital abnormalities.

CHAPTER TEN

WHEN Hunter and Kirsten arrived at the destination hospital, Tia, Amy Masters's mother, was shattered and her fear wasn't helped by the fact that, as a single parent, she was without family support. It was a chilling insight for Kirsten to see a mother trying to cope without the person who would most understand her distress.

Two-day-old Amy had suspected coarctation of the aorta, or narrowing of a section of the aorta at birth, which could seriously decrease the blood flow from the heart out to the rest of the body.

Kirsten introduced herself and Tia clutched her, almost gabbling with distress, repeating the same story over again. 'I should have noticed earlier but I thought she was just cold.' Her eyes darted across to her baby and back again as if to reassure herself her daughter was alive. 'Just cold! What a fool I was!'

Kirsten took the woman's shoulder and steered her into a seat. 'Tia, sit down. Someone will get you a drink. You really need to stop feeling guilty and pat yourself on the back for noticing so soon. Often babies with Amy's condition aren't picked up until day three. So you did really well.' She caught the eye of one of the hospital nurses and smiled. 'Could you get Tia a cup of tea, please? I think she's in desperate need of one.' She hugged the woman and stood up. 'I have to go and see Amy. I'll be back shortly.'

The nurse came over to help. Kirsten was pleased to see the young woman sit down beside Amy's mother and put her arm around her while she asked her preferences. As she walked away she heard Tia tell the nurse how guilty she felt that she hadn't noticed her baby was sick.

The MIRA crew stabilised Amy as quickly as they could because they were limited in what they could do prior to surgery. During the flight, Kirsten slipped her phone number into Tia's pocket and comforted her as best she could. 'If you need to talk, give me a ring.'

The transfer was completed and Kirsten heard Tia tell the new staff how guilty she felt.

'That poor woman. It must be hard, coping with this on her own.' Hunter looked back as they left Tia safely ensconced beside her daughter's crib in NICU. 'You did a great job supporting her, Kirsten. Any idea what happened to Amy's father?'

Kirsten grimaced. 'Tia told me he wasn't interested and wanted Tia to terminate the pregnancy. She refused and he walked.'

'She's better off without him.'

'What a good idea—except Tia still loves him,' Kirsten said dryly. There was a lot she could have said and she was actually close to forming the words, but Hunter was stopped by the director of NICU and Kirsten walked ahead and out of the unit.

Hunter gave only half of his attention to his boss as he watched Kirsten walk away. He had the impression she'd been about to say something important and that fleeting, crazy thought swirled in his brain again. She couldn't be.

'Hunter!' Professor John James wasn't used to being ignored.

Hunter switched back to where he was. 'Sorry, John. You were saying?'

Slightly mollified by Hunter's smile, the director repeated himself. 'I said I have a fellow in my office who wants to see you. Jack Cosgrove. Said he worked with you in Dubai.'

The last people he'd expected to see walking across the unit towards him were Eva and Jack Cosgrove, but there was no doubt the doctor he'd last seen in Dubai had business with him.

'Jack! I thought you and Eva were in Canada?'

'Hunter.' Cosgrove nodded his thanks to the director who bustled away. Cosgrove's face was serious. 'We're back to see an obstetrician.' The older man couldn't hide his pride in his coming fatherhood, but he was obviously on a mission. 'If you've got a few minutes, there's something Eva needs to tell you.'

When he looked at Eva, Hunter noticed that, while she looked uncomfortable, there was something different about her. Then he realised the latent bitterness in her eyes was missing and she seemed somehow softer.

'Sure. Come across to the coffee-room.' He glanced at Gloria Westerland beside the crib and the charge sister nodded that she would ensure his privacy in the staffroom.

Hunter led the way. He had no idea what this was all about but it must be important if Jack had dragged his wife up here.

They arrived and Hunter flicked the kettle on in case they wanted coffee. There was silence in the room as the Cosgroves exchanged looks. Hunter cleared his throat. 'So how was Canada?'

Eva shrugged. 'Canada was fine but we're here because of something that happened in Dubai.'

Hunter raised his eyebrows as the premonition firmed in his mind. He beat her to it. 'I know you lied about Kirsten.'

Eva jumped and glanced one more time at her husband. She must have received the support she needed because she sighed and then straightened her shoulders. 'I, um, may have given you the wrong idea about Jack's relationship with Kirsten Wilson.'

Hunter raised his head and his eyes burned into Eva's. His voice was very quiet and very cold. 'Why would you do that?'

Eva flinched. 'I knew your past and I knew it wouldn't take much to turn you off her. Kirsten was only listening to Jack's complaints about me. I knew they weren't having an affair.' She glanced at Hunter as though willing him to understand, but she couldn't read his expression. She went on reluctantly. 'But I didn't like the fact that Jack was leaning on her for support and I thought if I turned you off her, I'd feel better.'

She looked at her husband. 'When Jack found out in Canada what I'd done, he made me promise I'd come and tell you the truth when we came back to Australia.' She looked at her husband as if for approval, and he moved across and put his arm around her.

'It was wrong, and we're both sorry for any problems it may. have caused you and Kirsten.' Jack smiled down at his wife. 'If it wasn't for Kirsten telling me to give my marriage another go, I'd probably have gone straight for a divorce. I should have complained to Eva and not Kirsten, but…' Jack smiled down at his wife. 'This baby is going to open a whole new world for us and we wanted to start with a clean slate.'

Eva may have lied but Hunter had believed another woman over the one he professed to love. He'd been just as guilty.

Jack held out his hand and Hunter forced himself to shake it. He shook Eva's as well and they were quick to leave Hunter standing in the coffee-room by himself, wondering if this new knowledge would make it easier or harder to win Kirsten's trust.

The conversation he and Kirsten had had on the way to Maggie's birthday celebration came back to him. The words repeated in his head like a script.

She'd said, 'Think about it, Hunter. Do I hug a lot of people? Hug all my friends and the parents of the children I nurse? Did it ever enter your suspicious little mind that maybe you were wrong about me? That you threw away something precious we both had because of your insecurities?'

The fact that he'd decided he needed Kirsten regardless of her past didn't excuse him. He should never have believed someone else over the woman he loved. He'd thrown something precious away. And if he wasn't mistaken, he'd nearly thrown the chance to share something equally as precious. The chance to be a father.

He could even understand why she hadn't told him. Then he remembered the cave and how he'd given up and she'd used the last of her strength to save him.

He couldn't give up now because Kirsten needed him more then ever. He would spend the rest of his life making it up to her. He'd do anything for this woman.

Her soul was as pure as a hidden pool in an untouched cavern and he should have known that.

He'd been a fool to trick himself into abandoning her because of his fears that he'd never recover if she betrayed him. Kirsten would never betray anybody—least of all the man she'd given her heart to. No wonder she'd been devastated when he wouldn't admit to being wrong. How would she ever trust him not to doubt her the next time she uninhibitedly threw herself into someone's arms?

Finally he could see that emotion and joy and warmth and the ability to share herself was a part of the Kirsten he loved and would always love.

She didn't need a coward like the old him—she needed someone fearless who would take her love and be proud of her nature. The cave he'd cowered in for the last five years was more restricting than any mountain place. Kirsten had shown him the way out into the light and he'd been too frightened to follow her. But not any more.

He glanced at his watch. It was almost the end of the shift. In another ten minutes she'd make her way over to the paediatric intensive care unit to see Lachlan and her sister. He could beat her to it if his pager didn't go off.

When he walked in Lachlan was asleep and Abbey was by herself, reading a magazine. She smiled a greeting and he knew that she would help if she could.

'May I sit with you?' He dragged a chair over and Abbey lifted her eyebrow in amusement at his clear intention.

'Of course.' She waited and he thought again how restful she was. But he wanted someone different, someone who would drive him mad with her energy and ensure he knew he was alive. This was no time for pussy-footing.

'I love your sister.'

Abbey looked unsurprised. 'And you're telling me this because…?'

'I don't think she can forgive me for not believing in her.'

'Then you don't know her very well. We Wilson girls give our heart and it stays given. If you believe in her, Hunter, you will make her one of the three happiest women in the world.'

He had to smile at her teasing. 'The rest being the other two Wilsons, I take it?'

Abbey smiled and then she saw her husband approaching with Kirsten. 'Here's your chance. Don't blow it.'

Kirsten saw Hunter with Abbey and her heart sank. 'Is Lachlan OK?'

'Of course he is. Hunter's here to see you.'

Hunter glanced across at the family watching and then back at Kirsten. 'Do you mind?'

She shook her head. He drew a deep breath and in front of her family he said, 'I love you more than life itself.' And drew her into his arms. 'Can you forgive me for ever doubting you?'

Kirsten backed away. Now what was he doing?

A part of her wanted to believe in his confession so much but the more prosaic side doubted his sincerity. Why now? Why in front of her family, unless he thought he'd enlist their support?

He must have found out about the baby. Abbey and Rohan moved away and Kirsten wasn't sure if she was glad or not.

'Why the sudden change, Hunter? Why now?'

He shook his head. 'It's not sudden, Kirsten. I thought if I said it in front of your family, you might believe me this time. I've changed, exorcised old ghosts and laid the groundwork for a new wonderful future if only you will forgive me my doubt. I love you, Kirsten, and I'm so sorry I hurt you with my lack of trust. Let me spend the rest of my life making it up to you.'

He sighed. 'Or maybe it's me that needs to see that my dream isn't yours. Have I let you down so much that you can't forgive me?'

'Shh.' She pushed her hand against his lips. 'I will always forgive you because I do love you, so much.' She reached up and rested her lips against his. 'Please, kiss me.'

He felt the catch in his chest as years of ice splintered and gave away. 'That's what you said to me in the cave and it was as if my own angel was there for me.'

'I'll always be there, because I love you more than anything in the world.'

He couldn't believe that she was in his arms and what he was reading in her face. 'Will you marry me, Kirsten, please? Be my wife, and spend the rest of your life with me.'

There was no fear or doubt or conditions in that question. He wanted her and he wanted her for ever.

Kirsten's eyes filled with tears because she'd never thought they would find their way to this point, but this was really happening. 'I would love to marry you, Hunter.' And then he kissed her and all the fears and doubts and worries disappeared because she would always be a part of him.

'There's something I have to tell you,' she said, and it was his turn to silence her.

He ran his hand gently over her stomach and she realised he knew. 'Did Abbey...?' He shook his head.

'Things you've said, a tendency to shield your stomach and some of that "lousy" instinct you say I don't have. Besides, I love you. How could I not tell?'

He lowered his face to hers and they both closed their eyes. Her lips were soft and pliant but this was not the place he wanted to do this. He stepped back and gently took her wrist.

'We'll come back and see the in-laws shortly.'

They went up the stairs to Kirsten's bedroom and when he closed the door behind them Kirsten felt that surge of excitement she always felt before an adventure. But this was the greatest adventure of all because she could finally see that Hunter loved her.

He lifted his face. 'I hear Gladstone might have a vacancy for a paediatrician in a couple of years. Could be the perfect place to bring up a family.'

'As long as I'm with you, anywhere will be perfect.' She kissed him and then tilted her head with a mischievous smile and he could see a little of Abbey and Bella in her face. 'But I think you'll enjoy being a part of the family.'

CHAPTER ELEVEN

IT WAS a strange place for a wedding reception—an airport! But Gladstone, like many regional centres, had lost its daily commercial flights. Left, was a lovely little terminal perfect for a social venue and an enormous bitumen apron area for visiting aircraft under a cobalt blue sky. Balloons and streamers hung from the departure gate where the married couple would leave from later.

On this day, there was a fixed-wing air ambulance poised for a quick getaway and two MIRA helicopters and several private planes from Camden Aero Club to complete the collection. It was more like the picnic races than a wedding except when you saw the radiance of the bride reflected in the eyes of the groom.

Kirsten wore a three-quarter-length white sheath and a white straw hat, and the windsock in the corner of the airfield flew parallel to the white scarf around her new husband's neck.

Earlier, in the tiny church on top of the hill, Hunter had taken his bride's hand for the final vows and the look that had passed between them had brought tears to the eyes of the two maids-of-honour. Abbey and Bella had sought their own husband's eyes across the pulpit and young Lachlan had gurgled in the thin arms of his Great-aunt Sophie.

*   *   *

A month later, back at MIRA headquarters, Kirsten Morgan held her husband's hand as they paused outside the building before going in.

'A quiet married life suits you, Mrs Morgan,' Hunter said, and she blushed.

'Quiet isn't a word that springs to mind, but loving you is my greatest adventure.'

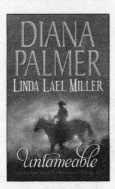

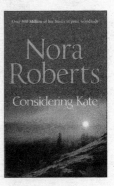

The World of Mills & Boon®

There's a Mills & Boon® series that's perfect for you. We publish ten series and with new titles every month, you never have to wait long for your favourite to come along.

Blaze. — Scorching hot, sexy reads

By Request — Relive the romance with the best of the best

Cherish™ — Romance to melt the heart every time

Desire™ — Passionate and dramatic love stories

Have Your Say

You've just finished your book.
So what did you think?

We'd love to hear your thoughts on our
'Have your say' online panel
www.millsandboon.co.uk/haveyoursay

- Easy to use
- Short questionnaire
- Chance to win Mills & Boon® goodies

Visit us Online

Tell us what you thought of this book now at
www.millsandboon.co.uk/haveyoursay

YOUR_SAY